LOVE OR DECEPTION

Morgan K. Wyatt

Romantic Suspense

Secret Cravings Publishing
www.secretcravingspublishing.com

A Secret Cravings Publishing Book
Mainstream Romance

Love or Deception
Copyright © 2014 Morgan K. Wyatt
Print ISBN: 978-1-63105-287-3

First E-book Publication: April 2014
First Print Publication: July 2014

Cover design by Dawné Dominique
Edited by Larriane Barnard
Proofread by Rene Flowers
All cover art and logo copyright © 2014 by Secret Cravings Publishing

PUBLISHER
Secret Cravings Publishing
www.secretcravingspublishing.com

Dedication

Appreciation goes to my tireless editor Larriane, talented cover
artist Dawne, and Rene.
Extra special thanks to my supportive husband, Scott.

To Patsy,

Enjoy.

Morgan K Wyatt

LOVE OR DECEPTION

Morgan K. Wyatt
Copyright © 2014

Chapter One

"I love you," Mark whispered into her hair as he slipped one long, muscular leg over hers.

Amy snuggled closer to him, nuzzling his neck. Ah, she loved this time, right after a rousing lovemaking session when they were both sated and drowsy, drunk on the idea that in a world of mismatched couples, somehow they found each other. Mark's slight snore alerted her he'd dropped off to sleep. She should get up. There was so much to do before work. Instead, she stayed, breathing in the peace of the moment.

Hard to believe she was a bride. Not that she had anything against marriage. She just hadn't foreseen it happening to her. How could it? All she did was work at Theron under major security scrutiny. The only people she saw were other employees, with the majority being women. The confidentiality clause she'd signed forbade fraternization between employees. The company must have a reason for being so paranoid. Right now, she didn't care. All she wanted was her husband to awaken.

"Honey, do you remember our wedding?" Using her index and middle fingers, she made slow circles across his wide shoulders and around his muscular arm. The barbed wire tattoos encircling his biceps always surprised her, not that they didn't look good on his tanned skin. They did. No, it was that she never imagined herself as a woman with a big gorgeous husband who could easily be a male stripper or a porn star with his looks. Nope, she never expected to marry. Even if a part of her held out hope,

she never expected anyone without a heavier eyeglass prescription than hers.

Mark held up one arm, stretched, and twisted it enough to make his bicep pop. He noticed her eyes following the play of muscles. His deliberate wink made her giggle a little. Geesh, just another sign she was way out of her depth. Truth told she never dated much, period. School, then work consumed her every waking moment.

He rolled to his side, facing her, and yawned before answering. "I do remember our wedding since I was there. Plus it was only two weeks ago."

"Yes." All that was true, but it wasn't what she wanted to hear. By mentioning the subject, he might tell her how wonderful it was or even describe it in detail. Did she expect him to gush about the meaningfulness of their vows? No way, she'd admit that she had issues bringing their wedding into focus. All she could see was a couple and minister on the beach with the sun setting in the background. With the shadows falling on them, it was hard to tell if the couple was even white, let alone if it was actually them. The sun was setting in the west, which worked since they married in Tahiti. Still, it had the same feeling of looking at a magazine ad for honeymoons.

The woman had on a short dress, and the groom wore a loose white shirt. That she could tell. They did have a whirlwind romance. Was it possible she was drunk when she married Mark? Was that why she couldn't remember anything very well? Her hope was, by mentioning the wedding, he might also confess how wildly in love he was with her. It might ease her fears about the two of them being an odd couple.

Her Aunt Remy raised her with a healthy self-esteem. Being worthy of her handsome husband wasn't an issue. It was more a case of like going with like. She'd heard enough comments when a couple showed with one partner being more attractive. When the woman was more beautiful, people assumed the man was rich and powerful. Charitable women might think he was charming and good in bed. Unfortunately, it never worked that way with the women. People seemed genuinely baffled and usually predicted a future break-up. Rather unfair if you asked her. Couldn't the woman have some great trait? Maybe she was smart, interesting, and a decent conversationalist, even reasonably good looking with a slender build and short blonde hair. Her nose crinkled once she realized she'd just described herself.

The curve between his shoulder and neck beckoned her to nuzzle. The simple action reassured her that they were actually married and together. Everything happened so fast. A slow roll of her body had Amy looking up at her husband who pinned her to the mattress. "I think I know what my own Dr. Death needs." He wiggled his eyebrows and leered at her.

* * * *

"Ma'am, ma'am, could you take a look at this?" A man with a wrinkled jacket and mussed hair pushed Mark's appointment book into her hand. An appointment book, how quaint, when everyone else relied on cellphones and laptops for date keeping. She blinked twice wondering why the man with the short, abrupt-sounding name handed her the book. What was his name, Burt or Bark? She couldn't remember. Was it just yesterday, the day before, or even longer ago when she laid in bed enjoying the warmth of Mark snuggled up next to her? She lolled in the security of his embrace and now she was sitting alone in their living room, except for Bark and his partner.

"Ma'am, I need you to look at the book. Is this his? Does the writing looking familiar?" The detective stared at her as if dealing with a particularly recalcitrant child. He nudged the book as if she wasn't already aware that it was in her hand. It was Mark's day planner filled with his illegible scrawl. How could he be gone?

"Detective…" She hesitated unsure of his name, even more, unsure of what she was going to say. How did this all happen? It seemed like a fog encased her normally sharp mind. She was smart once. She couldn't remember anything clearly, but she had a vague memory of being intelligent. She even held down an important job of some sort.

A woman's shrill voice called her name. "Amy!" She turned in the direction of the voice as a woman hurried toward her all blues and greens and vivid red hair. She should be able to see better than this. Her glasses, she needed her glasses.

The woman reached her, hugging and enveloping her in a cloud of familiar scent. Something tugged at her memory. She knew this woman. A slight smile graced the woman's face, conveying both pity and solace simultaneously. Touching her face, she looked up at the woman in entreaty. "My glasses?"

"Amy," the woman stroked her back as she talked, "you quit wearing glasses after your Lasik surgery, remember? You said you wanted to look younger and flirty, not like the scientist you are."

Scientist. She was a scientist. Yes, that's right, but what did she study? Why was it so hard to remember anything? Maybe the woman knew Mark. Odd, she couldn't even remember that she no longer wore glasses, but she could remember Mark, the feel of him next to her, his smile, even his snorty little laugh that made him sound a bit like a pig, something she never mentioned, knowing it would make him self-conscious. She burst into tears, as a wave of desolation swept over her again like a hungry tide pulling her downward.

"Don't worry, Amy. Aunt Remy is here," the woman promised as she wrapped her arms around her and rocked her slightly as if she were a baby.

"Ma'am," the detective protested, "you're crushing the book. It could be evidence."

Remy pulled the book from Amy's unresisting fingers and handed it to the officer. "You'd think if it was so important you'd be dusting it for prints."

"Yes, ma'am." The disheveled man didn't answer her question, but managed a strained smile before taking the book. He walked over to his partner.

The two detectives spoke in hushed voices stirring Amy's curiosity. Her tears stopped as she sat up trying to hear them.

"Great another one who watches every police drama. They all think they are CSI experts. Did you find out anything, Maxfield?"

"Not much, the wife called the police stating her husband disappeared while she was in the shower. I don't know, Burt, it sounds peculiar."

Amy noticed Burt's measuring look and heard his comment. "She doesn't look like the type to off her husband." His partner huffed her disagreement. "Besides, I heard they were newlyweds."

Maxfield raised her eyebrows before commenting. . "Newlyweds kill each other every day, especially if the will favors them. I heard Amy Newkirk is one of the top scientific minds in biological warfare. They call it something else, but that's what it really is. A woman who devises ways to kill off entire populations without a sound is not a delicate blossom."

Burt's head swiveled back to stare at Amy. "I don't think so. Those aren't movie tears. That woman's heart is broken right in two. Besides, what is the motive?"

Maxfield aimed a cuff at her partner's arm. "That's our job to find out before they call in the FBI."

Their conversation added to Amy's distress, restarting the tears she'd almost stopped and causing Remy to shout at the chattering detectives. "Will ya'all just shut up or move to a different room? She can hear every word you're saying. I can too, and I'm not liking it."

Wiping her nose with the offered tissue, Amy surveyed the room, trying to pull her thoughts together. The woman whispering to the detective with the short name said she worked on killing people. That couldn't be right. She'd know if she was a killer, wouldn't she? She looked up into Remy's concerned brown eyes. If she were a killer, would Remy hold her so tight? Did they think she killed Mark?

Blinking twice, she tried to clear her eyes of the vision-blocking tears. Everything still looked vague and blurry. Touching the bridge of her nose, she asked again, "My glasses?"

Remy jumped up surprisingly fast for such a large woman. "You stopped wearing them, but if you think you need them, I think I might know where a pair is, you being so organized and all."

Remy reappeared with a black case in her hands. Amy opened the case to reveal a pair of plastic horn rimmed frame glasses. No wonder she stopped wearing them. Placing them on her nose, she peered through the lenses bringing everything into slightly better focus slowly as if adjusting a camera lens. There, she had it, mostly. The edges were a little fuzzy still. It was like one of those photos where the camera focused in on the center object and intentionally blurred the surroundings. Her eyes took in the plain walls stacked with boxes and one lone framed photo on the wall. Standing, she walked to the picture, which featured a grass shack perched on wooden stilts over water with palm trees in the background. No figures stood near the shack or even peered out its lone window. The photo gave her a sense of peace.

"That's probably from your honeymoon. In Bora Bora or was it Tahiti? You remember?" Remy nodded at her as if she should remember.

She shook her head no. "I don't remember anything. All I know is Mark is gone. My memory went with him. Those people," she pointed in the direction of the whispering detectives, "keep asking me questions I can't answer, and my head hurts."

"Oh, sweet darling, come sit down. Can I get you some aspirin? Maybe a glass of water? How about both?" Remy led Amy back to the couch, before bustling off to the kitchen. On her way back, her outspoken aunt, stopped in front of the detectives who conversed only a couple of meters away from the couch.

"What is wrong with you people? Can't you see my niece has been drugged? Why aren't you investigating that instead of having your heads up your asses? Standing over here making conjectures about how my niece might have killed her husband. Don't think I don't know how your lazy police minds work. Never wanting to do the legwork, just pin it on someone nearby, and call it a day."

"Ma'am," Burt said, only to have his partner interrupt.

"What makes you think she's drugged," Maxfield asked, opening her keypad on her cell to take notes.

"Did you even look at her eyes? Her pupils are dilated. She didn't know who I am, either. I practically raised her when my sister Cici ran off with some Marine. She stood and stared at a picture from her honeymoon and didn't recognize it. My gal is smart. She went to college on scholarships, has both a medical degree and a doctorate's in biochemistry. She's no party gal who does recreational drugs in case you were going to suggest that."

Amy fought the grin that tugged at her lips. True, she didn't remember much, but the sight and sounds of her Aunt Remy lighting into the detectives felt familiar.

Placing both hands on her hips, Remy continued chastising the two. "I mix up enough potions to recognize the signs of poison.

Part of my business is to know when someone is hexed or poisoned."

Burt took an involuntary step back at Remy's revelation while his partner stood her ground.

"What do you know about Mark?" Maxfield asked.

Amy pretending not to eavesdrop picked up the discarded appointment book and flipped through it.

"Ah, Mark." Remy's smile could be heard in her voice. "I wish Amy could tell it. There was such joy in her voice when she told me about him. Suffice to say, she loves that man more than life itself. Your job is to go find him."

Remy turned and hurried over to her and flourished the glass in front of her face. "Drink it up with the aspirin, Sweet Pea."

Amy took the proffered tablets and sipped the water slowly listening to the detectives.

"She doesn't know anything about Mark," Burt commented. Maxfield mumbled her agreement.

"I suspect if Amy is as in love as her aunt declares, then all she would do is talk of her beloved, especially considering they are newlyweds. Keep in mind, this is a very smart woman, probably smarter than ninety percent of the population, so finding a boyfriend will not be easy for her. Especially if she wore those awful glasses."

Amy noticed the woman's shudder. She retrieved the glasses from her head to see if they were that terrible. Sturdy no nonsense dark frames surrounded sizable plastic lens. Obviously not that fashionable, but they served a purpose. If the glasses could talk, they could tell her all that she couldn't remember. No sudden influx of information came causing her to put the glasses on a nearby table. Her best bet would be to listen to what other people had to say and just maybe she might be able to piece together the missing parts.

"That means Amy knew very little about her new husband too." Burt stroked his scruffy beard. "Then we need to start there. Looking into who was or is Mark Schaeffer."

Maxfield shook her head. "Actually, we need to do a drug screen on Amy before it is out of her system, especially with all that water her loving Aunt Remy is pumping into her."

* * * *

Amy held the test tube in her hand turning it over. It stirred a memory of several test tubes on a black topped lab table. Why? A nurse bustled in with a long needle and a suspicious stare. The police wanted her blood and urine to prove something. She wasn't sure what. The flowery smelling woman called Aunt Remy wanted her to do the tests to prove she didn't make Mark disappear. As if, she would. The thought of him opened up a hole inside of her, a place he used to fill. Where was he? She tried to form an image of him. The last thing she could remember was his voice, low and husky whispering he loved her. Their bodies entwined, and the slight wheeze of his breathing. Seasonal allergies worked him over good. Mark blamed her cat Samson for his congestion.

"Ma'am, I need you to make a fist." The nurse's voice broke into her memory. Shooting the nurse an irritated glance, she balled her fist and tried to recapture the fleeting image. Mark had allergies, and she had a cat named Samson. She watched the nurse wipe her nose with the back of her hand as she filled the test tubes.

"Those are contaminated!" The words exploded out of her mouth. The nurse glanced back in surprise, her mouth opened as if to protest. "I saw you wipe your nose. There is a chance of your mucus entering my test tube. If you can't be one hundred percent certain, there is no purpose in running a test." She bit out the last sentence almost rote, as if she had said it many times before.

"Are you telling me how to do a drug screening," the nurse snapped back at her.

A slender man in a lab coat walked into the room. He pushed up his slipping glasses and smiled in Amy's direction before speaking. "You'd be well advised to listen to Dr. Newkirk. I meant Schaeffer since she is one of the top bio-chemists in the country."

Biochemist. That's it. That's how she knew the nurse was messing up the results. The man's concerned face tugged at her memory. Hadn't she seen it often, even daily? He obviously knew her. In addition, he was here, past the police guard. Did that mean he had some sort of authority?

"I am sorry, Dr. Korman," the nurse murmured the words and bobbed her head respectfully. She made brief eye contact with Amy before adding, "Sorry, Doctor, um, Newkirk."

Sorry now that suddenly I am a peer, as opposed to some possible axe murderer. Of course, I could be a murderer who is also a doctor. Amy mused on the irony but quickly shut down the thought. She knew she wasn't a murderer. A slip of a conversation flashed into her head. Mark jokingly called her his own Dr. Death. Even though she chuckled with him, she didn't really appreciate the comment. It was hard to explain to people how she actually saved lives as opposed to taking them. It was hard to say anything at all since she signed a confidentiality clause. Maybe that was it. Perhaps she said too much to Mark. Could she be the cause of his disappearance?

Korman, he must know what she did for a living. She had to know. "Dr. Korman, do we work together?"

He placed his bare left hand on her shoulder. Amy stared at his hand wondering if such a gesture was normal between biochemists. His eyes were surprisingly shrewd, the eyes of a scientist, no doubt.

"My poor, dear Amy. Your Aunt Remy told me you lost your memory, but I couldn't fathom how a mind as brilliant as yours could ever stumble. Yes, we work together at the research center. We've worked together for the last twelve years." He squeezed her shoulder as if trying to imply something Amy couldn't quite grasp.

He picked up the file and snorted, then muttered to himself, "This makes no sense."

Amy wondered what he was reading. "What?"

Dr. Korman looked up from the paper. "Oh, your medical orders, or I should say lack of them. I would have thought with the injury to your head an MRI or at least an X-ray. Just blood work and it appears they can't even do that right."

So far, she'd discovered that she was a biochemist at a research center. The doctor with the familiar face acted as if the hospital was not treating her right. Did they not want to? Was it because of her profession or something else? The detective said something about biological warfare. Mark called her his own Dr. Death. Did this make her a bad person? It couldn't be. She would know. Would this man stand beside her, squeezing her shoulder if she were a bad person? Maybe, if he happened to be just as corrupt. Amy tilted her head to give him a thorough once over. He didn't look particularly anything, definitely not evil, maybe a trifle academic, and the type to talk about new pharmaceuticals over a romantic candlelight dinner.

Where did that thought come from? Dr. Korman continued to rest his hand on her shoulder as if it belonged there as he discussed the reasons against drawing more blood at this time. She knew him. No doubt about it. Maybe her mind couldn't bring up the details, but her body recognized him. There was no jump in her heart rate but, still, a quiet acceptance. Maybe it was the years they worked together, but it felt like something more. The way he boxed her in as if protecting her from the rest of the world made her wonder. Maybe Aunt Remy would know and could explain it to her.

As if hearing her thoughts, Remy bustled into the room. Dr. Korman turned at the disruption and smiled at her. "Remy."

"Ryan," she acknowledged. "I came to check up on my girl. I figure there had been plenty of time to draw blood. Besides, those detectives are milling around out there wanting to get at her. I thought maybe I could buy her some time, at least till her memory comes back more."

Ryan Korman rushed out of the room with a determined look in his eyes. The nurse excused herself as Remy helped a still shaky Amy out of the hard plastic lab chair and over to a softer, upholstered chair.

'Remy, I know my memory isn't that good, but how do I know Dr. Korman?" She relaxed in the chair while Remy pulled up a matching chair.

"You've lost your memory for sure. He picked you as his research assistant. You were probably the sharpest knife in the drawer, so it wasn't surprising he picked you. He shepherded you through the medical community advising you what specialty to pursue, what conferences to speak at, and he just always seemed to be there. If he were a bit older, I might consider him fatherly. The fact that he never married began to make me wonder…" Remy broke off looking at the wall with a bemused expression.

"Wonder what?" Amy thought she knew, but she wanted to hear Remy's opinion.

"You scientists always wanting cold facts, never seeing what is in front of you. Never taking a walk on the emotional side."

"Remy, do you think the police think I had something to do with Mark's disappearance," she asked, hating the break in her voice. Scientists didn't cry, at least she thought they didn't. Apparently, she worked with the instruments of biological warfare. Anyone who did that had to be a tough cookie and not someone who whined about unjust accusations or misplaced husbands.

Remy pillowed her head on her overflowing bosom. "Don't cha worry about nothing. They will point their lazy fingers your way. Ask some questions about if you were happy, and all that. If you answer honestly without a lot of jawin' about how happy you both were, then they'll believe you. Liars always have big elaborate stories with all sorts of fancy details about the love note she wrote him that morning since they know they are going to be asked."

Amy sat up quickly. "Love note. Will that make me look guilty? I think I did stick little love notes all over the house for Mark to find. Is that what murderers do?"

Remy wrapped her large fleshy arms around Amy and drew her back into her embrace. She patted her on the back before murmuring, "Love note was a bad example. I suspect most murderers do not write love notes." She threw the nurse an irritated glance when she walked back into the cubicle. "Besides he's only gone, not dead. Probably went out for the proverbial pack of cigarettes. That's what happened to my man. Left for a pack of Lucky Strikes and never came back. Many a woman got lucky when their man went in search of Lucky Strikes and never came back." Remy laughed at her own joke causing her body to jiggle, upsetting Amy's headrest.

Amy tried to laugh too, but coughed instead, sounding more like a tuberculosis victim than a grieving wife. Maybe it was just as well she coughed. She wouldn't want the police to think she found anything entertaining about the situation. Remy gave her a few firm slaps on the back that almost propelled a lung through her chest.

"You okay, sweetness?" Remy asked cocking her head birdlike to peer into Amy's flushed face.

Blinking twice, she gasped to pull air into her lungs. Why did the simplest bodily functions seem so difficult? No doctor, outside of Korman, had come to talk to her. Just a tired nurse who couldn't even take a blood sample correctly. Things were not okay. "Is it possible I could see a doctor, possibly my doctor?"

Remy looked in the direction of the nurse, as did Amy. The woman in white huffed a little and disappeared almost silently in her crepe-soled shoes.

"I bet she's going to get a doctor," Remy offered.

"Thank goodness." She managed to murmur the words with her head still pinned against Aunt Remy's chest. Her aunt stroked her hair reminiscent of petting a cat. She'd thought she'd mention her sudden thought when a memory crowded it out. Her mother left her on Remy's doorstep rather like an abandoned feline to chase after her newest man. She remembered her aunt stroking her hair similar to now as she cried her eyes out, certain she'd never be happy again. At the time, she found it comforting. The human touch signaled that someone was there for her.

Ryan Korman entered the room with a concerned look. "Nurse Delancey said you asked for me." His lips quirked up in an almost smile.

Amy was about to clarify that she had asked for her doctor, as opposed to specifically him, but she noticed the thought that she asked for him cheered him. It was puzzling, but she chose to hold her tongue and simply nodded.

Ryan hurried to her side, picked up her right hand, and held it lightly. Not exactly proper procedure unless he was taking her pulse. He wasn't. With Remy patting her head and Ryan grasping her hand, she felt like little more than a bone between two dogs. There were things going on in her body she needed to document. As a doctor, she could use this information to understand the drug involved. Even in her lingering haze, she realized it might be up to her to investigate what happened to her, and, more importantly, Mark. She managed to shake off the ministering hands and sit upright to speak.

"Dr. Korman," she started, noted his hurt expression, and immediately corrected herself. "Ryan, I would like to document the various issues I am presently suffering to get a grasp of what is going on inside my body. Would you be willing to do this for me?"

He nodded his head while extracting a small legal pad and pen from his coat box. "I would be delighted to help you. The fact you thought of it means your senses are starting to return back to normal."

He was right. "We need to hurry then. Remy, you can help."

Her aunt squeezed her shoulder so hard it hurt a bit. Amy smiled up at her, not mentioning it. The woman might be as rattled as she was.

"Remy, you saw me a couple of hours after I called the police. How was I?" She turned slightly to look up at the woman hovering over her similar to a guardian angel. Make that a vengeful one.

Shooting one hand through her wild curls, Remy sighed. "You were messed up, staring off in the distance and not seeing anything. You asked for your glasses. Couldn't remember that you had Lasik surgery and didn't wear them anymore."

Ryan wrote rapidly and then looked intently into her eyes. "Can you see me okay?"

"Yes." She touched her face, assuring herself she wasn't wearing glasses. "When I put the old glasses on, they helped some, but I still couldn't bring things fully into focus." She thought about the picture she tried to view without much success.

Ryan clicked the pen a couple of times as his lips twisted in thought. "You'd have difficulty looking through two different sets of corrective lenses. That's what happens when you look through your old glasses with your Lasik-corrected eyes."

Amy bobbed her head in understanding to encourage him to continue.

"Your inability to focus was not your eyes, but more whatever drug was introduced into your system that dampened all your natural responses. What else did you notice?" He had the pen suspended over the paper again.

Rubbing one hand over her face, she tried to bring back that initial panicked moment. "It's odd really. The police tell me I called them in a panic, telling them my husband disappeared from our bed, but I don't remember doing this. They arrived, and I was wet from the shower. I could barely say my own name. I couldn't remember what I did. I barely recognized Remy. The only thing I knew for sure was that Mark was gone."

The doctor wrote down a few slashes and looked up. "I know you're upset, but do you think he could have just left?"

Amy nodded her head slightly. The detectives kept asking her that too. "I know it has to be forty-eight hours before a person can be considered missing, but there was blood on the bed. His blood, I know it. It wasn't a lot, just a bit on the pillow."

Ryan's pupils widened, and he wrote some more.

Remy moved closer to the man to peer over his shoulder. "I thought we were documenting Amy's physical situation to figure out what's going on here. Looks to me you're turning all detective. We got two horses' asses in the next room thinking Amy might have helped her husband vanish. The way I see it, we don't need another one."

"Oh no, just made a note to type the blood." he offered, throwing an uncertain glance at Amy as if asking for approval.

She managed a puny smile for her former mentor. "You're right. I want to continue writing down my symptoms before I forget." Her eyes danced across the battleship gray walls and unwelcoming plastic chairs. As unpleasant as her surroundings were, it did indicate her sight was returning. "You ready?"

At his head bob, she continued, wondering why she didn't remember much about a man who seemed so entangled in her life and past. "My body felt heavy. I was sitting when you came," she looked at Remy. "I couldn't even stand. It felt like gravity was fighting with me and definitely winning. My hearing was either dampened or distorted. It sounded like everything was coming down a long metal tube. I couldn't feel anything. Nothing. Not heat, not cold, not the chair I was sitting on, or even the notebook the detective shoved into my hand. The only thing I felt was pain. Grief opened up a big gaping black hole."

Her colleague's pen raced across the paper. His top teeth bit down on his bottom lip indicating intense concentration or even pain. He must have felt her stare because he looked up, revealing anguished eyes. They must be very good friends, she rationalized, if he feels agony over Mark's disappearance too.

"Even though I had no clue what was going on, I remember thinking I felt like the marshmallow man with my hands absurdly large, unable to be of any use." She shook her head. It was an odd thought to pop into her head when she needed to document actual events. Why couldn't she remember any?

Remy stepped behind her and rested both her hands on Amy's shoulders, probably tired of trying to read Ryan's writing. As she remembered, it was even worse than the usual chicken scratch that constituted most doctors' writing. That's the reason most all hospitals switched to computers for orders, prescriptions, and especially surgery assignments. Her eyes moved over the man earnestly trying to capture her words. Something happened between the two of them. Not romantic, no, much more important, some type of medical experiment that went horribly wrong. Was it because of his handwriting, she wondered. Yet, another thing she couldn't remember. Just as well, he wouldn't appreciate her recalling it.

"Is that it?" Ryan asked, as he clicked his pen shut, denoting that he considered himself done.

"For now. I might remember something later. I'd like a copy of your notes. Is it possible you could email them to me?" She'd go over them with her pharmacology book tonight to see if any drugs matched up with her symptoms. She had her doubts she'd not find the drug used in a textbook, suspecting it hadn't been approved for the common market. It probably had no purpose but to temporarily paralyze and discombobulate a person. Not exactly, something you need for a physical disorder. Nope, it sounded more like something the CIA might use.

Ryan used the tablet to tap her on the knee, gaining her attention. "Tell you what, I'll type them up and bring them to your house. You will be at home this evening?"

Amy looked at Remy not sure what her schedule would be. She couldn't imagine going anywhere. The only place she wanted to go was home. She needed to be at home when Mark returned.

Remy assured him that the two of them would be home. Ryan stood, nodded to Remy, and touched Amy with the legal pad again before leaving. He gave her a slight smile, but it didn't reach his troubled eyes. As soon as the door closed, her aunt whistled.

"That boy has got it bad for you. How come you never noticed? Gave him the time of day?" She cocked her head to one side, regarding Amy. "Never mind, you got enough to concentrate on. I'll go see if the Keystone Cop twins will set us free."

As if hearing Remy's words, the detectives entered. Maxfield flashed them a strained smile, acknowledging she heard the comment. "You can go home now, but stay close. No long trips."

Befuddled, Amy stared up at the woman. "Why would I take a long trip? I need to be at the house when my husband returns."

Remy grabbed her arm as if she were an invalid. Amy allowed the red-nailed grasp to remain because she was still feeling woozy, but not so foggy she didn't hear the detectives' comments.

The woman mumbled maybe more to herself than her partner. "She sure isn't acting super intelligent."

A small sound similar to a smack or a rough pat reached her ears, perhaps the sound of a rude partner getting a reapproving tap for the remark.

"Give the woman a break. She lost her new husband. That means they were still at the *I love you and good sex* stage. Of course, she's grief stricken, probably drugged too. Too bad, we drew a mediocre nurse."

The woman cleared her throat before speaking. "I don't know about that. I think it is all contrived. She wasn't drugged. Everything is an act."

Amy cocked her head listening. Remy tightened her grip, probably feeling the tensing of her muscles at the last remark. The urge to go back and correct the woman tantalized her. That's what the old Amy would have done. That's one thing, she felt certain, but she didn't have the energy.

The door started to close on Maxfield's comment. "What motive would she have for misplacing her husband?"

That's right. Why would I not want to be married to the most wonderful man in the world?

Memories poured in like a busted gallon of milk flooding her brain. Mark smiled at her seductively as he unbuttoned his shirt. Another picture replaced the former image. He was running down the beach clad only in his shorts, and the setting sun silhouetted him. The likeness morphed into him propping up his head with one his hand as laid next to her. His lips were moving, and she could make out the words.

"Did you enjoy yourself, Dr. Death?"

A shudder ran down her spine as she considered the peculiar pet name. Most people wouldn't want their romantic names aired in public. No one wanted their co-workers to know at home they were often Sweet Cheeks, Hot Legs, or even Viking Warrior Princess, but Dr. Death? Talk about creepy. It made her wonder why her husband christened her with such a name.

Chapter Two

Remy placed two bowls of soup on the table. A couple of spoons appeared next to them almost as an afterthought. Her aunt settled into her chair with a hefty sigh of relief.

"All this going on, caused me to miss Samson. What happened to that ol' Tomcat? He might consider himself a wild one, but he was smart enough to recognize a soft touch in you."

The spoon slipped from Amy's fingers. "I'm not sure"

Remy's soup-laden spoon stopped on the way to her mouth. "Good Lord, you lost Samson. That's hard to believe. You doted on that ugly Tom. I'd always figured since you never married up that he served as your family. Whatever happened to you had to be powerfully strong to make you lose track of Samson."

Powerful strong would be a good description. This must be how a computer felt after its hard drive was wiped. Still, she remembered some things. "I need to go look for Samson." She half-stood, but Aunt Remy's hand braceleted her wrist.

"Sit down, Sweet Pea. Ol' Samson is used to living on the streets. He's a cagey one, and he'll return when he feels like it."

Aunt Remy's words made sense. They usually did, but somehow it felt disloyal to sit and eat.
Amy used her spoon to chase a noodle around in the broth. Chicken noodle soup was one of her childhood favorite meals. Her aunt probably thought it might bring her some comfort or at least assuage her hunger. Alphabet soup would have been more useful. At least, she could create words instead of chasing a single noodle. Why wasn't she hungry? Doing the math, she realized it had been almost twenty hours since she and Mark had shared a pizza while watching a DVD on how the brain worked.

Her natural response should be hunger, but something blocked that drive. Grief, pain, loss seemed to be appropriate answers. They might be the right ones, but she shouldn't discount whatever drug was in her system. She'd make sure to add suppressed appetite to her notes.

The doorbell rang. Talk about fortunate timing if it was Ryan with the notes. She stood to answer the door only to have Remy rush past her. Besides being a big woman, Remy had to be in her sixties, but she could move.

Walking slowly into the living room, she found her aunt in an animated discussion with two people. The woman struck a responsive chord, but she couldn't put a name to the face. The stern faced man drew no response. They both turned at her entry. The woman made a wide circle around Remy to reach her and grabbed both of her hands.

"I am so sorry to hear about what happened? How are you?" The woman stared intently into her eyes.

Noting the look, Amy decided she must be a colleague, someone with medical knowledge. Even now, the woman would observe her blood shot eyes, cold jaundiced skin drawing her own deductions on how she really was. It would be helpful if she shared those conclusions. Her male companion managed to get past Remy too. He apparently couldn't feel the evil eye she fixed on him. It'd be enough to cause folks in Terrebonne Parish some major unease.

Of course, the man didn't know Remy's reputation as the conjuring woman of Madeline Street. She'd never seen her make poppets or a hex sign, but people there always tried to stay on her good side. Another memory from her past, things started to come back, she realized. The frowning black suited man did not appear to be the type who worried about potions, curses, or even crossing the path of a black cat.

He crowded the concerned woman out of the way. Beth tossed him an irritated look. Beth, her name was Beth. They were friends, work friends really. Never associated outside of work that she could recall, but since she spent so much time in the lab, it was just about the same. A clause in her confidentiality contract forbade her from socialization with other employees. She remembered that too.

It seemed a bit strange to put in there since most of the employees had so little social life anyhow. Most were single with a few couples working for Theron. Her whirlwind courtship and marriage disturbed management terribly. They acted more like a hurt father, claiming they hadn't had time to investigate Mark thoroughly. She emphasized she understood the confidentiality clause and what it entailed. Part of her knew they'd react in such way. That's why she kept the relationship private, that and her fear something so precious might be easily dissolve. Ignoring the man, she smiled at her newly remembered friend. "It was so nice of you to come and see how I was doing."

Her friend managed to regain her position in front of Amy by stepping in front of the man and giving him a tiny hip bump. A bold move for Beth, Amy somehow knew.

"I was very worried about you. Have you heard anything?" She used her head to block Amy's view of the man and in turn his view too.

The blocking was something they did in the lab when talking about men, sex, and anything else not pertinent to the project. Every moment they were in the lab, the cameras were filming. That's why they'd developed a system of blocking the camera with their heads, bodies, or even a handy lab tray. A system of coded words meaning other than what they usually meant evolved between the two of them. They chose references to food and lunch because it was something people would mention, and it probably convinced security that being slender women they must have been harboring tapeworms to obsess about food so much. Mostly, they just mouthed what they wanted to say as long as they had their backs to the camera. They came up with these procedures in the restroom that with any luck wasn't bugged too. They took adjoining stalls and kicked a notebook between them, plotting their interaction.

It all came back with that one head move of Beth's. She smiled, delighted at the first signs she might be returning to the woman everyone seemed to remember. Then a sudden rush of resentment hit her as she remembered how much she hated the cloak and dagger atmosphere of the lab. The worst part was the daily inspection. Walking through an x-ray machine and a metal detector wasn't good enough. No, the guards had to run their hands over them as if they were attendees at a heavy metal concert.

This awkward procedure had her ditching her purse and not wearing any dresses. They suffered the humiliating search procedure on the way out too, maybe more intensely because in some ways bringing anything from the lab would be more harmful than taking it in.

Beth mouthed the words *Are you okay?*

A good question and one she couldn't answer. What the hell was going on? She mouthed back *I don't know.* She figured Mr. Frowny must be security, there to put even more of a damper on her day. No doubt, Beth's presence was to get the door open and offer her some type of assurance that no matter how outrageous the request was, it would be for her own good. Of course, she was supposed to think, 'Look, they brought a friend along. It must be a good suggestion.'

The man must have thought enough female bonding had gone on because he simply pushed Beth aside. "Pack a bag for a week. You're going on a vacation."

Amy wanted to peek under the man's shirt, maybe poke him with a needle to make sure the lab hadn't finally succeeded in manufacturing the cyborg they once theorized making. Not a single human emotion crossed the man's face. If this was their new creation, they needed to develop it some more.

The total lack of emotion identified him as security. Somehow, the guards learned to wipe all human emotion off their countenances. This blank demeanor served them well when feeling an employee's ass for possible contraband. Beth and Amy were relieved they hadn't started cavity searches. She'd declared she'd quit then but wondered if it were possible to quit knowing what she knew. His words didn't surprise her. In a tiny corner of her brain that still functioned, she rather expected them. As soon as she remembered the confidentiality clause, she wondered if they'd remove her, try to probe her mind to assess what information she gave out in her drug-induced stupor. Theron needed to monitor her to make sure she wouldn't ramble, giving away secrets that many governments would kill for. Maybe she should go with him. At least, there would be some semblance of safety.

Remy yelped. "What! Have you lost you ever-lovin' mind? This girl doesn't need to go nowhere. I'm here to take care of her. That's all she needs." She placed her arms akimbo on her hips and proceeded to move between Amy and the man who failed to identify himself. Remy had settled herself in for a fight.

In an effort to diffuse the situation, she peeked around her aunt to talk to the man. "I didn't get your name, sir." She tacked on the sir to let him know just how rude he had been. He appeared not to notice.

"Simpson. We'll wait while you get your bag." He folded his arms doing a great imitation of a brick wall.

A standoff. Time to put her much-lauded brain to use. She had to stay. Amy knew that much. Theron would try to get her back to work, no doubt about that, but she wasn't ready, not when her gut feeling was her job might have had something to do with Mark's disappearance. What to do? She knew Theron did not recognize "No" as an acceptable answer, but it did recognize there were entities they did have to play lip service to, such as the police.

"I can't leave. The police told me to stay put. What if a kidnapper tries to reach me?"

A brief flicker of anger flashed across Simpson's face before he could appropriately blank it.

Must not know her if he thought she'd offer no resistance. Why did they hire intelligent people and expect them to behave like cows? Simpson did remind her of a robot who received a command he didn't understand. He stood for a second, then stepped away to palm his cell phone and move into the kitchen. Beth gave her two thumbs up. She wasn't sure if the two thumbs up were for outsmarting the security drone, but she figured it was.

After an abrupt conversation, Simpson stepped backed into the living room. "We are leaving, Beth." He turned to eye Amy. "I'll be back. Do not go anywhere."

"I wasn't planning on it." She bit back the desire to bait Simpson. Was that part of who she was, someone who baited security because their petty tyrant ways sickened her? Beth's upraised eyebrows seemed to confirm this assessment.

Simpson stood at the door giving her a final stare-down. "Don't say anything."

"Say anything about what? Should I not talk about the love of my life disappearing while I was showering? Maybe I shouldn't say anything about my obsession with Belgium chocolate, especially the truffles." Obviously, she answered her own question about being the type of person who tweaked security's nose any time she could.

"You know." He directed an intense glare her way.

Simpson was probably disappointed he couldn't make death rays shoot out of his eyes and fry her on the spot. She wanted to share her observation with Beth but didn't quite know how. She looked at her friend, who slid her head toward Simpson the tiniest little bit. Oh, she knew. It was almost as if they had telepathy.

She stiffened her hand, saluted, and clicked her heels together. "Orders received, sir."

Simpson allowed his face to register disgust before slamming out of the house. Beth followed him, giving a small wave through the uncurtained picture window.

Remy shook a warning finger in her face. "You go too far, missy. The charming gesture you just did was enough to make the man irate."

Thinking back on her visitors, she snorted. "I think that man was born angry. Not much I can do will change that."

Remy turned toward the kitchen. "I might as well clear the dishes since you haven't touched a bite."

Amy slipped around her. "Not yet, I think I'll nuke my soup. Simpson's visit made me hungry."

"Really," her aunt wondered aloud as she eased her bulk into one of the new, Windsor chairs Mark and she bought to go with the pedestal table. "How's that?"

Pushing the numbers on the microwave, she tried to figure out what happened, what changed that caused the fog that surrounded her to dissipate in spots. "I don't remember everything by a longshot. Simpson standing there so rigid and condescending made me think of daily searches performed by black uniformed security. You'd think with as many women as we have on staff, they could employ some female security personnel, but they don't. Every morning and every evening one of those men would run his hands over my body, even checking through my hair. That's why I cut it all off. I suspected the one guard who always seemed to search me enjoyed it a little bit too much, even to the point of sniffing my hair."

Remy slapped the table. "Tell me his name. I'll fix him good."

Wait a minute, she remembered Simpson stepping into the kitchen for a few unsupervised seconds. A crawling sensation coated over her skin, and she held up her hand for Remy to be silent. She didn't need Remy threatening to castrate some guard, and then something bad happened to him. She pointed to her ear, then placed a finger over her lips as she began opening and closing cabinet doors searching for a bug the man may have hidden.

The hidden microphone could detect the sounds of a search too. Knocking a few glasses together, she made sure her voice was overloud. "Remy, I need something more than soup. My stomach is starting to dine on itself."

Remy look like she was about to say something, but chose not to. Instead, she reached under the stove for a heavy cast iron skillet. She managed to get the skillet up on the stove, but not without hitting it a few times on the stainless steel stove.

"I know what you need. Some hush puppies. It's a shame I don't have any catfish to fry up with it."

Amy grinned at her aunt and hoisted herself up on the counter. Her sock footed feet slipped as she tiptoed to peer into the upper most cabinets above the fridge. Her fall caused her to tumble against the appliance, which shifted under her weight. Her hands grabbed at the wall in panic. Her fingers slid over the smooth wall only to encounter a bump.

That was odd. Kneeling on the counter, she peeked behind the fridge. There was a small black bump on the wall. Half afraid she might be touching a dead insect, her fingers traced over it. It was a bug all right, but not the six-legged kind.

Clever putting it behind the fridge since the fridge might get pulled out once a year to vacuum behind it. Grabbing a piece of paper, she wrote instructions on how to act around the bug.

If she destroyed it, then they'd probably just try harder to remove her from the house. No talking in the kitchen except about food, and they needed to use as many electrical appliances as possible from the blender to the dishwasher keeping the room awash in a plethora of sounds. She turned on the radio, tuning it to a rock station and boosting the volume so she almost didn't hear the soft knock at the door. Remy turned to stare at the kitchen door.

Someone was at the back door. Was this Grand Central Station? The top of Ryan's head was visible above the curtains. Putting one finger to her lips, she hushed her aunt as she opened the door. Keeping her finger at her lips, she pulled Ryan in. His rounded eyes signaled his understanding as she led him to the farthest room from the kitchen, her study. Unpacked boxes crowded the room, which served as part storage and part office. She pulled the man between the towers of boxes and whispered into his ear. "Theron has bugged my kitchen. That's why we couldn't talk."

Ryan shook his head. "I'd figured they'd do as much. That's why I came in the back door. I imagine someone is watching the house."

She hadn't considered that. "Did they see you?" Ryan was breaking the socialization rule, not that they were socializing, but they were together in a non-work environment.

"No, I planned well. I left my car at the park about a quarter mile away. I walked through the woods to get to your backdoor." He sidled to a window and peeked out the blinds. "There is someone out there in an older sedan watching. Theron should at least try to be less noticeable."

Great. Suddenly, she felt like she was in some movie of the week. Her hand gripped his forearm. "What is going on?"

His long fingered hand covered hers. He gave her a reassuring squeeze. "I wish I knew. I do know you're in danger. The very fact you were gassed says it all."

"Gassed? I bet it happened when I was in the shower, the perfect time since the room was already steamy and small."

Ryan nodded, still holding onto her hand. "My thoughts too. Were you supposed to survive? I think the water may have negated some of the effectiveness of the gas. You managed to stay alert enough to call 911."

She nodded her head, trying to capture a vague memory of her shower that day. It was today, wasn't it? "It's Tuesday, isn't it?"

Ryan immediately felt her forehead. She brushed his hand away.

"I would know if I was feverish, and I'm not. What day is it?" She was almost afraid of the answer, but she had to know.

He placed the folder he brought with him on a box before cupping his hands around her shoulders. "It's Thursday. Are you sure, it was Tuesday? It is easy to get confused."

There was a calendar in the room, one of the first things she put up to help her be organized. She also saw it as a way of blending their two lives together. She had starting writing both their appointments on the calendar. She used blue for Mark and red for herself. Whipping out of Ryan's loose hold, she took three steps to reach the calendar and pointed to Monday. "See I had a doctor's appointment. Because of that, we just had pizza for dinner. The pan should still be in the sink if Remy hasn't cleaned it up."

Ryan stared at the calendar, pointing to the scrapbook workshop on Wednesday. "Did you pay for that or register in some way?"

Scrapbook workshop? Where was it? She only had a vague feeling she liked scrapbooking. An image of a box-shaped store painted a peculiar shade of green apple came to mind. "I know the shop. Aunt Bee's Craft Closet. It was only ten dollars. They provide all the supplies you need to complete the project. There should be a record if I attended."

Ryan smiled at her encouragingly. If she hadn't, then where was she? She couldn't have taken a shower for two days. "Ryan," she turned slowly, "I think I am missing forty-eight hours. I need to tell the police. That means Mark has been missing for forty-eight hours. He really is a missing person. What about Theron? How could I not show up for two days?"

"Amy, think this through." He pushed the office door closed, gesturing in the direction of the kitchen. He placed his lips near her ears and whispered the words. His closeness didn't make the words any less chilling. "Tell no one. I think this is a setup. I am not sure how or who. If you've been out of it for two days or more why has no one shown up until today? As a high security clearance employee, your absence would be acted upon immediately. Nothing happened. Don't tell the police because it just makes you look a bit unbalanced. They will pass this off as a man who decided he wasn't quite ready for the married life."

His words did make sense, especially as chunks of memory started falling in place. Ryan had always been good to her. He showed her the ropes with amazing patience when she was a newbie, an irritating curious one too. Even though he served as her mentor, he was only about ten years older than she was. There was a time she thought he might be attracted to her romantically, but she pushed aside that notion as being fanciful. She'd been working with him in one way or another for almost ten years. Outside of Remy, Ryan was probably the only person she could totally trust. Part of her mind reminded her that she should trust her husband, too, but she never told him all her secrets as she did Ryan. "Tell me what you think happened. I respect your opinion."

"Sit down." He motioned to a rolling desk chair. "I've given this a great deal of thought. Even took the rest of the day off to consider it. It was not a case of robbery. Now that we suspect there might be a missing forty-eight hours, it thickens the plot. An outside influence such as a rival company or even government kidnapping could happen, but they'd not return you. Secondly, Theron would be on top of that in a heartbeat. Wipes out that theory. Besides, your husband would report your kidnapping."

She sighed. "You told me what it wasn't. I thought for a moment that the gas might have been Sarin. I had most of the symptoms, but I wouldn't have them for forty-eight hours."

"You're right as usual, Amy. I mean Dr. Schaeffer. It's hard for me to get used to the name change." Ryan pushed his slipping glasses up his nose.

She smiled at her friend while he paced the tiny area deep in thought with his hands behind his back. The man knew something, or he thought he knew something, but he wasn't sharing. "Out with it, Ryan, I know you well enough to hazard you've come up with a couple of theories."

"I have. Don't know why I bother to try to hide anything from one of the sharpest minds I've ever encountered." He stopped pacing and looked around the room for a seat. Not finding one, he pulled up a sturdy-looking box. "Here's what I have. You remain. Mark is gone. No signs of a robbery. Your muddled thinking is a result of a pharmaceutical blocking your memory. The blood on the pillow is minute. It could have been a simple cut, a nose bleed, or even intentionally planted."

Amy's attention caught on the blood significance. "How did you know about the blood?"

"Did you honestly think Theron wouldn't run its investigation? I saw the pictures, and they typed the blood. It could be anyone's who is O positive." He waited, giving her time to think about it.

She should have considered that Theron would do such, but her memory returning in chunks made it hard to keep on top of it. "Yes, you're right. They'd do a better investigation than the police in reality."

"Here's the troublesome part." He leaned closer, cupping his hand around his mouth. "I wondered if it might not be Theron. Perhaps they were trying something on you as a guinea pig. When Mark objected, he disappeared."

The heaviness of her limbs, her foggy memory, her impaired vision, hadn't they worked on something like that for the military? It was a serum injected into prisoners of war. It caused them to confess. They often admitted to things they never did or even to things that never existed since it tended to blur memories while releasing inhibitions. She thought they shelved it. On the other hand, maybe someone else was using it. "It's a possibility. What else do you have?"

Ryan rubbed his hand over his face, knocking his glasses askew. He pulled them off and put them in his shirt pocket. Inhaled deeply, he opened his mouth to speak but then closed it without saying a word. The man was dithering.

"Spit it out." The words came out more sharply than she intended. It had been a long day or maybe a couple of long days. Who knew for sure at this point? "Please," she tacked on.

"Okay." Inhaling again, he spoke. "Mark hasn't been in your life long. How much do you know about him?"

"Mark," she whispered his name but stood at Ryan's nefarious suggestion. "How dare you accuse Mark?"

Ryan stood, too, meeting her toe to toe. "Hear me out before going all ballistic on my scrawny white ass."

She laughed, remembering the line from a popular movie. Waving her hand in a circle, she motioned for him to proceed.

"Amy, we live odd lives, never talking about our work and probably having very little opportunity for socialization. People talk all the time, especially non-Theron employees. They whine about their job, complain about their siblings or parents, sometimes both. They talk about their hobbies, their favorite teams, restaurants, television shows. Sometimes they curse whatever political party or religion they don't like. If they have an ex, there is usually an ongoing litany about that person." He stopped and stared into her eyes.

"Your point to all of this is?" She raised one eyebrow. He had a point. Ryan always did. He just took his time getting to it, which was the major difference between him and her husband. Mark was always action, always moving.

"Out of everything, I mentioned that people talked about on a daily basis, what can you tell me about Mark?" He said the words softly, but they still landed with a big impact.

"Okay." She flashed an uncertain smile. "Remember my memory isn't what it used to be."

His lips tightened at her comment, but he refused to saying anything more, putting the burden on her with his silence. She heard cops did that to get people to talk. Well, she knew plenty of things about Mark. "He doesn't have any siblings, and his parents are dead." She folded her arms, nodding her head.

"Did he say they were dead? Did you assume that? Did he ever show you a photo of them? Are his grandparents dead too? What about cousins, did they all die too? What were his parents' names?"

He lobbed the questions at her like water balloons, and she had nothing to lob back. Why didn't she know these things? She should. Everything happened so quickly from meeting him at the pharmaceuticals conference to getting married. "I don't know."

He tugged on his ear, a nervous gesture. Ryan felt bad about pressing her, but she did ask him, which meant she had no grounds for complaints. He was on her side even if she didn't like what he was saying. "We talked about us. That's it."

"Did you mention Remy? Your mother? The half-brother you've never seen? Me?"

She was surprised he tacked on the last, but it all made sense. He certainly rated above her mythical half-brother. "Yes, I told him, even about you."

"Amy, can't you see he was keeping stuff back from you? I can't tell you why. Might even be married to another woman. Since you didn't marry in the states, they don't check that when you marry out of the country. Wait, his parents' name would be on the marriage certificate. Do you know where it is?" He looked expectantly around the room at the various boxes, trying to read the words printed on each one without much success. He pulled his glasses out and perched them on his nose.

"You'd think their names would be on it, but it's Tahiti. I'm not sure if I put my name on it. I don't know where it is. I let Mark take care of that since he's an accountant, which means he's organized." Ryan rolled his eyes when she mentioned the word accountant, or was it the organized word that earned it. "I saw that. What's wrong with being an accountant? Not as wonderful as being doctor, is it?"

"It doesn't have anything to do with a doctor. It is a generic job. One that is hard to check out. I believe most of the Mafia claims to be accountants. Have you ever met his co-workers? Even know the name of his company?"

She brightened remembering Mark had told her that. "It's Accountants' Accounting. He laughed and called it a stupid name."

"Did you ever look this up to see where it was? Maybe you might like to surprise your husband on his birthday. You do know when his birthday is?"

Caught. She didn't know jack about her husband. The caring eyes of her friend didn't help any. "Roman Catholic, born July fifteenth, loves Mexican food, Los Abuelos is his favorite restaurant, never married, graduated from Tulane with honors, enjoys bicycling and gardening. He enjoys watching *Nova* and *Scientific American*."

Ryan sighed. "I find it amazing you share the same likes. You even have the same birthday. Went to the same college. What disturbs me more is that you would lie to me. I am your friend. I'm here putting my career in danger to try to help. All I get is a sheet of lies that a five-year-old could have done a better job putting together. Maybe we aren't friends at all. Perhaps I was only fooling myself thinking so."

Great, she lied to her friend and pissed him off in the process. God! She covered her face with both hands. The tears slid down her face unexpectedly. Crying wasn't something she did. It was for the pampered girls with rich daddies, not her. Amy realized that children thrown away like half-grown puppies don't get the luxuries of tears or bemoaning their fate. Everything she had, she earned, except for Mark, who appeared in her life like a pop-up thunderstorm out of nowhere.

A suspicion that Mark might not be who he pretended to be was growing. Actually, it wasn't a new thought. It had always been there, but as long as Mark told her how much he needed her, how beautiful she was, and how much he loved her, she ignored it. The sex was great too. It seemed like they were always in bed. If not in bed, then just getting out of it. It was too much on top of a very long day. Her tears flowed, as her heart broke a little more. She felt arms close around her and recognized the smell of the antibiotic soap and rubbing alcohol on Ryan's clothing. The cologne of doctors she used to joke. He'd remind her that it was one-step up from smelling like a vet.

Remy opened the door, her face gathered up like a thunderstorm ready to let loose on someone. "What are you doing to my girl?"

Amy backhanded her nose, wincing at her action. "I'm okay. It's just been a long day."

"Alrighty then, I'll give you two a couple more minutes, but Ryan needs to go because you need your sleep." She closed the door quietly.

Amy placed her head back on Ryan's chest, liking the comfort of another person. It didn't change anything, but it made things seem okay for a little bit. "I am overstressed to be sure. I didn't like what you mentioned about Mark. It hurt me because, for a change, a man was crazy about me. I wasn't just some brainy chick to mock. He was the only man who cherished and loved me in my life. I don't want to believe it might have been a lie."

He tightened his arms around her, laying his head atop hers. "I don't want it to be a lie, either. I want what you want, but we do have to check out all angles."

Amy sniffed, reaching out for a tissue box on the crowded table. Her hand landed on it as Ryan pushed the box closer. He was always there trying to make things easier for her. "You're right." It felt like Ryan kissed her hair, but that didn't make sense.

"I happen to know that Mark is not the only man to ever love and cherish you." Ryan loosened his embrace and straightened.

Using the tissue to sop up her tears, she caught his words. How like Ryan to try to make her feel better. "If you mean my father, you'd be wrong. Never met him. I doubt he even knows I exist."

Ryan opened the door and stood there a moment. He had one foot in the hall before turning to say over his shoulder, "I wasn't talking about your father." He pulled the door shut.

The house seemed eerily quiet after he left, but Remy was there somewhere. It wasn't a big house. She picked up the folder Ryan left behind. She walked out into the living room where her aunt watched some type of game show, yelling out answers and squealing with glee when she got them right. Remy took so much joy in her game shows. Her aunt smiled and pointed to the kitchen. Yep, they were being monitored she almost forgot. Her aunt asked, "I changed the sheets on your bed, Sweet Pea. I'll sleep on Mark's side. Is that okay with you?"

"Sounds fine. I am going to take a bath, then go to bed." What she really was going to do was search the bathroom for some sign of a propulsion agent that injected the drug into her body. A needle, vial, maybe a handy container with the name printed on it. No one would be stupid enough to leave evidence. On the other hand, she'd be the foolish one if she didn't look. If she'd been out of it for a while, then whoever did it had time to remove any evidence, but she still had to search.

* * * *

Simpson drove the conservative sedan to Beth's house. The woman had been quiet most of the return trip. When they first left Amy Newkirk's house, she'd been quite talkative. Volatile might be a better word. No one had told her he was there to take Amy back with him for quarantine and observation. Nope, she didn't like it at all. He stopped in her driveway. Beth unbuckled her seat belt, reached for her purse, and slammed the door all without a word to him. True, he didn't need words to know when a woman was pissed.

He waited until he was out of the neighborhood before calling headquarters. "Simpson here. The mission failed." He tolerated the stream of profanity aimed at him but felt obligated to defend his actions.

"No, sir, you're wrong. The women must not have been as close as you thought. It is hard to tell with women. I did place the bug. It is activated, so you should be able to hear what is going on in the house."

Really? It was hard for him to believe he was babysitting some scientist who apparently lost her husband and memory at the same time. Convenient, his cynical side added. Headquarters refused to elaborate on the significance of the case. Instead, they sent him to be Theron's errand boy. Obviously, they left out some vital info. Why? He handled matters that could topple nations. What merited such cloak and dagger tactics? Maybe the bleary-eyed blonde-haired woman did murder her husband. She wouldn't be the first. Theron might want her to get away with it, so she could keep developing biological warfare delivery systems. Amy Newkirk wouldn't be the first person to get away with homicide. Of course, he kept coming back to the reason why. The voice in his ear pulled him away from the one in his head.

"Yes, sir, I will post a surveillance team on Newkirk's house." He mentally reviewed whom he would call on to watch the house when he couldn't. Probably would be an extremely boring job, but that's the way things rolled sometimes. It sure beat being in a weapons crossfire and out of ammunition.

Names of wanna be private eyes came to mind. If they had any ambition and money they'd have their own businesses, instead of being available for hire. As was his custom, he sized up the local talent. In a town the size of Dallas, there were always plenty willing to observe, record, and do a little bit more if promised none of it would come back on them.

Yeah, he wanted the type willing to work for a buck, but not intelligent enough to realize nothing could be promised. There was a careful balance about hiring local talent. Too eager ones bungled a job convinced they could handle it due to the hours spent in front of the television watching crime dramas. One told him confidently that he always knew who the killer was at the start of the show.

A heavy sigh escaped him. Kids today. Did none of them know how to think anymore? Had to bite his tongue on that one and not explain that all the viewers knew who the killer was. The show was about being able to tie the guy to the crime. Too often, that didn't happen in real life.

On some of the cold cases, Simpson was the man who slipped in and out without a trace. Giving out too much information could get him killed. Other times, his habit of collecting intimate details of people's lives saved his neck. He kept that jewel to himself. Occasionally, when hiring locals, he got a wise guy who asked too many questions. They were the troublemakers. Thought they knew enough to cut him out of the picture and collect all the dough. They thought wrong.

Tony, an old special ops bud, who went into security, gave him a handful of names starting with the most capable to the least. For this, he'd start at the bottom. It didn't appear to be any more than watching and taking notes. It really was an insult to his skills. Couldn't understand why the agency was so on fire for him to take the case. They even pulled him off a power shift in an oil rich South American country. Damn, they needed that country, too, with the price of gas shooting up.

It didn't feel right. He'd flimflammed plenty of people. Some might even call him an artist at telling lies that resembled the truth, even under torture. Yeah, he was that good, which meant he could sniff out an incomplete truth or a smokescreen. It made him wonder why they were working so hard to fool him.

* * * *

Amy, dressed in her oversized nightshirt, smothered a yawn. She was tired, but more likely she suffered from drug related symptoms. No matter, sleep would help eliminate the drug residue in her body and the fatigue. Later, Amy was glad for the familiarity of Remy's warm body in bed with her. It would be almost impossible to sleep alone. She rolled closer to her aunt. "You don't think they can hear us in here?"

Her aunt giggled. "Nope, I turned on one of those late night talk shows. It will take them a while to figure out it isn't us. Who knows what crazy things those guests might be saying too?"

She kissed her aunt's cheek, getting her lips greasy in the process. "I forgot you put that night cream junk on your face."

"Takes more work for women my age to attract the male eye, not like you who has men falling prostrate in front of you." Remy rolled over with her pronouncement.

Her aunt makes some cryptic comment, and then pretends to sleep. She should be used to it since that is what she did while Amy lived in Terrebonne, but not this time. She elbowed her aunt gently. "Tell me what you meant."

"I know your heart is broken with Mark's disappearance. Somehow, you came up with the idea that he was the first man to love you. That's why you're so crazy in love with him. He wasn't the first man to love you."

Her half-cough half-laugh filled the room. Seriously, her aunt saw her with eyes of love, not as she was. Men weren't exactly breaking down the door for skinny scientists with super short hair. True she did forget a lot, but she hadn't forgotten the basic things like walking, talking, and that men did not crave the attentions of women smarter than they were. It made her wonder just how smart she was or better yet how intelligent Mark was. Her being a brainiac didn't scare him off. It was another reason she loved him. A pang of loneliness stabbed her reminding her that once again she was alone.

The smell of talcum powder and Remy's night cream were oddly comforting in the dark. She never realized how dark the room was. Squinting, she tried to make out the shape of the wardrobe. No luck, tomorrow she'd buy a night light. She was— no, she meant is—crazy in love with Mark because he is so open and obvious about his love for her. It made her wonder about Ryan's parting remark though. "Remy, when Ryan was here he made me realize I don't know anything about Mark. I don't even know the names of his people. I told him that Mark was the only man that loved and cherished me, and he told me I was wrong."

Remy muttered from her side of the bed. "God have mercy on the men folk. Some of them have such bad timing it's no wonder they're alone."

Chapter Three

Simpson read the agent's report on the last twenty-four hours observing Newkirk's home. Amy and her aunt visited the library, the local health food store, and the animal shelter. He made a mental note to find out what books she checked out at the library. If she was doing research on the library computers, she probably didn't login under her name. Well, he'd have to order a search on the library server for the time she was there. All he had to do was eliminate all the porn and near porn sites, the adolescent boys searched as well as few of the older males. No fashion sites or celebrity addresses searches for Amy Newkirk. With any luck, no hopeful mystery novelists were busy Googling how to kill a husband or dispose of his body.

The health food store was somewhat significant because headquarters wanted to know what the subject was consuming. Food would be his automatic response, but they wanted more details than that. With that Cajun relative squatting in her house, they were probably tucking into crawfish and dirty rice. His stomach gave a rumble reminding him that the coffee and a half of a stale cheese Danish he consumed made a poor meal. Shaking out a cigarette, he lit one hoping to stave off hunger pains. Smoking didn't help him drop weight, but the demands of the job did keep him from eating regularly. Nope, people would never think of him as a James Bond type, which was good. Sophisticated, debonair men tended to attract both male and female eyes. The modest spare tire around his middle helped him to be less noticeable.

What he really needed to do was get into the house and check out things. With either Amy or her aunt always at home, it wasn't easy. Word was she requested to return to work. If they couldn't observe in her in a quarantined setting, then work was the next best thing. Theron had so many cameras, guards, and bugs demonstrating they were even more paranoid than the tobacco companies of material leaving the premise. With her at work, he could get in and see what the geek girl had in her house. Of course, you think someone would have done that when she was out of the country.

Sure, he heard all the talk about how smart she was, but so far, he wasn't impressed. The woman misplaced her husband and, as far as he could tell, wasn't too upset, even able to return to work. He'd observed plenty of cold-blooded killers, and he'd put Amy Newkirk, make that Schaeffer near the top if she could keep her cool after offing her husband. Even he kept forgetting her married name.

The police already wrote the husband off as a reluctant groom, which may or may not be true. It could be true. It was hard to know with the intellectual set. Was the husband as smart as his wife was? Did he feel threatened by her intelligence? The compact bungalow did not hint at the money Newkirk's financial records indicated she possessed. Obviously, she squirrelled away somewhere. Newkirk appeared to be one not to spend cash in obvious ways. It could be the reason for a fight. Man expects to share in his wife's money, but when he expresses his opinion, he disappears. Some folks act as if they never heard of divorce. Then again, many people felt they were smarter than the law. Was Amy one of them? So far, she played the confused victim well.

* * * *

Amy managed a weak smile as her co-workers peppered her with questions while their faces wrinkled up into a reasonable facsimile of concerns. Did they know what happened to Mark? Was it related to her work? Hard to say, but she certainly wouldn't find out anything by staying at home after two weeks with Remy hovering over her or visiting the spa the firm recommended. The facility they wanted her to visit probably resembled a sanitarium more than any spa. A suspicion that once she entered the grounds, she might never leave also nagged at her. Work was her only acceptable option. It allowed those who were leery of her missing husband and memory to monitor her. It would also give her access to the lab to discover if she dealt with anything that might instigate a kidnapping.

Kidnapping seemed to be a moot point since Marks's disappearance never merited a ransom demand. Did she have something to do with it? Could she have offed her husband like the detective implied? Maybe had a psychotic break, and, as a super-smart scientist type, she knew how to rid herself of a body. Never mind that she never had a psychotic break in her life or had a motive. Her colleagues' eyes followed her as she prepared to work. Turning her back to them, she buttoned up her lab coat, no reason to see their anxious expressions, which indicated concern about their own safety. A few of the women threw her pitying glances she caught in the reflective surfaces of the equipment.

They were part of the group that thought Mark left her. Oh well, the police came to that conclusion too. Detective Maxfield had assured her they had a watch on his credit cards while patting her hand. She'd added, as if woman-to-woman, more than in the official capacity, "You know if he doesn't want to be found, he won't."

She knew that better than anyone did since he'd worked so hard at revealing so little of himself. It didn't make sense to marry her, only to leave her. What would compel him to woo her and then abandon her? Even though he chose not to talk about himself, she'd deduced his intelligence by his astute observations on life.

Pushing her safety glasses in place, she observed Beth headed her way, balancing a stack of notebooks tall enough to block her vision. The woman had to crane her neck to peer around them.

Amy caught a look on her friend's face. She wanted to say something but not in front of the other employees. Her safety glasses cut off most of her peripheral vision, making a silent message more difficult. She stripped off her engagement and wedding rings with a mild pang, placing them in her top drawer along with her wristwatch. Company policy forbade the wearing of jewelry in the lab. Before it hadn't been an issue since all she ever wore was a watch. Normally, she wouldn't have even bothered to wear the rings to work, but taking them off severed her last connection with Mark. He slipped the simple wedding band on her finger during their beach wedding. It hadn't been off her finger since. How long had it been? Biting her lips, she counted the days, almost a month. Beth dropped the notebooks on a counter with a sigh.

"Thank goodness, I caught you before you started." Her friend fairly panted the words.

"Why? I've been gone too long. There is a great deal for me to get up to date on and even more for me to do." She flicked on her computer, cheered by the thought. Work would keep her busy, not busy enough not to obsess over her missing husband, but perhaps enough not to fall into a pitiful, sniveling mess of shattered dreams.

Beth's eyes darted around checking out who was monitoring the conversation. Amy knew she fought the desire to stare at the cameras mounted throughout the lab. A glowing green light would mean the camera captured their every look and possibly every word. Making a half turn to reach her latex gloves, she glanced up at the corner the camera hung suspended from with its glowing green eye. Yep, it was recording, no surprise there. She touched her nose allowing Beth to know their video status.

As if being cued, Beth cleared her throat, angled her head to the notebooks scattered across the counter. "You aren't on Project Morpheus anymore. It has been reassigned since we were unsure when you would be back."

"Reassigned!" Her voice bounced on the stainless steel surfaces. Her tinny, shrill tone garnered looks from her curious colleagues. Not good, not good at all. She should have suspected as much, but somehow, she kept running smack into a wall wherever she turned. The walls appeared out of nowhere, causing her to skid into them. If only she had a sliver of a clue of what was happening, maybe she could piece it together. Lowering her voice, she stood directly in front of Beth using her friend's body to block the camera. Luckily, Beth even had a few inches on her. It would appear on playback she was talking to herself or even just standing. "What's going on? I am lead scientist on the Morpheus Project. No one knows more about it than I do."

Beth spoke loudly, aware of attentive ears and cameras. "I am so glad you are willing to take over Project Blowfly. People tend to underestimate the dangers of the common blowfly."

Firming her lips and blinking her eyes, she managed to fight the urge not to roll them at blatant flattery used to coat her assignment to such an asinine project. Was this punishment?

"I'm your girl," she tried to inject some cheer into her voice, but not too much. She'd be willing to bet that she never had a reputation for being perky or cheerful. Deadly serious would be more appropriate since her work was serious stuff. In a whisper she mouthed, "Who has my project?"

"Wilkenshire," Beth whispered back, interlacing her fingers together to prevent any wayward, telling gesture that the camera might catch.

Wilkenshire, she couldn't believe it. She'd bet this lame blowfly project was his baby. "Lord, have mercy on us all," she murmured, realizing she spouted one of Aunt Remy's trademark phases. It certainly suited the situation. "Where do I start?" she asked, aware that she should be saying something with so much silence between the two of them.

Beth pushed a blue binder toward her. "You might want to transcribe these notes into a somewhat coherent narrative." She grimaced, maybe imagining her friend's outrage, before walking away.

Transcribing notes? Really? She couldn't believe it. Grunt work suitable for the lowest peon on staff, not for one of their top scientists. She might even be the top scientist, especially in her field. Holding onto the binder, she plopped into her desk chair and scooted to her computer. Pulling off her latex gloves, she aimed them at the trashcan and missed. Screw it. Let maintenance do their job.

Theron insisted that safety was its number one priority. It was the reason behind the lack of jewelry, lab coat, and even gloves to type up a simple report. A person never knew when they might encounter a dangerous toxin. Currently, she wasn't feeling like a rule follower, especially when she'd to work on a joke of a project. Even a middle school student could figure out that flies were not a security threat.

Typing in her password, she watched the circle icon blink to indicate loading, but it seemed to take extra-long. Her screen flickering to life featured a verdant field screensaver she'd never bothered to change. The familiar screen struck her as peculiar for a reason. Squinting, she realized all her Morpheus Project files were gone. They ripped her files away from her. She straightened hearing soft footsteps. What now? What else could they take?

Ryan Korman's image was superimposed over the verdant field screensaver. She saw his raised hand hover over her shoulder. "Don't," she hissed the word. The image of Ryan touching her shoulder, even compassionately, might result in unfortunate results for him. His hand landed on his lab coat, worrying a hanging string as if his original intention. His smile looked false, as she pivoted her chair, but not as stiff as his words.

"Good to have you back with us, Dr. Newkirk. No, I mean..." His eyes rolled up, and his lips twisted as he struggled to recall her name. "Never mind." He turned sharply and stalked away.

Well, that didn't go well. Unfortunately, Ryan probably felt she rejected his comforting gesture. For a smart man, she certainly flustered him, to the point of him forgetting her new name. Not like him at all, but she wanted to keep him out of the strange quagmire that surrounded her. There was no need for him to stick his foot in the mess. Still, how could she reassure him when streaming video of all her activities inside the facility went to someone's office? All the labeled videos sat on shelves to serve as a backup whenever questions arose. The video with her conversing with Ryan would be the one watched the way her luck was running. Her friend didn't need that type of grief.

Opening the blue binder, she looked at the scribbled notes and winced. Wilkenshire's handwriting taunted her. "A third grader writes better," she grumbled as she began typing her notes. Her mind wandered as her fingers typed. The situation puzzled her, but solving puzzles is what she did. True, most of them were of the chemical nature. Something wasn't right, besides a missing husband and forty-eight hours she couldn't recall.

Theron was the unopposed leader in chemical options. A tag line a cunning vice president developed, saying it inspired confidence and misled the public. It also hid the fact that most of their products could cause compliancy, deviant behavior, and death. Ten years ago when she signed on, she didn't realize that was the company's overriding objective. Instead, her early projects were positive ones, including increasing crop yield and developing plants resistant to disease and pests. Of course, that one didn't turn out as well as she planned, either. Published reports from watchdog groups blamed genetically altered crops for everything from migraines to autism.

The company policy of keeping a low profile from their product kept the reports from actually naming them as the creators, but Amy knew. Her guilt propelled her into the Morpheus Project that somehow she could eliminate the horrors of war. At first, the project aimed to create a substance that would negate the aggressive war-like tendencies of humans. Airplanes could disperse it in the air. Civil wars tearing countries apart would halt immediately. It would be like an anti-depressant for the masses. Soon all the soldiers would be reaching for a cocktail instead of a weapon.

It sounded so good in theory a small smile crossed her face at the image of soldiers throwing down their weapons, unstrapping their helmets, and walking off into the sunset. She had almost single-handedly perfected the drug and the propellant needed, but suddenly the project changed. There seemed to be no market for something that stopped wars. Too many people profited from continual wars, which resulted in a huge market for something that would crush the other nation with as little property damage as possible. By that time, she'd chosen to visit the pharmaceutical conference in Albuquerque. She'd referred to it as research, but she just needed a break from Morpheus.

One of the researchers strolled by her workstation and glanced at her computer screen. Amy followed the woman's path wondering if she were spying on her. Was Ellen's interest in her screen just normal curiosity? Maybe even a type of career competiveness where she compared her project against Amy's? If that were the case, Ellen won big time. Nothing could be worse than typing notes that didn't make sense half the time. The hash marks and abbreviations served as a type of code for Wilkenshire. On a good day, she might try to unravel them, but not today.

Instead, she included the hash marks and the abbreviations into the notes. She didn't expect anyone to read the notes or even conduct the research. Blowfly was a dead end, busy work so to speak. She wouldn't be surprised if tomorrow they assigned her another aimless task. Apparently, she'd have to prove herself again. Mark's disappearance resulted in her exhibiting shock symptoms. The word instability occurred more than once within her hearing, making her a loose cannon and incapable of working on a sensitive project like Morpheus.

As a trained medical doctor, she knew the signs of shock. Probably the reasoning the higher powers used to remove her from the project, but there was much more than that, starting long before, even before she met Mark. Her big mistake was publicly questioning the direction the Morpheus Project took. *Odd, she remembered that, but couldn't remember Mark's birthday.* After that small display of noncompliance, Theron was glad for her to take her doubts to Albuquerque pharmaceutical conference where they hoped she'd forget her dissatisfaction.

It worked, in a way. She met a charismatic man with gorgeous eyes and a charming manner. Mark literally swept her off her feet when she tripped over a mass of power cords taped to the floor rather like an impromptu speed bump. He caught her about the time she would have taken a header into the male erectile dysfunction booth scattering pamphlets featuring grinning, virile, mature men. For that, she owed him a major thank you as he steadied her back on her feet. Instead of thanking him, his sparkling green eyes cast a spell on her, causing her mouth to fall open, without a single word coming out.

He helped her over to a round plastic table with equally frail plastic chairs. The unknown man came back with a soda and urged her to drink it. A sugary drink was an excellent cure for shock. Amy smiled, already impressed by his actions. Her savior introduced himself as Mark. At first, she thought he was in pharmaceuticals because she remembered he talked quite knowledgably about the products at the conference. As they got to know each other a little better, he showed less medical expertise, finally admitting to being an accountant. Oddly, she accepted his profession without question.

Stupid. Idiot. She scolded herself for her attentiveness to a ready smile, flirtatious banter, and a pair of broad shoulders. Maybe she should have Googled him or even hired a detective to investigate Mark Schaeffer. None of this occurred to her because she was in love, hopped up on oxytocin. Her system pumped the hormone into her bloodstream with every sexual encounter they shared, making her bond to Mark, not only emotionally, but also physically. If he did have a medical background, he'd know this. Many men without medical backgrounds managed to deduce this fact. Did he really love her, or did he pretend to love her? If he did pretend, what would be the benefit to him?

Her lips twisted in a grimace, thinking it might be likely he had walked as opposed to some nefarious ending. No ransom note, which killed any interest the local police had. A man caught up in an affair where he flies to a tropical island and marries in a beachside wedding that may not be real either. Yep, that sounded like a man who might walk. Why did Mark pick her? There were plenty of scantily clothed cuties promoting products at the conference, especially around the male erectile dysfunction area.

It had to be something else. She knew what she was, a slender thirty-something woman who recently hacked off her long blonde hair. No femme fatale for sure, so why the attraction, and why was it so immediate? Her Aunt Remy would tell her she had plenty of good features from her kind heart to her crackerjack mind, but those things did not get you dates, especially with men who looked like Mark.

Maybe her desire to be married and have children overrode her logical mind. Heaven knows her hormones played havoc with any logical thought processes. Somewhere in the corner of her mind, she hoped to marry. Being in her mid-thirties made the concept of children a vanishing one. She knew enough about physiology to know her peak childbearing years were mostly behind her. Wait any longer and the rate of birth defects skyrocketed. Maybe that pushed her into running off with Mark. That would involve thought, and, as far as she could remember, she went on pure emotions. Couldn't say it wasn't an amazing trip, though.

As a brainiac, she never expected such exhilarating highs, one right after the other. First, Mark announced he had to have her, and then he loved her, followed by a proposal and a runaway trip to Tahiti. He managed it all in less than two months. Amy pecked away at the keyboard to demonstrate to the slow moving employees who managed to saunter past her desk that she was not only working, but she was okay. Was she?

She acknowledged the interested personnel with a head bob. Her usual persona never went for jibber jabber. Why change now?

Besides, that would only indicate something wasn't right, confirming the management's theory of her being a loose cannon. Couldn't afford that now, especially being on her own. Aunt Remy headed back to Terrebonne today, rather begrudgingly.

Amy knew her aunt didn't think she should be alone, but, apparently, the good folks of Terrebonne felt they couldn't manage without their Remy. One man even drove to Amy's house to beg Remy to return to concoct a potion for his digestion. The mischievous smile on her aunt's face indicated another body part might be involved. Most folks just settled on calling, a few even texted, which surprised Amy. The old hometown never served as a haven for the technologically advanced. It was more like something time left behind. She practically pushed her aunt out the door this morning, and not because she wanted her to go, quite the opposite.

Still, as vulnerable as she was, two weeks was long enough. She'd become dependent on Remy if she stayed. Stirring up a pot of gumbo, doing her laundry, chit chatting about nonsensical things to keep her mind off her current life, all sounded good. It wasn't what she needed if she was determined to figure things out. Aunt Remy would tell her to let sleeping dogs lie, even if one of those hounds happened to be her missing husband. No one in this strange, twisted drama acted as he or she should.

Police didn't accuse her of causing her husband's disappearance but there wasn't much effort in finding him. They shrugged their shoulders murmuring about Mark getting cold feet. The female detective tried to assure her that it wasn't uncommon by pointing to celebrity marriages that ended mere weeks after they started. Amy's lips twisted to one side remembering how hard she fought to keep from shouting she wasn't some drunken pop star who married in a moment. Before the words passed her lips, she checked them. Why did she run off in such a hasty fashion to marry a man she just met? It made no sense. It took her almost six weeks to decide on the appropriate hiking boot when she decided to take up hiking.

Any hope of returning to normalcy and rescuing her previous life depended on figuring out what happened. She needed to concentrate to do that, without the distractions of other people. Of course, that meant driving home to a dark house and climbing into a cold bed, she shared with Mark and most recently Remy. Maybe she should get rid of the bed.

Feeling eyes on her, she glanced up, only to find Wilkenshire regarding her with a smug smile. She half-rose in her chair, ready to tell the man what she thought of his sloppy records, but she stopped. It would only attract attention she didn't want. Sure, the old Amy Newkirk would have, probably, but then she hadn't been trying to be low-keyed. Remy hinted the old self stepped on a few toes in her quest to do things her way—that happened to be the better way. No doubt, she'd treaded on Wilkenshire's a few times. Hard to believe someone bumped him up to Morpheus.

It could only mean that the project was finished, or they felt he could do no harm. He certainly couldn't help. Using her hand to scratch her head, she peeked through her fingers at the irritating man. No reason to let him notice her interest. It would give him even more reason to gloat. The disheveled man gave the appearance of trying to channel Einstein with his uncontrolled graying curls. It baffled her how he even worked at the facility since they insisted on scientists who were the crème of the crop. Must have a relative on the board was the only logical answer.

The remainder of the day crawled by with nothing to distract her, but the blowfly notes that were mostly gibberish. Her opinion of Wilkenshire dropped several more degrees after reading them. Amy would have bet at the start of the day that it would be hard for her opinion to get any lower. Instead of writing Kelvin, he wrote Kevin for temperature unit. On further examination, she realized he should have at least used Celsius, a laboratory guideline, as opposed to a personal option. Nothing he wrote made any sense in a type of rambling fashion with a scientific word thrown in now and then for flavor. How could the man call himself a scientist?

* * * *

Simpson looked at his watch. Four-o'clock, he cursed when he saw the time. Parking his sedan on a side street, he carefully made his way through the copse of trees. The suspect's neighbors worked, but before long, they would all start heading home, including Amy. He hoped to be in and out of the house much earlier than this. Unfortunately, Theron's president wanted him to analyze the tapes from the bug in the house. There wasn't much to analyze. There were sounds of cooking, the radio, even the dishwasher, and all sounds of daily life. If he knew, what they were looking for then, he might be more likely to find it. No one was willing to give him any clues. The best he could do was find any Theron files she may have taken home that would provide legal grounds for suing or terminating her services.

His breath caught a little as he scampered nearer to her house. Not in as good of shape as he would like, then again, it was probably the damn smoking. He stopped to finish the cig in his mouth, and then ground it out under the toe of his shoe. The dry leaves crackled under his feet reminding him how hazardous a fire could be. The butt was lifeless and flat, presenting no hazard to the surrounding leaves. He picked up the butt and placed it in his pocket leaving no evidence of his visit. Good, he pulled on his latex gloves smoothing out the fingers. At first, he found wearing the gloves awkward, but now he found there was little he couldn't do with his latex clad fingers. It was past time to check out the house.

An elderly woman with an equally old schnauzer strolled down the street. *Could they walk any slower?* When he felt they were clear, he slipped out of the woods, glancing both ways to make sure he wasn't observed. Using his burglar pick, he popped the back door open. "Could have used a credit card on that flimsy lock," he muttered to himself and then stopped. He didn't want to be on the audio tapes. It was a point of personal pride that he could toss a house and leave no trace.

Opening kitchen cabinets silently, he noted Amy was not a collector of wine glasses or even dishes for that matter. She had the very basics—three plates, two bowls, and assorted flatware. A skillet, a pan with a lid, and a stockpot compiled her entire cooking arsenal. Everything had a well-worn look as if it were a hand-me-down or purchased at a yard sale. Not a single new item that could be a wedding gift. Strange.

He opened the pantry to find it sparsely stocked. Not too surprising since she had been out of the country. Not everyone kept their cabinets stocked as if they expected a blizzard. Simpson smirked to himself, knowing that his mother back in Nebraska would consider anything less than six weeks of food on hand inexcusable.

Ah yes, Amy was southern-raised. People who believed you could get milk whenever you wanted it as opposed to keeping a box of dried milk on hand. So far, nothing, but then again people usually didn't hide things in kitchens. He checked the freezer to encounter a half loaf of millet bread and two ice trays. Damn, the woman lived like a bachelor with the exception she had no beer in the fridge, just a container of gumbo.

The living room, besides a couch, chair, and coffee table, held an afghan and the latest edition of *Popular Science* and *Astronomy*. If the woman was trying to look like a geek, she had it down. The sound of a car had him peeking through the blinds. An orange Camaro definitely wasn't a factory color and, better yet, not the doctor.

He headed for the office, glancing at the picture in the hallway. That was peculiar. Sure, he wasn't an interior designer, but there wasn't anything on the walls in the kitchen or living room, so why put a photo in the hallway? Once in the office, he forgot about the out-of-place picture. The laptop set on a computer desk charging and open. How convenient, he thought as he powered it up. The screen flickered to life, bypassing the need to enter a password. Never a good sign because people who didn't use passwords didn't have anything to hide. Typing in a directory prompt, he scrolled through the files looking for a hidden or encrypted file. Nothing. Plugging in a jump drive, he downloaded everything.

While the files downloaded, he poked around the stacked paper boxes with carefully printed identification such as winter clothes, books, and rocks. Not surprising, he found clothes, books, and rocks. The only thing unusual was they were not in the appropriately marked boxes. The doctor's house didn't yield any evidence or anything vaguely interesting. The woman saved her textbooks. Lord knows she had a ton of them. She had medical journals going back years. As far as he could tell, she was a typical over achieving female. A woman like her would be lucky to hook a man.

His watch alarm went off alerting him he needed to leave. He closed the box lids, replacing the tape. The duct tape mainly adhered to the cardboard. Any slackness in the tape, the suspect would conclude she'd opened the box previously. Word was she lost her memory. With that in mind, it would be hard for her to remember if she opened a box or not. Grabbing the jump drive, he powered down the computer. Placing one gloved hand on the computer, he felt a slight residual heat. It should dissipate before the suspect entered the office. The fact the laptop was in the office showed she didn't overuse the computer. Avid computer users often left the computer where they used it last, beside the bed, on the kitchen table, or on the couch.

He passed through the kitchen on cat feet, pulling the kitchen door closed behind him. Standing in the shadow of the tress, he waited for the good doctor to return home. Did he lock the door? A doubt nagged at him, but the neighborhood traffic picked up. A loose puppy ran down the street with two children chasing it. Before he knew it, a couple of adults joined in the chase. It would be best if he stayed in the shadows. Of course, that canine could veer off the sidewalk to the woods. Better to fade into the woodwork, so to speak. He smiled at the thought. Yep, few were good as he was when it came to blending in.

Only problem was he came up with nothing. No matter, his job was mainly observation, and that part was ridiculously easy. Tonight he'd return and attach a tracking device to her car. Her house only offered a carport instead of a garage, which made it all the easier.

* * * *

The clock read 5:00. Several employees hung up their lab coats and readied themselves for the departure search. Normally, Amy was one of the last to leave, but not today. Her head hurt from trying to make sense of the notes. She tried inserting missing words into the sentences at least to make it grammatically correct, but they still didn't make any logical sense. After about three hours, she decided the man wrote pages and pages of garbage.

What was his purpose in the lab because she was willing to bet he never passed a biochemistry class?

Saving her dubious files, she decided to leave. Eyebrows rose when she hung up her lab coat. Not exactly in character, she knew but refused to type another bogus page. Nodding at Emery, a reticent biologist, whose high hairline and blond eyebrows always managed to give her a startled appearance, she said, "Not quite up to long hours."

Emery's head bobbed frenetically in agreement. "Understood. Say no more." The biologist wasn't known for long conversations, but she seemed unusually panicked that Amy might want to continue the conversation. *Geesh, be gone a couple weeks, have your husband disappear along with your memory, and a person becomes a social pariah.*

She looked around for Beth, longing for a friendly face but didn't see her. Her least favorite guard stood ready to search her. Roman was the nickname Beth christened him with due to his hands going where they shouldn't. As far as she knew, no female scientist had successfully hidden files, notes, or even flash drives in their bras, but Roman was determined to be sure. He confided once that he'd read about a Civil War spy smuggled notes in her hair, which made him determined to finger and sniff her hair. Roman was the major reason behind chopping off her long blonde fall of hair.

The sun started its descent while she was still on the highway, making her consider the season. Halloween wasn't far off. It was always a big deal in her hometown. It acted as a warm-up to the Mardi Gras. Coming fast behind Halloween would be Thanksgiving, then Christmas. Theron actually became generous around Christmas, giving the employees several vacation days. Had she thought during her beachside wedding ceremony that it signaled the end of her lonely holidays? To be fair, she usually drove down to see Remy at Christmas.

She tried to remember what she did for Thanksgiving last year. Jumbled memories of Chinese food and Ryan filled her mind. Still, it should be her and Mark's first holidays together as a couple, only it wouldn't. Maybe he'd return before then. Amy realized she'd accepted the detectives' conclusion that Mark got cold feet and left on his own.

The small house came into view. The closed blinds gave the house a sleeping aspect. Maybe it, too, was waiting to start its life, rather like her. Too bad, she hadn't at least left a light on to welcome her home. She'd try to remember to do that tomorrow.

Flicking on a light, she headed to the fridge. Aunt Remy would have left her something delicious. The short, fine hairs stood up on the back of her neck. She reached back to verify they were actually standing up. They were. She began to back out of the house. Apparently, a primitive sense allowed her to know things weren't right. Tapping down a sense of panic threatening to well up, she ran to the neighbor's driveway. Punching in 9-1-1, she hoped that standing in the public view would offer her some protection.

The police car careened around the corner going too fast for a residential neighborhood. At least they responded promptly. A young officer approached her. Her neighbors' faces appeared in windows and doorways, no doubt attracted by the siren. The downside of living in the modest subdivision with houses mere yards apart was that often she could hear her neighbors, especially when they didn't even bother to whisper.

"Isn't she the woman who misplaced her husband?"

"Who's gone now?"

Ignoring the curious onlookers, she turned to the cop. "Sir, someone has been in my home while I was at work. I called immediately. I didn't touch anything, but the back doorknob, light switch and the fridge handle."

He nodded, introduced himself as Officer Ramos, and proceeded to walk toward her house. Amy followed, reluctant to enter. When she realized she'd have to sleep there tonight, an involuntary shiver shot through her body. *Amy, get ahold of yourself.*

Ramos entered the kitchen and turned full circle with his hand on the butt of his gun. He motioned for Amy to come in. "The intruder is long gone. If he wasn't before you came in, the fact you left gave him enough time to escape."

No one left. She'd watched the door. The house looked about the same, but it was different, disturbed. She left the bug undisturbed in the kitchen, so Theron would know she called the police. If her visitors happened to be work-related, then they would know their visit did not go unnoticed. The officer walked slowly through the house turning on lights as he entered each room.

What did he see? A painfully clean house with labeled boxes still packed. Amy stared at the boxes with her precise handwriting. That one held books, the next one held books, but these were fiction. The boxes detailed her life in a way. This one enclosed winter clothes. The other contained Christmas decorations. Not one of them was Mark's. He joked about traveling light. Amy chose to ignore his lack of possessions, putting it down to some eastern philosophy he practiced. Now the lack of boxes indicated a man who did not intend to stay. The police noticed that possibility sooner than she had.

The officer returned from the back rooms, flashed a concerned look her way, which featured unsmiling lips, alert eyes, and a slight furrow of his brow. "I didn't see anything, ma'am. What made you think someone entered the premises?"

It felt different didn't seem like a response with any merit. She lied. "I am horribly OCD," That part wasn't a lie. "I noticed some of my things were moved out their regular spots."

He nodded as if listening, but Amy knew better. The man had already placed her under the Nervous Nellie file for women who call about a loose screen door banging in the wind. It would be hard to prove someone had been in her house since the person had been professional about the entire thing, not leaving any real sign, but she knew.

The air smelled different. Smoke? Cigarette smoke, that's what it was. Her intruder may not have smoked in her house, but smoke smell clings to your clothing. "I smelled smoke. I don't smoke."

The officer's nostrils flared as he tried to take in the smell. "I agree. There is a slight tang. Does no one in your family smoke?"

"No one. I just bought this house, haven't had it more than two months."

Ramos placed his hat back on his head, ready to leave. "Well, that must be it. The former owners must have been smokers. Changes in weather bring out the smell."

There might be some validity to his argument, except they were experiencing a drought. "Dampness brings out odor."

He didn't acknowledge her statement or didn't want to. As far as he was concerned, case closed.

Amy watched the black and white drive away, sending the neighbors back inside their own undisturbed homes. She turned back to the house. Where was the darling brick ranch she fell in love with a little more than three months ago? Mark appeared on the scene after she made plans to purchase the house. He didn't seem to mind that his name wouldn't be on the title. At the time, she regarded that as just another sign that he was a very modern, open-minded type of man. Now she was unsure what type of person he really was. In the scheme of things, she'd spent more time delving into work projects than spent with her husband.

Walking into the house, she threw the deadbolt, knowing it would do little good against a determined predator. Still, it gave her some sense of protection. The fridge yielded up shrimp gumbo, perfect for a fall evening. Punching numbers in the microwave, she mentally reviewed her plans for the night. Should she go in another room without a bug? Although she hadn't planned to talk to herself, maybe it would be best.

Cradling her bowl of hot gumbo, she glanced back at the wine bottle on the counter. Would drinking alone make her pitiful? She deposited the soup on the office desk and returned for the bottle and a wineglass. Technically, she was pitiful and might as well enjoy some of the benefits, not that she planned to get drunk on a half-bottle of Riesling. That was for when you had other people to watch out for you, which she didn't.

Grabbing the small weather radio, she carried it too. The sound quality was horrible, but it was good enough to serve as a filter, making it difficult for whoever was listening to discover anything. Turning on the radio, she turned it to a heavy metal station that should annoy her eavesdropper. It certainly rode ragged on her nerves. She longed to turn it to the local jazz station but fought the urge.

Booting up her computer, she took a spoonful of gumbo, closing her eyes in appreciation. "Ah ya, now that was cooking."

Folks wondered why she wasn't twice her size with Remy's delicious cooking. Remy answered that quickly enough by saying she worked too hard to gain any weight. That she did. Terrebonne,

58

Morgan K. Wyatt

while not being a bad place, was not for her. Working, saving her money, and earning scholarships seemed to be the way out for her.

Lifting another spoonful of the piping hot gumbo to her mouth, a shrimp tumbled to the floor. She slurped up her spoonful, and then leaned down to search for the shrimp. Samson, her cat would normally clean up the dropped delicacy. Where was he?

Her head almost touched the laptop as she felt for the shrimp under the desk. Smoke, it was on her computer. Amy jerked up quickly dropping the shrimp she'd located. Her computer too. Was nothing sacred? Her intruder would be mighty disappointed with her laptop. She believed in leaving work at work. Outside of a checking account and a photo finishing software, there really was little of interest on her computer. She mainly used it to surf the Internet, which she planned to do tonight.

An urge to search for the cat surfaced, despite Remy's words about the feline coming back when he pleased. Did Mark take her cat or maybe allowed him to escape. Samson was declawed and overweight not exactly ready to return to the wild, but he took every opportunity to get outside.

Opening the exterior door, she walked around the perimeter of her home calling for her pet. A shift in her neighbor's curtains cut her search short. Hard to believe what her neighbors would say if they discovered she lost her husband and her cat. It would probably be best to locate them one at a time. Tonight, she'd work on the husband and hoped her cat would return like he usually did from his outside forays, dirty, hungry and anxious to return to the safety of the indoors.

A tired smile crossed her face as she considered recent biological research revealed that animals were unable to ponder a poor decision. The ability to do so was located on the brain stem. It explained Samson's many attempts to escape. What about her though? Why would she take up with a man she knew nothing about?

Opening the house door, she vowed to remedy the situation. Research was her strong point. The house felt even lonelier with the absence of the familiar and often vocal Samson. Ryan joked the cat's hoarse meow reminded him of a chain smoker.

Back at her laptop, she typed Mark Schaeffer. Hundreds of names came up, with the majority of them being doctors, a couple lawyers, three writers, and one businessman. Some had pictures and links, but none of them was her Mark. The name seemed to be as common as John Doe. No, it was more common. Was Mark his real name? He seemed to answer to it. Hard to say. If not, it was a good workable name that seemed to fit him.

She wondered if she should take notes on what she found but hesitated, concerned about the smoke smell. If her unknown visitor handled her computer, then the person could return for another looksee. Might have installed a keystroke device that would count the number of her keystrokes identifying what she typed. Grabbing a pencil and paper, she wrote down the information. Not that it yielded that much, but it allowed her to not repeat searches she'd already done. Aware her home invader might return she wiped out the history. Where could she hide the paper?

Cautiously, she removed the picture in the hall trying not to make any sound. Since she only had one photo in the house, it wouldn't be hard to trace her activity. Sliding the paper behind the photo, she replaced the back. Now it was time for bed, only problem was she couldn't sleep in their bed alone.

Chapter Four

The cell phone's chime drew Amy from her fitful slumber. Reaching blindly for the source of the noise, she rolled and tumbled to the hardwood floor. Blinking, she stared at the living room walls in a daze. The bedroom seemed to be the epicenter of all the chaos that shook her from her moorings. It would be foolish to try to sleep in the room, especially alone.

Aunt Remy offered some solace, but she'd left. In fact, that was probably her calling. Crawling across the floor with her eyes half-opened, she located the phone still in her purse. Sloppy of her, she usually plugged it in every night to charge. The battery indicator glowed brown, a symbol of her forgetfulness. Odd, she could remember how she used to be, but couldn't return to being the same person, even though she tried.

Her colleagues at Theron treated her the same way they'd treat an unknown pathogen, with extreme caution. Maybe they thought she killed her husband and dumped his body in the river. Local police didn't think so, but they had no real motivation to investigate what they viewed as fallout from a hasty marriage. Most damning was Mark's car was missing too. Murder or even kidnap victims seldom take their own car. There were incidents on police shows where the victim left the scene in the trunk of his own car. She chose not to mention it, not after that female detective reamed out Remy for mentioning CSI and their procedures. Apparently, television did not mirror real police action. She knew that on one level, but what if it did?

What if the man she briefly called husband was a hostage held somewhere? The phone vibrated in her hand. A picture of her aunt appeared on the view screen along with her number. Thumbing the answer button, she held it up to her ear. It felt good to be in touch with someone familiar, even though her aunt seemed to have a hundred questions for her. She'd do her best to answer them.

"No, Remy, I didn't sleep in the bedroom. I couldn't." She nodded her head as her aunt warbled on about the waste of a good bed. The image of the bug planted behind the fridge came to mind.

Not that she was saying anything important, but, still, no one needed to eavesdrop on her conversation with Remy. She stood, murmuring inanities, while walking into the kitchen and switching on the dishwasher. Never mind that there were no dishes inside. The house inspector pointed out the dishwasher was loud, dated, and needed replacing as soon as possible. For now, she'd hold off replacing it since it served her purpose.

The automatic coffee maker had turned itself on, but, instead of brown warm stream of life-giving fluid, it just sprayed out water, albeit hot water, but water. God, she forgot the coffee too. What was wrong with her? She turned to walk out of the kitchen, deeper into the house. She assumed there were no more bugs, but how could she be sure? No one babysat the house yesterday, which allowed her smoking visitor plenty of access time.

Her aunt asked where she slept, interrupting her silent search for possible other bugs.

"In the living room on the leather sofa." Remy's tsking came over the phone loud and clear, making Amy smile a little. It almost felt like she was there. As if reading her mind, her aunt's voice blasted out the phone. "I'm coming back up, girl .You need me. You won't say it, but I can feel it."

"No." Her voice lacked conviction because she wanted the comfort of someone in the house, especially a presence that would stop all the home invaders. Still, she didn't know whom she was dealing with here. As powerful a force as she regarded her aunt, she was no match for a knife or a bullet. No way could she put her in harm's way. Trying to muster up some conviction, she said, "Please don't, you'd be bored with nothing to do. Besides, the good people of Terrebonne need you."

Her aunt grumbled but gave up the challenge easily. Maybe she didn't want to come up, but family obligation pushed her into offering. Aunt Remy's intuition was something a betting man or woman could place money on and win every time. If she sensed something, then something was going on, and it was Amy's job to uncover it. No reason to bring her aunt up here, but she had to quell her fears.

"Ryan is coming by to check on me. Making sure I'm okay." She murmured the words while crossing her fingers behind her back. Her only problem was she never successfully told a lie. A snatch of a memory surfaced with Amy's old college roommate, Bertie, telling her she could never play poker or date successfully because she couldn't lie worth crap. For the most part, her words rang true.

Ryan could come by, so it wasn't exactly a lie. If he came by, then they could discuss her symptoms. It would be nice to get his opinion. Ryan happened to be one of the premier neurologists in the field. If she were suffering from a drug hangover, he'd know. Of course, it could be shock, resulting from all the major life events, but she tended to think it was the first, as opposed to the latter.

Her aunt's voice perked up a little. "Well, if Ryan is coming by, then I won't worry."

Heavens, her husband was missing. At least, she thought he was her husband. Her aunt already had that tone in her voice. The one she assumed when she suggested possible matches to people. Didn't her aunt like Mark? Didn't she want him to come back? Maybe she knew he wasn't coming back. Folks believed her aunt had 'the sight,' but it seemed to come and go at will. Certainly would have been handy if she managed to 'see' what happened that fateful morning.

Her aunt bid her goodbye without her even realizing it. The dead phone signaled she had hung up. Did she even say goodbye? Maybe she should call her back. A glance at the time on the phone indicated any calls would have to take place in the car, after she charged her phone. If she hurried, she could stop by the gas station on her way for coffee.

The red neon lights of the service station beckoned her. Swerving into the station without bothering to turn on her signal earned her a long honk and a one-finger salute from the man behind her. It served him right since his behemoth of a truck sat on her bumper the past mile. Grabbing her purse, she slid out of the car wondering what type of driver she used to be. Her eyes passed over the handful of folks filling up their cars. Most leaned against their vehicles as if not quite reconciled with the thought of starting the day. A young woman with glasses startled and looked up. The widening of the woman's eyes signaled recognition. Maybe she should say hello.

The woman's feet angled a path across the pavement, instead of toward the mini-mart. What would she say to a person she couldn't recall? The woman did a slight shooing motion with her hands as if she didn't want to talk to Amy. She kept the motion close to her body as if she didn't want to attract a great deal of attention either. Maybe they had quarreled, and they weren't speaking. It was just as well since she had nothing to say to the woman.

Amy stood in the middle of the gas pumps station looking like the lone girl not picked at a barn dance. Awkward. She jogged to the paper towel dispenser in the center island to grab a paper towel. Rubbing the towel across her dry hands, she pretended to wipe off something offensive. Did she care before the incident what others thought of her? She wasn't sure. Amy only knew now she cared very much, probably because people deemed her crazy, incompetent, or even murderous.

Inside the mini-mart, she walked slowly up and down the aisles considering whether any of the prepackaged food looked edible and would not undo years of careful eating. The chocolate cupcakes seem to call her name. There were only two small cupcakes. How much sugar and sodium could they contain? Turning over the package, the 5-point font print mocked her as she tried to read the ingredients. Intent on deciphering the various chemical additives, she hadn't notice the female from the gas pump slide up close to her, picking up her own snack cake.

Not looking at her, but at her sponge cake treat, she whispered, "Do you have anything else for me?"

Amy turned her head slightly to look at the woman, causing her to hiss, "Don't look at me. We mustn't be seen together."

She snapped her head back to peruse the various treats passing themselves off as food. She wasn't supposed to look at the woman, and they couldn't be seen together. Were they lovers? Wouldn't Remy have expressed great surprise that she married a man if she were a lesbian? What was their connection? She wanted to ask, but she doubted the furtive acting female would answer her.

The woman asked again, "Is there anything you want to tell me? Any information you want to pass on?"

Amy blinked twice. Odd, and people thought she was unbalanced. "No," she said the word low, playing along with her would-be spy. The woman dropped the snack back on the shelves and turned to leave. Normal height, medium straight brown hair cut in a classic bob style, which gave her a professional appearance. Khakis and an oxford shirt indicating she was probably heading to work where the dress code wasn't too stringent. The brief look at her face revealed unlined skin with a touch of acne in the T-zone area. Probably in her twenties, not any older than thirty, she decided, but how did she know her?

Maybe she didn't. Could be that the woman pretended to make contact with people and pass along information. What game was she playing? Was she pretending to be a James Bondesque spy or maybe a police informer? Maybe she was an investigative reporter ready to blow the lid off a big story. The last thought chilled Amy rather like someone walking over her grave. Oh well, she came for coffee. Eight different pots steamed lightly on their various burners. Grabbing a Styrofoam cup, she reached for one with the Breakfast Bold label. It sounded like something she would drink. Her hand hovered over the cream and sugar containers. No doubt, both items would be horrible for her body. Plain coffee was enough. There were definite benefits to a shot of caffeine.

Coffee in hand, she headed for her car. Fragrant steam wafted from the cup making her sigh in delight. Too bad, she hadn't picked up any food to go with the coffee. Espionage girl rattled her, and she forgot her quandary about the granola bar and the cupcakes. She really wanted the cupcakes. That, she knew without even remembering whether she liked cupcakes. Her stomach growled adding its vote for the iced cake.

"Silly woman," she complained, unsure if she was more upset with the girl or herself. A quick check revealed the chick had hit the road, perhaps to sidle up to other strangers and ask bizarre questions.

Still, Amy wondered as she opened the car door. The woman looked familiar. She felt a twinge of recognition. Maybe it was possible she did know her. If she did, what had they spoken about? The thought consumed her, running through her mind like a rat injected with the equivalent to five cups of coffee. That's how she knew coffee could jump-start your day.

* * * *

"Hey, Beth, how are you?" She called to the woman she recognized from the other night. Hurrying up the walkway to the facility, she fell in step with Beth. A few precious seconds they could talk relatively unobserved. She didn't doubt there were cameras all over the grounds monitoring any attempts to bring cell phones, recorders, or even flash drives into the facility, but two employees walking shouldn't excite them too much.

Amy cradled her Styrofoam coffee cup between her hands, inhaling deeply before taking a sip. Nectar of the gods, she couldn't live without a good cup of java.

Her friend shot her a slight smile while raising a questioning eyebrow. "What are you drinking?"

What a stupid question, and they were worried about her. "Coffee. What else?" She took another appreciative sip of the brown stuff. Holding it in her mouth and savoring it as if it were a fine wine.

Beth stopped walking and just stared for a couple of seconds. "You hate coffee. Can't even stand the smell of it. You're a dedicated diet soda drinker. Always have a can of diet soda before the ten o'clock break."

Coffee? She didn't drink coffee. She spat out the liquid. My God, did she have memories implanted in her that were not her own? Looking at Beth, she knew she had to ask. "I never drink coffee?"

"Nope." Her friend shook her head confirming her answer. "I told you once it was rude of you when your friends might want coffee, but you laughed and told me to get it at the gas station."

Yep, she got it at the gas station. She woke up craving coffee, feeling like it was an integral part of her life. Maybe she did like coffee and the diet soda was the lie. She looked at the confused expression on her friend's face, wondering how good of an actor she was. Bringing the cup up to her lips, she took a sip of the brew. Nasty, bitter, why would she want to drink this? "This is awful. I'm tossing it."

"Wait," Beth said, placing her hand on Amy's. "I'll drink it. I happen to like coffee. I wondered if my eyes were playing tricks on me when I saw you drinking it. When you bought your house, I even gave you a coffee maker in hopes if you had me over you might make me some."

That explained the coffee maker at least. It made her wonder how good of friends they were. Beth expected to be invited to the new house and apparently, she hadn't been. Another twist in a life she couldn't quite remember.

Mentally measuring the distance to the doors, and the guards, she felt she had time. Being out in the open made it hard to place bugs. "You probably noticed I've not been eating. Can you tell me what I was like before?" She hesitated, not knowing how to put it. Before she misplaced her husband or before Mark absconded. If he did take off, at least he had the courtesy of not cleaning out her back account. He could have. She shared everything with him, accounts and passwords. "Um, the incident."

Beth took a final swig of coffee, tossed it at a trashcan, and missed.

"You missed," Amy noted, and they both kept walking.

Beth did a double take. "Before you would have picked up the cup and put it in the trash."

Amy looked at the partially crumpled cup on the ground, experiencing a yearning, almost a compulsion to pick it up. She jogged back to deposit it in the waste container despite her friend's request to leave it.

Standing with her arms folded, Beth tapped her foot playfully. "That's the Amy I remember."

Gasping for breath, as she sprinted back to her friend's side, she decided she must be out of shape. "Tell me more about myself."

"Well, you weren't much for a joke. I think it was because you're too much of a literalist, which might be a good thing in a scientist." Beth pulled a ponytail holder out of her purse. Bundling her hair up, she made a face and mouthed the word "Guard."

Yep, she remembered that, the searching of the hair. Her lips tugged up. She remembered something real, or did she? "Did I cut my hair because I didn't like the guard searching it?"

Beth placed two fingers across her lips, thoughtfully, before she replied, "I don't like the guard searching my hair, either, but yours caught on fire while using the Bunsen burner. It wasn't that long ago."

Her brows pinched together giving Beth a troubled look. That made her reason another false memory. No wonder they took her off the Morpheus Project. She was a train wreck. The real question was what caused the train named Amy to go off the rails. At this point, she wasn't really betting on being married. She knew now she didn't like coffee, and she cut her hair because it caught on fire. The building loomed closer. "Beth, hurry and tell me a joke."

"Okay, here it is. Why did Cinderella get cut from the softball team?"

Amy looked at her friend. "I asked for a joke, not some absurd question about fairytale characters."

Beth hugged her hard, surprising her. "You're back. That is something the old you might say. The punch line is because she ran from the ball."

"I am familiar with the story of Cinderella. She leaves the ball afraid of the carriage changing back into a pumpkin. How is that funny?" Amy wondered briefly if she should stop talking as she pushed the door open. Wouldn't sudden silence look more suspicious, signal her misgivings?

Beth sighed. "Cinderella did run from the ball, but it has a secondary meaning of running from the softball, which would mean she would not make a good player." Beth forced a little chuckle.

Amy got it, once Beth explained, but would she have gotten it before? "There was no mention of softball in the fairytale. Therefore, it does not serve as a legitimate joke." The guards grinned at each other demonstrating she struck a responsive chord.

Throwing her keys into a bowl that had to go through the metal detector, Beth spread her legs to have the wand waved over her body. "Jokes aren't legitimate or illegitimate. They don't have parents."

Amy managed a chortle. "Now that was funny."

Beth slanted an evil look her way as she waited for Amy. "It wasn't a joke."

She knew that. Did this mean she wasn't acting the way the old Amy would? There was even a chance that the old Amy existed in a world where she erected an elaborate façade, acting in a way that she thought people expected her to act. What if the old Amy knew what was going on and tried to create a mental breadcrumb trail to lead her home? It made sense. Maybe knowing what she did, Project Morpheus wasn't at all what she remembered it was, but what they wanted her to remember.

Apparently, Detective Maxfield thought she killed people for a living. Not with her bare hands, but by creating some nerve agent that would rid cities of its human pestilence. It wouldn't be the first time someone created a biological warfare agent. Most countries had some type, although they claimed not to. The anthrax scare of years ago was an industrial creation. Some facility tested it out with frightening results. They usually conducted those tests in other countries. Often they would recruit college students with the offer of money. They had to dilute the product to a miniscule level because people tended to get upset when college students died, especially in great numbers.

The horror of it made her stumble into the wall. Leaning against the wall, she peered around her. No one was watching her, except for the camera in the corner. No way would she have condoned testing on college students. Of course, she was only at the development end, not the testing end. She never asked about the test subjects, but this time she did. A memory of her standing in a room arguing with three men about testing on college students solidified and took shape. She watched the scene unroll as if a movie or maybe as if she were a spirit flitting about the room observing.

One of the older men argued that they wouldn't be liable if the students signed a waiver. The bald man crossed his arms, wiping his face clean of emotions while Amy ranted about their inhumanity to humanity. The bearded man, who seemed to be in charge, stroked his whiskers, simply observing, before speaking.

"You have a point, Dr. Newkirk. College students are valuable to both their families and the university. If anything went wrong, it would compromise the testing." He pinned the first man with a stern look. "Nathan, a waiver is the equivalent of using a

washcloth to wipe up an oil spill. It would do little to nothing. It is essentially a piece of paper, best used for wiping your ass."

She knew that wasn't her reason not to use the students, even without seeing the scene in its entirety. How could she be involved?

The sound of footsteps coming down the hall caused her to push off the wall. Inhaling, she tried to calm her thoughts, clearing all emotion from her face just in time as two white coated women walked toward her engaged in an animated discussion. When they were almost a foot from her, both heads pivoted in unison, and they chirped.

"Good morning, Dr. Newkirk." The two bobbed their heads.

Amy gave a slight hand wave and managed to mumble her reply. "Good Morning." Her mouth may have hung open as she tried to recall their names. No matter, they moved away fast, never noticing her hesitation. Perhaps, she should have reminded them that she'd married and her name was Schaeffer. It tended to emphasize her missing husband, so she never bothered. Most women in science kept their surnames for career purposes.

She watched the women for a few seconds, noting their similarities. About the same height, both Caucasian, wore glasses, had the same pasty colored skin and both had their hair clubbed back. Could they have succeeded on the droid/clone hybrid? The droid was for reconnaissance missions, not lab work. A female model never existed in the planning stages. At least she couldn't remember one.

They called her Dr. Newkirk. Most people did. Were they trying to be sensitive to Mark's disappearance? Could be they never knew she was married. Remy hinted she'd been closed mouth about the whole affair. Her aunt implied the only mention she had of Mark was when she was flying off to be married in a tropical paradise. Her aunt acted somewhat out of sorts because she never heard any details of the courtship or the proposal. Walking slowly, she tried to remember their courtship.

Their meeting at the pharmaceutical conference shone in its completion, crowded beside a collection of half memories and false memories. Strange, it would be easy to say she remembered the meeting better than anything else because she loved Mark.

Still, she loved Remy, but she didn't even recognize the woman who raised her when she first arrived at the house. In her shock, her nose recognized her first. The same strong perfume she'd worn all her life triggered hidden memories of tight hugs, snicker doodle cookies, and whispered confidences. The scent brought her a feeling of peace that nothing else could.

Her slow ramble brought her to her workstation a little later than usual. Beth looked up from her monitor and gave her a slight smile, reluctant to draw too much attention to their interaction. Amy gave a nod, acknowledging her. She turned on her computer while she prepared for work. Slipping on her lab coat, she reached to pull her hair back, only to realize it wasn't there anymore. It was as if her body did not recognize this new Amy. She knew the feeling.

Another day of typing up Wilkenshire's bogus notes, trying to make sense of the rambling nonsense convinced her that the man was no more a scientist than she was a pro baseball player. She may have forgotten many things, but she knew she did not have the physique to be a professional sports star.

Theron's regulations specified passwords would change every six weeks. What was her password? Samson's name brought up a box with an error message. Three wrong passwords would lock up the machine and earn her a visit from IT. What would a woman deeply in love choose as a password? The name of her beloved, of course, she pecked out Mark and the screen came to life. That was odd. How would she remember the password, when she'd forgotten so much? Maybe the password was a false memory too.

The green hill shimmered on her screen promising serenity and a warm summer afternoon. The computer company knew what it was doing when it chose this as a default screen saver. At first, she thought it bland, devoid of any structures, animals, even flowers. Still in its pristine beauty, it represented a simplicity she coveted. The hill didn't doubt it was a hill or wonder if it might have been a mountain or an architect of genocide.

People assumed she had her memory back completely. Something kept her from grasping it. Flickering images of birthday parties, graduation ceremonies, and a man leaning over her danced at the edge of her consciousness, vanishing when she attempted to bring them in focus, rather like a ghost or a dream. There was always the question of what was real or what wasn't.

Ryan's voice pulled her from her internal questioning. "Good morning."

Pivoting in her chair, she smiled up at him, glad for a welcoming face. Most everyone else acted as if she were the carrier of some gruesome disease. They kept their distance, while observing her as if she were the infected party in an experiment. Her smile slipped a little as the thought grew. Could she be part of an experiment?

"Amy, is something wrong?" Ryan's brow furrowed, and he leaned a little closer as if to diagnose a malady.

The word "wrong" seemed to grab her colleagues' attention scattered across the lab area. She felt their eyes pinned on both her and Ryan. The open area consisted of various workstations with cubicle walls, but none of them higher than three feet. At first, she thought it strange, rather a façade of a cubicle, which offered no privacy or noise cancelling benefit. When she first started working at Theron, she expected to interact with other employees to brainstorm solutions. That sounded good, but, of course, they never did. Theron's searches, confidentiality, and intellectual property agreements, plus the camera created an atmosphere of watchfulness and paranoia.

The other scientists did not share ideas or data. She barely knew if any of them were married or had families. That's how little they actually communicated. With one word, she felt a spotlight was on her, as if there hadn't been one already. The camera might even be zooming in on her. Fighting the urge to look at it, she managed a weak smile.

"My stomach is giving me some issues. Yesterday, I stopped on my way home and got one of those chili cheese tacos in a bag."

The eyes turned away almost in unison. Nausea might be an area for concern, but attributed to a spicy, high fat concoction that passed for food was of no consequence. Ryan raised one eyebrow questioning her food choice. Suddenly a memory slipped through, a certainty that she was always very health conscious buying her food at the local farmers market. She felt her cautious attitude was somehow, linked to her job and work with genetically altered crops.

Ryan touched his nose with his finger before replying. That simple motion triggered a memory, but not one completely accessed. She only knew it meant something. She should know. Was it a sign? They spent the last ten years together, according to Remy. Did they have certain signs? Maybe it was just a nervous gesture.

"Amy, I can get you some antacid tablets."

"No, I am okay." The words popped out of her mouth without thought, and then she realized they made her earlier excuse into a lie. Sloppy of her, she had to be more careful since she didn't know who to be on her guard against. "I mean," she hurried to add, "I'd like that. Then I think I'd be okay."

"Will do." He gave a small salute and made a sharp pivot to turn. His lab coat flapped behind him at his rapid exit.

Her eyes followed his weaving path between cubicles out to the central hall. Remembering the camera documenting her every action, she spun back to her computer screen. It wouldn't do to show too much interest in the departing doctor. There was no reason for him to enter into this mess. There had to be some way to warn him off. He couldn't come to her house because of the bug and the unmarked sedan parked at the end of her street. Her fingers started typing madly without any conscious thought. She was trying to look busy without even opening Wilkenshire's notebook of horrendous scribbling.

A sulfuric cloud filled the room, probably the result of Rangasami and Johnson's work involving decomposition. Her nose wrinkled at the odor, wondering why they worked more in an auditorium as opposed to separate rooms. A few individuals did earn the right to separate rooms. Somehow, they'd proved themselves in some way. Why hadn't she? Why was she stuck doing grunt work? Worthless grunt work at that.

The words on the screen made no sense while her thoughts took over picking out various words and stringing them together. *The drug is still in my system. Must cleanse system. Food in house is not safe.* A sea of random letters and punctuation surrounded the words obscuring them unless a person looked for them. She saw them because she was supposed to see them. Was her subconscious trying to contact her, or was it another false memory? Using her mouse, she highlighted the area and clicked delete. That wasn't good enough. Switching off the machine would clear the memory. Slipping her shoe off, she felt around with her toes until she found the surge protector. Using her big toe, she pushed it off. Her computer went dead, along with her desk light.

Slipping her shoe back on, she threw her hands up in the air. "What's wrong with this piece of crap?"

Johnson walked over from his experiment, cocked his head at her blank screen, and pushed the power button. Really, did he think she wouldn't have thought to push the power button? He shrugged his shoulders and walked away. The other people in the room were vaguely interested, but not enough to investigate.

Ryan entered the room with a bottle of water and a medicine cup, most likely with the promised pills. Noting the black screen, he commented, "What happened to your computer?"

Biting her lips, she tried to look perplexed. "It just went dead."

"Okay." He put the water and medicine cup on her desk. "I bet I know what it is." He bent to peer under her desk.

His head was at her knee level. She bent, looking under the desk too, which put her mouth close to his ear. "Meet me at Maybelle's diner at the end of town. Don't bother to answer. Just be there at seven."

Ryan crawled farther under the desk to flick the surge protector back on. His hand rested briefly on her ankle and squeezed it as a reply. Backing out from under the desk, he brushed off his hands and announced to the room at large, "You must have kicked off the surge protector with your foot."

"That must be it," she muttered her response, refusing to look at the man. It might be better to keep their relationship distant for the all-seeing electronic eye.

Reaching for the notebook, she powered up the computer. Her mind fast-forwarded to her future meeting at the diner, making attention to the illegible notes more difficult. Amy decided she made better sense typing what she knew about fruit fly behavior as opposed to transcribing the nonsensical notes. There was the danger of making Wilkenshire look more intelligent than he actually was. Busy work, that's all it was, anyway, and probably would never be read by anyone.

The day crawled by, especially the lunch hour, which she decided to forgo. Theron's cafeteria provided free lunch since employees weren't able to leave the premises. It would necessitate too many more searches and more opportunity for one to sneak out work files. A mental snippet of an employee smuggling out files materialized in her mind, but that didn't mean it happened.

Even though her stomach growled, she refused to heed her hunger pains. Why would she see the word, cleanse? If the food in her home, the very food she and Remy bought together, was possibly tainted, then why trust the cafeteria food? The bottle of water Ryan bought her provided her sustenance for the day. Holding the bottle to her lips, she parted her lips for a sip, but stopped. Where did the bottle come from? It only took Ryan minutes to return from fetching it. Her hand lowered, setting the suspect bottle on the desk.

She remembered twisting off the lid. Lifting it slowly, she brought it up to her nose. No smell, but many agents had no discernible odors. She tilted the bottle slightly catching a water drop on her tongue. No taste, but many toxins have no tastes including ethylene glycol used in anti-freeze. Adding the toxin to lime gelatin was a popular way to get rid of deadbeat boyfriends or redneck husbands. Some women made the mistake of bragging about getting rid of the nuisance, unaware there was no statute of limitations on murder, even if the man needed killing.

There was an article in a chemical journal about a scientist who dropped a few drops of dimethyl mercury on her latex glove. Even though she disposed of the gloves promptly, thinking nothing of the matter, she still died four months later from the poison.

An involuntary shudder shook her. Poisoning had to be a horrible way to die. Some paralyzed your body preventing you from crying out or naming the culprit while your mind raced trying to find a way to stop the inevitable demise.

The lab area was quiet since everyone left for lunch. If she stayed, it wouldn't be that unusual. Standing, she decided to visit the lunchroom and grab some food, not to eat, but, as a cover. She'd push it around her plate while forcing someone into conversation with her. The delicious aroma of beef stroganoff floated in the air causing her stomach to rumble its discontent at its empty state. Rather sadistic of them making mouth-watering food as a delivery system for a toxin, but, wait, that made no sense.

Why poison some of the best scientific minds around? Sure, they might be replaceable in one sense, but these scientists' willingness to go along with Theron's over the top secrecy and long hours, limiting both a family and social life, was probably their most attractive quality. Her casual glance took in the other diners. Their recruitment must have been a delicate dance of crawling through their personal files while wooing them with financial reimbursement possibilities. Most people ask questions, even make demands, and scream about their rights. No one was like that here. Instead, they were a herd of introverts, biddable brainy recluses with no clear leader. Theron, with its strict rules and procedures, served as both their god and religion.

Compliant, rather like a bunch of sheep that tended to operate on the fear principle, they did what they were told, fearing the consequences of not following along. What result would be so horrible? Wouldn't it be a simple loss of income? With their skills and education, another promising job shouldn't be that hard to come by, especially for people willing to move. Most of them were probably single. No one to hold them back but also no one to notice any changes in their behavior, which might be the real reason for their suitability.

The possibility of ingesting drugs during the day was limitless from the water to the food. Even the ventilation system could pipe in minute amounts of an invisible gas. Were they lab rats in an experiment? If so, did the others lose their memories or have false memories? Would Ryan remember anything? Was he part of the plan? It might be possible. It would be clever to insert a familiar face with a warm manner to encourage her to confess her fears. She had to tread carefully, taking his measure without revealing her own doubts. The diner appointment suddenly seemed less appealing, but, at least, she'd have drug-free food. Albeit, a little greasy, but still reasonably edible.

Chapter Five

The M and B in the neon diner sign weren't functioning. Instead of Maybelle's, she drove to *ay elle's* in the misty night. The rain didn't surprise her as she pulled into a gravel parking lot. It'd been raining when she left work. Maybe it was the tail end of a hurricane. Hadn't paid much attention to local happenings with so much going on with her life. Back in Terrebonne, they'd be nailing plywood over the windows to keep them from shattering. Dallas, not being a coastal town, didn't panic at the mention of a hurricane. The best they got was a few days of soaking rains, like today.

Amy jogged across the parking lot, trying to avoid getting too wet. There might have been an umbrella in her car, but she doubted it. She figured the person she was didn't worry about her hair overly much because she existed on a cerebral level. Still, her Aunt Remy said she had Lasik. That meant she took a walk on the vain side of town recently. No matter, she stood inside the brightly lit restaurant and shook her hair, rather reminiscent of a dog. Great, her short blonde spikey hair ought to look even more disheveled. The aroma of cooking burgers and hash browns drew her stronger than any magnet.

Who cares if Ryan shows up or not? For once, she was going to eat greasy spoon food and like it. Amy picked up the laminated menu and perused the various burger platters. Maybe the Maybelle special with a dressed burger, hash browns, a side salad, and an order of onion rings. Her stomach gave an approving growl. A waitress in a polyester orange smock with Trixie stenciled over her right breast moseyed in her direction. Amy wanted to shout at her to put on some speed since she was starving, but it might not be advisable. Trixie had a hard look, the type that begged someone to start trouble.

Her shoulders slumped with tiredness, but her attitude was pure belligerence. She'd probably been on her feet all day, causing her joints to stiffen up due to the concrete floor. All she got for her efforts was a couple bucks in tips and a jar full of change. The woman was too old to be waiting tables, but probably didn't have the skill to do anything else. Yeah, Trixie would wait on folks, but she didn't have to like it.

Definitely, didn't want trouble. Maybe she could start with pie as an appetizer. That sounded good. She smiled in the hard-faced server's direction, hoping to hurry her along. The gum-chewing purveyor of fried food finally arrived at her booth. She cracked her gum before asking, "What can I do for you?"

The bell rang above the door, causing both their heads to turn. Ryan walked in, a little damp, but, still, he was a welcome sight. She put up a hand to wave to him, then, put it down realizing she was the only customer in the small diner. You'd think she'd get better service. The server's eyes traveled over him, starting at his topsiders, moving up his chinos and windbreaker, only stopping at his mussed hair. Nodding her head in his direction, she asked, "Do you want to wait on your boyfriend?"

What, another ten minutes while Ryan perused the limited menu. It would take him a while to make up his mind. She wasn't sure how she knew this, but she did. "No, I want to eat as soon as possible. I haven't eaten all day."

Ryan slid into the booth just as she spoke, raising his eyebrows at her starving comment. She continued talking to the server and nodded at the doctor. "I want the Maybelle platter with French dressing on my salad. Sweet tea and apple pie. You can bring the pie now."

Trixie turned to Ryan, who was polishing his glasses on the edge of his shirt, readying himself to read the menu. "What would you like?"

Looking up, he opened his mouth, but before he could announce he needed more time, Amy piped in, "He'll have the same."

The waitress scribbled on her pad, then turned to walk away muttering under her breath, "Ballbuster."

Amy's head went up. That woman meant for her to hear. Her earlier thought that she wouldn't start trouble forgotten. She sat up ramrod straight, staring daggers at the departing Trixie's back as she slid behind a swinging door.

Ryan's hand covered hers as he spoke. "Let it go. You have more important battles."

Exhaling, she slumped in her seat, pulling her hand out from Ryan's and found she missed the warmth and contact of his hand. Too bad, she couldn't slip her hand back under his fingers. It made her feel a little less alone. Who knew if she could trust Ryan, but Remy did, and she was a good judge of character. Glancing at his beard shadowed face, she expected anger since she ordered for him.

He winked at her. "So did my little ballbuster have a rough day?"

She aimed a kick at his legs under the table but ended up ramming her toes into the hard wooden bench platform. "Ouch."

Ryan peeked under the table, and then shook his head. "Tsk, tsk, see what happens when you react in anger? Amy, you aren't a fighter. You're a thinker. I know you are frustrated right now, but you need to quit reacting, or you're just going to end up hurt. I'm not talking about bruised toes, either."

She might hurt more than her toes. It sounded like he knew something, maybe more than she did. Well, it wouldn't take much. She sat up, scooted to the edge of her seat. "What do you know?"

Trixie swung back through the door with two slices of pie in her hands. She headed toward their table just about the time Ryan was ready to speak. She yelled in their direction, "You want your pie heated up with butter on it?"

Amy didn't want the woman to come any closer. It was hard to know whom to trust. Trixie had the look of someone willing to pass on information for money. Actually, she'd probably do a lot for money. "Sure."

Ryan wrinkled his nose. "You do know you agreed to have butter put on an already calorie-rich dessert that is not good for your heart."

Her eyebrows shot up. She did. "Oh well, no help for it. It's on your pie too. Go on, I just didn't want her eavesdropping."

"I can't say much. No one was more surprised than I was when you got married. Never heard you talk about your engagement or even mention Mark's name. No one did. Then you took off, which was surprising in itself since you almost never use your vacation days and very few sick days."

Ryan looked off over her shoulder. Amy turned to see if anyone was there, but there wasn't. A thought, an outrageous one, formed in her mind. So incredible, she almost didn't allow herself to even think it. "Ryan, did you ever meet Mark?"

His lips twisted to one side. "I heard about your marriage and his disappearance all in the same sentence."

No one seemed to have met Mark. Why did she keep him so low-key? Women were supposed to be excited about their marriage and honeymoon. Even someone as introverted as her should have bubbled up with a little excitement. Smiled more, giggled, even gushed about her beloved. "Did I seem happy before I took off?"

Trixie placed the steaming pie wedges in front of them. She pulled wrapped flatware out of her pocket, making Amy grateful for the flimsy paper barrier. "There ya go." She aimed her grin in Ryan's direction. "I'll be right back with your tea."

The pie smelled wonderful despite the melted butter pooling around the crust before soaking into the pastry shell. Picking up the fork, she attacked the pie. Shoving a loaded fork into her mouth, she watched Ryan's eyes flickering upward trying to remember.

"I wouldn't say you were happy. No giddiness, but rather more introspective than usual. I figured it had something to do with Project Morpheus. You'd been putting in long hours. I'd have advised you to take some time off if I didn't know you'd give me a hundred excuses why you couldn't."

Trixie returned with the tea, saving her smiles and attention for the man. Ryan acknowledged her with his own smile and nod. Great, now we'll never get rid of her. It was better when Trixie and she grudgingly tolerated one another.

She watched her friend enjoy his pie, while she finished off hers. Preoccupied she questioned herself. Did that mean she had doubts about her marriage, Mark, or Project Morpheus? It could have been all three. Why? The Mark she remembered was charming and handsome. What girl wouldn't want to show him off and brag about him to other women? It would be hard for even an antisocial woman not to toot her horn a little. While parts of her life remained lost, short vignettes appear revealing a little, but leaving more mysteries in their wake. One thing she did know was she didn't date much. Wouldn't this make Mark a big deal? Maybe she was a person who didn't show a great deal of emotion.

"Ryan, do you remember me being excited about anything?"

He chewed thoughtfully before he answered. "You were very animated when you got that vintage camera at the thrift store. You had to order black and white film online. Drove across town to get it developed, then I was forced to look at endless photos of trees, rocks, and a very patient squirrel that allowed you to take endless shots of it."

"Were my pictures that bad?" The thought of herself as an aspiring photographer intrigued her. It was as if she were learning about someone else.

He pointed his now empty fork in her direction. "No, just the opposite, you show real promise with the ability to capture a moment that makes a simple photograph into a story."

"Did I get excited about anything else?" Finding out more about herself filled in the holes in her past.

Ryan managed to fend off obliging Trixie with a hand wave before answering. "Recently, you started taking scuba lessons down at the Glenview Middle School pool. You even tried to get me to take lessons with you. Talked about all the beautiful things you would see when you took a diving trip as a form of enticement to get me to join you. Not a strong swimmer, I demurred. Did you have a chance to do any diving on your honeymoon?"

Good question. Did she do any diving on her honeymoon? Sucking in her lips, she tried to access the memories of her honeymoon. A vague image of a beach wedding immediately materialized but nothing else. Wasn't she gone two weeks? Surely, they would have gone diving in such a beautiful area or even snorkeling. Nothing. She couldn't recall even swimming or playing in the waves. "No, I don't think so."

His hand reached for hers. "My mistake, I didn't mean to bring up painful thoughts."

Amy managed a distracted. Shrugging her shoulders, she added, "There are no memories to be painful or otherwise. That's the problem."

Squeezing her hand, he murmured, "I'm sorry. I had no clue. I knew in the beginning that things were foggy, but I thought your memory was back. "

"I want others to think that. It might be better if they do. Let this be our secret, okay?" She knew she might be taking a chance trusting the earnest doctor, but it didn't feel like it. The sad thing was she was unsure if she could trust her feelings. Some drugs and nerve agents did manipulate emotions, often causing feelings of paranoia or euphoria. As far as she knew, no trust drugs existed, and if there had been, wouldn't she trust everyone?

"You can trust me." His brow furrowed a little. "That sounds like something a con man might say. Still I think you know what I mean."

She nodded, distracted, as Trixie placed a laden Maybelle platter in front of her. The succulent aroma of cheeseburger made her drool. Without a thought to manners, she picked up her burger and bit into it, eating rapidly, trying to assuage her hunger. She polished off the burger in a couple of minutes and started on her salty fries.

Ryan ate slower, watching her with interest. "I never saw you eat comfort food. Only organic wholegrain and such. You didn't feel odd consuming that cheeseburger?"

"No, not at all. It was delicious. Remy said something about me being a health food nut. It must be true, especially with all the natural food stuff in my house. I may have lost my memory, but I doubt everyone else around me did too." She shook her head at the thought but continued to scarf down the greasy fries. "This is delicious."

Trixie, standing closed by, folded her arms and smiled appreciatively.

Ryan chomped down his burger with equal enthusiasm. "Hard to believe this is the same woman who would scold me as a doctor for ingesting so much sodium and fat."

The hand carrying a fry to her mouth stopped. "You're right I would. Still, an occasional flirtation with grease and salt won't kill us, right?"

Ryan's laughter attracted Trixie who reacted as if he called her.

"Need anything?" The server directed the question to her companion.

"Oh no, everything is fine. Wonderful even." Ryan's words caused the waitress to light up, straightening her spine, and pushing her bosom out. The doorbell tinkling put an end to Trixie's impromptu show as she turned away to wait on the new customers.

"Why did you laugh?" Amy asked, uncertain of his behavior, but she was sure it wasn't for the server's benefit.

"You were quoting me when you spoke of a flirtation with salt and grease."

"Really?" She poked at her dressing drenched salad. "That would mean my memories are still there. There must be some way to access them. I just wish I knew how."

"If we knew what agent you were exposed to it would be easier to decide on how best to reverse the process." He pushed up his slipping glasses in a habitual gesture.

"You mean you think I was exposed to something that caused a loss of memory?" At last, someone who thought the same way she did. Aunt Remy thought her overcome with grief at her new husband's disappearance. She didn't say it outright, but the signs were there, including the trite phrases, the pat on the back, the kind expression in her eyes. The same way her aunt reacted when Amy screamed in terror, convinced monsters lived underneath her bed. Wait, the monster memory was new. Maybe her memory was coming back. Don't most kids fear monsters under the bed? That means it was a plant. She slumped against the vinyl seat and sighed, not sure what was her actual memory and what posed as her memory.

"I do believe you have either inhaled something or had it injected into you. I've worked with people with amnesia and those in a coma. Your symptoms are like neither. In some ways, you are more like a person coming out from anesthesia. People dream while under and often confuse their dreams with what went on in surgery." He pulled off his glasses looking into her eyes.

Did he mean she was dreaming all of this? This was no pleasant fantasy of winning the lottery. The thought raised her blood pressure, aggravating her already exasperated state. Biting her tongue, she managed to not vent her spleen on the one friend she was 86% confident was on her side. The tinny tingle of the bell drew her eyes as two guards from the center meandered into the diner. "Guards from the center." When Ryan started to turn his head, she added. "Don't look."

Inhaling deeply, he leaned across the table blocking their view. "Do you think they followed you here? If so, what are you going to do?"

Her eyes measured the space from the table where the guards sat to the door. Too close. Maybe there was a back exit through the swinging doors. If nothing else, she could sprint through the kitchen. She had a feeling Trixie might be doing most of the cooking tonight based on her long disappearances. Cutting her eyes back to Ryan, she whispered, "It might be coincidental, but it won't be good to see us together. I am heading to the restroom to find another exit, which means I am sticking you with the check."

She fluffed her hair, pulling it up in clumps making it look more punkish. Retying her plain oxford shirt under her breasts created a midriff-baring top. Unbuttoning the remaining blouse top exposed her breasts with traces of the lace bra cup peeking out.

Ryan coughed. "If you want the guards not to look at you then I would say you are going about it the wrong way."

The look on her companion's face seesawed between concern and interest. She looked down at her breasts prominently displayed in her tied up shirt. It made sense, he was a man, and men responded to visual cues. No more than that or was it? Certainly not the time to explore her relationship with the doctor. "I just want them not to mistake me for the serious scientist type."

"Trust me. If they do see you, I doubt they'll even bother looking at your face."

"Thanks, I think." She slid out of the vinyl booth seat, squeaking as she went.

She refused to look back but put an extra sway into her walk, just in case the guards looked up.

Past the jukebox and through the swinging door, she found herself in a short hallway with restroom doors and an Employees Only door. It looked like it was the Employees Only door as far as an exit. Surely, the staff had to get deliveries somehow, which equaled a back door. Besides, last time she looked, Trixie was out front chatting up the guards.

Pushing the door wide, the smell of hamburgers cooking and the underlying smell of old bacon grease assaulted her nose. A large beefy man in a white T-shirt and pants leaned against an industrial mixer. Her eyes traveled over the bald man with arms the size of Tennessee hams trying to think what she should do. He was in the act of lighting up a cigarette. Her first instinct was to pull it out of his mouth and stomp on it. He looked up.

"Hey, what are you doing in here," he questioned while his eyes made a thorough survey of her attributes.

Trying to stay in character, she sashayed up to the brute. Taking the cigarette out of his mouth and praying she wouldn't die from some unknown infection, she took a puff and handed it back to the man. "Thanks. Be a doll and point me to the exit. Ditching a date. The nerdy fellow with glasses. So not my type. Back door seemed my best chance." She spotted the door and headed in that direction.

Smokey peered out into the dining area while she almost made it to the door. He appeared beside her in a heartbeat proving big men can move fast. The slap on her butt was not only unexpected, but it lingered, causing her to choke.

"See what you mean, sweet cheeks. Why don't you hang around a bit? I'll be done here in a jiffy."

Luckily, her pants had enough sheen in the fabric, she was able to shake free of his oily grasp. "Got to run." She stepped into the rain, suiting her motions to her words. The cold rain pelted her, slicking her clothes to her body. There was no need to look behind her to see if the amorous cook was watching. She could still feel his eyes. Once in her car, she looked back toward the restaurant and picked out the outline of Ryan standing next to the window. What was he thinking? Lights off, she slowly maneuvered the car through the parking lot. *Ignore the car in the parking lot.* It wasn't exactly a look away spell, but it would have to do. Creeping up to the road, she waited for a break in traffic. Flooring the car, she threw gravel as she merged into traffic. The car behind her flicked its brights to alert her to her lack of light situation. When she judged she was a good eighth of a mile away, she turned them on.

Her mind raced as she turned into her neighborhood. Did the guards follow her? Was there a tracking device on her car? It made sense. They could have put it on her car while she was at work or even asleep. Why? Was she just a lab rat of sorts, or did they fear what she might know or do?

What should her next move be? It was hard to decide especially when she couldn't talk out her options. Ryan seemed to believe her, but she couldn't talk with him too much, or they might start tailing him, if they hadn't already. Cutting the engine, she stared at her dark house. Sure would be nice to have someone waiting inside. Preferably, someone she knew and liked, as opposed to some goon, hoping to pry secrets out of her. The joke would be on him. She couldn't even decide what was real in her own life.

Driving her key home, she unlocked the door, pushed it open, and sniffed for the stench of smoke. Nope, nothing, maybe her home wasn't molested today. It made her feel a little better. It also meant they probably found what they wanted yesterday or just gave up.

Since she ate, she didn't have to worry about fixing a meal. All she had to do tonight was think. She flipped the lights on and turned to punch the radio on when she noticed a cloth poppet doll on the counter. She recognized it since Aunt Remy made plenty. The movies would have you believe they were evil. Aunt Remy made them mainly for protection, even to attract a lover. This one was blue. She picked up a knife out the silverware drawer and poked at it. A swatch of golden yarn for hair and embroidered eyes and mouth, it was well constructed, not done on the run. It even wore a tiny peasant blouse and skirt that struck a responsive chord, but not a memory. She had to call Remy, not on her own phone either.

Switching on the radio, she went to her hall closet to don a ball cap along with a windbreaker. If she chose to walk to her local dollar store, she wanted to be halfway comfortable. She turned on the lights in the house to look like she was home. Remembering some burglar on a radio interview telling that the bathroom light concerned him, the most since you never knew when someone might come out.

* * * *

Simpson stood in the rain and watched Amy pull the hood of her windbreaker up as she walked away from her home. Most people did not take walks in the rain, especially when they didn't have a dog. Her behavior was suspicious, considering he'd witnessed a woman earlier carrying something blue in her hand furtively entering the house. He'd love to get into the house and see what she'd left.

Should he follow the odd-acting scientist or look into the house? A quick glance at his watch noted the time. Problem was he didn't know how long Amy would be gone since he didn't know where she was heading. Couldn't be going far or she would have used the car. His window of time was short. So far, Amy had given him a fat zero as far as information. Perhaps the woman left some evidence. Maybe she'd handed off something. That's why he hadn't located anything before. He had to get inside. The answer to why he was even on this assignment could be inside.

Next door, a teen on a cell phone leaned against a primer dotted sedan talking animatedly. The fact he wasn't boasting, cussing, and went silent for long periods meant he was talking to a female. Lucky him, a smitten male stopped him from making his move. What was wrong with the kid? Didn't he notice it was raining? His cell phone would short out on him eventually, but he didn't have time for natural consequences to take effect. An irritated middle age woman in a housecoat slammed the screen door open and shouted at the boy. "You fool boy, come out of the rain."

Thank goodness, for mothers. Sometimes they made his job easier by being so predictable. His tucked his small black burglar kit—that he referred to as the ultimate house key—into his left pocket. A brief spurt of speed took him from his car to the shadowy side of the house.

Most people would underestimate his athletic ability and that's the way he liked it. A dog barked in the distance stopping his slow slide to the back door. The dog could be barking at him, but it didn't matter if the owner didn't react. Most didn't. Too often, their dog barking at nothing had fooled them or at least that's what they thought. Most were clueless how many times crime brushed near them, even death, only to be turned away by an alert canine.

After no response to the brief bark, he moved silently under the overhang until he reached the backdoor. He wiped his hands on his shirt, which stayed reasonably dry under his jacket, before pulling on his gloves. Despite powder inside, they wanted to stick to the residual moisture on his hands. Gloves on, he managed to open the door but remembered his dripping jacket, shoes, and hat.

"Damn," he cursed as he shed them at the back step. They'd be wet and uncomfortable when he slipped them back on. It also took time, something he didn't have. He ditched them and stepped inside the house lit by the kitchen ceiling light. A blue doll sat by the microwave. He blinked. It looked rather like one of the dolls the Amish children had. Drug traffickers often used dolls to transport drugs. Why would the doctor be any different? He grabbed the doll, tucking it inside his shirt. He slipped his damp shoes back on. Glad he'd worn canvas slip-ons as opposed to lace-ups. Hat in place, jacket zipped up. He disappeared back into shadows to return to his car.

In his car, he turned on the heat to dry out some. He pulled the doll out and stared at it under the meager illumination thrown by the car's dome light. Seeing it up close, it didn't look too much like those dolls the Amish girls carried. Instead, it looked like a voodoo doll. He dropped it, not that he was superstitious or anything. Plenty of people practiced voodoo in the bayou and coastal areas. Might just be a sign that the doctor had more than one person to worry about. He'd turn it over to Theron and let them poke at it, just in case bad intentions could rub off on whoever handled the doll. At least, he was wearing gloves. Mentally, he decided to keep the gloves on until he turned the doll over. He drove slowly through the neighborhood not to attract attention. All he wanted was to get rid of the doll he felt sure was emanating evil from its spot on the passenger seat.

* * * *

Amy finally reached the store. Why did places seem so far away when one had to walk? At the store, she purchased a prepaid phone and minutes. Huddled against the store's exterior wall, she activated the phone while the gutters leaked, targeting her with every other drip. Phone working, she called Remy.

"Remy, it's me, Amy." She knew her aunt might hesitate to answer an unfamiliar number, but then, she had all sorts of people calling her for charms or spiritual advice.

"I know it's you, even though your voice sounds peaked and strained. What is it child?"

Her warmth managed to flow over the airwaves, giving Amy a little comfort while she curved her body away from the neon light of the sign.

"I came home tonight and there was a poppet in my kitchen. You didn't stop by, did you?" She knew it was a silly question expecting Remy to drive five hundred plus miles and not stay for dinner.

"Oh my, a poppet you say. I wasn't there. Poppet might not be a bad idea, depending on those who left it. What color was it?"

"It's blue, a pretty little thing with blond yarn hair and an embroidered mouth. I didn't touch it. I walked all the way to the store to get a new phone that didn't have any type of bug on it. So what do you think?"

A couple exiting the store eyed her until she stared them down. They climbed into a battered truck and took off in an oil rich plume of smoke.

"That's good. It means it's a healing poppet. The embroidery shows intention, not something dashed off in the moment. Odd someone would make you a poppet. That's something you do for someone close to you. Got any witchy friends up there?"

"None I can remember. Is it okay to have it in the house?" She was unsure what bothered her more. The doll or that someone entered her house to leave it. Both bothered her, but her visitor bothered more.

"Depends on what is it. Go home open it up and tell me what is inside. If it is just healing herbs, maybe quartz, turquoise, or amethyst, that's good. Even be a bit of garnet to protect you from blood disease. Someone sees you suffering and wants to help. On the other hand, it could mean evil too, someone slyly dressing it up as if it were for good. Call me when you open it up. Do you have a camera on your new phone?"

"No, it is the cheapest phone they had. I'll call in about twenty minutes." She powered off the phone and walked home, glad the rain had tapered off to a drizzle.

My God, she was using a prepaid phone like a drug dealer or a man cheating on his wife. Is this what her life had come to ducking out of greasy spoon through the kitchen, doubting her memories, hesitating to talk to Beth or Ryan because somehow they might end up entangled in the whole mess?

Hearing about her love of photography and scuba lessons had been nice. The details helped her feel more like a real person. There were specifics to his recollections. That was what was missing from her memories with Mark. Nothing special, or unusual, didn't most women want to get married on an exotic beach?

Her husband didn't seem to know her favorite color or foods. He didn't take her scuba diving, which she would want to do in such a magnificent location. The fish and the reefs had to be spectacular around Tahiti. She didn't have any, photos either, which was odd since she was such an ardent photographer. Maybe she did, and she just needed to find her camera. She'd do that after she dissected the poppet.

She placed her hand on the backdoor knob, and it felt loose, not locked. Pushing it open with one finger, she peered inside. It didn't feel like anyone was there.

Just in case, she called out, "Hello, is anyone here?"

No answer, she stepped inside with intentions to grab the poppet and step outside for her follow up call. The poppet was gone. The butter knife she poked it with remained. Someone took it. Why? The most obvious answer was they wanted her to doubt her senses. The next thought was that they knew it was a healing poppet, and they didn't want her to get better. Neither of them gave her any comfort.

Standing on her stoop, she called her aunt and explained the situation.

"Hmmm, Amy child, this perplexes me. Someone has an eye out for you. If so, they will continue to make charms for you. God and his angels will look after this kind soul." Her aunt cheered herself with the thought. Amy, on the other hand, figured she had just one more person in her house while she was gone.

"That's good. I thought maybe someone didn't want me to get better, and they took the poppet," she said, revealing her fears.

"That's a possibility, too, a rather grim one, since they have a ready-made poppet and can choose to stuff it with other things to bring on a different outcome."

"Thanks, Remy, that helped a lot. I may not be able to walk into my house now." Her darkened neighborhood with beams of light coming out from various house windows didn't look too frightening, which made her wonder why she was so scared.

Chapter Six

A man's form gained more definition as the fog began to burn away. He was heading her way. Amy narrowed her eyes trying to recognize the approaching figure. Was it Mark? If so, then that meant he was alive. He hadn't been kidnapped, either. Maybe he could explain what was going on. "Mark," she called out his name and reached out both arms to him.

A sudden battery of knocks jerked her awake with enough velocity to roll her off the couch. Smacking her face against the hardwood floor merited a curse as the knocking came again.

A masculine voice yelled from the other side of the door. "Amy. Amy. Are you okay?"

Stunned by her rapid exit from the dream, she lay on the floor, feeling her heart race. Was it fear that caused it to race or love? Did the possibility of seeing Mark's face do that to her? The knocking came again, along with some doorknob wiggling. Ryan, she recognized his voice. Theron would probably recognize his voice too. Scrambling to her feet, she rushed to the back door, flinging it open.

Putting her finger up to her lips in a hush motion, she said loudly, "Thank you for bringing the plant seeds by. Sorry, I didn't come to the door right away. I was in the bathroom." She pushed Ryan back with one hand, allowing her enough space to stand on the outside stoop with him. She leaned forward to whisper a reminder about the bug in the kitchen. Of course, now the bugs might be all over the house. She hadn't had time to check.

Her friend's eyes roved over her attire of an oversized T-shirt featuring the slogan 'Nerd? I prefer the term Intellectual Bad Ass.' She pulled the shirt away from her body to read it and raised the hem level, exposing an inch of her orange panties. A smile tugged at her lips. She had a sense of humor, a rather dry one, but one all the same. What if this wasn't even her shirt, a plant to make her think of herself other than she really was. Best to double check her assumptions.

"Ryan, do you think I'm funny?"

His eyes appeared to linger on her legs. He shook himself and looked up with a blush and sheepish grin. "Of course, I don't think you are funny looking. You're beautiful."

His words pleased her but didn't answer her question. "I asked if I was funny." She pointed to her shirt. "I am wearing a humorous shirt, which would mean I must have a sense of humor."

Ryan nodded enthusiastically. "I understand now. You want to know if you're funny because of the shirt. It indicates a sly, but subtle sense of humor that doesn't shout its existence to all, but rather lurks, waiting, like a cat waiting for an unwary sparrow."

"Yes." She threw her hands up in triumph, raising the shirt hemline once more.

Ryan put a hand on her elbow to turn her toward the door. "You need to get dressed. Can I come in?"

Amy's eyes drifted to her neighbors' homes to see if any of them might be stirring yet. "I'm not sure if that would be a good idea. That might give the wrong impression, especially with me having misplaced my husband."

His eyebrows shot up. "You're kidding me right? Standing outside in just a T-shirt and orange panties, talking to me gives them the right impression?" He slid his hands into his khaki trouser pockets and jingled his change and keys, a sure indication of his frustration.

Placing a hand on his arm, she leaned forward slightly. "You're aggravated. Am I right?"

Ryan nodded, opened his mouth, closed it, and opened it again to speak. "In more ways than you can imagine."

Nodding, she found his remark cryptic. She pushed the back door open while motioning to her ear. He followed her silently to the den as she moved over to a calendar and marked off another day. "It helps me to keep track of time since I seem to keep losing it. Today's Saturday, which might explain your appearance. Actually, it doesn't. Why are you here?"

His index finger pushed up his glasses, another tell she recognized. He shrugged his shoulders. "We're friends. You can remember that, right? I even gave you that T-shirt."

Her shoulders drooped. That meant she wasn't funny. All the talk about the sly sense of humor wasn't about her at all. Damn it.

Why couldn't she have any type of characteristics? She was as bland as a clean white board.

Ryan removed his glasses and polished them. "I know you're upset. What is it? It can't be the shirt. You picked it out from that catalogue I brought to work. You dithered between that one and the one that said, 'You read my T-shirt. That's enough social interaction for the day.'"

Her laughter surprised both of them. It was half relief finding out she had at least one positive characteristic besides intelligence, part recognition that she did have a real friend in Ryan. "I'm sorry to say the social interaction shirt sounds exactly like me." She rolled her eyes up trying to recall the conversation. "Did you say 'Not that shirt, it will feed into your hermit existence'?"

Grabbing both her shoulders, his eyes lit up. "I did. You remembered."

"I did!" Her exclamation bounced off the walls of the almost empty room. Realizing her mistake, she added, "I have to stop talking to myself."

Ryan smirked at her and pushed the door closed. His eyes held hers and gave more significance to the fact she only had on a T-shirt and panties. She reached for a robe she must have abandoned in the office earlier, wrapping it around her. The plaid unisex robe didn't seem particularly feminine. She stuck her nose in it and inhaled. It smelled like her, though.

Stepping closer, Ryan asked, "What are your plans for the weekend?"

Part of her thought the words sounded like an inquiry for a date. As if, she may not have gone on many dates, but she still recognized the protocol. Still, that would be odd because she was a married woman. Her eyes darted around the room as she considered her answer. Thank goodness, she kept the blinds closed. The blank walls mocked her, reminding her of her current state. She didn't want to commit to anything until she understood what had happened to her. Maybe she would move from this tidy little house. "How long have I lived here?"

His brow furrowed, and his eyes flickered upward. "Two months. I even helped you move in. Do you remember? You were lucky because the former owner wanted to leave immediately. She allowed you to move in before you even owned the house. You paid her one month's rent." He walked over to a box labeled Office and hefted it up with a grunt. "I remember carrying this box. Boy, do I remember. I wondered if you had rocks in it."

Amy tried to take the box from him and staggered a little bit under its weight as they both eased it to the floor. Strange, she'd never unpacked anything. Two months gone and everything still sat in boxes. She lifted a flap of the heavy boxes, finding other boxes inside with lettering. She pulled out one shoebox labeled Jasper and pulled off the tape to reveal several specimens of Jasper, some rough, some polished. Ryan picked one up holding it up to the light.

He winked at her. "I suspected I was carrying a box filled with rocks. Looks like I was right."

"Minerals," she corrected. "Many people believe Jasper has amazing healing properties. It is also believed to increase sexual desire." Ryan's lips formed an O. "I must have been experimenting with them somehow." There was something more about the box, something important, she couldn't recall. Could it be related to the reason she told the detectives she only lived here a month?

Ryan nudged a few boxes around until he located a smaller one. "I thought it was in here. I may not have the photographic memory you have, but I can remember a few things." He picked up the smaller box and carried it to her. It bore the label Scrapbooks.

The tape had also been torn, then re-taped, making her aware she might not be the first person to view the contents. A chronological timeline of her life with pictures would be a big help. It would patch up all the holes in her memories. She ripped open the flaps only to discover textbooks. "Textbooks," she identified the contents with disgust.

No help there, a fragment of her packing items for her move materialized. The phone rang about the time she wrote scrapbooks on the box. Unlike most people, she labeled the box first and then packed it with the item. The work-related call had disturbed her, which caused her to pack her old medical books in the scrapbook box instead. That would mean her scrapbooks would be in the box marked textbooks, possibly. They were probably sitting side by side waiting to be loaded with appropriate goods. "Look for a textbook box, and I should find my scrapbooks."

They pushed various boxes around trying to find the right textbook box. She even looked in her closet. Under two boxes of Encyclopedia Britannica, she found the box. "Help me," she pleaded as she tried to wrestle off the two heavy boxes that seemed to be slowly squishing the bottom box. Why would she have piled boxes in that manner? She would have if she thought they were books. Her breath came faster, perhaps due to the exertion or the possibility of finding out more about her very elusive past.

Ryan wrestled off the two boxes, while complaining, "You never told me what your weekend plans were?"

Excited about the smashed box, she pulled it close to her. It certainly did not look like something that contained heavy books. She shook it, didn't feel like it either. Tape covered the flaps too. She began to tear at the tape, not really thinking about her response. "I thought I'd head out to Albuquerque to the Kiva Conference Center where I supposedly met Mark."

"Supposedly?" His words came out choked, causing her to look up.

Oh no, she did it. Said what she'd secretly been thinking and revealed her doubts about Mark, her marriage, and pretty much the last month of her life. Ryan's alert eyes reminded her that she could not palm off some silly excuse such as misspeak. She'd have to brazen it out instead. "That's the plan."

His voice reflected surprise and speculation. "Really?"

Turning back to the box, she tore at the stubborn tape without success. Bending she grabbed one end and tried to pull it with her teeth in desperation. Sure, she could get up, go to the bugged kitchen and get a knife, but she couldn't wait. Incisors clapped down on the tape and brought her face close enough to the dusty floor to start her coughing.

Holding out a pocketknife, Ryan said, "Use this."

She took the proffered knife, smiling up at him. "Always a boy scout." The phrase clicked, she looked up at her friend whose face showed equal astonishment. "I used to say that, didn't I?"

His nod confirmed her initial suspicion. "You said that every time I brought out the knife my grandfather gave me. At first, I thought you were mocking me, but then I decided it was just your way." His lips twisted up in a wry expression.

Maybe it was her way. Hard to say with her current memory issues. Slicing through the tape, she opened the box to reveal a few tattered scrapbooks with a newer one on top. She hadn't lost them. Opening the first book, she saw a picture of herself in front of her current house and then another photo of her and Ryan in front of the house.

Ryan peered over her shoulder, pointed to the second picture, and remarked, "The realtor took that one. She thought we were married. Made a comment about how we bickered back and forth like an old married couple."

She hurriedly flipped through the album. There were several black and white photos of trees, squirrels and rocks reflecting her photography habit. That story was solid, but what surprised her were the photos of Ryan wedged in with photos of Aunt Remy, her visit back to Terrebonne, and pictures of her minerals. Placing the book on top of the box, she bent to carry it back to her room as she dressed. She didn't want to take a chance on losing the evidence of her life.

His gaze flickered to the box in her hands. "Afraid I might abscond with your photos?"

Biting her lips, she tried to determine if he was joking or serious. No smile and a creased forehead, she concluded that he wasn't kidding. "Nope, just want to keep my memories close as I dress. In fact, I am taking them with me on my way to New Mexico. Things have a way of disappearing in this house." She put out one hand to turn the doorknob, but Ryan's comment stopped her.

"About that road trip, you're not going alone. I am not even sure if you should be driving, considering you think your car might have a tracking device on it. Get dressed, and I'll explain my plan. Pack an overnight bag, just in case. Leave your phone, since I am sure it's bugged too."

When did he turn so alpha all of a sudden? Amy glanced at her friend in a new light with his shoulders back, a determined glint, and his nostrils flared a tiny bit as if scenting a challenge. The take-charge attitude looked good on him. His arm came around her to open the door. He nodded, well aware the bug might pick up his voice.

Taking the box with her, she entered her bedroom. Once she pulled on her jeans, she considered how the scrapbook would help her unravel her life story. She'd be like an anthropologist digging through her own records and trying to piece together a profile for herself. If Ryan chose to be dominant, then he could drive, leaving her plenty of time to peruse the scrapbooks. Although ten hours might be a bit much to expect, no matter how good of friends they might be.

The shirt halfway over her head, she reconsidered changing. Somehow, it pleased Ryan that she was wearing it. Maybe she should keep it on, but a bra was definitely in order. The mirror, never kind, revealed what a bird's nest her hair resembled. A quick rinse under the sink faucet might help bring some order to it. Her inability to sleep soundly always left her with bad morning hair. Did she cut it because the guard played with her long locks or because she caught it on fire?

That one guard did seem way too handsy, but he was probably that way with most of the females. Anyone creating memories would know this. Wouldn't they also know she caught her hair on fire? It was hard to know what to believe. Just like her house, did she move in one month or two months ago? Flipping back to the photo, she noticed the time stamp on the photos was ten weeks ago.

Brushing her teeth, she wondering why the architect of her false memories got that part wrong. She didn't close on her house until a month later. All the legal documents would reflect this, but moving in early was between her, the owner, and apparently Ryan. It could be they didn't know. The T-shirt Ryan rejected reflected pretty much how she felt about social interaction.

Pulling on an athletic shoe, she realized she would be the perfect subject. She lived alone, no husband or children, and only Samson, her cat, but now he was gone. No close relatives nearby or even those who checked up on her often. Work consumed her, so she had no social life to speak of, no one to tell her how things used to be. Yep, if she were unethical, she'd use someone like her. Tying her shoe on with vigor, she was almost dead certain she'd been the test subject for a less ethical scientist. The unanswered questions centered on the agent used, to what purpose, and how did Mark fit into the experiment.

Crimping her wet hair with hair gel, she regarded herself in the mirror. The pixyish haircut emphasized her eyes. The woman in the mirror bore no resemblance to her ID card with the long straight hair and no nonsense glasses. It could be part of the experiment, an effort to reshape her into something or someone else. She may have even agreed to the procedure. If so, why not tell her.

Flipping on the bathroom fan, she left the room. A slight hand gesture at Ryan indicated it was time to go. Turning on the radio as she passed in the kitchen, they both wordlessly left the house and hiked a few blocks through a wooded park and up the hill to reach Ryan's late model sedan. He opened the door for her before walking to the driver's side.

The sun peeked out of the clouds, throwing a few sunbeams and drying up the puddles left from the night before. It might turn out to be an Indian summer day. The thought cheered Amy. Of course, it would be a nicer day if she'd get to indulge in a late brunch followed by laundry and possibly topped off by grocery shopping. Who knew she'd find mundane chores yearn worthy? It had to be better than backtracking the few things she could remember. Her glance fell on Ryan, how did he fit into her other life, the one she couldn't quite pin down.

As if feeling her gaze, he commented without taking his eyes off the road. "We'll stop by my house. I'll grab a bag and Burton. Plus, we'll switch cars."

Who was Burton? Could she trust him? "Why are we picking up Burton?"

Braking for the stop sign, he shot her a confused look. "Burton can't take care of himself. For Pete's sake, he's a bulldog. They can't even effectively reproduce without assistance, let alone feed themselves. Remember you like Burton."

An image of a bulldog with legs seemingly too short to support his stout body came to mind. "Does Burton have a brown and white coat?"

Ryan grinned. "Last time I checked. Sometimes it is all brown if it's muddy outside."

A dog certainly changed things. Maybe sneaking in and out of Albuquerque might be a little harder. Her plan included not attracting attention. The car slowed to turn into the driveway. A click of the garage opener drew her attention as the door slid up revealing a gleaming 1965 Mustang convertible. "Where did that come from? Should I remember it?"

Ryan parked the car and turned to wink at her. "You don't remember I spent years restoring this baby."

Punching his arm, she said, "Don't be cruel to the woman with memory issues. If you had this primo ride, wouldn't I have taken a picture of you with it?"

He transferred her box and bag to the Mustang's backseat. "You're right," he admitted. "I bought this off some guy whose wife informed him it was either her or the car, right after I heard about your marriage."

Interesting. She never thought of him as a classic car type of guy. "It'll burn major gas."

"No worries, I think, between the two of us, we might be able to afford the fuel. I just need to get Burton, my bag, and change my clothes." He jogged in the direction of the house. Amy followed slower, wondering what was wrong with the clothes he was wearing.

Burton welcomed her with a wet tongue swipe. At least the dog remembered her, even if she didn't totally remember it. The inside of the house was neat and orderly as she suspected it would be. A black and white framed photo caught her eye. She approached it realizing it was a shot of Burton. It looked like her work. Odd that should come to mind when she couldn't remember whole sections of her life. Another framed photograph sitting on his desk drew her.

She picked up the wooden frame photo of a laughing woman throwing back her hair with attitude. She stared at it. Could it be? It looked familiar, but she'd never seen a photo of her old self when she was this carefree. Why was it on his desk? She assumed he worked at his desk. That would mean he'd stop now and then and look at the photo. He must have taken it.

Ryan came out of the bedroom in a pair of plaid shorts and polo shirt. That in itself was enough to shock her. She wasn't totally sure she'd ever see seen his legs before. A ball cap stenciled with some tourist destination completed the outfit.

"I thought we'd play 'tourist' today. A tourist never attracts attention, while some stranger asking odd questions does. Watch and learn." He looked at the picture she still held. Taking four steps in her direction, he reached for it. "I always liked this photo. It was so hard to get you to relax. I think Burton finally got you to laugh. He was just a puppy then."

She watched as he carefully replaced the photograph. What she wouldn't give to have her memory back. Even if she did, there was probably a lot about this man she overlooked or perhaps never noticed. "So your plan is to roar into town in your gold convertible, pastel shirt, and bulldog. Somehow, this will not attract attention."

"We attract a little attention by being noisy, loud tourists, but we are soon forgotten. If we came in as deadly serious scientist types we would attract more and be remembered." Ryan nodded as if agreeing with his own statement.

"Won't people remember the ride or even Burton?" She didn't think folks were that non-observant.

Pointing his finger, he explained, "They might. All the better. Do you have a classic Mustang? Do you own a bulldog? Do you have a styling guy who dares to wear pastels?"

Amy shook her head. "No to all. I think that last question should be do I have a gay best friend?" She smirked at his feigned look of outrage.

"It was either this or the Kiss T-shirt. I thought this worked better. C'mon girlfriend, it's time to hit the road." He used his extended index finger to tap her nose making her laugh.

Ryan pranced out the door with Burton high stepping beside him. Who was this man? Did she ever really know him?

Chapter Seven

Ryan kept the top up on the *Stang* as they crept out of town. They decided not to go into their tourist mode until they were well out of town and out from under the watchful eyes of the Theron Corporation. She'd like to think she left tracking devices behind since she left her cell phone in the kitchen and her car in the garage. Still, she wasn't one hundred percent sure. The missing time she couldn't account for would be a perfect time to insert a tracker in her. Rather like the microchip, they put into dogs. She tried to do a thorough search of her own body for cuts, wounds, unexplained punctures. There was a tiny hole between her fourth and third toe. It could be a needle mark or something else. Maybe she stepped on a needle or a tack.

Maybe she could ask Ryan to inspect her scalp. The man played with the radio trying to find a station before settling on some heavy metal oldies station. He grinned at her, probably aware of how much she didn't like listening to some rocker screaming, "I'm back." Oh well, it would only last so long before they lost the signal and then they'd be forced to listen to one of the many country stations that abounded in the state. That thought didn't cheer her, either. What did she like?

"Ryan," she strengthened her voice to shout over the screaming singer. "What kind of music do I like?"

He twisted on the volume off before answering. "Not that, I am surprised you lasted as long as you did." He chuckled, catching her eye, then, looked back at the road. Burton took it as his cue to try to climb in the front seat. His short stubby legs made a valiant effort to hurtle between the seats and over the console, but didn't quite make it.

"Burton back," Ryan delivered the command in a stern voice, causing the struggling dog to desist. Looking at the dog sprawled between the seats and over the console, Ryan sighed. "Amy, can you shove him back and up on the seat? He's not terribly coordinated. Besides, you're in his seat."

Unfastening her seat belt, she twisted to her knees to lift and push the challenged pup. "C'mon, Burton. You need to do your part. I'm tagging you passive aggressive if you don't put more energy into it." A powerful shove sent the resistant pup back into the backseat and Amy sprawled across the console. She rested in the awkward position considering why an intelligent man would intentionally buy such a pet. Wiggling she managed to get her knees under her even if it stuck her butt in the air. Grabbing onto the back of Ryan's seat she carefully slid her body around fighting the wind resistance from the open windows that threatened to topple her. A sharp toot from a nearby semi air horn gave her a start, but Ryan's arm whipped out guiding her back to her seat.

Tears gathered at the corners of Ryan's eyes from laughing so hard. Unfortunately, she seemed to provide entertainment besides canine wrangling services. She quipped, "That concludes the comedy portion of our show," settling back into her seat and snapping her seatbelt in place.

Ryan patted her knee and laughed one more time before adding, "It was a very nice show. The trucker beside me enjoyed it so much I was afraid he might swerve into us."

"Thanks, I think. You could have pulled over and helped me. As for that trucker and his stupid horn, I almost jumped out of the car." She cut her eyes at him.

"I should have helped you, but I did keep you anchored to your seat." Ryan was quick to agree. "Burton's never been in the backseat. I had no clue he would be so difficult. Tell you what, maybe I'll let you drive. Then, I'll do dog duty."

It sounded good in theory. "Ryan, do I know how to drive a stick?"

He felt around the edge of his seat, until his fingers latched onto an eyeglass case. Prying it open with one hand, he pulled out a pair of prescription sunglasses. "I may need your help. Can you take off my regular glasses and put on my sunglasses?"

She undid her seatbelt and replaced his regular glasses with his sunglasses. Surprisingly, she found the act intimate. Something you'd do for someone with whom you were very close, like a spouse or a best friend. How close had they been in the past? Remy thought they were good friends. She even hinted that Ryan might have romantic aspirations toward her. Could she ask him that? No way. He hadn't even answered her music question.

As if reading her mind, Ryan responded, "As far as music, you're a jazz fan. You like some of those 1940's songs, too, with the swing bands and those singers who sing torch songs. The one where she bemoans how sad and lonely she is, or the man that got away, and such."

It sounded somewhat familiar. "Can you sing me one?"

Ryan coughed to clear his throat and then belted out, "That old black magic has me…"

Amy tilted her head, considering the words. "Am I a witch or a Wiccan?"

Ryan stopped singing to answer. "Nope, I don't think so, but if you were, I doubt if you would have told me. You'd say some things are private. Probably the same reason I don't know if you can drive a stick, and I've known you longer than anyone at Theron." His lips settled into a mulish line.

Watching her companion's face, she could see her need to be private upset him. This necessity to secret everything away was making it hard to figure out who she really was. "I wish I hadn't been so private. It would be a great deal easier to find out more about me. How about you? Aren't you on the quiet side too? After all, you never mentioned you purchased this car?"

"You're right. In my defense, I figure people don't want to hear about how I choose to waste my greatly inflated salary. Ever wonder why we're paid so much for what we do?" He flicked on a turn signal, switching lanes.

"Nope, I hadn't given it any thought since I am more consumed with how I misplaced my husband and memory all on the same day." Amy shook her head in frustration. She really didn't need one more thing to throw in the mix. Didn't she have enough to think about?

The car came to a stop in front of the tiny food mart attached to the gas station. Ryan reached across to pull down the roof latches to release the convertible top. "Only reason to have a convertible is to drive around with your top off." He wiggled his eyebrows suggestively. The top slowly folded back, attracting attention from a man pumping gas.

Angling her head toward the man, Amy remarked, "There's someone who envies you for your car."

Opening the car door, he stepped out and grinned back at her. "Sure, he envies me, not just for the car but also the beautiful woman with me."

She perked up at his remark. There it was again. He called her beautiful. As a scientist, she recognized people had little choice in how they turned out. It was more a genetic crapshoot. Nothing the offspring had anything to do with, but, then again, it was a matter of perception too. Ryan perceived her as attractive, and, surprisingly, she found she liked that. Perhaps she was vain too. Realizing she'd been quiet for a while, she wondered what to add to the conversation when Ryan spoke again.

"And the handsome bulldog."

God, he grouped her with the dog. This would explain why they had no romantic relations between them despite the ten years they'd known each other, geesh. She searched for her sunglasses, hoping to veil the shock in her eyes. Was he always like this? If he was, then she must be used to Ryan's ways. Glasses on, she stared at him. Hand resting on the door, he looked slightly flummoxed, maybe even a little red. He'd just put the top down, so it couldn't be the sun. It could have been something he said.

"Ah ha," she said, excited that her excellent brain figured out the riddle that was Ryan. He was trying to compliment her but then felt awkward, so he tacked on the dog comment. That was even worse. Now he stood tongue-tied, not knowing what to do next. "Can we leave Burton in the car alone? He won't jump out?"

That surprised a chuckle out of him. "He can't even crawl over the console. Forget jumping over the side."

"Yeah, you're right. I thought I'd go inside and get something to drink." She opened her door to join him.

Inside the tiny market, the narrow aisles stuffed with the necessities of road travel, including beef jerky, sunflower seeds, trashy novels, and batteries, made it hard to get past anyone. She fingered a novel. It might be nice to read, especially if Ryan was driving. She held up a book where the heroine seemed to be in the process of losing her clothes.

Ryan drew close enough to whisper into her ear. "Good thinking, it will add to your tourist disguise."

She didn't bother to tell him that she planned to read it. Clutching the book, she headed back to the cold drinks. Opening the door of the drink case, her hand hovered over the bottles as she read the various names. A shiny can caught her eye, and she reached for it.

Ryan carried a Coke, water, and a package of beer nuts to the counter and glanced to see what she snagged. "Diet soda, huh? You're still drinking that stuff?"

Sniffing, she elevated her nose the tiniest bit before answering, "I happen to like it."

Back in the car, she wondered aloud, "Did I always drink diet soda?"

Ryan carefully backed out, avoiding the influx of cars that felt the need to replace his newly emptied parking spot. "As far as I can remember. It always surprised me, you being a health nut. I figured you for a water only gal or at least green tea."

Amy bit her bottom lip. It didn't make sense that a person who went to the trouble to buy organically raised food would drink a chemical bath of manufactured sweetener, dye, flavoring, and half dozen unpronounceable ingredients, but she did. "Maybe I should have gotten water like you?"

"The water is for Burton. Could you pour it into his bowl for him? You'll probably have to hold his bowl, so it won't spill."

Amy rolled her eyes. The dog was more trouble than a child was.

Ryan merged back into the traffic. "I saw that eye roll."

Amy poured cool water into the plastic bowl. "I'm not sure how you could since I'm wearing sunglasses, and you weren't looking at me." Burton managed to slosh at least half of the water on her hands as he drunk.

"Doesn't matter," he replied, shifting into a higher gear as the car picked up speed. "I know you. You tend to roll your eyes whenever I ask you to do something for Burton. In fact, you asked me why I couldn't get a more self-sufficient pet like a cat."

Wiping her hands off on her pants, she asked again, "Why didn't you get a pet that took less care?"

"I'll try not to take it personally that you didn't commit my answer to memory. I wanted a pet that needed me. If I couldn't be important to someone, at least there is something that needs me." Ryan nodded his head. "This is when you tell me how pathetic I sound."

Actually, she was wondering whether she was so crass that she actually said that before. Obviously, she had. "No, uhm, I was thinking that was sweet."

"Liar," he teased, before speeding up to pass a semi.

Speeding down the road in a vintage gold Mustang convertible with a bulldog in the back, nope no one would think to look for her on the road to New Mexico. At least, she hoped not. So far, it looked like she was not a successful liar. The best she could hope for is no one realized her memory was starting to come back in chunks. Her best bet would be to remain a bit vague. Ryan apparently knew her better than anyone did. To test her theory, she asked, "Tell me something that the two of us did together no one else would know about."

"Okay, I'm thinking." His lips pursed, then, he smiled. "If you don't remember any of this, I'll be devastated."

Amy landed a playful punch on his arm. "That is so not fair since I don't remember most anything. Sometimes I wonder if what I do remember actually happened. The other day I was drinking coffee, rhapsodizing about how much I like coffee, and Beth told me I never liked coffee, ever. Once she said it, I spit the coffee out. It tasted horrible."

"Hmm, interesting, rather like some of the experiments you were working on for the Morpheus Project," Ryan yelled his comment, passing another semi.

She wondered briefly if they should be talking about this while driving at high speeds on the open road. If, somehow, she overlooked something, if a bug existed in the car, then they'd have to dial down the road noise, the wind, the radio, and Burton growling along with AC DC's *Giving the Dog a Bone*.

"Is the dog singing or in pain? What did you mean about the experiments?"

"Burton is singing, a rather unusual trait for a bulldog. You referred to it as crying because he discovered he was stupid and ugly."

"What a bitch and we're still friends?" Amy shook her head. It could turn out she might not like the person she really was.

Ryan nudged her hand. "You were joking. You always liked to tease me about Burton, but I knew you liked him. Jealous because your cat Samson ran away for days being all independent and such."

"I didn't remember having a cat immediately. I thought I did, but there were no signs of a cat in the house. That seems odd because even if he ran away, wouldn't I expect him to come back?" An image of an oversized tiger striped cat with a torn ear prowled in a corner of her mind. "What did he look like?"

Ryan laughed. "You called me pathetic when it came to Burton, but Samson is a mess. He was a stray, on the old side with a torn ear, and practically as big as a bobcat. What he lacks in looks he did not make up for in personality. He's difficult at best and only likes you. No one else. He tolerated me, just barely. You had him declawed and neutered, exacerbating his mad at the world attitude. That's why you kept him inside so the neighbors wouldn't call animal control on him."

She could remember a cantankerous cat pacing the living room, looking out the window. "What did I do with him when I went on my honeymoon?"

"Good question, I never thought about it. I was too surprised you got married. A little hurt, maybe, but still surprised." Ryan's foot pressed down on the gas a bit, shooting the car upward to ninety.

Amy knew the stomping on the gas pedal tied into their conversation. She wasn't sure why he was hurt when she got married. Maybe he thought if they were good friends, she would have told him. On the other hand, maybe, she looked at the speeding, sober-faced man, Aunt Remy was right. Ryan had deeper feelings for her than she suspected. Talk about bad timing. She didn't need any more complications in an already convoluted life. "Slow down, it's bad for Burton. He might become airborne since he doesn't have a seatbelt on."

The Mustang's speed dropped significantly, as he backed off the gas, even switching to the slow lane. Ryan glanced at her, then back at the road. "God, I'm sorry Amy. I don't know what came over me."

She started to say emotion but bit her tongue. It would only embarrass him more. The tension around the two of them shimmered. It was time to change the subject for everyone's comfort level. "Tell me about the Morpheus experiments. I thought the formula would make people less aggressive."

"Well, as you probably guessed, you absolutely were not supposed to talk to me about Morpheus. It was in your confidentiality agreement, but you did anyhow because you were concerned. The subjects you tested the compound turned passive but open to suggestions. At first, you were all for giving them positive suggestions like going home and working on the farm. Not everyone's suggestions were as benign. They brought in animals and had the test subjects kill them. They did the killing without any visual display of emotions. That's when you came to me. The implications were horrible. Morpheus could create assassins. Once the drug wore off, the subject never remembered his or her actions. Needless to say, this upset you. Shortly after that, you disappeared—on your honeymoon." Ryan's lips compressed again, but his gas pedal foot didn't.

The implications staggered Amy. Theron did do research for the defense department at times. If CIA or Army could inject the drug into anyone and sent him or her, out to assassinate a target subject. It would be hard to trace back to where the original order came from since the assassin wouldn't know. Troops of one nation could turn on their own troops, especially if the product were airborne. She must have argued about this. Aunt Remy mentioned she went ballistic about the fallout from the genetically modified crops. No wonder she only ate organic.

"Ryan, I consider you my friend. I must have shared my doubts with you. Didn't it seem strange that I would disappear for two weeks, reappear later with a story about a runaway marriage, and a missing husband? Then there's my cat. All traces of him are gone. I think I am part of the experiment. That's why we have to find Mark or at least find out if he ever existed. I hope he never existed."

She sighed deeply, almost unwilling to consider the natural expansion of her stream of thought.

Ryan agreed. "I hope Mark never existed, but I'm betting not for the same reason you do."

"Tell me your reasons, and I'll tell you mine." She almost wished he wouldn't tell her his. She didn't want to share hers. The landscape flashed by reminding her that for most people this was a glorious extension to a long, hot summer.

"As a man of science, I try to keep my emotions under control. I learned how to do this early in life since I was skipped ahead a few grades in school. Being smaller and smarter than the other kids made me an easy target. I was determined to show that their taunts didn't bother me. I carried that attitude with me, which kept me from telling you how important you were to me."

Spotting a rest area, Ryan signaled to turn before moving into the exit lane. He pulled into a parking space away from other cars. Burton sat up and looked around with interest. "C'mon, I need to take Burton for a walk. It will give us a little privacy as opposed to screaming our innermost thoughts at eighty miles per hour." He clipped on Burton's lead before opening the door. The bulldog eagerly jumped out, but his back legs became tangled up in the seatbelt.

"I bet you thought he was going to get away from you," Amy teased, knowing the dog would not leave his owner's side.

Ryan shook his head and walked over to the grass. "Nope, but some folks have strong feelings about dogs being on a leash. Amy, you and I are rule followers. You know we are. I wanted you to know how I felt. I gave you hints."

"What hints?" Sure, she'd lost her memory, but she remembered more and more every day. There was nothing about any hints, especially if they were of the romantic nature.

"We've been friends for the last ten years." Ryan winked at her.

It made no sense. "Of course, we're friends. I am sure you're my best friend. I don't understand."

Shooting a hand through his hair, Ryan sighed. "I picked you as my protégée because you were so much brighter than the other residents. That was the logical side, but my masculine side picked you because you were attractive, single, and fairly close to my age."

Her resident memories were a little hard to recall, but she did remember a little. "What about that chick with all the hair and the big tits, Lauren. I'd think you would have picked her."

He snorted. "If I wanted a roll in the hay, I would have. She was as dumb as the day is long. She must have slept and cheated her way through medical school. I fear for her patients. I wanted someone I could talk to. At that time, I was only thirty-four and still had hopes of marrying and having a family."

"You're only forty-four, you still could. Plenty of men start families after forty." She thought her words sounded hopeful. Why would he give up hope so early? He was smart, attractive, and fun. Any woman would be lucky to marry him.

"That may be, but once I found the perfect woman, I really couldn't consider anyone else." He shrugged his shoulders while Burton pulled on the leash heading for a tree.

"Oh, she was married?" That was the only reason she could think of for it not working out. Well, maybe. "Was she not into men?"

He shook his head. "Not married until recently."

This was perplexing. Amy mentally tried to catalogue the women that Ryan was in daily contact with. The problem was people seldom talked about their social lives. Most of the people she saw sported latex gloves. They didn't even wear jewelry because of the chemicals and the fact bacteria could slide under a ring and cause all sorts of problems. There was the policy, too, about jewelry. "I give up. Who is she?"

"Really? You don't know?" Ryan dropped the leash, and put both hands on Amy's shoulders. "It's you. It's always been you." He lowered his head to kiss her, barely touching her lips before a flurry of barks and shouts broke out.

Burton could run if a female poodle was involved. An elderly woman clutched her beribboned dog, cursing the bulldog who danced around her feet. Ryan sprinted to grab the leash of his wayward canine companion. He was still apologizing by the time Amy joined him.

The woman, not easily calmed, gave them both a baleful look. "If you paid less attention to each other, then you'd be better dog owners." She stomped off into the building that clearly displayed a No Pets sign.

"Now, I know what my problem was. I was spending too much time on being a good pet owner," Ryan commented, giving her a sheepish grin.

Suddenly lighthearted, Amy exclaimed, "I can't believe you were crushing on me. I thought of you as my friend."

"People call me clueless sometimes in matters of romance. Men don't want to be friends with women. If a man is your friend, rest assured he wants something more." Ryan said the words slowly.

Amy heard him, but she wasn't sure she understood him. "We are friends. Are you saying you don't want to be my friend? Were you pretending to be my friend to get me to sleep with you? If so, you're playing a long game."

Ryan sighed. "Of course, I want to be your friend. Since, I revealed my deep dark secret. It's your turn."

They strolled back to the car, passing families herding children in front of them like so many cats. "I'm afraid," she stopped, hesitated, not sure she could go on. Ryan nodded encouragingly. "Well, if I am married, I think I may have killed my husband as part of an experiment."

Ryan didn't act shocked or revolted as she expected, just thoughtful, as usual. "If you are part of an experiment, which I suspect you are, I think they want you to believe you killed your husband. To what purpose I'm not sure. That's why we need to find out more about the mythical Mark."

It made sense. "If I killed my husband, the guilt would consume me. I'd end up in the psych unit. I certainly would lose any credibility as a whistle blower. "

Ryan opened the car door and assisted Burton into the backseat. He held the door open for Amy then walked to the driver's side to get in. "I will admit to hoping you would reveal deeper feelings for me as opposed to admiring my analytical abilities." He put the key into ignition and started the car.

Amy reached over and turned it off. Ryan started to speak, but looked at Amy's hand still covering his, then into her eyes. "Ryan Korman, this would have been a lot easier if you were a little more upfront. I sure don't know what your hints were, but let me give you an example of what would pass for a hint. I like you, Amy. I would really like to go out with you. We deal well with each other professionally, let's try unprofessionally."

Ryan grinned. "Do you honestly think that last one would have worked?"

"Not really, but it would have got me thinking. Instead, I'd think he's such a wonderful man why hasn't any woman snatched him up. If they got the same hints I did, then it is self-explanatory. I do like you, Ryan, in all ways. Let's see if we can find my husband and figure out what's going on. I want my name cleared before it tangles with your name. There's no reason for you to be knee deep in the mire too."

He kissed her briefly on the lips. "Then we're okay. Two brilliant minds like us should be able to clean up this mess. Then we should work on hints and such."

Her fingers touched her still tingling lips. She never expected the kiss, especially after assuring him that she might be a murderer. "I might still be married. We need to be careful."

"I seriously doubt you're married. You missed all my hints over the years. It doesn't seem likely you'd dash off with someone you just met. Doesn't sound like you," Ryan replied, starting the car.

"I didn't think so, either. That's why it all seems so peculiar. I wanted love, so I just accepted it. It takes me forever to pick the right type of tofu." Ah, she remembered something else. They drove slowly out of the rest stop. A man standing near an SUV caught her attention. He looked like someone she'd seen before, and he stared hard at her as if he knew her. An uneasy suspicion crept up her spine, suggesting that somehow their association wasn't good. She tried to view him in the side mirror, but lost sight of him.

Ryan nudged her leg. "Is something wrong?"

"Yes, no, I don't know. I thought I saw someone, but I can't bring a name to the face." She shrugged, not willing to admit to being uneasy. There wasn't much to go on.

Ryan grinned at her before merging back into traffic. "I do that now and then, and I haven't even lost my memory."

Chapter Eight

Two rest stops and one lunch stop later, the mountains surrounding Albuquerque drew closer. Burton sat up in the backseat attracting the attention of children in a nearby SUV, who pointed to him excitedly. Amy glanced back at the dog, and she'd swear his lips curled back in a canine grin. More likely, the speed pushed back his lips into a happy countenance. No two ways about it, he was one funny looking creature.

Grabbing her backpack, she pulled out the notes to determine where she needed to go. Did she tape back the back cover on the picture where she hid the notes? She hoped so. Still her car was in the driveway, and she'd left the radio on inside. No one should decide to venture into her house today. Considering the various folks who had been in her house, mostly uninvited, she should install a rotating door.

The mountains puzzled her. Shouldn't she remember them? It is rather hard to overlook mountains. If she flew in, then she would have definitely seen them. She couldn't imagine she'd willingly undertake such a long drive on her own to attend a pharmaceutical conference she only had marginal interest in. Sure, if she knew the love of her life was waiting for her, then she'd walk the distance, but she hadn't.

Ryan sang with gusto to an old country ballad demonstrating a pleasant baritone timber. He certainly embraced the tourist image. No one would think he had fears about being tailed, implicated in a crime, or possibly killed. The kiss had surprised her. Maybe the fact it felt so right was the biggest shock. Heaven knows it was a long time coming. The oddest thing was she didn't feel married. No thoughts passed through her head of how appalled Mark might be. She could calculate it had been over a month since the wedding and heading toward two weeks since he disappeared. Local police assumed he left. She was beginning to think likewise, but more so, in that it was his intention all along, which made no sense.

As if feeling her inspection, Ryan stopped singing, reached for the volume knob twisting it off. He gestured to the mountains. "Did you have any time to hike the Manzanos?"

Looking back at the mountains, she considered his question. He asked her if she hiked through the mountains. That would imply she liked hiking. Holding up one finger, she took a mental inventory of all the memories she could recall. In a few, she wore hiking boots and used a stick to assist in her footing through hilly terrain. In her thoughts, she joked about not being a runner to a man. Who was the man? Was it Mark? Were they in the Manzano Mountains?

Looking at the glorious mountains, she knew it wasn't. While her memory yielded up hilly terrain, it was no mountain. The sun silhouetted the man making it hard to see his face. A ball cap shielded his face, making his identity more difficult to determine. Whoever he was, she felt safe, at ease, and playful in her memory. It had to be someone she felt at ease with, someone she'd known long enough to let down her guard. "We used to go hiking, didn't we?"

Nodding, he pushed his hat back to scratch his head. The wind caught it. Ryan grabbed for it, as did Amy and managed to capture the hat. "Good thing, you caught it or I'd have to wear the hat with the hula girl who moves on it."

Amy chuckled at Ryan's remark more because he thought it was funny as opposed to thinking his remark actually packed humor.

"I don't believe you have such a hat."

Ryan waggled his eyebrows. "You don't believe." His voice grew louder with pretend shock. "I can't believe you don't believe me."

Did she insult him? It could be possible he owned such a hat. After all, she didn't expect the car. The man appeared to be full of surprises. He winked at her dispelling her fears that she'd somehow upset him.

"No, it has a palm tree on it and the words, 'It's five 'o'clock, somewhere.'"

Their back and forth banter relaxed her. It felt like coming home after a long, uncertain journey. Her pretending he was funny was something friends did for each other. Rather like driving across two states to make sure she didn't imagine a husband and not once questioning her sanity.

"We hiked once, as much as you can in a place as flat as Dallas. We had to drive west to reach the Austin Chalk Formation to get any type of hill. Even then, it wasn't much. You commented you were a hiker, not a runner. I laughed because I was neither. Do you remember that?" he asked, turning slightly to watch her face.

Excited that he confirmed her memory, Amy grabbed his leg touching the bare skin where his shorts rode up. "I do. I do remember. This is so wonderful. It might mean my real memories are starting to break free."

Would her actual memories take over the ones she had added during her missing period? She seriously hoped so. Afraid she'd talked about things that never happened or no one was familiar with, she talked very little, not wanting to expose her faulty recall. Trying to decide what was authentic only made things tougher. At first, she thought if she could locate Mark, then she'd get him to tell her what was real and what wasn't. Her simple premise would not only have her husband telling all he knew, but that he had loved her once. Their sudden passion propelled them to race off to a tropical island to marry. Even if Mark was an impulsive person, she wasn't. Maybe she could measure dubious actions against the Amy that Remy knew. Glancing toward her companion, she realized Ryan would know her better than most.

It was obvious to her, finally, that he considered her more than a friend. No doubt, he paid close attention to her habits and preferences. He stared ahead, handling the car confidently. Why had she never thought of him as possible marriage material? They had much in common. The things they didn't share just added interest. Would she possibly want someone exactly like herself? She doubted it. She'd read enough on successful marriage partner traits to know the components that ensured a pleasant union. Marrying someone just like you usually resulted in boredom. Because of her research on the state, she would have known better than to cast her lot with an unknown factor like Mark. Yet, she had. Logically, she should have discussed her doubts with someone, but she hadn't.

Her courtship and marriage appeared to be a secretive affair with it only made public after the fact. Only Aunt Remy received a phone call. Honestly, she didn't even remember making the call. The only details she knew were the ones Remy related about her being so crazy in love with Mark and dashing off for a tropical wedding. Remy couldn't even tell her what island they chose for their wedding destination. Sighing heavily, she looked at the mountains, wishing she knew what the hell was going on.

Ryan patted her knee. "Not much longer now. I heard that sigh. Where do we want to go first?"

Looking at her paper, she read the words to him. "Kiva Conference Center." She remembered seeing the words in her mind. She even looked it up on the Internet, and it did exist.

Ryan pointed to the small glove compartment. "Get the GPS out and program in the address."

Looking at her paper, she typed in the address wondering why nothing about it rang a bell. Maybe when they drew closer, she'd see a building or a landmark she'd recognize. Tall office buildings lined the street along with colorful shops and restaurants. Every now and then, she'd spot an unusual bit of art squeezed into the bustle of the major city, which surprised her. It was New Mexico's biggest city, according to the Internet article, and yet they passed nothing recognizable. They passed a McDonalds, Starbucks, and a Wal-Mart, but they seemed to exist in every town, so that meant nothing.

Ryan made all the appropriate turns, stopping at the lights when needed to arrive in front a huge set of buildings with a sign announcing it was the Kiva Conference Center. Her heart fell. Nothing about the center struck a chord. She could pretty much bet she'd never been there before in her life, but she had to check it out. They located an underground garage to keep the heat off the car.

Burton jumped out of the car on his own, determined to go with them. Ryan shrugged his shoulders. "I'll need to walk him around some since it has been a long trip." They walked slowly through the dark garage with Ryan keeping the bulldog away from car tires he wanted to mark as his own territory. Outside, the sun was blinding, but they turned in the direction of the center. A uniformed guard stood by one of the doors.

Amy approached the guard without any conscious thought. He seemed young, at best in his twenties, with sharply creased trousers, and alert eyes. His nametag identified him as C. Lopez.

"Officer Lopez," she called out, earning a smile from the guard.

He bobbed his head, before replying. "Yes, ma'am. How can I help you?"

Amy wondered how to frame her question without sounding like a moron. If she attended the conference, then surely she'd know if it was at the Kiva Conference Center. Not knowing, made it sound like she was bombed out of her mind or a total airhead. Trying to figure out the right line of inquiry, she decided to go with the business viewpoint. "Yes, I think you can help me. I represent Argo Pharmaceuticals. I was hoping to stage a conference like the one you had here a few months ago. Maybe you could put me in contact with the right personnel."

The guard sucked in his lips and used his hand to rub his chin before speaking. "Well, uhm, stage, there is one. I am not sure who's in charge of it. I just started work about two weeks ago. Macy handles all the bookings." He gestured to the double doors.

Ryan and Burton lingered along the row of small trees that tried valiantly to grow in the heat. She'd bet Burton's form of irrigation wasn't helping. Catching Ryan's eye, she motioned to going inside the building. He nodded, pointed at the dog, and motioned to go in. Placing her hand on the door handle, which was surprisingly cool, she opened the door.

Not what she wanted, but it was what she planned when she decided to follow her absent husband's trail. There was no one to help her retrace her path. After all, outside herself, no one ever met Mark. That in itself was a bit peculiar. It wasn't as if she'd never had a beau. The ones she did have often faded away before they even got up the gumption to ask her out. Amy decided early not to end up like her mother, falling prey to a smooth line and a pair of wide shoulders.

Her determination allowed her to find something wrong with almost every man who had a minimal interest in her. After a while, men stopped asking her out for a drink. Eventually, they didn't even bother to ask her opinion. The only male who willingly and consistently kept her company was Ryan. With all this in mind, why would she fall madly in love with a chance-met stranger?

Her footsteps echoed in the empty hallway as she attempted to find the elusive Macy. Amy chafed her arms surprised at the coolness. Looking at the high ceilings and wide corridors, she tried to imagine it filled with people bustling about with goodie bags on their arms and paper coffee cups. She could do it, if she tried hard enough, but it didn't feel right. One door stood ajar to an exhibit hall. Peering into the cavernous room, she tried to imagine booths dedicated to various drugs. There'd be the long legged models passing out pamphlets along with the ubiquitous Power Points. Someone would have one of those annoying air people jumping around in the belief it would attract people to their display. Turning away from the door, she was almost positive she'd never attended a conference here.

Bringing back her first meeting with Mark, she focused on the surroundings as opposed to the smiling man who grabbed her when she stumbled. The ceilings were lower in her memory and surfaced with acoustical tiling, rather dated, indicating an older builder. Not here, but she remembered seeing the sign Kiva Conference Center. Could there be more than one?

Another guard appeared to her left, noticing her inquisitiveness as far as open doorways and made a direct path to her.

"Do you need help?" he asked.

The subtext could have been 'why are you in rooms where you don't belong?' Raising her eyebrows, she did her best to look surprised. "Oh, I was looking for Macy."

The guard nodded at her response, then gestured to the north hallway. "Ms. Grimes' office is close. I'll escort you."

"Thank you." She pushed the words out, trying to sound grateful, but miffed that he put an end to her snooping. She followed the uniformed guard, wondering if an older part of the building may have hosted the conference. If she'd ever been in the building, wouldn't something be familiar?

Her head swiveled taking in the various closed doors, signs, and kiosks. Nothing rang a bell. The center looked like great place to have a convention. Albuquerque, as a major city, had much to recommend to conference visitors, from restaurants to friendliness.

Perhaps it was cheaper than Boston or San Francisco. She remembered a conference in Anaheim. Theron put them up in a four star hotel, but they still had homeless people lingering near the building for a handout until the door attendant chased them away. Odd, she remembered that conference, which was, she rolled her eyes upward trying to remember, seven years ago. Ryan attended with her.

The guard knocked on the door and waited until someone bid him to enter before pushing the door open. Amy smiled at the guard, who she felt certain was anxious to put an end to her roaming ways.

A dark haired woman drummed her lacquered nails on the desktop while frowning at the monitor. "Yes, what is it?" She snapped out the words without looking up.

Whoa, not exactly friendly, Amy cleared her throat, stalling for inspiration. She'd wished Ryan was here and not for the first time, either. The woman looked up, spotting Amy hovering near the door and managed to wipe away all signs of irritation. Standing, she held out her hand.

"Hello, I'm Macy Grimes, Conference Coordinator. How can I help you?"

Amy stared at the hand. Remembering she should shake it, she grabbed her hand and pumped it a bit too enthusiastically. The petite Asian woman did well to stay in her stiletto heels. Okay, she had to keep the same line of questioning in case the employees spoke to one another.

Glancing down at her casual clothing, she realized no one would mistake her for a corporate warrior on assignment. "Ah, I was passing through on vacation. I thought I'd bop into the center, and…" Did she actually say bop? How unprofessional.

Macy looked a little confused but continued smiling, although it looked more like a grimace.

Amy plodded on, aware she sounded less than authentic. "My company was thinking about a conference. We heard what a great job you did with the pharmaceutical conference back in August."

Macy's brows levered down, which didn't seem to be a good sign. "What month did you say?"

"August." Amy counted the weeks off when she met Mark, while Macy hustled back behind the desk. Scrolling down a tablet, she mumbled to herself.

"Mary Kay, Fitness Trainers, Compact and Subcompact Car Dealership, Motivational Speakers Forum, Star Trek Convention, and Comic Con. Nope, no pharmaceuticals or even medical conferences." She looked up, directing the last words at Amy.

No conference, it couldn't be. She had to be wrong about the dates. "Oh, did I say August? I meant July."

Macy scrolled a little more and laughed. "I am shocked I forgot about that."

"The pharmaceutical conference?" At last, she had proof that she wasn't imagining everything.

"Oh no, we had to close the center down for renovations. Some stupid lawsuit about the place not being suitable for people with disabilities. We had to modify everything from the elevator doors to bathrooms. Originally, the building had such modifications in place, but someone showed up with a tape measure. Apparently, some places were an inch or two shorter than specifications required, which made it harder for the extra wide wheelchairs to get through. I took my two weeks' vacation then since no conferences were held." She shook her head, perhaps marveling at the workers enlarging doors or the fact someone measured them.

It wasn't July; she couldn't go back any farther. "Maybe they were scheduled here, and you had to send them somewhere else."

Macy folded her arms as if sensing her professionalism might be in question. "Oh, people schedule events years ahead. We did have Civil War re-enactors along with the genealogy folks scheduled. The Enactors were glad to move to November. The genealogy people went to Salt Lake. It is hard to beat out the Mormons when it comes to having genealogy records."

Amy nodded, convinced no pharmaceutical conference happened here in the past two months. "I see." It had to happen in the six-week time span for her absences to make any sense.

Macy picked up a clipboard and attached a check sheet to it before passing it to Amy. The paper detailed what rooms and services they got in various packages. Taking the clipboard, she knew she'd have to play this charade out to the end, discussing vendors and bandwidth.

Thirty minutes later, she stumbled out of the center amazed that people could afford to put on conferences. Vendors would have to garner a lot of business to underwrite the rental agreement. Amy mumbled something about showing it to her boss and shook Macy's hand again.

Ryan sat on a shaded bench with a panting Burton by his feet. He looked up when Amy approached. He stood, causing Burton to lurch to his stubby legs. "Did you find anything out?"

Inhaling deeply, she considered her reply. "The two of us can't afford to host a conference, even at our glorified salaries."

Rubbing the back of his neck, Ryan snorted. "Well, hell, I knew that even before you went inside. Did you discover anything else?"

A sense of unease prickled the hairs on her arm. Two workers steadied a wrapped statue on a dolly. A sunglass-wearing mother pushed a twin stroller down the street with two screaming babies. Nothing that out of ordinary to cause the unease she was feeling. Over there by the only decent size tree in place, there was movement as if someone had ducked back behind the tree. There was no one there now.

It could be the man from the rest stop. Even it was, he could be coming to the same place. It was the only major city in the area. Oh yeah, then there was the fact she was paranoid due to a missing or sabotaged memory.

"Let's walk." She started walking, not waiting for Ryan.

He looked like he might object. Maybe he had enough walking with Burton. Still he managed to catch up with her, keeping pace, but Burton struggled. She slowed down wondering what appeal the dog held for Ryan. "Why didn't you go for a real dog like a Labrador or even a Greyhound?"

Ryan laughed. "Goodness, how many times are you going to ask me the same question? Same answer as before, Burton needed me. He couldn't make it on his own."

That's for sure. Amy fought snorting. The street was crowded with colorful boutiques and restaurants promising everything from Tex Mex to Vietnamese food. Pointing to a gallery across the way, she looked both ways before crossing the street. She waited until Ryan and the dog made it safely across, then headed for the gallery that caught her interest.

The window featured a placard on a trestle that advertised Denis Paul Noyer lithographs were available inside. Ryan looked at the sign and chuckled. "Now I get it, you and your obsession with Noyer. Why don't you break down and buy a lithograph?"

Her admiration of the French artist returned along with several of his lithographs she'd stared at in various galleries and museums, coveting them. This shop didn't figure into her memories. "You know how cheap I am. I think I will go into the store to see how long he has had the lithographs. Do you mind?"

Amy wasn't ready to tell him the whole trip had been a waste, pretty much laying out the fact that there may not even be a Mark. That would mean she was never married. It would also mean someone implanted those delicious sexual encounters in her mind. That would be enough to make someone very wealthy. Would she have agreed to an implant? Definitely, in theory and on ethical grounds.

The gallery owner came out of the backroom as soon as the door buzzer announced her arrival. The white haired gentleman was more than pleased to show her the Noyer lithographs. "I took a chance on these." He motioned to the prints beautifully matted and hung out of the sun's damaging light. "Got them about four months ago, I figured maybe the locals or even the tourists would like something different than wolves baying at the moon and wounded Indian warriors. I figured wrong. I only sold one in four months."

"Really, four months. I am sorry to hear that." She wasn't too sorry to hear that Noyer hadn't sold but more that she hadn't been here. No way, she would have missed a chance to stare at Noyer's work. His depictions of an earlier period gave her a sense of calm. Something she could use right now. Motioning to a smaller Noyer picture of a Victorian house surrounded by palm trees, she said, "I'll take that one."

The man removed the painting from the wall with a grin. "That will be eight hundred dollars."

"Oh." She had never asked how much the pictures were before. She always assumed she could not afford them.

Noting her hesitation, the shop owner hurriedly said, "Seven-fifty, okay?"

"I guess." She wasn't bargaining with him, even if he thought she was. Instead, she was certain she'd never been to Albuquerque, not once. That meant she never walked through the Kiva Center before today. No reason to since no pharmaceutical conference occurred there. If there was, why didn't Ryan go? She certainly never walked into this gallery. More importantly, she never fell madly in love with Mark. They never got married and had lots of exquisite sex. That probably disappointed her the most. The euphoria felt almost drug-like, maybe because it was.

She handed the shop owner her debit card. He managed to talk himself down to seven twenty-five without her even bartering. If she hung around long enough, he'd probably thrown in an extra picture. She went for the small picture because it would fit in Ryan's trunk easily. It was a small price to pay for little bit of peace to put on the wall. The portrait with the grass shack used to bring her that until she realized she never took it. Probably was from some Internet file. Maybe her memories of Mark came from a romance novel.

A young girl squatted by Burton to pat him on the head, making him squirm in delight. At least someone was enjoying the trip.

Nodding to the wrapped bundle under her arm, Ryan commented, "It is about time you gave in and purchased your heart's desire."

Amy blinked twice, stared at Ryan, then realized he was talking about the Noyer, not Mark. Yeah, if it were that simple wouldn't women line up to buy memories of a whirlwind courtship, a handsome husband, and delicious loving? She would. With this in mind, she began to question the Morpheus Project. Maybe it did start out as a military project, but other uses materialized that drug companies jumped on. Of course, down the line, when side effects showed up, too many to count, it never stopped the pharmaceutical segment from marketing the drug out the wazoo.

The consumer stood a fair chance of blindness, paralysis, stroke, and death. Men still popped blue pills in the millions, aware they could lose their vision, hearing, often memories, and, due to drug interaction, their lives. Most pharmaceutical companies believed disclaimers and heavy hitter lawyers protected them.

"Oh, yeah, the Noyer, I caved. I should say the shop owner caved. He kept lowering the price. If I hadn't left, he'd probably paid me to take it. The man could use lessons in the art of salesmanship." They walked aimlessly, not heading in any direction. She knew Ryan expected her to say something. After all this was her trip. "I think the trip was a bust. I didn't find out anything."

The slanting sun's rays indicated the sun was on its way down, which wasn't too surprising. At least driving in the dark meant it wouldn't be as hot. Ryan's hand landed on her bare arm, bringing comfort with it. He'd say something profound. She was sure of it.

His pulled down his sunglasses to look into her eyes. "Let's get something to eat."

Okay, she was wrong about profound. They stopped at a little cantina with outside tables. The owner brought Burton a pan of water and a plate of mystery food. Whatever it was, it didn't last long under the canine's assault.

The restaurant featured brightly colored lights stretched over the outside dining area. They came on once the sun settled behind the mountains, giving all the diners' faces a festive air. The lights and tequila made life seem a little less serious. Maybe she'd think about it tomorrow. Sunday was soon enough to decide if she'd been part of a nefarious experiment. Tonight, she'd relax, enjoy her food, and maybe drink a tad too much since Ryan was driving.

Reaching across the table, he covered her hand. "Tell me what you found?"

She wanted to toss back the rest of her margarita, but that would involve shaking off his hand. She didn't want to do that. He'd take it wrong, and right now, he was the only person she felt she could trust. "Nothing, that's what I found. There was no pharmaceutical convention here. When I walked around in the building, the modern lines didn't mesh with the cramped building in my mind. I never walked down this street. I never stopped in the gallery. I am damn certain I never met a man named Mark. Let alone married him. On the upside, that means he didn't leave me. On the downside, it means something bizarre went down. Worst of all, I will admit to being sad that no one loved me so much that they wanted to run away with me and get married."

Tears pooled in her eyes, and she wanted to wipe them away before Ryan noticed. He squeezed her hand but kept his grip. He cleared his throat as if he had trouble speaking.

"I suspected that Mark didn't exist from the start and not because I didn't believe you. I did believe that you thought he existed. I knew that if the man ever met you, knew you like I did, fell in love with you, that there was no way on Heaven or Earth that he would ever leave you."

Chapter Nine

They decided to stay the night at a small hotel before making the drive back, part of Amy's original plan before Ryan invited himself along. The letters in the Star Lite Star Brite Motor Lodge were burnt out in a few places, inviting weary travelers to visit *ar ite rite Moto Lodge*. It sounded more like a rite of passage or an entrée in a foreign restaurant, except for the lodge part. Ryan turned when he noticed a pet friendly sign stuck into the small patch of grass in front of the aging motel.

A few children splashed in the postage stamp sized pool. It reminded Amy of the few trips she made with Aunt Remy. They never stayed in plush hotels with actual lobbies and warm cookies. They mainly traveled to reach her various clients, and money was always an issue. Some hotels would frown on the unusual clientele parading through the lobby to get a hex lifted or a love potion.

It wasn't too surprising since some of the folks had scared her. Sometimes she'd hide in the bathroom and peered out at the parade of old women with canes and rheumy eyes, desperate women clutching a photograph in one hand and wrinkled money in the other, drag queens teetering on platform shoes, immigrants barely able to speak English, and one-eyed men with eye patches. Not everyone looked as if he or she belonged in a cult movie. Often conservatively dressed folks slipped in when no one else was around. Ironically, they usually wanted revenge, a curse, or even a voodoo poppet to torture. Remy didn't do that. She helped people.

It was a concept that puzzled the revenge seeker, who probably taught Sunday school. They carried deep inside them hatred so deep, it didn't matter what roads they took as long they assuaged it.

Hate, dislike, and fear rode people hard. The women who came to Remy usually wanted love potions. Her aunt did her best to advise them because some of the men they wanted weren't worth having. In the end, they were probably sorry they got them. Amy bit her lip, thinking about the women making return trips to have themselves shed of the man they originally wanted. Exhaling deeply, she realized what they wanted, pretty much what every woman wanted, was the experience of being madly, deeply in love.

Ryan steered the Mustang into a parking slot. With his hand on the door, he turned to look at her. "I'll try to get two rooms close to each other."

A quick glance showed the parking lot only held about a dozen aged minivans, station wagons, and pickup trucks. Two rooms shouldn't be a problem. Of course, it meant she'd be alone in a room in a strange city. Lately, she had a hard time falling asleep in her own house, unaware of what might happen when she closed her eyes. "Could you make that one room—if you don't mind?"

His eyebrows shot up. Seeing the question in his eyes, she hurried to add, "Two beds, of course. I don't want to be alone. Is that okay?"

His eyebrows settled back behind his glasses. His lips tried to push up into a forced smile but didn't succeed. His expression resembled more of a toothache than anything else or a man who'd received a sucker punch. "Sure, no problem. I understand." He turned to the lit lobby where the night clerk smoked a large cigar while watching a tiny television. Better him than her. She had no desire to inhale the noxious fumes.

Ryan definitely resembled a tourist in his pastel polo and plaid shorts. Talk about a square peg. He certainly stuck out among the straw Stetsons and boot flare jeans usually worn with the belt buckle won at the local rodeo. His point was to vanish by not trying to blend in with the locals. Sure, there were plenty of tourists in town. Some with flashy cars, a few wore polo shirts, and some even had small yappy dogs. All the same, none of them had a flashy car, questionable attire, a petulant bulldog, and an amnesiac scientist companion. Despite his reassurances, Amy felt exposed. Why hadn't she asked him to put up the car top? It would be giving into her paranoia.

Burton sat up tall in the backseat, trying to scope out the area. He didn't seem anxious. Animals were supposed to be more sensitive to threats and weather, but she figured he was an exception. The children who'd been in the pool started back to their room, yelling and arguing in the process. Burton felt the need to add his commentary and began barking, attracting attention. Oh great. She slid down in her seat but tried to grab Burton between the seats. Might as well have a lighted arrow pointing her out, but neither the children nor the parents appeared to care.

Ryan exited the lobby, calming the canine without any common sense with his voice.

"Hey buddy, what's going on?"

The dog's lips tilted up as if he were smiling at his owner. Burton's little stubby tail shook so hard his entire body shivered. Such obvious adoration probably dismissed a variety of faults. Brandishing a key with a green star attached to it, Ryan opened the car door. "We're in Lucky Number Seven."

They drove the short distance to their room. Ryan opened the door, which released a miasma of stale cigarette smoke and even older beer. The pine scented room deodorizer scent rode lightly over the other smells. A dollar room deodorizer could only accomplish so much. Shouldering her bag, she entered the room with reluctance.

Two full beds covered with avocado chenille spreads dominated the room. A small spindly bedside table stood by each bed with western theme lamps more appropriate for a children's room. Make that a child from the fifties. There was a worn wing chair with vinyl upholstery. A bulky television squatted on the dresser. Framed pictures of sunsets over the desert were the only decorations. Heavily lined drapes kept out the sun or car headlights. She peeked into the tiny bathroom to discover a tub that smelled of bleach. Good, at least she knew it was clean.

Ryan came in after walking Burton and putting the top up on the car. "It is a bit of a dump. We can go elsewhere."

Two doctors who made decent money would not stay in a ramshackle motel. That was the reason enough to stay. "How did you register?" She asked him not to use her name, so her movements couldn't be traced.

"Talked up the clerk, man to man. Told him I was here with my girlfriend. Paid cash. He agreed that he never saw me. He assumes I am married. Registered as John Smith, which is rather surprising since there are three more John Smiths staying here tonight." Ryan tossed his hat on the bedside table, removed a pillow from the bed, and placed it on the floor for Burton.

The clerk's probable speculations on Ryan's nocturnal activities were definitely better than the truth. The clerk would be disappointed if he knew the real story, but, then again, Ryan probably was too. Squatting by the dog, he patted the canine, making her think he'd probably be a decent father. He certainly was patient with what had to be the most challenged canine in the world. The words popped out of her mouth before she had time to edit it or even think about their appropriateness. "You would have made a great dad."

Straightening to his full height, he ran one hand through his hair. "Possibly. Hard to say since I never had any children. I might have been able to rent out a surrogate mother. I've heard there are women who do that, but..."

She playfully punched him on the arm. He knew what she was asking but turned the question aside by joking. "Never mind, I shouldn't have asked. Was I always this abrupt?"

His face lit up with a grin. "I can answer that with one word, yes."

Sighing, she shook her head. "I was afraid of that. Forget I said anything. I figured you were so good with Burton that you'd be natural with children of your own."

Ryan cast a glance back at the dog. "You hear that buddy? She thinks you're as much trouble as a child. Not hardly." He reached for Amy's hand, surprising her.

She hadn't seen that coming. He tugged her toward the bed, perching on the end of it. She sat uneasily beside him. Remy insinuated that they both were too blind to see the noses on their faces. He turned a little more to face her and reached for her other hand, surprising her even more. "Ryan, what are you..."

"Listen, that's all I want you to do. Just listen, and then think. That's all you need to do."

She started to open her mouth, but he shook his head. Exhaling, she allowed her hands to relax in his grasp as he brought their joined hands to rest on the bedspread between them.

His somber eyes met hers. Then he began to speak. "In the beginning, it is hard work to get established as a resident. Some residents came already married to the program, which was good because there's certainly no time for socializing, unlike what you see on television." A low chuckle escaped possibly at the television doctors hooking up everywhere and having plenty time to hang out in restaurants and bars.

He licked his lips, but continued speaking. "I always thought I would marry and have kids. I came from a happy family and pretty much believed I would imitate my parents. Of course, that would involve a wife. I dated a little but not successfully. I am not what you consider charming. There was even one woman I tried to impress by taking her to a fancy restaurant and talking about new pharmaceuticals about to come on the market."

This she remembered. "It was that night I recalled when I saw you at the hospital. I couldn't understand the memory. Why go to a French restaurant with a strolling violinist to talk about the latest drug breakthroughs?"

"You have hit on why I'm single. I took you to the restaurant to tell you how I felt about you, but chickened out at the last minute. I settled for shoptalk. I figured it was better to preserve what we had than to throw it away on something that might never happen. Then I convinced myself I misread everything, maybe you didn't even like men."

His words shocked her enough that she jerked her hands free. "What? What, did you think I was a lesbian?" She knew rumors of that nature usually proliferated about unmarried women.

"No." His answer was loud and hung between the two of them. "I just figured you didn't have any use for anyone, man or woman."

That certainly didn't make her feel any better. She stood and paced the small room, throwing questions in Ryan's direction. "Was I so unlikable, unattractive that no one would want me? Did you think I was some type of asexual being, rather like a plant, or a being from a science fiction novel? Did you think I relieved all my sexual longings with BOB, racy romances, or both? "

His brows drew together. "Bob? Who's Bob? I only knew about Mark and Dirk several years ago."

She sighed. Had to bring it up, didn't she. "B-O-B stands for battery operated boyfriend. In other words, a vibrator."

Ryan nodded and wisely chose not to elaborate on the subject.

Amy tried to place Dirk. Good heavens, she wasn't sure she could even remember him. Not just because of her problematic memory, but that he mattered so little. "Dirk, wasn't he the liaison from the defense department?"

"Yeah." He gave up the word with pained expression. "Ex-marine, tall, broad shoulders, had a Marine tattoo on his sizable bicep."

"Sounds like you spent more time observing him than I did. Why would a guy like that be interested in me? We both know I'm not the Bambi type." She vaguely remembered him but not as being overly interesting. She was unsure what it was about her that appealed to the man. She stopped pacing and stared at Ryan.

Pushing off the bed, he stood and walked toward her, placing both hands on her shoulders. "You have no clue how beautiful you are. I find your intelligence incredibly alluring, but I think Dirk was interested in you because you were the only female in the building who wasn't panting after him."

He called her beautiful again. Not the most effusive compliment she'd ever received, but then she hadn't received many. All her compliments dealt with her work as opposed to her appearance. Theron didn't employ models for their research. The chemicals used in the labs, along with safety features, made flowing hair, skirts, and even cosmetics undesirable. Of course, the skirts were more about the searches. No woman wanted to have the guard pushing the metal wand underneath her skirt during the twice-daily searches, even if in many ways, they were just drones for the company.

"That might have been true. I can't recall why I went out with him. I do remember him to be lacking in intellect."

Ryan's lips twisted up in a smirk. "Yeah, that's what all the women want in a guy. I am not totally sure if they care if he can talk."

His hands still rested on her shoulders. It wasn't uncomfortable. She considered it reassuring, but puzzling. Her memory might be lacking in many aspects, but she was sure they were not this touchy feely with each other. Ryan's anxiety showed in the way he held his shoulders. Odd that she'd known that, but they'd been working together almost a third of her life. "What is it? There is something you want to say, and it's troubling you."

He sighed, dropped his hands, and turned away from her. He ran his palm over his face a couple of times. He wasn't going to tell her. She read that in his body language. Whatever it was, he was wrapping it up to store it away. "Ryan, don't do this to me or you. First, you work yourself up to tell me something. Then you stop. How long are you going to bottle things up? Maybe I need to know." Her voice gradually rose with each sentence, fearing he kept back information about Theron or possibly her murderous past. "What is it?" she yelled while throwing her hands up. Knowing anyone outside could hear made her wince. She probably sounded like some ill-tempered drunk.

Ryan spun around at the question. Calmness settled over him, which settled on Amy too. He reached for her right hand, bringing it to his lips, kissing it. "I love you, Amy. I think I always have to some extent. I'd make up excuses, telling myself I only admired you or your work. I even tried going out with other women. A single doctor is still a catch, but all I could think about was how they weren't like you."

His words hit her with the same impact of an anvil falling on her head. At least she would have seen that coming. Maybe. *Ryan loved her.* It seemed right. He did love her. Did anyone else volunteer to drive ten hours to see if her husband actually existed or was merely a drug-induced fantasy? Nope, no one else offered to drive. Still, the thought of her being so appealing that other women in comparison were lacking was hard to conceive.

"Those other women probably wanted to talk about something other than retroviruses and the efficiency of using anthrax as a biohazard. I could see how that might be off-putting."

"It was," he agreed with a smile as he turned her hand over and kissed her palm causing her skin to heat. "I figured before we even made the trip, that Mark never existed. Your sudden marriage and honeymoon tore at me, but it made me aware you were open to marriage and a relationship. You seemed pleased by the whole event, except for the disappearance."

"I was." She tried to remember the sense of euphoria she usually had when she managed to bring up a memory of Mark. "The whirlwind romance, the pet names, the beachside wedding, and the sex. A woman had to have come up with the sexual fantasies. I doubt any man could."

"Hey," Ryan interjected as he rubbed their clasped hands along his jaw. "I would like the opportunity to prove otherwise."

The Mark memory must have been a whole insertion, rather like programming a computer. Her runaway wedding and honeymoon was the time her brain learned to accept a life and love she'd never experienced. Of course, everyone was surprised she came back married because she hadn't mentioned it. She must have called Remy sometime. She thought she called her from Tahiti, but that would be easy enough to disapprove. Were there times when she was lucid, walking around? Did she spend the two weeks in a coma while someone sat beside her imputing memories? That seemed the more likely scenario. How could they do this, if she'd been unwilling? Ryan's words penetrated her ponderings. "What? What did you say?"

"You heard me. I did not want to lose this one chance of letting you know how I feel. You don't have to feel the same way. Most relationships are not equally balanced. Often the woman loves more. I would just like you to think about it." He still held her hand, giving it a small squeeze.

Odd, she thought she felt a tingle. Probably did. He was sexy in a clean cut way. His compassion and gentleness were endearing too. Something held the two of them together for the past decade. Their relationship lasted longer than many marriages did. "Okay."

How would she put what she was feeling into words? "I am not against exploring our feelings, but I'm the woman everyone thinks is married. I must be such a horrible wife that my husband fled from me. We can't announce it was a drug-induced fantasy until I discover the reason behind it. As far as I can tell, it might be dangerous. That means if you're around me too much, then you might get sucked in. You'll need to keep your distance."

Ryan used their clasped hands to pull her into his embrace. "Like hell, I am going to stay away, especially with you in danger. We are top scientists at Theron. With that in mind you'd expect working together, we could figure something out. They have no idea you've regained your memory or at least most of it."

That was true. "I told everyone my memory was fine." Of course, she told them that when she thought she drank coffee too.

Ryan rubbed slow circles on her back similar to her Aunt Remy's method of lowering her anxiety. She leaned her head against his shoulder thinking of how well he knew her. Of course, he had forever to learn her ways, but until Ryan, no one cared to. His voice rumbled against her ear. "If your memory was fine, wouldn't you be freaking out that you were used like a lab rat?"

He was right. "Yes, so if I keep acting calm, they will assume I remember nothing. I should show some concern about my missing husband, but that's it. Maybe even some anger that he'd desert me."

His smoothed one long fingered hand through her hair. "That's good. So what is your next move?"

Amy tried to think about it, but it wasn't easy. He kept distracting her with his body. As a scientist, she could recite passages about why the smell of his pheromones excited her. On the other hand, she also knew not all pheromones reacted the same way on everyone. If they did, there certainly wouldn't be any lonely people on the face of the earth. They'd all be humping like rabbits. The image instead of being giggle-worthy became stimulating. She didn't want to fall in bed with her best friend and possibly her ally because she was horny. No, Ryan deserved so much more. They needed space. Pulling out of his arms, she grabbed her bag and headed for the bathroom.

"I need to take a bath," she called over her shoulder, refusing to look at his shattered expression. She needed time to think, and the bathroom appeared to be her only refuge.

* * * *

The hotel bathtub was a little short, causing her to prop her feet on the waterspout. At least there was a bath. A shower wouldn't give her time to think or stall. Hot water eased some of the tension from the long drive but not all. Her situation perplexed her. Was she in danger? It was hard to think otherwise when someone was tailing her and searching her house. Apparently, Theron thought she was enough of loose cannon that they pulled her off Morpheus. Maybe she threatened the project, but not in the way Wilkenshire would, failing to adhere to protocol. No, it was much more. As an intelligent person, she had to realize she must have put some failsafe measure in place.

Somewhere, somehow there had to be notes, documentation, evidence she'd managed to hide. That's what they were looking for. Closing her eyes, she tried to think of how she'd hide something. A jumble of memories crowded into her mind, including hiding a birthday present, she made for Remy when she was ten. Something a little more recent would help. An image of her in the company restroom squatting over a toilet to shove something up her vagina, that wasn't a tampon. God, she did secret information out of the firm. The guards were thorough in their searches, but they hadn't reached that level. Most of the scientists would probably quit if they did. Even nerdy compliant introverts had stuff they'd not accept.

Lathering up the washcloth, she tried to bring in the image clearer as she washed her leg. In her mind, she looked at the thumb drive before wrapping it in cling wrap. The drive chafed. It made her glad the day was almost over. She made sure to flush the actual tampon and use the inserter wand to push it up. A feeling of horror and desperation flickered over her, causing her to shiver in the hot water. What was on the flash drive that would drive her to such drastic measures? These were not the actions of a woman wildly in love. What did she do with the drive? Did she go anywhere? These incomplete memories caused more questions than they answered. Maybe Ryan could help.

A tiny voice whispered in her head that Ryan could be part of the conspiracy. The very best part because he had her trust. She sat up suddenly and reached for a towel, anxious to flee. Realizing she was responding to the primitive fight or flee mechanism, she dried her body and dressed. She couldn't leave without Ryan. Running out of the motel room desperate to return would tip off Theron. Better if she didn't show her hand.

Cracking the door, she peered out to see Ryan watching television with one hand resting on Burton's head. The two of them didn't look like double agent types. The canned laughter from the sitcom made Ryan laugh hard, pulling off his glasses and wiping his eyes with the edge of his shirt. Nope, he couldn't be working against her. Just in case, she should watch what she said.

They both doubted the reality of her marriage and courtship. It would be prudent not to mention the flash drive.

Opening the bathroom door all the way caused Ryan to look up and blink. Probably trying to bring her in focus without his glasses, she grinned as she walked toward him. His upturned face lit up as she drew closer. His delighted expression tugged on her emotions. They had shared so much over the years. A comment Remy made about not seeing what's right in front of them returned. Ryan was definitely in love with her.

A certainty settled somewhere around her heart. As a teen, she wanted to hear the words desperately. Armand Fournier was more than willingly to whisper the words in her ears as he removed her panties one sultry summer night. Despite his protestations to love forever, she never heard from him again. Some of friends mentioned he joined the military. She was never too sure. For a week, she cried emptying numerous tissue boxes certain that, her heart cracked right in two. Aunt Remy never asked what happened, probably because she knew just like everyone is the parish did. Smooth-talking Armand managed to relieve the majority of the local girls of their virtue. Remy gave her a foul smelling potion to drink while reminding her that a man's actions always meant more than words.

Ah, yes, how could she forget such true words? Ryan patted the spot beside him. She slid onto it wondering if she were making a mistake. The old Amy would have no reason to hesitate, but then the old Amy thought they were friends.

He pushed back on his glasses. "I was beginning to wonder if I should check on you to see if you fell asleep in the tub." The remote sat between the two of them. Using two fingers, he pushed it toward her. "You pick what you want. I'm not committed to this show."

Picking up the remote, she held it to her heart. Fluttering her eyelashes, she teased. "It must be love. He let me have the remote." She only meant to joke, but, when she saw the serious expression, she knew she stumbled when she only meant to be lighthearted.

Reaching for her hand, Ryan held it, pulling her a little closer into a half embrace. "I am glad you finally realized it."

His face drew closer. He intended to kiss her. Now would be an excellent time to stop him. He loved her, and she didn't know what she was, except vulnerable. Her hand lifted, but instead of landing on his chest, it stopped on his glasses to pluck them off and fold them against her chest. "Maybe we should put your eyewear someplace safe."

He took the glasses and placed them behind him on the nightstand. "Let me see if I remember where I was. Amy, Amy where are you?" He pretended he couldn't see placing his hands in front of him waving them until they landed on her legs smoothing up to her hips. "Oh, there you are."

She giggled and attempted to scoot up higher on the bed. No, she definitely didn't want to get away. Ryan surprised her by pinning her to the bed with his body. A move she didn't expect. Twisting one way, then the other trying to loosen his hold, but suddenly she wondered why she tried to get away. He felt good on top of her, not too heavy, but enough body weight and testosterone to pin her to the mattress. When was the last time a male pinned her to the bed?

Hard to say. It wasn't recent despite her pseudo memories of Mark. Indistinct images of sweaty bodies entwined, whispered endearments, and labored breathing was what she remembered. It was rather like viewing an NC-17 movie through cheesecloth, nothing was that clear. Ryan's face drew closer. Beard stubble darkened his chin. His pupils dilated. His breathing came faster and harder signaling a more rapid heartbeat. Her own heart beat faster. Anticipation built as his lips lowered to her, and then it hit her, stiffening her body.

Ryan stopped so close that it was hard to bring his face into focus. "What is it?" His face drew away as he sat back on his haunches, a look of resignation on his features. He shot his fingers through his already disordered hair.

Revelations certainly had bad timing. She wanted Ryan to kiss her and more. The odd dance the two of them had participated in, either knowingly or unknowingly, was about to reach the crescendo in the music, but then she had to ruin it all. Amy knew talking about memories of lovemaking with another fellow would not add the amorous mood. Far from it. Although she had read about those individuals who did enjoy watching other men with their women, a quick glance at her disgruntled companion assured her he was not in that small group. How could she explain and retain their former closeness of seconds before? She couldn't.

Pushing against the mattress, she worked herself into a sitting position, to be at least be at eye level with Ryan. Lying on her back, sprawled across a motel bed put her at a disadvantage while speaking. At least she thought it did since she couldn't remember doing it before. Her hand reached out to touch his face, tenderly. "I am so sorry. I wanted you to kiss me."

Ryan's eyebrows lifted in inquiry. "You did?"

"Of course, I did." Amy noted his surprise. "Who wouldn't want a handsome man, like you, to kiss them?" She chose to ignore his remonstrations. "It's just as I watched your face grow closer, the memories of making love with Mark came back."

Ryan fell back on the bed and covered his face with both hands, which did little to stop his words. "Damn it, I finally tell you how I feel, and I am bested by a fantasy rival."

Getting to her knees, she crawled to Ryan's side, pried his hands on his face, and rested their joined hands on his chest. "You haven't been bested. Unfortunately, my mind kept working on the puzzle that is Mark while my body was responding to you. I was focusing on your face. How sexy you looked with the stubble on your face. Then, it hit me."

"What?" Ryan chose to stay in his position but allowed his stiff fingers to bend and wrap around hers.

"The angle of this vision, the perspective was wrong. Right now, I am looking down at you. At best, I can see my hands and yours." Amy leaned her torso back while keeping her hands on his chest. "Now, I can see my arms, knees, but that's about it. In my memories of Mark, sometimes I would look at his face close-up, but other times I saw the two of us in bed as if I were a voyeur, a spirit in the corner of the room. There is no way I would be able to see that." The perspective had bothered her.

Biting his bottom lip, Ryan waited, probably weighing his words or conclusions before speaking. "Okay, you are describing a third person viewpoint. Do you think a third person could have watched you and Mark? Maybe even filmed, these images part of some kinky activities the two of you willingly participated in?"

Amy cocked her head to one side and stared at her friend. "Really, you think I'd do that?"

Realizing his mistake, Ryan tried to backpedal. "I'm sure you wouldn't. You don't like having your picture taken, even with your clothes on."

His obvious discomfiture made Amy laugh. "It isn't a clothes thing. I don't like having my picture taken because I do not like the result. It never seems to be how I think of myself. It's as if the person in the photo is a stranger. That's why I dislike it. As for the scenes of lovemaking, I don't think it's me in the images at all."

"Then who?"

Amy lifted her hands from Ryan's chest and scooted back to rest against the headboard. It looked as if the foreplay session was over, and they were back to discussing the case. It definitely needed solving more than she needed any type of sexual interaction with Ryan. *Well, not exactly true, most of her body and part of mind disagreed. Damn, her logical side. No wonder she never had any fun.*

She watched him push up on his forearms thinking how incredibly sexy he was. How could she miss this? Somehow, he managed to hide behind his lab coat, glasses, and slightly officious manner. He asked the same question she asked herself. Yet, how did she know it wasn't her that Mark made love to? Using her hands, she placed them about a foot apart in the air. "It was like I was watching a movie of sorts of two people in bed. I couldn't see them all that well as if I was looking through a curtain. The slender blonde on top was me, and the man below was Mark."

Ryan grunted his response to her description.

Amy chose not to honor his grunt with a reply, but continued. "Several things occurred to me. Now, it's possible that whoever is involved in this scenario has seen me naked since my first recollection is being wet in the shower, but they haven't seen me making love to any man because I haven't had any relationships to witness. Have I?" She stared at Ryan as if expecting an answer.

"I am supposed to know this how? Would you be running off and having one-night stands and confessing them to me later?" He ran one hand over his face. "Geesh, really, I am supposed to help you on this? I can tell you that you outlasted almost everyone at

Theron as far as long hours. You burned the midnight oil outstaying your colleagues. Since you already know how I feel about you, I will admit to staying late, too, just to be near you even though more of my work centered on live patients at the nearby hospital, as opposed to projects in the lab. When would you have the time to meet these men?"

Her lips pressed together as her eyes rolled up to the ceiling. "You're right, of course. I couldn't remember any men, either, but more importantly, besides the third person perspective, the woman in bed was not me, I think."

"Why is that? Besides the third person view, I mean," Ryan asked.

Amy blushed, a little, wondering if she should look away from Ryan when she confessed the truth. "This blonde woman I couldn't see that well was very, uhm, I am not sure how to say this. She was, uhm, very assertive in bed, imaginative, and I think she may have had a horsewhip near the bed. That's another thing I didn't recognize, the bed. Now I realize it could be in a hotel room. What I could see of the room looked wrong. Not like a hotel room should look." She motioned to her surroundings.

"What was wrong with the room?" Ryan kept his eyes on her face.

Discussing the images was making her a little uncomfortable and possibly somewhat aroused. Using her two fingers, she measured her pulse, definitely rapid. Why would a man who didn't exist excite her? Ryan's hazel eyes stared into hers. Okay, she was sitting on a bed with a handsome man who already confessed to loving her, talking about sexual images. People called her intelligent. They might seriously reconsider if they saw her now.

"Pulse is rapid, isn't it?" Ryan asked with a slight smile.

"Yes, yes it is. Why do you ask?" Her words sounded particularly stupid to her. Of course, he was a doctor and cared about her welfare.

"Not surprised, go on, and tell me about the room," Ryan insisted, making a circling motion with his hand.

"Um, yeah, that. At first, I paid attention to the couple on the bed and my feelings. I felt love, joy, and happiness. Wait, let me try something." She slid over the few inches that separated them and swung her leg over his prone body until she straddled him with her buttocks lightly balanced on his thighs.

Ryan's hands reached up to circle her waist helping her balance. "I like this already."

Perched on Ryan's thighs, she surveyed the room. She could see a great deal, certainly more than his face and chest. "Let me try something else." She lowered her body, allowing her breasts to rest against his chest. Resting her face next to his she could still see the right side of the room with their luggage on the floor and Burton looking up at them inquisitively.

The room also seemed much warmer, or maybe it was her. Ryan's arms had moved, embracing her, holding her in position. She liked it. Rubbing her check against his, she enjoyed the feeling of his five o'clock shadow. Her tongue flicked out tasting salt and a slight chemical mixture on his face. The salt she'd put down to sweat, but the slightly acrid chemical taste perplexed her. She didn't consider the air alkaline. She licked him again for another sample.

Ryan laughed, and then said, "I never picked you for a licker."

"Hmm, I was trying to figure out the chemical composition on your skin." She snuggled her face into his neck enjoying his aroma, comforted by it. In some ways, it was rather like coming home. Strange, only minutes earlier she wondered if he wasn't part of the scheme. If they wanted a top-notch doctor to observe her reactions, they definitely couldn't do better than Ryan Korman, noted physician and medical author.

Ryan's hand lightly stroked her hair, pausing to curl the short tendrils around his fingers. "Ah, beautiful words of love, how long I've waited to hear them. The chemical composition you're trying to break down with your tongue is cologne."

It didn't stop her from wanting to lick him, sniff him, rub her cheek against his, or anything else for that matter. He pulled her head down to his. Somewhere she knew there was a reason not to kiss him, but she misplaced it along with her doubts and her inhibitions. The first brief kiss left her wanting more. Cupping her hands around Ryan's head, she lowered her head for another long kiss. Heat streaked through her body as she attempted to express her feeling using her lips and tongue. The heavy floodwalls that kept her emotional side restrained began to crumble.

The first crack formed when Ryan confessed his love for her. His hands caressed her ass, moving her body up and destroying the walls with each movement. Her lightweight clothing felt heavy and suffocating. Rolling off Ryan, she half kneeled on the bed to discard her shirt and bra under his appreciate gaze.

He stood to pull his polo shirt off over his head then tossed it way with abandon, right before he dropped his shorts. They both stared down at his erection outlined by his boxer briefs. Amy's breath caught knowing this was where it got real.

A silence fell between them that allowed the sound of the laboring air conditioner to fill the room. The slamming of car doors and a few yelled comments reminded her that thin walls and an even thinner door separated her from other people. People sure of who they were and their past and what they were doing.

The flickering television cast multi-color light across Ryan's body. Here was a man who was all about action opposed to words. Suddenly, everything fell in place. Not her memory, but knowing she wanted Ryan no matter what the consequences. She rolled to her back to wiggle out of her shorts. Ryan leaped for the bed landing with a bounce that jiggled the headboard as he captured her in a half embrace.

Her hand rested on his bare chest. Had she seen his chest before? It was nicely defined which demonstrated, despite his long work hours, he still managed to work out some. A slight mat of curling hair teased her fingers along with two flat male nipples that begged to be kissed. Leaning over, she did just that, feeling him squirm under her mouth.

"How did I know you'd like that?" She was surprised at her certainty even before her tongue touched his skin.

Pressing her head against his chest, Ryan sighed and spoke, making the sensation more tactile than audio as the words rumbled through his chest. "I told you the time we went swimming. I thought I was coming on to you, but you thought I was merely making comments about the male sexual response."

She pressed up to her forearms, taking in his closed eyelids and relaxed expression. "Did this type of remark lure viable females to your bed?"

"Viable females? What kind of remark is that? Never mind, I get it now. Women who would sleep with me. Nope, I only tried it on you because you were the only one I wanted. Since it worked so well on you, I decided to mothball it." His hand tenderly traced her backbone as if memorizing each vertebrae.

She allowed her legs to tangle with his hair-roughened legs. "This is what I would expect to remember from a sultry sexual experience. The sensory aspect."

Ryan twisted a little under her, presented proof of his attraction. "I'd have to say we haven't had a sexual experience yet."

"More than you might think. For the woman, most of it is in her head as far as finding satisfaction." She smiled dreamily and rolled off Ryan to consider all the sensations she'd experienced. They bore remembering. She could feel his shadow and heat leaning over her even with her eyes closed.

He kissed her neck first. "There speaks a woman who has truly had nothing of consequence to compare her intellectual responses to sex to, which is a crying shame. I am about to give you the measuring rod you need."

Amy giggled, even though she knew it was inopportune. "Measuring rod, that's funny. Meant to be a pun?" She worked her fingers under his waistband to fill her hands with the globes of his buttocks. How very, very nice and firm, which was probably her last coherent thought.

* * * *

The television droned in the background. Excited voices talked about the joys of a seal-o-matic. It must be a commercial. Why did she go to sleep with the television on? Then her eyes popped open when she realized she wasn't home. Normally, she didn't watch television since she never had time. Most of the shows that passed for entertainment featured stereotypical characters and canned laughter. She'd even commented to Ryan that television helped perpetuate the social ills. Ah Ryan, she was almost afraid to look.

Rolling to her back, she waited a moment, preparing herself for what she might find. As long as it wasn't a dead body, she was good. Turning her head slightly to her right, she was almost nose-to-nose with Ryan. One arm was over his head in abandonment while the second arm held the sheet in place over his more interesting parts.

Yep, it was Ryan. Thank God, it was Ryan. She looked up to the ceiling trying to remember everything. This wasn't another pseudo memory was it? She remembered the feel of his body under her hands, firm, warm and solid. His face, arms, neck, and the V his shirt had exposed were all a bit red. The rest of him was lighter reflecting a man who spent his time indoors. The fact he wasted his weekend driving her to a dead end spoke of incredible devotion.

She remembered some of the things they did. Amazed the two of them could be so inventive. It demonstrated they both were in relatively good shape, students of anatomy, and most likely in need of a good lay. The thought made her giggle.

Ryan rolled, allowing his arm to mold around her body. His sleep tousled face leaned over hers. "I was really hoping for more than laughter. Something like calling on your deity of choice would have been nice, a heartfelt sigh, or even a long summation of how wonderful it was for you."

Amy turned into his embrace, edging her face into the spot where his neck and collarbone met. Ironically, she had already developed a favorite spot. Her face seemed to fit perfectly, and it allowed her to draw in the essence of him. "I was giggling because I thought we both needed a good lay. You were wonderful. As far as I can remember, definitely the best I've ever had."

"Hmm," Ryan murmured into her hair. "Better than the mythical Mark?"

Amy considered his words, working out what she'd been thinking about only seconds earlier. "That's it. You hit the nail on the head."

He ran his hand down her torso, resting it on her thigh. "So that's what I did."

"Yes, you did." She scrambled out of his embrace to sit up, not caring that the sheet fell exposing her naked breasts.

Ryan watched her explain with a wry grin.

Holding up one finger and pointing to him, she announced, "I understand. I remembered these great sexual interludes with Mark that made me feel euphoric on one hand, but on the other hand, I couldn't tell you a damn thing about them. I can't even tell you if Mark had a hairy chest, if he liked having his nipples sucked, or if he was a good kisser." She was enumerating Ryan's traits. The smug expression on his face acknowledged his similar realization.

"Go on. Tell me more about what you don't know about Mark."

Ah, she was playing to his male vanity but also giving voice to her thoughts. "I don't know how he smells, or tastes, or even how his hair feels underneath my fingers. These things are important to me, maybe to all females, something to be savored later. They are an essential part of the lover and the experience. I remember nothing about Mark outside of what he looked like. I can remember our meeting and the beach wedding. Are my memories fading, or didn't they bother to give me very many memories?"

Ryan's index finger went to the bridge of his nose to push up non-existent glasses. "True, you may have limited memories of Mark. I am not sure what is involved in implantation. I wonder if they showed you some blue movie with foreign actors while you were in a drugged state to account for your sexual interludes."

Placing her fingers to her lips, she considered it. "I might be highly receptive in a drugged state. I should experience some arousal, but, because I was not the female in bed, I would not have any tactile impressions. True, they never really said much, just breathing, grunting, and moaning. Why foreign?"

Ryan nodded as if affirming his own opinion. "Well, this is a hypothesis. They probably figured you might recognize an American actor. Besides American porn usually features..." He placed his hands about a foot in front of his chest to indicate major cleavage.

"Yep." Her eyes flickered down to her medium-sized breasts. "I could see how that wouldn't work. Other countries don't feature oversized breasts on their porn stars?"

Ryan winked. "Depending on what country you're in, they don't consider it porn, just a movie with a sex scene between two normal looking adults. It could easily have been from Scandinavian countries with a blonde with short hair in it."

Her mouth twisted to one side as she considered the implications. Not those of her being drugged and subjected to watching questionable movies, but to Ryan's knowledge of European movies, especially those featuring slender blonde-haired women with short hair. "It makes sense. Of course, if they knew me, they'd know I don't actually watch much television, so I wouldn't recognize anyone."

"They couldn't take chances. " Ryan looked into her eyes, and his view dipped to her chest, then recovered.

"The feelings I experienced could have easily been manipulated. The question is did the drug introduce those feelings or was it something else? The lack of actual detail allows me to verify that I never met Mark or at least never had sex with him. What is the purpose behind all of this?"

Ryan inched closer wrapping his arm around her. "It would be so much easier to figure out if we had the data from the Morpheus Project." He began kissing her neck.

The slide of his warm lips on her skin made thinking hard. She had the data. It was stashed somewhere. She almost confessed to having the information, but a tiny bit of paranoia reared its ugly head. What he said sounded like something someone gathering information might ask. Maybe he was going to do incredible things to her body again in an effort to get her to reveal all. The joke was on him. Once he started to kiss her, she was likely to forget her own name.

Chapter Ten

Amy stared up trying to count the acoustical tiles that made up the ceiling, probably asbestos considering the age of the motel. Strange, the tiles still existed, but maybe that asbestos removal ordinance only applied to buildings like schools and hospitals where the occupants had no choice in their residence. People didn't have to come here. Lack of funds usually made the choice for them.

The neon motel light, along with the parking lot lights and the occasional beam of headlights flickered through the edges of the curtains, illuminating the room enough to see her suitcase with her contents half strewn across the floor. When did she become such a pig? It didn't seem like her nature.

Burton rounded the end of her bed and stared at her. The dog's wrinkled brow suggested he was questioning her. If he could talk, what would he say, "Are you my new mommy?" or maybe "What did you do to my master?" Her eyes drifted to a bare chested Ryan who snored slightly. Her eyes lingered, cataloguing his features. Without his glasses and his mouth half-opened, he looked so young. Hard to believe he was older than she was. Almost ten years, but it didn't feel as if they were that far apart. A memory of her teasing him about his upcoming birthday popped into her mind. He tried to act as if it didn't bother him, but it did. She could tell.

Men valued different things as signs of achievement as opposed to women. Most women expected to be married and have children by her age. Well, most of them probably expected to have it happen a lot sooner. The girls in Terrebonne had their future husbands picked out by the time they were fifteen, which worked out pretty well since they were usually pregnant by sixteen. She wondered if perhaps she was a different sort of female, the type who didn't long for marriage and kids. Seemed she was until Mark came along. The implanted memory of Mark she reminded herself, the programmed image of him. He wasn't real.

Her hand stretched across the bed to rest on Ryan's exposed chest as a reminder of what was real. The warm skin beneath her palm, the texture of his skin, and chest hair were missing from her memories of Mark. She couldn't even remember what he smelled like. Shouldn't she be able to if the man had been a living being? Couples talk all the time about being able to find their sweethearts in the dark by smell only. It'd be hard to find someone with no smell. Her nostrils flared trying to take in Ryan's scent. There was a touch of styling products from his hair, a spicy body soap or cologne, a hint of the Mexican food they consumed, and Burton. She sniffed again, definitely Burton. The bulldog edged closer to her, and then again, it could just be Burton.

Ryan smelled comforting and familiar. Good chance he hadn't changed any of his grooming habits in the time she lost. It was obvious they spent a great deal of time together. Her body recognized him even if her mind seemed confused. Ryan Korman did not strike her as a player, and she was damn sure she didn't engage in casual sex.

What now? Were they a couple? They definitely couldn't act like a couple. She certainly didn't want Ryan bird-dogged the way she was. Danger surrounded her like an aura. Unfortunately, not remembering everything made her unaware of what she should be worrying about, but she knew enough that she should be worried.

Her lips tipped up, thinking about their frantic lovemaking. They acted more like teenagers. Well, at least the first time. The second time was more relaxed. It was obvious even to her that Ryan loved her, probably had for a long time. Back when she actually remembered things, did she know? According to Ryan, she didn't. It made sense now and explained her aunt's comments.

He murmured her name in his sleep, making her heart jump a little. Maybe she loved him too. God, she knew better than to try to judge her feelings with oxytocin racing through her body, making her feel soft and warm toward the man beside her. He could be a murderer, and she'd still feel that way until the hormone wore off. Her lips twisted as she considered possibilities.

Even though they both worked in a gray area of moral ambiguity, she always thought of Ryan as being the more naïve one. That's why he only worked with human subjects as opposed to the chemical component as she did. They both took medical oaths as doctors, but no matter how she tried to get around it, she was still doing harm to people. Maybe she could rationalize that it would end wars saving nations and people. In the end, it was only a more efficient way of killing people. Maybe she rebelled against it. Maybe that's when she lost her memory.

Ryan would never ever do anything inherently evil, but, unfortunately, sometimes he never suspected that motive in others. He came from a happy home, no great traumas in his life. No reason to be suspicious of people in general, but, still, he signed all the same confidentiality agreements she did, so he had to know Theron wasn't exactly lily white. She never talked about her work, except in the vaguest sense. Often she was frustrated when the great ideas she started with didn't pan out. Maybe he didn't know.

If he didn't know, then he could be talked into assisting her for her own good. No doubt, Ryan would want to do anything he could to help her. Perhaps someone noticed the time they spent together, suspected his affection, and decided to use him to spy on her. They would be smart enough not to tell him. Maybe he was micro chipped similar to a dog. They'd be able to locate him wherever he was, which would be helpful if they were together. His scalp would be the best place for the chip since hair would cover the incision.

Inching up in bed, she hovered over his head, similar to a vulture, allowing one hand to ruffle through his hair feeling for a raised scar. Nothing, good clean scalp, no shampoo residue build up. His body shifted. Not surprisingly, his eyes were open.

"Already? You're certainly the tigress." Reaching for her hands, he interlaced their fingers and rolled her onto her back.

Looking up at his grinning face, she almost admitted she was looking for the chip incision. Just because it wasn't there didn't mean he wasn't being used. He just didn't know about it. His warm body weight settled on her torso distracting her, driving all thoughts of Theron and microchips out of her mind.

* * * *

The sound of a car door slamming and a toddler screaming woke her. Light streamed into the room from the parted curtains.

Amy rolled over, her arm hitting the empty mattress beside her. Empty, not again. Why was it whenever she decided she cared about a man he disappeared? Blinking, she pushed herself up into a sitting position. A downward glance confirmed she was naked, which would make sense if she and Ryan did do the deed, or did she just imagine it? Was this stage two of the experiment? Were they testing her libido or her memory?

A knock sounded before the door opened about an inch. Grabbing the sheet, she covered herself as Ryan eased the door open. Well, at least that answered one question. Burton greeted her enthusiastically as if he'd been gone a month as opposed to a…wait, how long had they been gone? "How long have the two of you been out?"

Ryan pulled the cell phone out of his pocket to look at the time. "Twenty minutes, more or less. Burton isn't fan of strange places. It took him a while." He leaned over to unclip the leash from Burton's collar. The bulldog rushed to her side of the bed to swipe her hand with a slobbery kiss.

Instead of responding to the canine greeting, Amy stared at the phone in his hand. He took his cell phone to walk the dog. Of course, he did. He must have noticed her staring at the phone because he grinned sheepishly.

"I was afraid you'd wake up all alone and might…" He stumbled on the words.

Amy knew what he was thinking, and he was right. "Be afraid that I dreamed it all and start wondering if Dr. Ryan Korman even existed?" She finished the thought for him.

"Yeah," he agreed. Grabbing his dirty clothes, he pushed them into his tote.

One-night stands weren't her thing. Is this how people acted the next day, awkward and tongue-tied? Then again, perhaps they didn't wake up together because one of them vanished in the night. The two of them, make that the three of them, would have a silent ten-hour drive home. She had to do something. Slipping off the bed, she arranged the sheet around her toga fashion and approached Ryan, who watched her from the corner of his eye. Placing a hand on his shoulder as he crouched to zip his duffle, she asked, "We are still friends, aren't we?"

He laid his hand over hers on his shoulder and slowly stood. Holding their hands in place, he turned and looked at her. Using his free left hand, he pushed his glasses, but since they hadn't slipped, they couldn't go up any more. A nervous gesture, a tell, that said more than he realized.

"I hoped," he stopped and cleared his throat, "we were more than friends after last night."

His furrowed brow announced his doubts so clearly that Amy felt obligated to kiss it. Rising up on her tiptoes, she placed her lips on his forehead, wondering how she could have doubted him. Hadn't she spent practically a third of her life with him? "Of course, we are more than friends, but until we get things worked out with my memory and bogus marriage, it should be our secret. Agreed?"

She dropped back on her heels, which made Ryan only a little taller than her. He nodded and brought her hand to his lips.

His lips softly landed on her skin, reminding her of the night. Her audible sigh made him smile. "I suppose," he started with a bit of a wry grin, "I can wait a few more weeks since I have waited years to have you in my arms. What is a month or two when I'll be able to have you in my life?"

Whoa, wait, that sounds rather final. "Are you saying what I think you're saying?"

Grabbing her other hand, he bowed one knee. Oh my goodness, she should stop him. No one had ever proposed to her that she could remember. She didn't want it to be in a cheap motel while wrapped in a sheet. "Ryan." She hissed his name and gave a definite tug on his hands. "Get up, I think I know what you might say, but I don't want to tell Remy that the moment occurred in the Star Brite Motor Lodge."

Chuckling, he got to his feet, loosening her hands as he apologized. "I bet Remy would understand, but you deserve something a little romantic. Don't worry, I will research the subject and provide you with the proposal of your dreams."

No doubt, he would. With his attention to detail, it should take a few weeks, buying her enough time to examine her feelings. Maybe by then, some answers might have surfaced, such as why, suddenly, she had more surveillance on her than a meth dealer did. Biting her bottom lip, she hoped it turned out that way rather than her fleeing to another country, changing her name and hair color. Of course, it was better than being the guinea pig of some mind control drug. Still, how did she know if this was real?

Instead of becoming surly about her rejection of his impromptu proposal, Ryan perched on the bed fondling Burton's ears and scratching between his eyes. She seriously doubted a manufactured memory would include a challenged bulldog.

Grabbing her clothes, she headed to the bathroom. "I'll be ready in a couple of minutes."

"Great," Ryan answered from his position beside the dog. "I think we should grab breakfast on the go."

"Good idea," she said before closing the bathroom door.

Thirty minutes later, the three of them sat in a long drive-thru line, the Mustang idling, as they waited for their chance to yell their breakfast choices into a tiny speaker. Ryan perused the brightly colored menu. "Well, at least they're still serving breakfast." He sucked in his lips considering his choices. "I think Burton and I will go with the sausage biscuit. How about you?"

Amy didn't really like eating at restaurants. Too much chance of consuming genetically engineered food, not to mention chemicals and questionable handling. Trying to consider what items had the least amount of modification, she decided on orange juice and a parfait. They crept toward the open window where the woman staffing the window fussed over Burton. Well, she pretended it was the canine, but Amy had her doubts the way the woman bent almost in half to hand Ryan the food bags, maximizing her cleavage. Yep, definitely Ryan. She'd never have gotten a show like that, not that she did too many fast food runs.

The bag thrust into her hands, ending her descent into jealousy. It was just as well. She passed Burton's food back to him, which he gratefully wolfed down. Ryan slowly moved across the parking lot, watching out for the random pedestrian walking in front of his car. Amy popped the straw in her orange juice and looked up in time to see a man staring the restaurant window. She turned to check again, but there was no sign of him.

"Weird," she commented more to herself.

"What's weird?" Ryan asked, as he eased his car into the flow of traffic.

"A guy in McDonalds looked like the man at the rest stop. The same one I saw yesterday while walking through in town. I guess it isn't too weird. I mean we might have been going the same destination, but I can't place where I saw him before the rest stop." She took another pull on her juice.

"You're probably right," Ryan agreed, smiling in her direction. They tabled the conversation as the traffic picked up.

* * * *

Simpson watched the Mustang ease out of the parking lot. He aimed his camera at the couple in the convertible slowly departing. The man wore sunglasses and a hat. Stubble dotted his face adding to his disguise. It also added to the mystery of Dr. Amy Newkirk. Apparently, the man didn't want to be recognized, which shouldn't be too surprising since Amy recently misplaced her current husband.

Yet, the flashy restored muscle car carried a different message. Could be Newkirk had a twin. Didn't everyone? He'd run the photo through the facial recognition software once he returned to his temporary office. Just to be sure, he hit his speed dial to reach his assistant, Jergens. He waited for him to pick up before he started talking. "Still keeping an eye on the house?"

"Yep, what else?"

Simpson's grimace deepened as he considering Jergens' response to be a little uncivil and definitely not the way a subcontractor should answer. He eyed the crowded restaurant and decided to wait until he was face to face to point out Jergens' failure to follow protocol. "See anything?"

"Nope, car hasn't moved. She hasn't even opened her drapes for Pete's sake. What is she a vampire?" Jergens chuckled at his own joke.

Simpson rolled his eyes. This one thought he was a comic. It did tell him one thing. That the blonde in the Mustang probably was the slippery doctor. How fortunate, he decided to head to Albuquerque to follow a lead. Could be the Newkirk was following the same trail. It would be nice if she'd do all the work for him.

Now all she had to do was head back home and sneak into her house. It would be a test of sorts to see if Jergens noticed. If he didn't, then he needed to replace him. "Okay, keep an eye on it. You might want to take a break now because it will be a long day. I expect you to stay all day until I get back."

Simpson chose to ignore the cursing. The youngsters they recruited had no clue what hard work was, all soft and whiny. His lips twisted as he considered his suspect. No one told him what was really going on with the good doctor, but he bet it was major. It had to be to hire him. Did they want him to watch her, eliminate her, or protect her from someone who wanted to eliminate her?

A perky clerk with a blue tinted ponytail pulled through her visor called out, "Sir, sir, can I help you?"

Simpson turned in reaction, noticing the other customers were gone. To leave now without ordering would just look suspicious. He scanned the menu board. "Number three with coffee."

Besides, he needed to eat. Not like those two were going anywhere but back to Dallas. He'd catch them on the road since a dog tends to slow people down having to stop and walk it all the time. That's why he didn't have a pet. It limited a person. Couldn't go anywhere without finding a pet sitter or a kennel. Then when you got back it, it would be all reproachful and standoffish because you left it.

Simpson handed the counter jockey a ten. He always paid in cash because he knew how hard it was to trace. He waited for his change with a little bit of a smirk. The benefit of following criminals and enemies of the state is he learned all their tricks. If he should turn, then he'd be better than most as far as evading detection. In fact, he could be a super criminal, a godfather of sorts, but no one would know him.

He carried his tray to a small table considering his potential felonious abilities. People are usually done in by their personal connections. Family members are more likely to turn in a relative for an award, more so than strangers are. Co-workers, even neighbors notice more than you might think. That's why he settled on a rental house out in the middle of nowhere. He'd lost contact with his father, and his mother was dead.

His last girlfriend, the one who gave him reproachful looks, after disappearing for two months, dumped him. Just as well, it wasn't good to get too close to someone. Sheila, or was it Susan, didn't have a clue what he did. He made the mistake of telling her he bought women's shoes to explain the ticket stub from his Italy flight. After that, she whined about how he never gave her any free samples. Likely, she left due to lack of samples more than anything else.

Relationships weren't worth the trouble to maintain them. He bit into his sandwich and chewed thoughtfully. Theron dropped a bucket of money on him to retain his services, and, yet, he was to do little more than tail a scientist, reminding him of his early private investigator work when all he did was trail cheating spouses. Make no mistake. They were cheaters. Slighted spouses found enough circumstantial evidence to make them hire him. The women usually wanted to know who it was, concerned about what she looked like. Ironically, the wife was usually angrier if the woman was less attractive than she was.

Men, on the other hand, wanted hard evidence to use in a court case or maybe to hold over their wives' heads. Then again, he wondered if the men the straying wives chose to cheat on ever disappeared with a little help. People went missing all the time. Like his suspect's husband. The most interesting thing about the case is no one seemed too concerned.

The police decided he'd walked. Theron was strangely mute on the matter as if the man didn't matter at all. The person to show the most concern was, Amy, his wife. Her current behavior of spending the weekend with another man indicated she seemed to be over it. The man could possibly be her husband.

He sipped his coffee contemplating the unusual possibility. That would make his services useless. Wouldn't it? He wasn't asked to find the missing man, only watch the wife. He'd run the image through his image bank. Of course, to get a match the man would have to be in the bank for some reason. The only reason he'd be in the bank was if he'd been arrested, in the news, or was a celebrity. He could search the BMV database, but he knew he'd get thousands of hits with the side headshot. Couldn't tell much with the sunglasses and hat.

License plate. He didn't get the license plate. Damn, he couldn't believe it. How could he be so stupid? He threw away the rest of his meal, anxious to find the missing couple. Angry he failed to take his usual careful scrutiny of his surroundings he almost failed to notice the two men watching him.

They stood when he did, leaving their food on the table as if they intended to come back. Instead, they slid into their own unremarkable sedan.

Simpson drove recklessly, cutting corners too fast, burning rubber. With difficulty, he made himself slow down. A ticket would make him memorable. He didn't need that. His reputation was based on his ability to blend in with his surroundings to get the deed done with no one being the wiser. This assignment was starting to bug him. It seemed little more than surveillance. Too many details eluded him, such as the mysterious husband and the fact no one seemed to care about him. It meant either they knew he walked or he was dead. If he was dead, they knew who killed him.

If the cool little blonde did the deed, then she was obviously much more valuable to them running around than locked up where she belonged. He could be working for the company even now. His job was to document everything. So far, he had nada. What could he report?

The woman disappeared for a weekend jaunt in New Mexico with a man and a dog. She stopped at a convention center that was not running any conventions at the time. She slipped into an art gallery and left with what looked like a wrapped up painting. The gallery seemed to be legitimate. However, he would have loved to take a gander at the large paper wrapped frame. Could something else been attached to it or even a message in the picture. He'd have a chance to examine it later in her house.

The green highway sign cheered him. Finally, he could apply some speed and catch his quarry. Simpson maintained the speed limit until he was five miles out of town. Most tickets happened near the city limits. The trip odometer he'd intentionally cleared clicked off five miles causing him to ease into the fast lane. A quick glance in his rearview mirror revealed a sedan had eased into the passing lane too. Odd, but maybe not, his job made him paranoid.

He floored the car well aware he'd lose the sedan at this speed. After a couple of miles, he cut his speed. When driving into the city he'd spotted a surveillance plane over the highway, probably checking speed and radioing the offender's plates ahead to a waiting car. Soon, there would be drones in the air doing such simplistic work. Doing a better job, too, since they wouldn't be distracted by cell phones, personal problems, or the need to light up a cigarette. Of course, no drone could replace him, not that he was doing such a stellar job today.

Cars doing the speed limit in the fast lane cut into his time. He cursed, and then swerved into the middle lane working his way to the right, finding a clear section, then flooring it. His eyes flicked to the rearview mirror searching for the navy Impala he spotted earlier. A flash of blue kept appearing on one side, then on the other side of a weaving rental-moving trailer. Simpson grinned, imagining the wrath of the car driver.

Thank God, it wasn't him. No one would want to be behind the moving disaster. Half the time the truck renters had no clue how to drive the vehicle. Enough moves acquainted him with rental trucks with loose steering or alignment issues that caused the truck to pull powerfully to one side. Simpson experienced enough of his worldly possessions banging against the truck walls making ominous rattling with each turn. The principal reason he jettisoned the possessions along with the fact it slowed him down. Things, pets, even people owned you and not the other way around as most assumed.

Maybe he imagined the car was following him. It was probably just male bravado, wanting to be in front of the other cars. Most people believed the muscle car owners or convertible drivers were ones to speed, but they'd be wrong. It didn't mean they never did, but they went more for visibility. It is hard not to be noticed when you are speeding 100 miles per hour, or at least for very long, and then there was the police. Nope, the only thing a person could do in a sedan was maybe pass someone.

The radio blared in the background. A mention of a recent murder in Albuquerque caught his ear. Last night, a murder, he wondered if his little scientist was involved. Watching the two of them calmly divide up their fast food breakfast in the parking lot did not give them the appearance of trying to slip out of town unnoticed. Could be they were two cool characters who didn't hesitate at the thought of murder.

His eyes kept checking the cars around him, no vintage Mustang convertible in sight. He pushed the speed a little bit more. How could they have managed to get so far ahead of him? Where could they be? Did it matter? It all depended on whether they were the type that casually offed people. Perhaps the object they purchased might disappear before they arrived back in Dallas and he had a chance to investigate it.

His phone rang. Simpson patted down his shirt searching for his phone. "Damn it," he muttered realizing he'd misplaced his phone. He blindly felt along the passenger seat feeling for the phone. His fingers encountered the vibrating square in time to bring it up to his ear.

"What?" he barked into the phone, not caring who it was.

"Sir," the voice of the newbie grated. "Sir, we have a problem."

His brows beetled, picturing a kindly old lady trying to talk to his employee, or worse the old dear called the police because the fool stayed in the same place for too long. "What is it?"

"Well, uhm, someone is breaking into the house."

Simpson blinked twice, wondering if he heard right. "Are you watching the right house?" Hard to imagine the quiet neighborhood suddenly experienced a major crime wave. A flash of blue in the rearview mirror caught his eye as the sedan bit into the shoulder flinging gravel to get past the orange rental truck. Looked like he was wrong, those jokers were following him.

They were close enough for him to see their faces in his mirror. Two white males with bad haircuts, stiff posture, and a single-minded determination that he usually associated with Russians. *Shit. What next?* Jergens' voice chirping in his ear reminded him.

"Did you get a look at the person?" he asked, while watching the car behind him. He slowed down, no use in speeding now. Better to see what these bozos wanted.

"Yeah, huh, I did. An elderly lady dressed in black, I think she had a cat under her arm."

Simpson winced. Newbie was probably watching the wrong house. "You are looking at a neighbor. Burglars do not carry cats."

The navy Impala sped up. All he could see was the car windshield and two grim faced individuals. It didn't look good. He could hear the newbie going on about something but placed the phone on the seat. He had a feeling he was going to need all his wits.

Chapter Eleven

Ryan insisted on walking Amy back to her house through the woods, with Burton, carrying her oversized painting. Her eyes rolled upward at the thought of the three of them attracting too much attention. Ever since the police came screaming up to her house after her first call, she served as her own reality show in her formerly quiet neighborhood.

The last rays of the sun illuminated the areas, but shadows increased in the woods as they walked. By the time, he could return to his car, it would probably be too dark for Ryan to navigate safely. Amy wondered if she should invite him to stay the night since their relationship had changed. Her eyes cut to Ryan, grasping the painting with one arm while Burton stretched his leash and arm with his single-minded mission to claim every tree passed. He was a good, kind man.

He'd hooked his sunglasses on his shirt when they entered the woods. Without his glasses, the beard stubble, and knowing what she knew about his in-bed manner, the man was damn sexy. Too bad, she never noticed it before, or maybe she did. The thought of him staying the night had merit, but before she could fully embrace the idea, reality stomped it out.

A strange man leaving her house would cause more gossip. Add to that her personal snoops would now start watching Ryan. That was no way to pay back him for his trouble. It would also make her quest to uncover the truth a little bit more difficult. In his own way, Ryan served as her secret weapon. No one knew about their relationship. His security clearance hadn't been zapped like hers. Perhaps he could delve where she couldn't. The thought made her smile along with the sight of her house.

Home at last. It was still new, but it was all she had as far as a home base. Hanging her newest purchase would make it more inviting. It would also remind her of Ryan and their trip, which wasn't a bad thing in her view, a legitimate memory and a good one at that.

Amy inserted the house key into the door, the same time Ryan spoke "I think I should go in and search the house first. Burton too."

The masculine attitude asserts itself, Amy thought, but she said, "Go ahead. I know the two of you will sniff out any wrongdoers. Be quiet, though. " She mouthed the word *bug* as she took the painting. The hall light left on beamed a small trail of light, but the rest of the house was dark due to the closed blinds. She flicked on the kitchen light only to hear a familiar meow and Burton's answering bark.

"Samson," she cried out in delight. Her cat came back. She reached for the oversized cat that met Burton nose-to-nose at the door, refusing to stand down or hiss like any other cat. Cuddling the cat, she rejoiced in the fact he'd returned. She pointed out the obvious to Ryan. "He's back."

Two steps carried her to the radio, which she turned on to an uncomfortable level.

Ryan leaned close to whisper in her ear. "Even more amazing, he reappeared in a locked house." Ryan's forehead furrowed, conveying his thoughts on such an unusual occurrence. "I'll check the rest of the house." He turned pulling Burton with him who resisted, wanting to renew his acquaintance with Samson.

Amy held out the heavy cat at arm's length. It looked like her cat. Putting him on the counter, she examined his front paws. They were declawed meaning it must be her cat. He even had on the same orange and black Halloween collar she'd bought on sale after the holiday had passed. The feline began to purr, a loud distinctive sound. Smoothing her hands down his back, she murmured to herself, "You always were the loudest purrer around."

Ryan winced when he walked into the kitchen. As much as he liked head banging old school rock and roll, the station was even too much for him. He drew close to her to ask near her ear. "So you're sure, it's Samson."

Her fingers smoothed the cat's head looking for all the scars her old pet bore. "Here's his torn ear." She rolled the cat on his back without a struggle. "No balls either. His claws are gone. You have to admit there are probably very few tiger, neutered, declawed cats his size with a torn ear and a Halloween collar."

Pushing up the bill of his cap, Ryan used his closed fist to rub his brow. He dropped his hand and nodded in Burton's direction. "Burton recognized Samson. You do realize he's afraid of cats."

Burton looked up eagerly at the purring feline, even wiggling his stumpy tail, which translated into shaking the back half of his body. Amy picked up the cat and placed him on the floor. The bulldog sniffed the cat eagerly while Samson regarded it with a patient mien. "They do know each other obviously, which answers the question if it really is Samson."

Ryan placed his baseball cap on the counter, ran his hands through his flattened hair. "Yeah, I know hat hair. The real question is how did the cat get into the house?"

Amy nodded. "Yeah, I know. Seems like strangers, invaders, burglars, whatever are spending more time in my house than I am." The thought gave her a little chill. Originally the image of men pulling Mark from their bed used to creep her out, but now that she'd decided Mark was little more than a hypnotic suggestion, the alternative presented itself. People entered her home at will to search for something and drugging her in the process.

As if tuned into the same wavelength, Ryan mused aloud. "Leaving Samson was a good deed, and one that would indicate someone had been inside your house. This is not something someone conducting surveillance or searching would do."

Samson gave a plaintive meow, stating his opinion on that matter. Amy squatted to look under the sink. "I hope I can find something for him to eat." She pulled out a small can of tuna and flourished it, causing Samson to press up against her. Popping the lid, she upended the food into a glass saucer and placed it on the floor for the hungry feline. Burton looked up at her hopefully.

Ryan laughed and bent to pat his dog. "I don't know about you getting food here. She'll try to feed you granola or a soy burger."

Amy opened her fridge looking for something to feed the dog. "I bet I can find something." Her nearly empty fridge mocked her assertion. She held up a slice of raw milk cheese. "Not exactly a feast."

Maybe she should buy some dog food if Ryan and Burton were going to be showing up on a regular basis. She pushed a container of food around looking for something the two of them could eat. Wait, the dish didn't resemble any containers she owned. She pulled out the dish and pried open the lid peering inside. Ryan joined her looking over her shoulder.

"Looks like chicken and dumplings. Looks good. When did you start cooking?" Ryan grinned. He grabbed the dish and placed it in the microwave.

Amy watched him in stunned silence. Mystery food shows up, and they were supposed to dig in. "Wait, I didn't make that. It showed up on its own rather like Samson."

Ryan's finger stopped on the finger pad. "It looks good, but I guess you are right. Maybe I should just eat it, and you can watch me for symptoms." He pushed the start button.

She placed her hand on his shoulder. "Are you losing your mind?"

He turned toward her, placing his arms around her in a loose embrace. Her other hand rested on his other shoulder. "Sweetheart," he started, "do you seriously think someone would put a drug-laced casserole in your fridge and expect you to calmly eat it?"

She sighed. "Put like that, it doesn't sound like a clever action. I guess the person who brought Samson, brought food too. It makes me wonder if it's the same person who left the healing poppet."

Ryan took the container and bowls to the table. Amy went back to the fridge for two bottles of water while he dished the food out. "Do you think we should write a note just in case the food is drugged?"

Ryan raised his eyebrows and patted down his pockets. He found a receipt and a pen. He wrote as he spoke aloud, "Eating chicken and dumplings hopefully not drugged."

She twisted both lids off the water bottles and handed one to Ryan. "Here's to us. May we remember each other after dinner. If I weren't so hungry, I wouldn't do something so crazy." They knocked their water bottles together.

With trepidation, she brought the fork to her mouth. "It smells good." The broth was thick and rich while the dumplings were light. She moved the food around in her mouth, hesitating to swallow, wondering if she should spit it out. The taste lingered on her tongue reminding her of her early days with Aunt Remy when she filled her full of comfort foods. "This is my Aunt Remy's recipe."

Ryan's fork clattered against his bowl. "This is delicious. If I am bound to be a mindless zombie under the control of an evil overlord, this is the way to go."

The fluffy dumpling she'd bitten into with such relish suddenly felt like mud in her mouth. The desire to spit it out grew strong, but inherent good manners quelled. Did she act like some mindless zombie? When was she the zombie? Better yet, what did she do for Theron while drugged? Previously, she only considered herself a guinea pig. What if she were more than that? Her appetite fled. Maybe it was best someone needed to observe Ryan who packed away the food.

Watching him eat, she realized she couldn't let him leave. What if he fell asleep at the wheel or became homicidal ramming someone with his car? Truthfully, she didn't believe the food was tainted. She tabled her indecision over allowing him to stay because their relationship changed due to the possibility of him becoming a mindless puppet. It could be the obviousness of the food should allay her suspicions, but it didn't.

Ryan finished his serving. Motioning to her bowl with his fork, he asked, "Are you going to finish that?"

Amy shook her head. Still, Ryan reaching for her bowl surprised her. He certainly didn't need a double helping of a possible mystery drug. She was about to tell him when he put the bowl on the floor for Burton. Samson managed to lick up all the food the dog spattered out in his quest to inhale the chicken and dumplings. She imagined all three of them in a deep sleep, or, possibly, they could all turn on her as if in some B movie horror flick. Then again, nothing could happen. One thing she did know was she had to go food shopping tomorrow.

Ryan picked up the bowl Burton finished and his and carried them to the sink. Aunt Remy would have remarked on the sighting of a rare animal, a human male who cleaned up after himself. Amy decided to keep that observation to herself, knowing Ryan wouldn't appreciate it. Instead, she said, "I want you to stay with me tonight."

This caused Ryan to wiggle his eyebrows playfully as if her words implied something more. Someone not privy to her paranoid thoughts might consider the words as a come on. Before she could explain her intentions, he explained his.

"I planned on staying. I am uneasy with you staying alone, especially with various folks stomping through your bit of real estate." He turned back to the sink and turned on the water as if his proclamation ended the matter.

He'd already decided as if that sealed the deal. Had the doctor always been so domineering in his decisions? He deferred all choices of the social nature to her. Then again, he could have been playing a long game, make that very long, to try to win her favor. It made her wonder enough to ask. "Ryan, did you used to agree to do things like hiking and that herbal class we took together just to please me?"

He rinsed the bowl he was washing and grinned in her direction. "Why do I feel like this is a trick question? I will admit to wanting to please you, but, on the other hand, I had nothing against those things. If you had suggested something I didn't like, I wouldn't have gone along."

"What things would you refuse to do if I suggested them?" Amy asked, watching Ryan thoughtfully. It would help if he'd turn, so she could see his face. As if hearing her thoughts, he turned to open a drawer and pulled out a dishtowel. The man went straight to the right drawer, demonstrating his knowledge of the kitchen.

"How did you know which drawer the towels were in?" It wasn't the question she wanted answered, but it still merited asking.

"Ah, your memory comes back in drips and drabs. I helped you unpack the kitchen. I put the dishtowels in that drawer." He used the towel to dry the bowl, then opened the cabinet and put it away. He reached for the other bowl and turned to face her again. "To answer your first question, I drew the line at protesting outside of Bronsant. I felt it would not only land us in jail but would probably cause us both to lose our jobs."

The name was of the seed giant known for genetically altered seeds, specifically ones that went sterile after the initial harvest making the farmers dependent on buying more. At least, she could say she wasn't guilty of that development, but there was a good chance someone in Theron was. That was the argument Ryan used to prevent the protest. She could remember now. "Good call on your part, I recall."

His lips tipped up. "Glad you think so now. At the time, you weren't too pleased with me."

Amy reached for the memory, feeling her distaste and anger that she worked for a company that often caused some of the problems besieging the common person. The seeds, her work on modifying the seeds, were her first insight that perhaps her work was not for the betterment of humanity, but rather for those who paid the most. "Did I ever express my dissatisfaction about my work?"

Ryan put up the second bowl and then turned to lean back against the counter. "Not exactly, but you did ask deep, penetrating questions that often poked at the ethics of whatever project you were currently working on. Not that you ever got your questions answered."

Amy felt the pieces shifting and coming together. "I was a malcontent. Someone who refused to do the work they wanted done. So maybe I was not a willing guinea pig, but someone whose voice needed silencing. Maybe this was more to see if I could be trained as opposed to eliminated." She spoke the words more to herself than to the man who regarded with her interested eyes. She could remember him being her friend, now her lover. Those were real memories, she was sure of it.

Then again, this could be some elaborate test scenario. Maybe even now, her body was in an induced coma and this information was fed into her brain making her think she was living this moment. All the wonderful emotions she felt flooding her body during lovemaking were simply the ability to activate the release of hormones. Oxytocin would make her feel warm and loving toward Ryan. Abused women often stayed in relationships because the men were smart enough to have frequent sex, which released the hormone into the woman's bloodstream.

If she and Ryan had a real relationship, which she believed they did because everything pointed to it, then he'd be the perfect person to turn to for help. The fact they were now lovers seemed suspicious since they'd existed side by side without making the jump for years.

She studied his relaxed stance against the counter. He didn't look like a man acting, and he did eat the food with gusto. Still, his volunteering to stay seemed too convenient. If the man loved her, wouldn't he want to stay and protect her? Maybe he should go. "Ryan, you have to go to work tomorrow, as do I. How will you manage that from my house?"

He rubbed one hand over his face. "I did think about that. I'll go in late. In fact, I'll login tonight and say I have a dental appointment that I forgot to mention."

It made sense, but she needed more time to consider all the angles. Now that she and Ryan were lovers, would she ever have another clear thought again? She knew enough about hormones to realize most couples drifted apart and broke up when they stopped having sex frequently. It allowed the woman to feel unconnected to the man. Suddenly the woman started reexamining the relationship and the reason they were together. Men operated differently and could often leave at any time.

Ryan walked the few steps to her chair and dropped a kiss on her hair. "Why don't you grab a shower and get ready for bed since you'll be going to work on time. I'll take Burton out for one last walk." He suited his motions to his words.

Amy watched him and Burton head for the door "Stay in the back, so the surveillance car doesn't see you." Ryan raised a hand acknowledging her request.

In the shower, she allowed the hot water to pummel her, taking with it her distrust. She wanted this relationship to be real, not a drug-induced fantasy. What if she got out of the shower and discovered Ryan was gone? No sign of him anywhere. Because she and Ryan managed to fly under the radar, no one would remember seeing them together. They would assume she was making it all up. That action would probably earn her the insane label. Who would have her committed? There were plenty of mentally unbalanced people roaming the streets. Why should she be any different? It made her almost afraid to get out of the shower until she heard Ryan call out.

"It's me. Burton and I are back in the house." The sound of his baritone relaxed her some. Picking up the bath towel, she patted herself dry, imagining Ryan in the kitchen rooting through the cabinets for a snack or a drink. Good luck with that. She had to grin over the barrenness of her cabinets. Burton would watch with close attention since treats for Ryan would equal something for him too. Samson would affect an air of amused disdain that cats manage so well.

Amy pulled on her pajamas printed with the various scientific formulas. She wondered if Ryan bought them for her. Not something, she could have picked up at the local discount store. Most of the good things she could recall in her recent life somehow centered on Ryan. Obviously, he played a major role in her life, which was probably why Aunt Remy made the remark she did. Opening the jar of moisturizer, she smoothed it over her face, wondering if she had anything better than pajamas. No nighties or sexy lingerie anywhere in the house, which should have tipped her off that she had not recently returned from her honeymoon.

Smirking at herself in the mirror, she knew she didn't qualify as a sex kitten. Still, even she would have bought something sexy and floaty for the honeymoon. That is where they messed up. Then there was the fact that Mark left no stuff behind. Even a box of old T-shirts or discarded sports magazines would have made things more believable. Lack of items to boost credibility showed haste, indicating a plan thrown together in a matter of days, perhaps hours.

A squirt of perfume might counteract the pajama effect, Amy hoped as she reached for the bottle. Clean teeth, fresh breath, and an application of lip-gloss should make her night attire acceptable. At least, she hoped it did. Her hand paused on the door handle while her doubts about Ryan vanished, especially when she heard him laugh. How could an open laugh like his belong to anyone with nefarious intents?

The door opened with a slight whine that she hadn't noticed before. Odd, she padded into the kitchen just in time to catch Ryan teasing both Samson and Burton with a strip of ribbon tied to a wooden spoon. Both animals watched the ribbon with avid attention, but neither tried to grab the ribbon. It looked like they were both humoring the man, who looked over his shoulder at her.

"Hey, you look great." His eyes lit up confirming his words.

She'd bit back the desire to hush him remembering the bug, but she didn't. Hadn't they talked through dinner with the radio obnoxiously loud playing next to the bug?

Gesturing to her outfit with one hand, she said, "Ryan, I have on pajamas, dorky ones at that."

He stood up, dropping the impromptu pet toy on the table. In two steps, he reached her, rubbing one hand in a circular fashion against her back. "Dorky pajamas. I bought those for you. Went to Einstein R Us."

Her eyes crinkled a little as she laughed. "I figured you did. That's why I called them dorky, but I still love them."

"Do you now?" Ryan touched his forehead to Amy's. "I'm glad you do. Took some work finding out what size you wore."

Fascinated by his closeness, she murmured, looking up into his eyes, "How did you do that?" She didn't care all that much. She just didn't know what else to say. *Kiss me, now, might be a bit forward.* Sighing, she wondered how she ended up in her thirties and still unsure how to act around a lover.

Ryan's eyebrows rose at her sigh, but he continued to talk. "I tried to be sly, but I was always trying to get a peek at the size of your sweaters. I didn't go with just one. I looked at several. Ironically, of the three I picked out, none of them were the same size." He wrinkled his nose, probably mentally reviewing his efforts.

"Welcome to the world of women's fashion." Amy grinned, trying to remember if she could recall a time when Ryan slunk around the lab trying to peer at a discarded sweater. "What did you do?"

His eyes rolled up as he remembered. "Cissy in area four almost caught me handling your sweater. She never made any mention of it, probably thought I had a sweater fetish. I took the sizes eight, ten, and medium to an elderly saleswoman in one of the upscale department stores. She told me to go with medium but then warned me, depending on where the pajamas were made, that they could run small. No wonder men never buy clothes for women or at least not successfully."

He looked so bemused she leaned forward and kissed him. He tightened his arms around her, which aligned their bodies, hip to shoulders. *Ah ha, that's all I had to do.* His tongue tangoed with hers, increasing the warmth between them and upping her emotional turmoil at the same time. With her eyelids closed, she felt as if a current ran from Ryan to her, and she sent one into him. It sounded more like an image from a horror movie than romantic love.

Dropping her heels, she eased out of the kiss. She decided to keep the disturbing imagery to herself. Ryan's eyes twinkled as he ran a hand through her hair, caressing her scalp. Sweetness in his expression alarmed her. It looked like he adored her, even loved her. Instead of bringing her happiness that most women would traditionally feel, dread, even despair crept over her, cooling her body temperature.

Turning slightly not to look at Ryan, but off into the living room, she noticed headlights going down her street, which was odd since the end was a cul de sac. One house was empty due to a job transfer. The other home belonged to a vacationing family. Their excited five-year-old shared the news while they were packing up the car. Oh well, whoever it was would realize he made a mistake and turn around, but the headlights didn't come back. Whoever it was, either turned off his lights, or decided just to stay. Neither option made sense, but was part of the peculiar life she lived.

Not mentioning the lights, she asked, "Are you going to take a shower?"

Ryan's mouth twisted a little. "Well, normally I shower in the morning, but then again I don't get to sleep with a beautiful woman. I think a shower might be in order. Do you have a razor I could use? Might start working on this beard to appear a little more civilized. Thinking of that, I need to call my answering service." He pulled his cellphone and began to tapping in numbers.

She stepped away from him to give him some quiet for the call. Her eyes strayed to the window wondering about the car that disappeared down her street. As if hearing her thoughts, a set of headlights lit up her room. Good, at least she knew there wasn't anyone lurking at the end of her street spying on her as she prepared to sleep with a man who wasn't her alleged husband. It didn't matter that Mark might never have existed. What did matter was people thought he existed, and the two of them were married.

Chapter Twelve

Simpson used the tip of his tongue to move his canine tooth. Loose, but it might tighten back up again. Teeth did that. He should know since he had enough loosened in various altercations. Lost two twice, but the ceramic replacements appeared to be tougher than the actual teeth. Could be age, his teeth were getting more brittle, just like his bones. This was a young man's game. Still, he got the jump on those two amateurs following him.

He grinned imagining their surprise when he used the semis as a blind to drop behind them and force them off the road. They jumped out of their car in surprise and anger. Before the short one could reach for his gun, Simpson busted the crow bar across his forearm. He spun and caught the driver before he could do likewise, putting both of their gun hands out of commission with one of his favorite tools. A bearded, burley trucker stopped to see what the commotion was about and jumped into the fight when one of them shouted an expletive with enough of a foreign accent to set off the good ol' boy.

Simpson got in a few good punches, took a few too, pretty sure, one of them was from the bearded trucker. A few other truckers stopped as well. He slipped away then and was well away on his way to Dallas when the police cars shot by him going the opposite way. With any luck, his new friends might get a cell for the night.

The rest of the drive was uneventful. He spotted Newkirk's car in the carport. The lights were on in the house, but, apparently, she left them on. He slowed his car down and flicked off the headlights as he reached Jergens' car. The younger agent got out of his car and waited for him to stop before climbing into his.

The young agent did a double take before whistling, "You're a mess. Who'd you piss off?"

Simpson grimaced, the action caused the skin to tighten around his eyes and shot pain across his face. The familiar twinge alerted him that at least one of his eyes was black, maybe both. His first instinct was to snarl about the run-in with his foreign friends, but he decided against it. Why give out any more information than needed? Keeping his mouth shut kept him breathing more than once. "None of your business." He growled the words, silencing any future questions on that matter. "Just report."

Jergens sucked in his lips perhaps trying to stop his obvious remarks. He cleared his throat, consulted a notepad computer, he carried with him. "No sign of suspect, no sign of entry from front, no traffic to house. Hard to tell if the lights were on during the day, but at 7:12 pm, I heard the sound of a dog bark, which seemed to come from the house. Lights came on then. That's it."

Simpson listened to the report with a sense of growing discontent. What did the youngster do, sit in his car for the past eight hours? Why didn't he check the house, especially after he heard the dog? If he got closer to the house, he would have been able to hear more. Instead, of airing his grievances, he kept them to himself. Apparently, he had to tell the kid everything to do. Too tired to do that tonight. "Go home, get some rest, I'll call you tomorrow."

Simpson watched Jergens drive off, knowing he should be doing the same, but he needed to do the reconnaissance work that Jergens failed to do. Glancing at his watch, he waited until the minute hand had made ten full sweeps. "Old school watch for an old school kind of guy," Klein, a colleague once remarked. Klein was dead now, not by Simpson's hand, but at his own. Not a suicide, but rather his failure to follow protocol had been the same as putting a gun to his head. There was something be said for following rules.

He switched off the overhead dome light so the car would not illuminate when he opened the door. Slipping out of the car, he gently nudged the door closed. A slam would not only alert Newkirk and whoever else was there of his presence, but it would also set off the dogs in the neighborhood. Dogs did more to discourage crime than most people would suspect. It wasn't the threat of a beribboned Maltese or an overweight Bassett hound that did it, rather the alarm of a yapping canine. An easy robbery ended with a wide-awake homeowner.

The dark amplified the sounds of the neighborhood. A mother stood at a door down the street, yelling for her child to put up his bike. Someone would steal it, she warned. The kid just gave her lip. He had half a mind to steal it to make the delinquent respect his mother more. Someone down the street was using a chainsaw in one of the few houses that had a garage. That might bear investigating, but it wasn't his job. He already had a job, he mused as he smoothed on his latex gloves. It never pays to be sloppy or leave anything behind.

Ducking behind the house he knew to be empty, he kept to the shadows working his way to Newkirk's cottage. Her blinds were the thick kind, maybe wood as opposed to vinyl. While they showed up as rectangles with light edging around them, they didn't let anyone see what was behind them. It was a good covering for someone who wanted to discourage peeping toms. An excellent plan for a woman living alone, something she probably considered. He slid around to the back, but his pants legs caught on a prickly shrub. What else could happen today? He pulled it free, standing at the side of the house. He could hear the gurgle of water and the stupid radio. Did she never turn that thing off? It was set to an especially raucous rock station that didn't fit Miss Newkirk's personality at all. It was as if she knew someone bugged her house.

It was exactly what he'd do if he knew. Never giving out any sign that he knew, but, instead, waiting to see what move the person who placed the bug would make next. "Damn it," he swore softly. How could he have missed the obvious?

Of course, she knew. Wasn't she supposed to be a genius? Theron and he both assumed she had lost her memory and only acted as if she knew enough to find her way around work. A genius would know enough to act as if she was someone without a memory, especially if that were her safest alternative. Following the same line of reasoning, Newkirk also figured out she was being shadowed. If she knew he tailed her, then what did her trip mean? Was it a cover up, a ruse, a trick to hide her real intentions? He ground his molars considering the prospect that he might have been played.

Simpson determined he'd figure out what the hell was going on. Everyone was holding out on him, Theron, his foreign friends, and the good doctor. Out of the three, she was the one who was least aware, he'd give her that much.

One window was brighter, indicating the blinds were open a bit more. He slid carefully to the small slice of light, approaching it sideways. From his previous tour of the house, he knew it was the office, the perfect place to hide secrets. He didn't find any before, but maybe he was looking in the wrong place or Dr. Newkirk never brought any home. He angled his body to make himself as small as possible. A person looking out into the dark wouldn't see him. Bending his knees, he moved his head the needed three inches to peer in the open space. His gaze met a pair of intent brown eyes. Below the curious eyes, a flattened nose and a lolling tongue completed the picture, the dog. It gave a sharp bark sending Simpson scurrying across the yard to his car.

It was time to leave the area. So far, he'd been lucky no one reported his or Jergens' car. The only person likely to notice was Newkirk. She'd been too busy doing other things to pay attention to what was going on outside her home. Bad news if the man in the car had teamed up with her. He slid into his car, started it with the headlights off, and crept out of the neighborhood, hoping not to attract any attention. Sure, a strange car with the lights off driving slowly through the neighborhood was perfectly normal.

The rearview mirror didn't reveal an enraged man training a rifle with a scope on his car. Men in new relationships could be incredibly courageous or stupid. In Texas, every man was packing.

Stupid dog, he muttered to himself. He'd heard canines couldn't see well in the dark. The dog may have heard him more than saw him. Either way he alerted the occupants.

Newkirk has more going on than he originally thought. He'd taken his briefing from Theron as gospel. He should have known better. No good asking for an update. It would only alert them about the discrepancies he'd found in their initial summary. Better, he find out on his own before his ignorance got him killed. Back to his makeshift office to run images of the mysterious man with his flashy car and annoying dog through the facial identity program. On one hand, he could be any man, but he was willing to bet he worked for Theron too.

* * * *

Amy sat on the bed petting Samson. Her feline appeared no worse for the wear, maybe even a little heavier. Whoever had him had been feeding him well. The fact she and Ryan tucked into food left in her fridge rated high on the risk taker category. Despite all the weirdness in her life, currently, she felt that the person who brought Samson and the food meant her no harm. It didn't make sense, but nothing in her life did. Waiting for Ryan to come sleep with her didn't make sense, either. How could she have worked with him for ten years without any romantic inclination, then suddenly they were all over each other like white on rice? Then again, he made it sound as if he had plenty of romantic inclinations toward her, but she kept missing his signals.

Hard to say, she pushed the cat off the bed when the shower stopped. Samson slowly walked over to where Burton lay curled on a pillow and joined him, entwining himself so they made a rather lopsided ying yang symbol. What would tonight be like? Would he expect another rousing session like the previous night?

He padded into the bedroom in a pair of boxers and a Corona T-shirt. She found herself automatically smiling at him. He looked so young and sexy without his glasses. Made her wonder why no one had grabbed him yet. He nodded at the pets in the corner. "Settled in together, amazingly well."

"Yes, they did," she agreed. "I am surprised since they don't know each other well."

He raised his eyebrows but said nothing until he reached the other side of the bed, lifted the covers, and climbed in. "Seriously, you don't remember. They've been together before. Makes me wonder how much you can recall about me, about us."

Amy reached for her bedside lamp and flicked it off. Perhaps there wouldn't be a repeat performance. Ryan turned off his bedside light and rolled to embrace her with one arm. *Here it comes.* He pulled her into a spoon position, cupping her body with his own. He kissed her hair, and then he was silent. Amy counted to one hundred before she realized he was asleep. Well, it had been a long drive.

Ryan was a good man, someone she trusted. It would be very insidious of Theron to use someone she cared about against her. The man wouldn't agree to it, no way. Unless they convinced him it was the best thing for her, or perhaps he, too, was part of the experiment. A post hypnotic suggestion could have been made that he always loved her. It made a person wonder when they worked so long together and nothing happened. Could she trust Ryan? God, she hoped so, because there was no one else.

The soft sound of his breathing comforted her but made her envious at the same time. It must be wonderful to go to sleep and know exactly who you are. She, on the other hand, tossed and turned most of the night, worrying about what she may have done, what people think she may have done, what might have been done to her, and then there were the watchers, the people she knew were watching her. At least, the police gave up on her. Decided her unhappy husband walked as many of them do, or they may have decided she never had a husband and was looney tunes. Whatever they thought, she knew they'd written her off.

No murder without a body, the female detective had so succinctly told her. Other than her, no one reported Mark missing. You would think especially after all the time that passed that at least his work would have made inquiries. This only confirmed the fact that Mark never existed or that he existed only in her implanted memories. The physical image of Mark was probably the features and body of some foreign porn star. A person she'd have never seen, unless she had a special yen for foreign porn. Maybe they investigated her. Of course, they did. No one could work for Theron if he or she had a weakness that could be exploited.

Gamblers, alcoholics, porn addicts, even gossipers need not apply at Theron. They checked your medical records and your credit score. It was probably much easier being a CIA agent. Once they had you, they couldn't afford to lose you. Amy knew Theron was a relatively young company. Did she know anyone who actually left? There was Duran, a night guard. Come to think of it, didn't he have a heart attack and die. A little peculiar for a person only in his forties, but he may have had a family history of heart disease.

Placing names to people she passed every day at work appeared to help solidify her memory. There was no real reason for her co-workers to be erased, or was there? At least, she should be able to call them by the right names, so she didn't appear too strange because then more questions might come up, not just the ones about her luck in love. She remembered a Linda Collins working with her. She was a tall redhead with sad eyes. Apparently, she came on board after the accidental death of her chemist husband. He worked for Theron's competitor, Westco. The lab explosion took out half the company. Linda didn't stay too long. Amy tried to remember why she left. Car wreck, a bad one, she was unsure if she survived, certainly never came back.

Nope, people didn't leave Theron. She was sure of it. What would have happened if she decided to go back with Remy to take a long unsupervised leave of absence? Most companies would allow it but would caution it would be without pay. A few would threaten to let her go. Theron wanted her to relax at their secret spa. Strange, she never heard of it until then.

People may not have left Theron in the past, but once she uncovered all the dangerous tendrils related to the incident as she now referred to her mythical husband, she'd be gone. Turning her head, her eyes strayed to Ryan whose mouth fell slightly open giving him a boyish aspect. With any luck, Ryan would go with her. Not only did Theron demand secrecy and long hours, which played havoc with a person's social life, it also appeared that being an employee shortened your life expectancy.

Amy sighed deeply, as if she didn't already have trouble sleeping. Should she stay awake and worry about what she didn't know or fall asleep and wonder if her dreams were real or manufactured? Everyone has had a dream or two that he or she would swear was real on wakening. Her struggle was to differentiate whether her dreams were about events that did happen or were part of new memories.

She closed her eyes concentrating on the rhythm of Ryan's breathing. Her mind drifted a little, stretching toward slumber when a name popped into her mind. *Stella.* It stood out in black bold font in her mind. It belonged to the woman in the gas station, the one who acted so peculiar. It could be a fake name.

The nervous woman came to mind. They met before, always in out of way spots, in odd manners that looked like they didn't know each other. Last time, she met her in a bookstore while she perused the science fiction section. The image came to mind as if she were sitting in a movie theatre watching it on an oversized screen. *She arrived earlier and taped the USB drive to the overstuffed chair placed there to encourage readers to read a chapter in hopes of garnering a sale. Pertinent details of the Morpheus Project plus test results were on that drive. She remembered the terror she felt knowing that incarceration was the least of her worries. Still, she had to stop the project somehow.*

Her hands sweated as she handled a collection of Ray Bradbury's stories. An oversized man sporting a Star Wars sweatshirt plopped down in the chair and proceeded to open a thick paperback. Stella arrived, glanced at her briefly, then at the chair. They both pretended to stare at the limited titles, occasionally giving sideways glances to the man. A bookstore employee announced they were giving out free samples of cheesecake at the coffee bar, which propelled the man into action.

Stella lunged for the chair. She sat her purse strategically in front of the taped leg. Amy watched her fiddling with a book she hung onto when she made her lunge. When was the woman going to make her move? Already the two of them could have been seen standing side by side. There was no rule against strangers looking at books together. However once Stella's report came out, then people would remember seeing them once standing together in a bookstore on a rainy Thursday night.

It wouldn't take much for them to make the leap to her as the informant. The screen closed on the memory, chilling Amy with her sudden knowledge. She was the mole. The one that caused all the heightened security, or maybe she was just another mole in a series of moles. It didn't matter. Suspicions would make her dead meat. No wonder her security clearance vanished for high profile projects. It all started to make sense now, the fake memories and the husband who didn't quite fit in. There was a reason. The urge to wake Ryan and confess all overwhelmed her. What if he served as a tool to retrieve information? He would not know it. She had to keep quiet. Sad, she could share her body with him but not her innermost thoughts and fears. Unfortunately, it sounded like most modern relationships.

Chapter Thirteen

Simpson cursed as he peered at the computer screen through his bleary eyes. Things were starting to get a little fuzzy around the edges. He'd imported the pictures he took at the fast food restaurant, and he got almost two thousand and one hits. It was maddening because he had the feeling the man was not a known felon, a celebrity, or someone in a political office. He took a sip of cold coffee, grimacing at the taste and temperature. Caffeine could keep him awake only so long.

The facial recognition software searched crime data banks first. Then it moved on to photos on the Internet. He often found very low profile individuals who never had a mug shot, but couldn't resist plastering their social media site with photos.

"A-holes," he muttered to himself, "when will they learn that the Internet never forgets."

Problem was as he scanned through the pictures, a portion of a strong chin with stubble, a nose profile, plus a bit of hair escaping from the hat didn't give him much to go on. Apparently, it was enough to evoke two thousand and one masculine images. He noticed one of the snapshots had a woman's name attached. "God." He shook his head. "I have to do better than this."

Thinking of the social media sites, he widened the picture to include Amy Newkirk. If they were friends or lovers, then there should be pictures of the two of them together somewhere, even if they blocked most people from viewing it. Simpson grinned remembering how easy it was to hack into social media. He snorted, not sure, why they pretended to have security features. He knew why. Otherwise, folks who put up pictures of themselves staring in the camera with a sloppy drunk expression and flourishing a bottle of Jack would think twice. The woman posing with male strippers would be shocked to realize her husband regularly viewed her site. The woman who posted her skydiving photo was unaware that the company lawyer scanned her social media site for reasons not to honor her disability claim. Yep, people could be stupid.

He entered the picture to include Amy, guy, and a bit of the dog who had his paws on the seat leaning forward to beg for food. He started the search, then, stood to stretch. Should he bother to make another cup of coffee? Eventually, he'd have to sleep. Maybe a sandwich would do the trick. That sounded good, especially since his last meal consisted of orange peanut butter crackers from the rest stop vending machine. Pouring coffee into an empty stomach wasn't doing his ulcer any good. As if hearing its name, a few shots of pain emanated from his stomach.

A swig of liquid antacid and food were in order. He rattled the filing cabinet drawer to get to his emergency supply of antacid. Not bothering with the spoon, he twisted off the lid, and held it up to his lips. He should buy stock in the antacid the way he consumed it. A sudden ping from his computer almost made him choke. Putting down the bottle, he wiped his lips with his shirtsleeve.

He leaned over his computer to see what bogus information it had for him. Were there five hundred similar couples? They say everyone has a twin. Since he started working with this software, he'd say the gene pool was a whole lot smaller than he originally thought. A snapshot of a grinning Amy Newkirk on a theme park ride with the man in question stared back at him. The man had on sunglasses and a hat. They were the same sunglasses and a hat from his original picture. Hot damn! The photo address was a theme park image bank. Could mean that they had no clue it existed. He looked at the date, which was over a year old. Ms. Newkirk and the man had been keeping company for a while, it seemed.

Simpson stared at the photo. They looked happy as if they enjoyed being together. The man leaned in toward Newkirk as if to be closer. He knew good and well that men didn't hang out with women to be their friends. His head angled toward hers in this picture too. Probably the reason behind why he got a hit. Mystery man was always staring at the woman, making Simpson wonder why.

His first thought was the woman might hurt him somehow. He had to keep her hands in sight at all times. He sighed. Nope, that was his life. Most of the women he met were trying to hurt or kill him. The man's head was away from the camera, so he couldn't see his expression well. He zoomed in on the image looking at the muscles in the man's face. They were on a roller coaster going sixty plus miles an hour. He should be screaming, laughing, or even gritting his teeth, but his muscles were slack. Ah ha, he'd bet he was looking at her lovingly. He placed the original picture next to the theme park picture on the split screen. "Hmmm," he muttered, "the man is besotted. A man in love can do stupid things."

Another beep alerted him to another match. He clicked on the photo of a younger Amy Newkirk in a graduation gown holding up her diploma. A man similar to the previous man stood beside her. This younger man wore glasses and a suit had benefited the occasion. He noted the photo came from Remy Newkirk's social media profile. She captioned the photo *my darling girl on her graduation from medical school, and her mentor, Dr. Ryan Korman.* Paydirt.

He wrote the name down, Dr. Ryan Korman. He glanced at the date of the entry. "Damn," he mused. Those two had been together longer than most married couples he knew. He typed the names into the search engines, then, decided to make a sandwich to give them time to work.

Two doctors, one mentored the other one. Could he have been breaking her into the fold or shaping her in his image? Not too much, age difference between the two. Despite the brilliant mind theory, a man and woman of similar ages together usually ended up with one conclusion. Depositing his sandwich-laden plate on the desk, he brought up the image of the two again. Yep, he could see them as a couple, a nerdy couple. Their serious, earnest features were the same type seen in advertisements about changing the world. Of course, those people were actors. How did those two plan to make the world a better place?

He checked the search on Ryan Korman. He briefly read the entries, which included outstanding scholar, graduated with honors, and various awards—a regular brainiac. What he didn't see was any wedding announcement, which was just as well if he was keeping such close company with Newkirk. No children, either. He authored many groundbreaking papers. There never seemed to be any hospital, college, or practice he mentioned in his writings.

That, in itself, was weird. He found a press release over twelve years old welcoming him to the medical staff of Theron Pharmaceuticals. That must have been back before the company became paranoid or corrupt.

He'd bet the good, or not so good, doc still worked there. Something was up, obviously something not mentioned to him. He had two brilliant Theron doctors in cahoots, a missing man no one seems to care about was still missing, foreign nationals trailing him, and a company that hired him not even telling him why he was watching a suspect. Good chance it was only the tip of the iceberg. Ignorance was not bliss. He knew better than most how important withheld information was to both his livelihood and continual wellbeing.

* * * *

Amy felt Ryan awaken, but she kept her eyes shut. Despite Samson's inquiring meow, practically in her right ear, she kept her eyes tightly shuttered. She had to until Ryan noticed the scene she set after he fell asleep. Fears that Stella might try to reach her after seeing her in the mini-mart plagued her. It made sense that Stella might call since she couldn't show up at work or at her home. Email records were easily traceable. Calling seemed like the only option. She pulled out the battery on her cell phone to erase any history. Then realizing even that action might be noticeable by whoever was listening to her calls, she decided to dunk the phone.

She listened to Ryan quietly pad out of the room into the bathroom. He uttered a soft curse. She imagined him reaching into the toilet bowl to retrieve the phone. His mutter reached her ears, "Amy is going to be so pissed."

Her lips twitched upward. She was relieved as opposed to pissed. Of course, they'd just bug her new phone, but she might wait awhile before getting a new one. Phone records were always used as court evidence, so why would she or Stella use such a visible method? It didn't make sense. Prepaid phones like the one hidden in the bottom of her purse. No wonder she immediately thought of that when she discovered her phone was bugged. She'd used one before. That meant she just trashed an expensive smart

184 Morgan K. Wyatt

phone. She sighed. Oh well, that's why she had insurance on her phone.

It just made it a little harder for Big Brother to spy on her. She opened her eyes when Ryan walked back to the bedroom. The man filled the doorway, holding up the dripping cellphone. "I got some bad news for you. It looks like you won't be making any calls soon."

He looked so distressed at her inconvenience, her heart turned over a tiny bit. She warned herself she couldn't be like this. Falling for him would put her in a dangerous position. Already he knew too much. If he knew she was the mole, it would put him in more danger, and might actually get them both killed.

"No worries," she commented, and perhaps acted a bit too casual at the death of an expensive phone.

Schooling her features into a woebegone bent, she climbed out of bed. "I must have knocked it off when I went to the bathroom last night. Strange I didn't notice it." Realizing her excuse sounded a bit odd, even to her ears, she tacked on, "I must have been wiped not to notice the plop." She forced a laugh, but noticed Ryan's expression changed to confusion as if she wasn't making sense. A slight upward movement of his eyes indicating he was trying to remember where she left the phone. It wasn't the bathroom.

Knowing he'd figure out her lie, she stood, stretched, and smiled at him. Taking the phone from his hand, she placed it on the bedside table. She looped both arms around his neck, leaned forward on her toes, and planted a brief kiss on his lips. "Who needs a phone when the only person I want to talk to is right here in my arms?" She cooed the words aware she was using them for a smokescreen, but they still carried some truth.

Ryan touched his forehead to hers. "I am glad to hear that, but eventually you might want to order a pizza."

She wrinkled her nose. "Who knows what non-food substances are disguised under a layer of cheese."

"Yeah, right. What was I thinking? Maybe you need to renew your library books," he teased, planting a kiss on her nose.

Amy slid her tongue out to touch the dimple in his left cheek before answering. "I can do that online."

He feathered kisses along her face to her ear, taking the lobe between his teeth and tugging. Releasing it, he whispered, "You might want to call me sometime. You will need a phone for that."

Warmth flooded her body, fogging her thinking, she said, "I can't want to call you because they will only bug my phone again." She blinked in surprise. The man kissed it out of her. Biting her lip, she wondered if he noticed her slip.

"Ah ha, I knew it was something. That's it. You trashed the phone intentionally. Why couldn't you tell me that? We could have thrown it out the window in New Mexico. Some semi could have run over it. Better yet some teenager could pick it up and start texting her two hundred friends. Good reason to leave the service on just to confuse your listener. Who do you think it is?" He looked directly into her eyes.

A moment of panic seized her. She knew who she thought it was, but she had no proof. How would Ryan react to the thought that the company they both worked for was playing a deep and devious game of chess, using the employees as expendable pawns? She had no proof, and as a man of science, he'd demand proof. She dropped her chin focusing on his neck. "I don't know who bugged my phone, but I do know it is bugged."

Ryan moved his hands to her shoulders and gave a slight squeeze, probably intending it to be comforting. "Look at me. How do you know? What makes you think the phone is bugged?"

Sighing deeply, she shook her head. "I wanted to keep you out of this mess." Her body relaxed in his embrace while her thoughts raced. It would be nice to share everything with him. Ryan could inadvertently tip someone off by saying the wrong thing to the wrong person. Even office gossip about them spending off hours together would be enough.

He kissed her hair, then, murmured, "That's obvious. I volunteered. I believe you need me. I doubt there is anyone who knows both you and Theron as intimately as I do."

"Well, you apparently know most of my actual life as opposed to the version I've been given. What surprises me is you were not part of the new memories. Well, come to think of it, no one from the lab was. Why?" She didn't expect answers. It was a thought that randomly popped into her head. If she designed such an experiment, the details made it real. They were sloppy, never even investigated that a new Kiva Conference Center had been built and didn't have any convention going on at the needed time.

Ryan tightened his embrace bringing their bodies flush. "Whoever chose to use you as a guinea pig did it as a sudden, impulsive, or reactionary move. It had a purpose. Maybe to silence you or discredit you so no one would take you seriously. It might also be a way to test out whatever you were given. The people following you could be gathering data too. Asking you the needed questions would cause you to wonder about the validity of your marriage."

Resting her head on his shoulder, she felt safe in his embrace. Could the incident be attributed to Theron knowing she was the mole? It was possible, but killing her would be easier. Maybe one too many people have disappeared from the ranks of Theron's employees. Her disappearance might trigger investigation by a certain reporter. They could test out a new use for their concoction if the military wasn't buying. "You're right," she finally agreed.

Samson intertwined his large furry body between their legs, which was no mean feat, purring loudly. "I should feed him, but I am not sure how much tuna I have left, if any."

Ryan released her to reach down and fondle the cat's head. "Well, I am sure we can find something to feed the animals."

"That would work." She glanced at the clock. "I need to get ready for work. Did you call in about being late?"

"Yep. Took care of that last night. It felt like playing hooky. Figure the answering service would hear it in my voice. Go ahead and get showered. I'll round up some grub for the four of us. The radio is still on so I doubt it will be too much of an issue." Ryan turned toward the kitchen followed by a hopeful Burton and Samson.

The cupboards were mostly bare. "Good luck with that. Wait." Thinking of the bug in the kitchen, she pushed past Ryan. Pushing a chair up to the counter, Amy scrambled up to grab the bug. Noticing Ryan standing in the kitchen doorway, she put a finger to her lips. Wrapping her fingers around the tiny bug, she carried it outside to her carport and placed it on the concrete.

Closing the back door behind her, she dusted off her hands. "That's done. I would like to spend one morning not listening to horrible music and having every sound I make analyzed. It will do whomever good to hear the sounds of the neighborhood. They will assume I have the window open."

Ryan stepped forward to place a hand on her shoulder. "You lasted longer than I would have. Will you replace the bug later?"

It made sense to replace it. Too much of cars rumbling down the street, kids yelling, and Mrs. Torres' overfed poodle yipping all day was bound to make someone suspicious. It would definitely be a respite from heavy metal music all day. "I should. Remind me." Ryan nodded his agreement.

A quick glance at the clock alerted her that time was running away from her like a dog with a steak in its mouth. Placing her hand over Ryan's, she gave him a smile before heading to the bathroom. A twist of the knob allowed the water to warm up. It took a while before it was acceptable. Her pajamas hit the floor the same time her eyes studied the corners of the room, searching for cameras or disturbances in the wall where a camera might hide. She saw none.

Stepping into the warm spray, she decided if she were observing a participant in a study that she definitely would video the subject. If that were the case, then why would they need to bug her house or follow her? They'd certainly know more than it appeared they did.

Did she bring this on herself somehow? Shampooing her hair, she faulted her naivety as opposed to her leaking information. That came later after she realized she was dealing with an entity that had no ethics. Did she suggest the romance application for the drug? She rinsed her hair free of the shampoo and reached for the conditioner. A blurry image came into focus.

Her colleagues on the Morpheus team stood around her in a loose circle. Seven males in lab coats, a few wore superior smirks. She could hear her voice and feel her agitation. "Have you even considered the ethics of what we are doing? We are taking control of people's minds for brief moments and inserting whatever thoughts we want in it. Ironically, we could have people line up asking for certain thoughts. Paying good money to believe once they were a war hero or a movie star. Women frustrated with dating might want to experience a great romance. Folks with weight issues want memories of being thin and desirable. Would we give it to them?"

Her colleagues looked intrigued and began speaking suddenly. The stern looking one with the crew cut and the horn-rimmed glasses exclaimed, "I think you've done it."

"Done what?" her past self had asked.

Amy shivered under the shower spray as if it suddenly went cold. She was the culprit. Thinking about the Morpheus team, she realized why her engagement and marriage was heavy on sex and light on romance. There was no woman to insert moonlit walks, picnics in the park, or even the important engagement scene. The details were missing, but then she realized she was the detail person on the team.

Turning off the shower, she exited the tub. She may have thrown out the idea as a joke, but they ran with it. She did not participate in the experiment because she would have planned it much better. Just as well that the majority of her colleagues were unmarried and didn't have a clue how to make women happy. They erroneously thought enough sex should do it.

She patted herself dry and pulled on a bathrobe. Ryan sang a rock ballad with gusto while Burton tried to sing along with it. Not certain of how sensitive the bug was, she was sure her listeners now knew she had a dog or might think it was her singing. Would it make the house visits less frequent? Somewhere in the house she had evidence, she had to. More than the flash drive, she'd passed on to the reporter. A new computer indicated the need to get rid of the old one. If she did that, where would she put it?

Walking into the kitchen, she had to smile. Ryan managed to scrounge up enough ingredients to make tea and toast. Ryan fixing a meal for her was another thing whoever made up her new memories would not have known. "I didn't think I had any bread."

Ryan pulled out her chair with a flourish as if they were at a fancy restaurant. "Madam," he waved at the toast smeared with a miniscule amount of peanut butter, "your feast awaits. I found some sprouted grain bread in the freezer. Sprouted grain?"

Amy raised her eyebrows in inquiry. "You call yourself a doctor and are unaware that sprouted grain has twice the B6 and folate as regular bread. It is easier to digest too."

His eyes danced over his mug as he sipped his tea. Lowering the cup, he set it on the table. "I figured it was something like that." For a few minutes, they acted as a normal couple engaged in a romantic affair. They ate their meal in silence, unlike Samson who voiced his discontent at eating rice.

Amy reviewed her daily plans mentally. She'd left her car because she thought it might have a tracker hooked to it, or at least a bug, which meant no talking in the car, either. The two of them got dressed with relatively little talking. Was it the awkwardness of their friendship venturing into an unknown place or the fear that they were being watched? Neither option was appealing.

Ryan and Burton planned to hike back through the woods to his car. An unexpected downpour squelched that idea. Leaning close to Ryan's ear, she whispered, "It's still dark. I'll drive you to your car. Get in on the left side, and I doubt you'll even be seen if someone is still watching my house."

Grabbing an umbrella on her way out, she apologized to Samson for leaving him with a bowl of rice. "I'll bring you something home tonight."

Amy turned on her radio to the same acid rock station. If she listened to it in the house, it would make sense she'd listen to the same station in the car. She missed her jazz music, but she hoped her subterfuge was ending. Pulling in beside the Mustang, she jumped out of her car and opened her umbrella, rushing to Ryan who was doing his best to encourage Burton out into the rain. The dog was even more particular than her cat.

"What service," Ryan remarked as she held the golf umbrella over the three of them. Ferrying them over to his car, she waited until Burton sat proudly in the passenger seat. No doubt, he resented her taking his seat the entire trip to New Mexico.

The two of them stood close under the umbrella. "Ryan, I was wondering if I ever gave you anything for safekeeping?"

"Actually you did. At the time, you were so peculiar about it. I asked you why you didn't use a safety deposit box. You said something about it being traceable," Ryan answered, but his eyes filled with unspoken questions.

"That's right, they are. Not as secret and private as you might think considering the bank employees have access to the contents.

It might even result in blackmail depending on the contents. Why didn't you mention this before? It must have been important." Amy narrowed her eyes wondering both what she passed onto him and the reason behind him not saying anything. "What did I give you? Better yet what did you do with it?"

The rain bounced off the umbrella, isolating them in a small sanctuary of perceived privacy. If followed, the two of them would be obviously standing in the rain, whispering, standing close like lovers. After all, who else would stay out in the rain?

Ryan held his hands out about a foot apart. "Your sudden marriage and disappearing husband wiped the box out of my mind, temporarily. You gave me a box all duct-taped up. I say maybe eighteen inches by two feet. You never told me what was in it, just told me to it keep dry and safe and you would ask for it when you needed it. The you that came back was different and had no knowledge of the package. I thought it best to wait until you asked for it."

At least she knew the computer hadn't fallen into the wrong hands, but that might depend on where he put it. "Ryan, where did you store it? I need it now. I think it might be the answer to all the craziness that has been happening around me."

"You gave it to me right before I went to check on my parents' cabin. I think I told you I planned to keep the lake cabin for when I eventually decide to get out of this rat race. I did have renters, but they moved out because it was even too isolated for them, and they were survivalist types. So I was amazed they found it too far out, but maybe they weren't committed to their whole end of the world theories. Maybe the lure of a Taco Bell and a shopping mall proved too much for them."

Normally, she found Ryan's ramblings amusing, but not now. Too much was riding on that one parcel. "Where is it?" She pushed the words out through her teeth. No one would accuse her of sounding lover-like.

"Bomb shelter. There's a bomb shelter on my parents' property. If that wasn't secure enough, I put it inside a safe inside the bomb shelter. The renters never knew about the bomb shelter. I was afraid if they knew, they would have shut themselves in. It even has a time-lapse lock on the shelter like a bank vault. That's more for when you are inside. I just use the combination lock. The guy my parents bought the property off of must have been one paranoid individual."

That sounded safe. "Good, did you ever tell me this before?" Amy wondered why she had no memory of what happened to the mysterious computer. It would have been easier to reformat the hard drive and store the information on a USB. She did apparently have one USB since she passed it off to Stella. Still, she didn't feel secure. She also wanted a verifiable record in case something happened to her.

"No, I never had a chance. I took off a week to go back home. When I came back, you were gone. Beth told me that you took off on your honeymoon. I thought at the time she had you confused with someone else. I knew for a fact you hadn't been dating anyone." He shook his head as if he couldn't believe such a thing. "It made no sense, and then the mysterious husband disappears before anyone had a glimpse of him. The next time I saw you, you were in the hospital when Remy brought you in. When you looked at me, there wasn't any sign of recognition in your clouded eyes. That floored me."

Amy placed a hand on his chest. "I'm sorry about your devastation. It was the drug, not me. When can we get to your parents' house or more specifically their bunker?"

Ryan's lips twisted to one side as he thought. "Well, we both had recent time off. I imagine they aren't giving you any more time off. We'll have to wait until the weekend and take the redeye, but that would make us traceable by buying tickets."

"Is there any other way? I realize driving is out of the question." Five days she'd have to wait. Could she pretend everything was fine and dandy for five more days? She inhaled, checked her watch. "Okay, let me know. I have to show up for work on time like normal." She started to turn away before Ryan's hand on her shoulder stopped her.

"Not so fast, you are forgetting something." He turned her to face him and swooped in for a fast, hard kiss. "Now you can go."

She gave him a lingering look before she headed to her car. Who knew a dormant romantic lay hidden deep inside that very fine scientific mind? Not her, clearly. Just think of all the years the two of them had wasted when they could have been pledging their love to one another.

Chapter Fourteen

Amy hustled into her workstation a little damp but on time. A quick nod and a few casual hellos were enough to establish she arrived on time. Pressing the power button, she looked for the transcription folder. No reason to lock the gem up she thought as she opened it. No one would want to steal it. Did they give her this mindless work to see how long she would docilely take it considering she wasn't exactly meek and retiring before the incident? Then again, it might just be part of the experiment seeing what she did remember. Would the memories of Mark stay with her forever? Was there a way to extract them?

The sounds of keystrokes sounded around her as she tried to bring up the image of Mark. It was difficult. Their first meeting was blurry. Her initial impression was that he was tall, with brown hair, and uniform features. Nothing special, the joy and elation the memory used to bring faded away. Was that a natural occurrence? Was the memory time related only lasting so many weeks? If so, people might line up for regular updates or a new updated imaginary lover. Sounded like something right out of a science fiction book.

Could her relationship with Ryan interfere with her ability to recall Mark? It made sense that a real lover would trump a fake one every time, especially one as considerate and passionate as Ryan. An involuntary smile crossed her face as she mused about their trip together. Caught up in her daydreaming, she didn't hear her unexpected visitor approach.

"Dr. Newkirk."

Amy looked up into the alert eyes of Dr. Lawrence Clemmons, chief chemist and CEO of the corporation. He spent most of his time in the corporate suite now, but his eyes and ears were all over the facility. She was well aware there was great intelligence behind those eyes along with greed and ruthlessness too.

"Sir," she answered, making her eyes to appear guileless, "quite the cloudburst we're having." Geesh she sounded like a character from a 1950's movie, not what she wanted.

He looked at her in a measuring manner before he cleared his throat. "I guess you would be a good judge of the weather considering how much time you spent on the road this weekend."

Her right hand jerked, pushing the binder off the desk. She reached to pick it up, giving herself time to compose her face. He knew somehow. Ryan hadn't even reported for work, so it couldn't be his fault. How? The image of the man at the rest stop, then in downtown Albuquerque materialized. He must be following them. Brazen it out was her only thought.

Sitting back in her chair, she looked up at the man realizing how much he resembled a hawk ready to attack a defenseless pigeon, but she never considered herself pigeon. "Me, sir? I think you must be confused. I've been home all weekend in bed. Touch of the stomach flu." Her hand fluttered to touch her forehead to see if she had a fever. "Still a bit warm, I'm afraid. My car didn't move from my carport all weekend."

She managed to fake a sneeze under his suspicious stare. Clemmons stepped back as if afraid she might contaminate him. "You shouldn't be here if you are sick, standard protocol."

"Oh no, sir, I feel much better. Besides, I need to work. It's hard being in the house with the memories of Mark." She managed a sniff and turned away to grab a tissue.

Waving his hands to ward her off, he said, "No need to go on, I understand." He turned and left the area with a fast step.

Amy dabbed at her dry eyes, eternally grateful for the Internet article that claimed men were unable to deal with women crying. It bought her a little more time. Too bad, she didn't take his suggestion to go home. She did feel nauseous realizing her time was up. Opening the binder, she looked for the sticky note that marked where she left off. Scanning the notes, she bit her lip, disgusted with the ramblings of a man who knew nothing about science. Wilkenshire's appointment to the Morpheus Project frustrated her. The man couldn't even document insect behavior appropriately. Disgusted with the futility of transcribing his notes, she stopped to consider his history with the organization.

For the most part Wilkenshire stayed out of her circle of colleagues. Try as she might, she couldn't remember him while she engaged in the genetic engineering of crops. Beth mentioned him when they were in the early stages of the Morpheus Project. Apparently, he made the mistake of hitting on her. Would be hard to imagine who was more shocked. Beth, who worked side by side with single-minded focus with some of the best minds in the world, never had one of them look at her as a woman unless it was to ask her a question about female response for data. No doubt, Wilkenshire earned a few slaps because of his abrupt manner.

Beth handled it well by continuing to act as if she was clueless about his meaning. Eventually Wilkenshire gave up. Could be his immediate supervisor reminded him that dating or any type of fraternization among employees was forbidden. In the end, Wilkenshire toned down his libido down a few notches. He didn't fit in. His was not an inquiring mind. Most of the other employees recognized him as a bully who harassed them on the playground and kept as far away as possible.

Not bothering to search the whole complex for the man, she went straight to Beth. Her colleague turned the fine adjustment knob on the microscope as she watched the image on the monitor blur and then stabilize. Immersed in her new slide, she didn't hear Amy approach. Leaning over her friend's shoulder to get a better look, she asked, "Is it contagious?"

Beth startled and shot an irritated look over her shoulder. "If it was, you'd have it by now, but no, it's not an airborne virus. You'd have to know someone pretty well to get one of these."

She watched the image morph and move across the screen for a second. "Speaking of knowing someone pretty well, have you seen any sign of Wilkenshire? I need to talk to him about his notes."

Spinning her chair to face Amy, Beth put down one foot to steady herself and both hands on her lab-coated hips. "Ha, ha." She said the words as opposed to actually laughing. "I guess that was your idea of a joke. Keep working on humor. You don't have it down yet. I haven't seen Wilkenshire in days. He used to stop by and tell me a science fact of the day he got from one of those desk calendars meant for grade school teachers."

Beth looked thoughtful. "No wonder it has been so quiet."

Amy located the camera in the room. Dropping the binder on the floor, she stooped to pick it up but managed to stand so her back blocked the view of Beth's answer. She lowered her voice. "You mean nothing, nada, haven't seen him anywhere?"

"That's what I mean. Why do you care? You can't stand the guy. I think you dislike him more than I do, especially after he got your place on the project." Beth's eyes gleamed with interest.

Glancing both ways, she made sure no one was eavesdropping. "I don't dislike him. I never said that. I don't understand why they allowed him to take my place when the man would not be able to come up with a decent science fair project."

Beth chuckled and put a hand over her mouth to cover it, pretending to cough. Inhaling deeply, she gathered herself. "No worries, then. I think he's gone, which leads me to wonder if the project is finished too."

Resting two fingers against her lips, her attention caught on the words gone and finished. If Wilkenshire had vanished, it could mean a number of things. Main one was that he was never a Theron employee but rather some type of liaison or military attaché. The project was finished because they lost funding, they found a proven use for it, or it imploded upon itself. All bore consideration.

"Thanks, Beth," she murmured half-distracted and turned to go back to her workstation.

Wilkenshire gone. If the military contract went bust, then it made sense he left. As for the Morpheus agent, it may not have worked out as planned, but, then again, maybe it did. Wilkenshire left because he had proof that the assassin agent worked. Theron would never give him the chemical composition. Oh no, they would only take orders for it. The real question was had she outlived her usefulness? The answer looked more and more as if she had.

One of her greatest tools as a scientist was her eidetic memory. Often she only had to look at something once to remember it, which helped her ace many a medical exam. After working months on the projects, she would know the chemical composition of Morpheus agent. When it came to being right and remembering something, her colleagues always deferred to her. In some ways, she was the most dangerous member of the team, especially after she threw down the ethics card. While killing her might appear to be the most efficient way to get rid of her, it could cast doubt on the final product.

Even though Theron needed credibility to attract moneyed clients, they didn't want their scientists to garner too many awards. Before you knew it, they might start thinking they could leave the corporation. Amy had attracted just enough for clients to insist that she'd be part of the team to manage their interests. What should have been a team effort of unknown professionals became the Dr. Amy Newkirk and supporting members show. The memories were starting to come together. If people thought teen girls could be petty, then they never ever worked with scientists. There was plenty of resentment over her name constantly used by clients. It didn't help that she operated from a stance of absolute certainty. No one liked to work with a know-it-all, especially if the know-it-all was right.

Her intractability set the scene for her own downfall. It all made sense. She doubted she volunteered to be a guinea pig. A person with her memory could break away from the firm taking the chemical recipe of Morpheus with her. Theron never patented anything since patents eventually became public knowledge and other companies stole your ideas and undercut your price. They relied on blind loyalty and implied threat.

Sitting in her chair, she prepared to spend another pointless day of typing worthless notes, but the good thing was it allowed her to think and suddenly remember. The mist that made the memories so difficult to recall burned off like the fog a little more each day. Pulling out a stick of gum from her pocket, she unwrapped it and placed it in her mouth. Thank goodness, she could still get gum in the facility. By the end of the day, her packet was chewed and nothing to bring out of the building.

Early on, she wondered why Theron was so generous with free lunches and beverages. It wasn't as if they made the products, so they weren't free to the company. The food was better than you'd get at the local restaurants. They brought in a chef to meet various dietary requirements of the different employees. On those days, when she tried to work through lunch, a caring staff member usually brought her food. It was usually a turkey avocado Panini on Ciabatta bread, her favorite, paired with a diet cola. That seemingly innocent act demonstrated the monitoring of food intake.

When she was working on genetically modified crops, she wondered if their product ended up on the lunch menu. It made sense. If they had confidence in their product, why not use it? Then, on the other hand, they could feed it to a collection of unknowing guinea pigs and watch for side effects. It didn't make much sense when you considered the value of the guinea pigs. While it would be too expensive and troublesome to replace someone who fell ill or died, it would be much better to keep them healthy…and compliant.

Her fingers stilled on the keyboard. Compliant? Wasn't that the original Morpheus Project's intention, to make people compliant? They may have used the word peaceful or docile, rather like a cow. Often, she wondered why so many brilliant minds willingly put aside any chance of romance, children, or a social life. Those on the outside might call them nerds or eggheads and implied such folks never had a social life. She did once, a social life that came and went in spurts but drained away once she joined Theron.

The closest she came to a social life was with Ryan. Apparently, their association was hush-hush as if they were guilty of practicing human sacrifice. Her eyes traveled over her peers hard at work. The ratio of men to women was in favor of the men, yet no office romances, no flirting, or prolonged eye contact. Wilkenshire was the lone lothario roaming the halls of Theron. He calmed down some after a few weeks. It could be after ingesting enough free Theron food and beverages, he felt more compliant and less interested in Beth.

Amy's initial decision to avoid the lunchroom didn't work. If she didn't eat the food the dietary aide brought up, it would be noticeable. If she threw it away, it would be noticed. It was better to go to the lunchroom, grab something, and push it around her plate taking miniscule bites. Often, she packed it in her jaw only to spit it out in the toilet later. Chewing gum helped pick up any residual chemicals left in her mouth and eventually swallowed with her spit. The gum helped her not to partake of the free beverages too.

At first, she was only trying to avoid the possibility of ingesting genetically modified food. Then, suddenly things started to seem wrong to her. For instance, the guards searched them as if they were criminals, especially Roman, who often patted her butt or breasts as if copping a feel. This would pass for a sexual harassment lawsuit in any other place, but the women took it. Her aggravation rose as she recalled, and she avoided eating anything.

Ryan didn't act as compliant as the rest of the staff. Well, at least when they weren't at work. Why was that? She pondered the few people who "acted out" as if they were wayward children not following the Theron guidelines. They vanished, but with a reasonable excuse, such as transferred to another facility or moved to Florida to care for an aging mother. Still, they never mentioned leaving, no goodbye parties, just gone the next day.

Much to her chagrin, Amy realized she never thought about them too much, too intent on her own work. Did that make her a bad person? She furtively looked around the room, watching other people go through the motions of scientific research. The word research really served as a euphemism because they were well aware of the end they wanted when they started the work. Did her thoughts show on her face? She hoped not. Already she attracted enough attention that they'd attempted to reprogram her with new memories.

In a way, that was a good sign. It meant she was too valuable of a commodity to lose. On the other hand, it was probably the slow road to destroying her credibility. It was similar to the story of the astronaut who drove across several states wearing adult diapers to make it in time to threaten her romantic rival. People loved it when brainy people went bad. She'd managed to stay out of the headlines.

Surprising how a weekend of eating restaurant food and leftovers in her fridge cleared her mind. No wonder Theron wanted her to go to their spa where she could be administered a diet that would help regulate her behavior. Good chance, every time she left the house, her food supply received enhancements. Better to eat out every night than to eat at home. Even her vitamins in her cabinet could be suspect. When they started working on the composition the formula should take, they tried different formats including airborne, liquid, and a small blue pill.

The male scientists thought it immensely amusing that it wouldn't be hard to get men to swallow the pill assuming they would achieve an astounding erection, which would lead to wild monkey sex. The tiny blue pill, she could see it in her mind. It could easily be ground into their food. The pill was one fourth of the size of her pinkie fingernail. So small, she could hide it on her body, if she'd decided to smuggle it out for additional analysis or proof. She'd done just that she felt certain. How did she manage it with Roman, the handsy guard?

Give some people a gun, and they think they're important. Roman, just liked to humiliate her by leaving a warm hand on her body too long, sniffing her hair, or even making comments on how she must be working out because she felt firmer. Obviously, he didn't dine in the company lunchroom much. Perhaps, his purpose was to intimidate the females into appropriate behavior. She never saw him search a male employee. They left that to a huge muscular thug with a shaved head, who looked like a villain from a comic book. The man would scare the bejesus out of just about anyone.

One day, Roman wasn't there. That was the day she palmed a few pills. The memory, which had eluded her, came back suddenly with amazing clarity.

She was almost to the door where they had to submit to the search process when she noticed old Anthony in Roman's usual position. The aged guard usually wished her good morning. He apologetically patted down the female employees with his eyes turned away.

Knowing this was her only chance, she turned to go back to the lab. Beth called after her, "What's wrong?"

She couldn't claim a purse because she never brought one, and she was wearing her jacket. "I think I left the computer on."

Beth shook her head. "That doesn't sound like you."

"I know, but you know how OCD I am." She sprinted to the lab. The lights were off, but the door remained unlocked. An oversight on whoever left it last. Realizing the cameras would still be on but would only get shadowy images, she pulled her hair into a bun, similar to Marybeth Lancer's hairstyle. She occupied the

lab next door to theirs. It was the best disguise she could come up with. She tidied up books, keyboards, as if her original intention while she worked her way toward the pills. Marybeth was even more OCD than she. It would be believable that she would do a bit of light housekeeping if the lab door were open.

Standing in front of the drawer that held the pills, she slid it open, taking two from the container. More than two would be noticeable. She slid them into her front pants pocket where the camera couldn't catch her. She managed to exit the lab, tidying as she went, never facing the camera. She hurried to the restroom, keeping her face away from the camera.

In the restroom, she stood inside a stall wondering if they filmed inside too. Dropping her pants, she sat on the stool forcing herself to urinate, which was difficult since she cut back on her water consumption. She doubted if she was being filmed or that they were that interested in her bathroom habits. Leaning over, as if constipated, she searched her pants pocket. Finding the pills, she placed one in each hand and tried to decide where to place them. Even though they were small, they might look like a bump even if stuffed into her bra. Putting one hand up to her ear, as if scratching it, she inserted one pill into her ear. Pushing it just enough to stay in the ear canal, then she did the same with the other.

Once secured, she flushed, pulled up her pants, and exited the stall. Luckily, no one else occupied the restroom. She pulled out the hair closure and ran fingers through her long blonde hair. Realizing her jacket was in the lab camera video she took it off and turned it inside out exposing its vivid plaid lining. When Remy gave her the reversible jacket, she never thought she'd ever wear the colorful side.

Her heart sped up as she approached Anthony. Her decision was to talk to him, making it more difficult to search someone he regarded as a friend. "Hey, Anthony," she called out as he searched the employee in front of her. He gave her an answering smile.

She took one-step forward when the scary guard loomed up in front of her. He waved her into the inspection block, never saying a word. Did the man ever talk? Sticking to her original plan, she smiled up at him. "Hello, I bet this is a hectic time of day for you."

His hands were the size of Ping-Pong paddles as he brought them close to her. They seldom bothered to wand the scientists because metal was not what they were concerned about leaving the facility. Too bad, they couldn't do a daily mind sweep since information was what concerned them. Unfortunately, they'd have to reinsert the data the next day.

Inhaling deeply, Amy controlled her trembling as the giant ran his hands lightly over her body. His face looked flushed, as if he found the experience as awkward as she did. He never touched her hair or even her breasts. He waved her on without saying a word. She thanked him and earned a surprised look. She passed. Proceeding to her car, her heart began to beat normally again. Where could she hide the pills?

The memory ended without divulging the fact where she hid the pills. Did she flush them down the toilet afraid she'd be caught with them? No, she didn't go to all that work for nothing. She kept them. She was sure of it. Fixing the time in her mind, it meant she hadn't moved yet. Somewhere in all those painfully organized boxes must be the pills. Probably what her intruders were looking for, but they wouldn't have found them. She would have been clever, very clever. At first, she thought her mislabeled boxes were symptoms of a rushed mind. Now she decided otherwise. She had a reason for what she did. If only she could figure it out. Not all her memories were back. They popped in and out like bad radio station reception. No help for it, she would have to unpack all her boxes. Isn't that what people did who moved into new houses? Still, she had the feeling she wouldn't be staying long.

Amy couldn't remember the last time she saw Marybeth Lancer. Hadn't even thought about her, she was ashamed to admit. Hadn't seen her in the past few weeks, or had it been longer? It wasn't as if they were friends. Rather they were acquaintances who nodded heads in passing. Did she dare ask if she was still there? Biting her lips, she knew the answer. It would only draw attention to herself, which she didn't need. If recognition of changes around her would alert the higher-ups that she wasn't consuming enough of either the drug-laced food or that it was losing its potency.

Her head went up. Ryan was here. She could sense it. Odd that she knew he was here. It could be because an actual live person had entered the land of the science drones. The clock denoted it was twelve forty-seven. He circled the lab greeting everyone, saving her for last, perhaps believing it wouldn't look too obvious. Keeping his back to the camera, he asked, "How's it going, Dr. Newkirk?"

She looked up, aware only he could see the obvious relief in her eyes at his appearance. Mentally, she began to divide Theron employees into three camps, unaware, somewhat aware, and gone. She knew she was dangerously close to the third camp. Ryan was the only person she knew in the second camp. Beth might be more aware because of her recently diagnosed lactose and gluten intolerance that caused her to eschew more of the lunch options.

"Hungry." Not the most romantic words or even reasonably appropriate, but it was what she was. Her stomach gave a growl to confirm her statement.

Ryan placed a hand by his ear. "It's almost lunch time."

Instead of spitting out the words she wouldn't eat anything in the lunchroom on a dare, she murmured instead, "Yes, you're right. I am looking forward to the vegetable lasagna. How about you?"

"I ate before I arrived. Never know how long it will take at the hospital. Someone was having a birthday, so a local restaurant catered it." He shrugged his shoulders as if apologizing for eating non-tainted food. Amy mouthed the word, "lucky," while wondering how often she'd seen Ryan in the company lunchroom. Not much, come to think of it. His working between the facility and the award winning hospital must make it hard to contain the man. No wonder he was thinking for himself.

"On the run the way you are, you probably make use of Theron's mega-plus vitamins." She raised an eyebrow speculatively.

"I take them every day, never fail. Andy from the research team, I believe, gave me a lifetime supply." He chuckled, and then winked.

He knew. Thank goodness. Had he known for a while? It was something she wanted to ask him but couldn't here. "As a single fellow, I imagine you don't have the healthiest diet."

"Nope." He nodded his head in agreement. "In fact, I will probably stop at Loco Taco, grab dinner, and take it home."

She touched her nose to let him know she received his message. Was home his house or hers? Would it be safe to drive to his house? No, she knew the answer. Her best bet was to go home after a brief stop at the grocery and see if he showed up. So many questions she needed to ask him now that her memory was coming back.

Chapter Fifteen

Amy snagged a cart with a stuck wheel and shoved the recalcitrant cart through the produce section. She picked up a bag of organic apples and then put it down. It wouldn't do her any good to stock up too much. To keep her food supply reasonably safe, she had to buy her food fresh daily or live on drive-thru fare. Neither idea appealed to her that much, though there was probably a decent chance Theron didn't have every fast food employee on their payroll. While the employees might sell drugs from the restaurant, she seriously doubted if they were putting them in the food. Amy made a mental note to use restaurants not close to her house and never the same one twice.

Selecting three Gala apples, she placed them in a paper bag. It should be enough for her and Ryan if he should stop by. Steering her cart to the pet aisle, she picked up a few tins of premier cat food. Whoever took care of Samson spoiled him rotten. She should know this person. There was a connection. Left food for Pete's sake, not the thing a burglar or a cat napper might do. Comfort food too. The thoughtful cook may have left the poppet as well. This had Remy's fingerprints all over it. If pushed, her protective aunt could probably name her cat rescuer.

Another one of the cart's wheel refused to move forcing her to shove it toward the health food freezer case for all the good, it did her. There was no sprouted whole grain bread. Not too surprising when they shoved whole-wheat chocolate chip waffles, along with sweet potato casserole, and dark chocolate éclairs in the case. Fingering the waffle box, her eyes scanned numerous ingredients. "Flour Enriched, Palm Oil, and Palm Kernel Oil with TBHQ." She stopped reading and chose to count the ingredients. "Forty ingredients and I don't know what half of them are."

An elderly lady wearing a crocheted beret looked at her curiously but continued pushing her cart past her. The woman sported a T-shirt that proclaimed 'The Aliens Are Among Us.'

Amy watched her go, realizing the woman thought she was the crazy one. She probably wasn't the only one either.

Glancing at her watch, she needed to put some speed on. Unfortunately, her cart fought her every step. Spotting a pyramid of stacked spring water flats, she grabbed a case. Not too many ways a person could tamper with a sealed water bottle. Ryan might even be at her back door with a bag full of tacos. Having him come over wasn't a good idea, but she was so alone. It helped to bounce theories and strategies off him. Frankly, he also served as her factual memory.

No wonder he hadn't been able to understand when he'd been told she'd snuck away and met Mark. It would have been impossible since they spent most of every weekend together. Of course, Theron didn't know. No one did. Amy had rationalized that they were just friends, so the stringent protocol didn't apply to them. She pushed her cart in line and wondered if she hadn't wanted more.

A flash of a familiar face caught her eye. It was Stella. She had to be the key to all of this. Amy held her hand up to flag her down, but the woman darted down an aisle as if being chased by a pit bull. The man from New Mexico jogged through the doors, scanning the area, and his gaze pausing briefly at her, but moving on quickly. He obviously wasn't looking for her. Then who? She halfway turned and caught Stella peering out from behind a stack of disposable diapers. The man was after Stella. Leaving her cart, she sprinted after the man.

Catching him in the dairy aisle, she latched onto his arm. "Hey."

He turned slowly, slammed her with an irritated stare. Then, his eyes dropped to her hand still gripping his arm. *Oh my*, Amy gathered she was dealing with a dangerous individual. She should have thought it through. That's what comes from running on adrenalin and limited sleep. He wasn't just the man from Albuquerque. "Aren't you the man who tried to make me go to that spa?"

His lips flattened into a forbidding line, but he stayed speechless. Instead, he looked at her hand again, wiggled his arm to get free of her hold. Tightening her fist, she held on imitating a snapping turtle. "Why are you following me?"

He opened his mouth, and then closed it.

The words dead and danger flashed through her mind, but this might be her only chance. They were in a public place surrounded by people. The kid stocking the yogurt could serve as a witness if he killed her. She sighed deeply. It would literally wipe out any future she and Ryan had though. Future looked highly doubtful at the present. Wanting to live and grabbing the promised future made her bolder and even more impetuous than before.

The scent of cigarette smoke wafted off him too. Leaning closer, she hissed, "Don't bother denying it. I know something is up. You've been in my house. You followed me to New Mexico, not to mention trying to strong-arm me into visiting the alleged spa. What do you want from me?"

People began to gather, causing the man to say through gritted teeth. "Not here, I'll contact you later." He slid away, melting into the crowd of onlookers.

Amy watched him go, then, realized she left her basket unguarded with her purse in it. Great, she'd be lucky if she still had car keys, not to mention a car. Rushing back, she found her cart had been pushed out of line.

The granny in the crocheted hat nodded in her direction, saying, "It's not wise to abandon your cart. The world is not a safe place."

Flashing an apologetic smile in the woman's direction, she pawed through her bag verifying she still had a wallet and keys.

Not finished with her scolding, the woman pointed an index finger at Amy. "I had to chase away a would-be purse snatcher. A young woman who didn't look to be the criminal type, but you never know these days, had her hands on your purse until I scared her away." The cashier waved the woman forward, sparing Amy the need to answer.

Peering into the dark confines again of her purse, she touched the items in there. Her fingers slid over her wallet, her keys, a hairbrush, lip-gloss, and plastic square of tissues that Remy insisted she keep in her purse. Never knew when a woman might have an allergy attack or a good cry. Her fingers bumped up against paper, an envelope, peculiar since she hadn't put one in her bag. She half pulled it out enough to recognize her name on it and knew immediately that Stella left it. Fighting the urge to tear it open and find the answers to some of her questions, she shoved it back. Not the place or the time to peruse it, her head swiveled to see if anyone was watching her.

After the display in the dairy department, you'd think people would be waiting for the next dramatic event. It probably wasn't very dramatic. Considering the children terrorizing shoppers by racing down the aisle with their miniature carts, people had loud, intimate conversations on their cell phones, and a mother in the bread aisle yelled at her child to stop crying, which seemed to make her cry louder, her little scene was unimportant. A sudden crash made her cringe. Turning slowly, not knowing what to expect, she watched a breadcrumb cylinder row across the floor. The tiny cart racers had demolished the breadcrumb pyramid. An incensed employee and a red-face mother both showed up to scold the children whose faces reflected their lack of repentance.

Amy fought a small smile as customers turned and commented on the children and their lack of parental supervision. No one would remember her little tussle or even Stella running through the store. Nope, any talk would center on the demon children who destroyed the display. Placing her items on the conveyor belt, her anxiety returned. It was such an intrinsic part of her life. Sure, she had reasons to be anxious, her official stalker promised to visit her later, and the unread letter in her purse, and the possibility that she might need to run for her life in the next forty-eight hours. It was almost certain. Another reason she went light on the groceries.

On the drive home, her attention flickered between looking ahead and checking the rear view mirror. What did it matter if someone followed her? It appeared that everyone knew where she lived. Not only that, but they had already made free with her house. It didn't seem like there would be much left to discover. The tiny pills could be hidden almost anywhere, even in her vitamin supplements. Could she have accidentally swallowed her evidence? A sinking sensation filled her stomach while she struggled to breath. "Dear God, no," she muttered the words hoping she hadn't.

Driving more out of habit than actually being aware of the surroundings, Amy arrived at home still involved in a mental review of all her actions from the day her pseudo husband disappeared. Remy showed more paranoia about her food and supplement supply than she usually did. Perhaps it was intuition because there was no way her aunt could know the various machinations of Theron Corporation, especially since she hadn't fully unraveled the complex web. The more she remembered led her to other possibilities, rather like a set of Russian nesting dolls where one doll opens to reveal another. Unlike the dolls, her discoveries became bigger and more threatening as opposed to getting smaller.

Deep in thought, she separated her house key and opened her car door. Her aunt threw away almost all of the food she had stored in her cabinets, even the supplements. Did her aunt throw away the supplements? Why was she so driven to throw everything out?

As the local conjuring woman, Remy did have the ability to ascertain people's true intentions without asking and often gave them what they needed as opposed to what they wanted. As a scientist, she knew her aunt's incantations and potions went against everything in most medical manuals, but not all. The power of the placebo triumphed in experiments repeatedly in various drug trials often exceeding the actual drug results. The humble folks who came to Remy believed. Still, knowing all that, Amy realized her aunt possessed something extra.

A shadow detached itself from the side of her house startling her. A small dog-shaped shadow joined it, calming her racing heart.

Pointing to the bug, she scooped it up and wrapped her fingers tightly around it. Amy inserted the key in the door and pushed it open. She held one finger up to her lips until she'd replace the bug behind the fridge and clicked on the radio.

Ryan rattled the fast food bag. "Food is getting cold. I was beginning to get worried."

Stepping closer to Ryan, she gestured at the dog. "I see you brought Burton."

"Had to, I expect to stay the night."

Just like that, she shook her head considering his announcement as opposed to asking. True, his calm presence would help. Not addressing his alpha behavior, she instead said, "I stopped by the grocery, which was amazingly busy."

Samson meowed his hellos as the door opened. His casual greeting asserted no visitors came calling today, not that Amy believed she had a psychic connection with her feline. Rather the oversized alley cat took every chance he could to escape to the outdoors. Samson could fool those not used to his wily ways, which explained his earlier disappearance.

Burton trotted in, greeting Samson with a nose touch. Ryan followed putting the food bag on the table and the duffle on the floor. "I'll go out and get the groceries."

"Wait." The warning to avoid observation seemed foolish. Especially considering the man she feared would see him would be dropping by later. The alpha male who invited himself and his dog in for the night would not hide quietly in a closet while she conversed with her visitor or visitors. Ryan looked at her inquiringly. Not knowing what to say, she waved him on.

Her neighbors might see him, but then they must have seen him in the past. In fact, they probably wondered why he wasn't her husband. Bringing in groceries would just confirm that image. Not to say she talked to her neighbors much. Make that not at all.

Opening the sack, she inspected the contents. Placing the burritos and quesadillas on a plate, she warmed them in the microwave. They'd have to eat the tacos cold since it would take too much work to pick out the tomatoes and lettuce, and she'd gladly munch down on cold, safe food. An image of the letter deterred her from laying out dinner.

Opening the letter with equal share of anticipation and anxiety, she wondered what she would find. Would she find out she was a bold whistle blower or malcontent determined to cause trouble for her employer? She read the first line written in dark slashing handwriting that indicated either great determination or rush, or both.

> *Dear Dr. Newkirk,*
> *I apologize for my behavior at the gas station.*
> *If you are reading this, then obviously I found a way*
> *to get this to you. The number I had for you didn't*

work. I realize you may have felt obligated to dispose of that phone.

When I first agreed to take the USB to expose the Morpheus Project, I was not sure how much I believed in your claims of a major conspiracy and a drug that could change the general populace to mindless drones and often murderous ones too. Now, I believe.

Even though I showed my initial draft only to my editor, repercussions happened immediately. Someone looking for the elusive flash drive trashed my home. My editor, a new parent, received a death threat against his newborn child. He may have wanted to publish, but his wife convinced him not to. Still, it amazed me who knew what I wrote.

I feel unsafe. My brother gave me a Rottweiler for protection since I live alone. My dog vanished from my house. Often, I believe someone is following me, which explains my peculiar attitude at the service station.

I do believe these odd happenings trace back to the information you gave me. I am even more convinced the information you gave me must be made public. I am determined to upload it to the Internet, but I must disappear afterwards for my own safety.

I tell you this because I feel you are in as much danger as I am, if not more.

Stella

The sound of the door closing caused her to look up. Ryan had the case of water on one shoulder and gripped two bags in the other hand. "What has you so transfixed?"

Brandishing the paper, she walked toward him. "Read it."

He put down the water and bags and took the proffered letter. His eyes scanned back and forth. Then he looked up, raising an inquisitive eyebrow. "Is there something you want to tell me?"

"I think I might be a regular Woodward and Bernstein." She blinked twice, considering her words. "Stella is Woodward and Bernstein, and, as the informant, I am Deep Throat, which might be the reason I was assigned new memories."

Ryan placed the letter on the table. Wrapping an arm around her shoulders, he pulled her close to his body. "I was beginning to wonder as much. They chose memories of love and marriage that they thought would confuse a female mind. Maybe an average female mind obsessed with marriage, not yours."

Sucking in her lips, Amy shook her head emphatically and sighed. "I don't doubt your theory. It makes sense. All my memories of Mark are composed mainly of sex as opposed to romance. No engagement scene, no wedding planning together, no walks on the beach, or even snorkeling, which we should have done in a beach paradise. Scenes cobbled together by men. Any woman, even me, would remember their engagement with fondness. I couldn't even remember what I wore on my wedding day. All I can see is a couple in the distance with a priest. How would I be able to see myself as a third person?"

Ryan stepped away to pull out a chair and indicated Amy should sit. "It seems like sloppy work to me. There are tons of chick flicks out there, which could serve as a blueprint on what to include in a romantic memory."

Settling into the chair, thoughts in disarray, her eyes followed Ryan as he cleared the table. He removed the plate from the microwave. "Do you mind room temp water?" he asked breaking two bottles from the case.

"I prefer it." Her smile reflected a trace of whimsy. There were all sorts of diets out there. She probably had the only one based on avoiding drug-laced food from her employer. Then again, from what she heard about human trafficking, maybe others were determinedly avoiding their employer's efforts to drug them. "Drugged workers may make more compliant slaves but not always the most aware ones."

Twisting his bottle lid off, Ryan looked thoughtful. "You do have a point. I doubt we'll find any data on the matter. People conducting experiments that exploit unwilling individuals seldom publish their work. The original henchman must have believed if he gathered enough brilliant minds and drugged them into compliance that he could do anything. In truth, we have no clue how much has already been done.

Taking a bite of her quesadilla, Amy let the information percolate through her analytic process. "It would have worked, except for Aunt Remy. I am not even sure who called her. I doubt Theron did. The woman tore through my cupboards and fridge dumping everything. She spent two weeks feeding me fresh, untainted food, which cleared my mind some. I tried to continue the process by only pretending to eat at work. Each day, I'd remember a little more or question some of my memories."

Holding up a water bottle, he saluted the absent relative. "Hooray for Aunt Remy, a woman who always seems to see beneath the surface. Do you think she even bought the story you got married to a total stranger on the beach story?"

Her brows beetled as she considered the possibility. "Remy never corrected me. She supported me and fussed over me, but she didn't seem overly concerned about Mark. In fact, she made vague references about you and me not seeing what was right under our noses."

Stroking his chin, Ryan mused, "I doubt it would take too much insight to realize I was in love with you."

"I didn't know." Amy started to argue, but then stopped. It didn't say much about her intelligence. The drugs may have dulled some of her natural abilities, but still missing something like that was major. Changing the subject, she wondered aloud, "Why weren't you affected as much by the drugs?"

Taking another bite of his burrito, he chewed. "I know I got some over the years. Some days I felt less energetic with little desire to do anything else besides sleep after work. This is how they destroyed the employees' desire for a social life. The original kept us docile and unquestioning. The new formula you were working on could change people into everything from assassins to sex workers. Imagine a world where a select few decided what your purpose would be."

The thought dampened her appetite. Depending on who wielded the suggestions, it might be an even better, cleaner world free of impetuous crimes. Although she doubted it, those who held power usually had felonious intents. "You never answered my question fully."

Unwrapping a taco, Ryan took a bite, ignoring the begging canine at his knee. "Hmm," he swallowed and then answered. "Theron wanted its own doctors at the local hospital. Ones who wouldn't be alarmed at the chemical soup found in the employees' blood streams. Sometimes I felt like our job was to run interference with phlebotomists. I didn't just appear when you had your blood drawn. I was alerted."

Amy narrowed her eyes. "The nurse who liberally sprayed mucus on my sample with her sneeze so it had to be trashed may have done that deliberately?"

Ryan nodded. "The detectives were told the results were inconclusive."

Food she chewed and tried to swallow stuck in her throat. Ryan was part of the plan. Why didn't she trust her doubts back in New Mexico when she first suspected Ryan? Choking, she pushed herself away from the table, staggered to a standing position while still coughing.

His hands interlocked under her breast against her sternum. A quick push by his joined hands ejected the bit of taco onto the floor where Samson and Burton both dove for it.

Breathing easier, she slumped a little against Ryan's body. He said close to her ear, "If I were working for Theron would I have saved you from choking?"

"Probably not," she murmured. She wanted to believe. She didn't want Ryan to be one of the bad guys. "Explain yourself."

Sliding back into his chair, he began to talk. "I began to expect Theron employees might be drugged when I found the same chemical compound in all their blood. The excuse was a mega vitamin to keep all their employees healthy. Clemmons even gave me a case, I did not use. I believed at first but chose not to take any. Your fear of all things unnatural touched me. You wanted to grow all your own food and shop at the farmer's market."

Amy nodded her head in agreement but waved her hand for him to continue his tale.

"I took a bottle of the vitamins to a friend I knew, a chemist. I changed bottles so he didn't know the origin of it. I asked for a breakdown of what was in it. He thought I was on some devious mission to break someone's patent secret so I could developed a competitive product. I didn't dissuade him of that notion." His lips tipped up as if pleased with his chicanery.

Taking a sip of her water, she waited. "Well, what was in it?"

Holding up one index finger for emphasis, he said, "That was the beauty of it. It did have folate, potassium, manganese, even fish oil in it. In truth, it was a vitamin. Clive, the friend I asked to do the review, also came up with a dozen chemical elements he couldn't classify. Never had seen them before. He did recognize alprazolam. As you know, you find that in some of your anti-anxiety drugs."

"That would explain the calm, almost stupor-like appearance of my fellow employees. I didn't start getting too contrary until I tried to eat more cleanly. It was like a light bulb coming on. I could see everything that was going on around me clearer. Why was I the only one?"

A knock sounded at the door, causing Burton to erupt into a series of staccato yips. Ryan stood suddenly, almost knocking his chair down. He caught it before it hit the floor. "Are you expecting company?"

Was she expecting company? The man in the grocery came to mind. She hadn't even mentioned the incident. "Well, yes, I think it might be my stalker."

Chapter Sixteen

Another trio of knocks sounded indicating impatience.

Ryan's eyes took on a steely-eyed glare with his lips flattened into a determined line. Amy half expected him to tear open his shirt exposing a giant S or even green hued skin. He growled the words, "I'll take care of this."

Flying out of her chair, she caused it to tumble, which scared both the cat and dog. Latching onto his arm, she slowed his progress to the front door. "No, don't, I need to talk to him. He may be our break."

Ryan continued walking, dragging her with him. "I doubt it. Could be he's just obsessed with your beautiful self."

Snorting at the idea that a man could fixate on her, she continued to hold onto his arm. "Be nice. He strikes me as dangerous."

Ryan stopped to stare at her. "I can be dangerous too."

The light bulb flickered on again. He could be dangerous, very dangerous. She never noticed it before. The shy, self-effacing manner fooled many a cocky intern. Apparently, it fooled Theron too.

He threw the open the door ready to growl and snap at the man who was on the other side. Instead, a tearful Stella greeted them, pushed through the door by a grim faced Simpson.

The red-faced journalist looked up at them both apologetically. "He made me come," she said, gesturing behind her.

Amy nodded. "I see. I understand he can be most persuasive. Don't worry about it. Before we go to the kitchen," she directed a glare at Simpson, "I'll remove the bug."

Simpson grunted in acknowledgment. "Smart. Never fear, I will replace it tonight."

Amy moved toward the frightened Stella, leading her to the kitchen. Pushing her gently into a chair, she offered her a bottle of water, which she took with a nod and an audible gulp. Grabbing the bug, she rushed it outside. Wondering what happened to the men, she returned to the living room to find Ryan and Simpson eyeing each other. His name returned when she remembered him showing up before with Beth. It was a tiny triumph since it showed her short-term memory still functioned.

Simpson stood at the front door staring back at Ryan who blocked his way. With his back to her, it was hard to know his expression, but the body language was obvious, a wide stance, fists balled, and slightly away from his body indicated aggression. Burton joined his owner by standing next to Ryan's right leg and growling menacingly. The almost absurd looking dog transformed into a threatening looking creature. Samson slid into the room gliding up to Simpson then arched his back and hissed.

Simpson glared at the three of them. "This is ridiculous." Jabbing his index finger in Amy's direction, he said, "If you had this trio defending you originally, maybe you wouldn't have ended up in this predicament."

"Ryan, Samson, Burton enough." The cat and man stepped down, but the bulldog didn't.

Simpson looked meaningfully at the bulldog that advanced a few steps in his direction.

Slapping his hands together, Ryan said, "Burton, no." The dog stopped. Turning his entire body, he looked up at his owner with a canine grin and a wag of his stumpy tail. Kneeling to pat Burton's head, Ryan said, "Good dog."

"Good dog!" Simpson huffed. "He almost bit me."

Amy gave the man a disgusted look. "Then he would have been doing his job. Dogs serve as a warning and security system. Why are you here? Why have you terrorized Stella?"

The man blinked, maybe surprised at Amy's attitude. She refused to be the quivering mass of gelatin like the woman in the kitchen. To be fair, Stella hadn't been harassed for the last two plus months and perhaps even drugged for another third of her life. Nope, Amy was past scared. Now, she was angry, and revenge sounded promising.

Simpson blew out a breath, inflating his cheeks, making him look more an aging choirboy and less deadly. He was stalling and milking his image as a doofus security guy. Amy never bought it for a second. When he came and tried to separate her from the comfort of her Aunt Remy, she had typed him as hard and unforgiving, even in her confused state. "I didn't buy your security guy cover image, either." She took two steps in the man's direction, ignoring Ryan's throat clearing. "Sloppy if you ask me. Didn't think I would know who worked for Theron? Or did you think I wouldn't see you lurking around?"

The man shoved his hands in his pants pockets. Ryan stepped in front of Amy. "Calm down you two," Simpson complained. "I am not here to hurt anyone. I just want information. I believe your company is not only using you, but playing me too. I don't get played. As for the security bit, I agree with Dr. Newkirk. I thought it was stupid and said so. They assured me that you were so drugged out of your mind you wouldn't know what was up. Could we go into the kitchen and work this out? I have the feeling we might be able to help each other out. I have a sneaking feeling this is bigger than either of us can imagine. Whadya say, Newkirk?"

Amy stepped out from behind the shield of Ryan's body. "Sounds good to me. How does Stella figure into this?"

They stepped into the kitchen to see Stella struggling with the door that tended to stick. Simpson started toward her, but Amy waved him off. "Stella, please stay. We are going to talk this out. No one gets hurt, and you will get a career-boosting exclusive." The woman at the door stopped wrestling the stuck door and turned slowly as she spoke.

"Okay, tell me more." Returning to her place at the table, Stella's anxious expression morphed into a curious one. Perhaps feeling embolden by the presence of others, she pointed to Simpson. "He was the one following me, even chased me into the grocery store. Cornered me in the parking lot and made me come here."

Simpson slapped his hands on the table and leaned forward as he spoke. "I followed you because you were shadowing Newkirk. There are some shifty types trailing the doctor. I figured you were one of them."

Amy turned her head to watch each person. It was similar to watching a tennis match. Ryan held up a hand for attention. "Wait, what's this about other people following Amy?"

Oh yeah, how did she miss that comment?

The man resembled a low-level management employee with his cheap haircut and pasty complexion. He cracked his knuckles, and winced at the action. Wiggling his fingers, he said, "Fingers still hurt from discouraging two foreign nationals from pursuing you. They wanted you but settled for me since I happened to be in the way."

Ryan's lips thinned, expressing his doubts with that one familiar action. "You managed to fight off two would-be spies with your bare hands?"

"Dr. Korman," he said, startling Ryan. "Yes, I know your name and that you spent the weekend with Dr. Newkirk. That's beside the point. If properly trained, you could have whipped those third world thugs too. I did use a crowbar, quite the effective tool in the right hands. Ironically, fighting alongside a highway tends to attract men itching for a fight. I left after a few truck drivers arrived. A few accented words remarking on the stupidity of Americans is all it took to set off the Knights of the Highway."

It made sense that other countries would be interested in a mind control agent that would turn the masses into little more than unpaid servants and sometimes, killing machines. Ideally, they'd want it before it could be used on them. If not that, at least be able to use it in a manner that they'd have a fighting chance. Sure, feeding the drug to the public might result in an untrained force, susceptible to any command. What they lacked in skill, they'd make up in willingness to do acts that simple moral decency or logic prevented people from committing.

The thought of using the drug to insert memories of loving relationships, while somewhat pathetic, was harmless, especially if the person paid for that service. Using the drug and a command directive to override personal will to make someone into a slave was something else entirely. In the wrong hands, the world as she knew it would change drastically. Instead of feeding nubile co-eds Ketamine to rape them later without any resistance or memories, they could slip them some of the Morpheus agent and have a sex slave for life. Plenty of nefarious types would pay millions for such a product. Apparently, Theron already had it. Only two things stood in their way from making an astronomical amount of money.

She happened to be one of them. The disjointed dreams and memories that didn't make sense were fitting together.

Her jokes about using the drug to insert memories of a relationship that never was, she employed as a test. Once she realized the potential of the drug, her goal was to see if others had similar thoughts. The team pressed forward, ignoring her comments about ethics. They even embraced her idea of using it as a form of dating help. The men thought it might work to allow men, such as themselves, to overcome their social awkwardness and become full-blown bad boys.

"Oh my God, I remember." She shook her head as if to deny the memories.

All three chorused at once, "What?" Ryan looked concerned, while Stella flicked open a tablet, and Simpson looked preoccupied. He pushed up from the table, looked around the room. "What did you do with that bug?"

"It's in the carport." Amy watched the man shove open the stuck door. The sound of stomping reached them.

Simpson returned, locking the door behind him, and reclaiming his seat. "Safety precaution, yours." He looked at each face staring at him. "I guess in truth it is for all of us. Right now, they think you don't know much. As far as I can tell, you're little more than a test subject, but once you start demonstrating knowledge and active memory, then you're gone."

That's what she thought, but hearing someone else say it made it sound so final and deadly.

"I thought as much." Ryan wrapped his hand around hers and gave it a squeeze. She forced a smile for him but knew they both were in serious danger. Make that all four of them.

Acting as an unofficial chairperson, Simpson nodded at both Ryan and Stella. "Realize now we are all tied up in the same web. No easy way to walk away. Together we'll need to decide on some action."

Stella nodded. "I understand."

Ryan objected, frowning in Simpson's direction. "I would never walk away."

"Don't overestimate the power of love, buddy. Even so, it's too late."

Amy narrowed her eyes at Simpson. She was the only one here who knew all the details; shouldn't she be the one throwing out edicts? Oh well, apparently this man knew more about extracting himself from sticky situations than she did. "Why should I trust you? This could be an elaborate hoax?"

Three sets of eyes settled on Simpson. "You're absolutely right. You have no reason to trust me. I'll tell you my side. In my line of work, I have to be alert to the double cross. It's not a rare occurrence. It seems to happen more and more. Greed encourages my employers often to try to cut me out. Sometimes it is a security issue because they figure I know too much. This job seemed a bit bizarre when I took it. All I am supposed to do is watch you and report back. For this, I am paid as much as I would be to eliminate a ruler of a small nation."

Stella scooted her chair away from Simpson and closer to Amy.

The man continued, smiling slightly at the woman's actions. "I knew something was wrong immediately since no one had any interest in the missing husband. If they knocked off the man themselves, then there'd be no reason to look for him. The second, more amazing thought occurred to me, what if he never existed. I'd been in the house, snooped around, nothing male oriented anywhere in the house. Not even any boxes to be unpacked with masculine scrawl on it. I asked some leading questions of my employer giving him the opportunity to call you a crazy chick who imagined herself in love and married. Strangely, no opinion was forthcoming. My orders were to watch you, which I did."

Ryan shot one hand through his hair. "You did a hell of a job following us to New Mexico. I thought we were amazingly sly."

Simpson laughed. "You were. I have to credit your disguise too. Truth is I wasn't following you but following the trail of the elusive husband. I left Jergens to watch the house."

"What?" Amy shouted the word, afterward felt abashed at her loudness. "I mean, how many people are watching me?"

"Good question," Simpson remarked. "Truth is I don't know. Of course, they hired me, and I hired Jergens to take over surveillance on the house. You are being observed at work as you probably already know."

She nodded her head in agreement, encouraging him to go on.

"If those spics survived their beat down, then they'll be in town right about now. Word to the wise, they don't play nice like I do."

Stella huffed at his comment.

Ryan's brow furrowed as he twisted his lips in thought. "We have to do something immediately. I don't believe Amy can walk into that building one more time and live to talk about it."

She let go of Ryan's hand to rub both hands over her face. She thought as much today. "Okay, I agree we need to take action. Here's what I have. I suspected for a while that the employees of Theron acted as if drugged. I realized employees fed a constant diet of the initial formula would be more compliant to meeting the demands of their bizarre contract. We not only cannot talk about our work, which isn't too weird, but fraternization with other employees on off hours was not possible according to contract guidelines. They did everything possible to hire intelligent, socially awkward folks with no significant others, often no siblings or parents, which meant they had no one to use as a sounding board or reveal damaging secrets to. At first, this probably worked out well since they tended to hire people who were already naturally compliant. Long work hours never left time to question the unreasonable demands. We had amazing benefits. Healthcare that cost us nothing, but we have to use company facilities and physicians. Some of the doctors are pretty fine." She winked at Ryan.

"We couldn't bring in outside food or beverages, but we had all the food, beverages, and snacks we wanted free of charge, which got me thinking. What benefit was it to Theron to feed us? They had actual chefs preparing delicious meals regular, vegetarian, and kosher, once Epstein and Mernard joined. We had generous salaries, and once a month they brought in masseuses, so anyone who wanted a massage could get one. Sounds like the perfect job. A person would be crazy to complain."

Stella rested her chin in her hand and sighed. "Too good to be true. When did you start to suspect you were being drugged?"

Amy held her hands about a foot apart with palms facing. "Since I just finished the genetically altered crop project. I was quite concerned about the side effects of consuming such foods. I began to eat less and less food at the facility. Even skipping meals at times, but surprisingly the kitchen staff would deliver my favorite foods to the lab. I had a clue my food intake was under observation when I chose to skip lunch. When I didn't eat, it sent up a red flag. I threw away a sandwich and the chef asked me the next day what was wrong with it."

"Wow," Stella exclaimed, "they were more invested in you eating than my grandmother is, and that's saying something."

Placing her hands on the table, she rocked back a little in her chair and then dropped the front legs to the floor before continuing to explain. "Without the drug coursing through my bloodstream, I became contrary, questioning things that the others followed blindly. I was literally upsetting the apple cart. I couldn't understand why the others couldn't see what was so obvious. I put my neck in the noose when I argued vehemently against using college students as guinea pigs for the drug, even though I believed the original premise that it would make people more peaceful. On one level, I knew the drug has the ability to lull people into a docile, vulnerable state where they were open to the power of suggestion. That suggestion could easily be to kill or to stop killing. That's when I knew I had to take a sample out of the lab to be tested."

Ryan's mouth opened, and then closed. Finally, he shook his head. "You smuggled something out of Theron? With their security? Why didn't you tell me?"

"Trust me, it wasn't easy. I even impersonated Mary Beth to do it. Have you seen Mary Beth lately?" Amy felt sure that the OCD lab tech vanished, but she needed confirmation. If anything happened to her, then she was partly responsible.

Ryan's eyes flicked up before he asked, "Is she the one with the straggly bun and always arranging items in descending order?"

Amy bobbed her head in agreement. Maybe Ryan did see her. That would mean she was okay and that she didn't majorly screw with her life by pretending to be her.

"No." Using his index and middle finger, he tapped the bridge of his nose. "Can't remember the last time I saw her. It's been over a week, maybe weeks."

She slid down in her chair. It was, as she feared.

"Wait a minute," Simpson held up a hand with all his fingers folded down. "Let's see if I got this." Straightening his thumb, he said, "Theron employees get amazing benefits but no social life." Raising his index finger, he continued, "You quit eating after the GMO research."

Burton's hackles stood up as he faced the kitchen window and emitted a few low growls Simpson got to his feet, placing a finger to his lips. Using a combination of grace and stealth, he slid out the backdoor.

Stella's face considerably paler than when she entered, whispered, "I'm afraid."

Amy reached for her hand, deciding not to reveal her fears at this time. Ryan started to stand as if to go after Simpson, but she managed to land a detaining hand on his thigh before he deserted them. No reason for him to run into who knows what. Besides, she needed him in here. His face reflected his disgruntled state, as she said, "Who could be out there watching if Simpson was in here with us?"

The man in question slipped back through the door in time to hear the question. "That's what I want to know. I'll tell you who it wasn't—an amateur."

His dour manner did nothing to reassure the trio. Amy had to ask, "Did you see anyone?"

"No, I didn't, but that means nothing. Burton heard or saw something."

Ryan forced out a laugh. "I hate to ruin your theory, but this is a dog who sometimes barks at leaves blowing in the wind."

Simpson shook his head in a weary manner as he pulled out his chair. "I have ten years on you, Dr. Korman, and a world of experience. Paying attention to dog growls, even leaf crunches has kept me alive. Do not discount anything. An amateur leaves signs from noise, footprints, dropped items, even scents. There was nothing obvious in the dark. Come daylight, I might find something I overlooked. Time is of the essence. I would caution you against sleeping here because you might not wake up."

Amy gasped, causing Ryan to stiffen beside her. "Do you have to be so melodramatic?"

Patting down his coat, Simpson pulled out a packet of cigarettes. "Mind if I smoke?"

Amy shrugged. "Might as well. It wouldn't be the first time you smoked in my house."

He lit the cigarette, inhaled to get it going, before answering. "Never had. I wouldn't be that stupid. It leaves a smell behind."

The memory of smoke hung in the house after she returned to work. If not him, then who? How many people trooped through her house looking for evidence or possibly chemical formulas? It would be quite a bonanza to grab the recipe without paying for it or killing anyone for that matter. Felt like her house might be the hot spot for agents, counter agents, and assorted terrorists. How many people watched her? An urgency to flee the home she so carefully chose with such high hopes overwhelmed her. The need to flee stiffened her spine. A cough returned her back to the conversation. Stella had a lit cigarette in her hand. A small dessert dish served as an impromptu ashtray. Instead of outrage at people smoking in her house, she only wished she could smoke. Maybe it would ease her nerves. As a scientist, she knew better, but it didn't stop her from wanting to smoke.

Simpson pointed his cigarette at Ryan. "I'm only telling you the truth. You don't like it because you need to take immediate action. It changes everything."

Stella, calmer with a cigarette in her hand, turned to give Simpson a doubtful perusal. "Why should we trust you again?"

"Glad to see you got your pluck back because you'll need it. I am not a do-gooder, unless the cause happens to be me. This time it is about self-preservation, but I'm willing to take the three of you along. While I realize you probably think I don't have an immense store of ethics, I do have some. Theron crossed that line, maybe a couple of years back. Their way of cleaning up loose ends is to bury them. I am a loose end as are the three of you." He cocked an eyebrow at Stella before lifting the cigarette to his mouth.

She stubbed out hers and sucked in her lips before speaking. "Self-preservation is number one in my book. What do we need to do?"

Amy and Ryan turned attentive faces to Simpson who used the water bottles on the table to design some battlefield formation. Flourishing the half-full bottle, he said, "Here are the foreign operatives I know about."

Grabbing a full bottle, he pushed it near the ashtray. "Here are the ones we don't know about."

Amy was ready to argue over assuming there was someone else, but a look from Simpson silenced her. He knew more about covert operations than she did. Simpson pushed a tin of cat food near the ashtray, designating it as Theron, and in turn, surrounding the dish. She didn't have to ask if they were an ashtray, she knew.

A knock on the backdoor, they looked at each other. Would a murderer knock on their door? One who wanted to get the drop on them might. Simpson motioned them to the other room, unholstered his gun as he approached the door, standing off to the side. Ryan grabbed her and pulled her deeper into the living room. Would drywall stop a bullet?

A woman's voice with a definite Cajun accent announced, "I've come for the cat and dog." Samson greeted the woman with an affectionate meow. Who was it? Amy pulled out of Ryan's grasp to see who was at the door. A middle-aged woman dressed in a broomstick skirt and dark top weighted down with so many necklaces and pendants that gravity should have made her stoop. Instead, she stood straight, without fear, looking straight at Simpson who held a gun on her.

Recognizing the necklaces, the attitude, Amy moved closer to the woman. "Do you know my Aunt Remy?"

The woman smiled at her. "I am Althea. I haven't formally met your aunt, but she did put out the call for someone to watch over you. I answered it."

Not sure how to ask, she held out both hands, moving them as if trying to form the question, "How did she contact you? Um astral projection?"

Althea reached down to pick up Samson. "Not hardly, takes way too much energy. The Internet. We conjuring women have a sisterhood. Now, I have come for the animals since you will be on the run. They could track you with the animals."

Amy was quick to agree. Grabbing a bag, she started putting the cat food in it. Ryan eyed the woman. "I doubt Burton will go with you." As if to prove him wrong, the dog moved to Althea's side.

Althea placed Samson down beside Burton. Removing a necklace bedecked with jade, Jasper, onyx, and obsidian beads with a six-pointed star dangling at the bottom, she placed the necklace over Amy's head. Kissing her on both cheeks, she said, "Be at peace, all is well in the universe." The words gave her a sense of peace despite her known world splintering around her.

Gathering up the pet food sacks, Althea left, followed closely by Samson and Burton. Ryan stood close to her. "Damn, how did she do that?" He asked the words with a type of reverence.

Simpson looked at the closed door, then Amy. He reached for the necklace. She took a step back preventing him from touching it. "Please, it is a protection necklace. I don't want you messing it up with your negative energy."

Simpson continued to stare at the necklace until Ryan stepped in front of Amy blocking his view. Deprived of observing the necklace, he asked, "How did she know you would need someone to look after the pets?"

Amy pushed Ryan to the side. It was sweet how he tried to shield her. Maybe the drug made her unresponsive to her attentive friend. Another reason to get rid of the formula. Who knew how many people were not experiencing real lives. "Can't say how Althea knows things. It's her gift. Aunt Remy may not know who is watching me, but she does know someone has answered her request. It's hard to explain since it is an entirely different realm than the one I work in, but I've seen enough growing up not to discount it. According to Althea, we are leaving tonight."

Stella drifted into the room. "What now?"

Motioning to the hallway, Amy said, "We're heading to the office to unpack boxes. Inside one is the drug that is causing so much trouble. I didn't label it as evidence or drug. It can be hidden in a tiny container."

The four of them ripped off duct tape and unpacked boxes creating jumbles of seasonal clothes and unsteady stacks of books. Holding conch shells up to the light, Simpson explained his plan. "I have a plane and a pilot who can fly wherever you need to go."

Ryan started to answer, "That's good. We need to go—"

Simpson interrupted before he could finish. "Don't tell me. Tell the pilot. The less people who know the safer you'll be."

Stella followed the conversation while turning a geode in her hands. Flourishing the geode, she interjected in the silence. "I used to crack these open when I was a kid in an effort to find the crystal caves inside. This one has a line all around it as if it had been cracked open and glued shut. Why would someone do that?"

Amy leaped over the empty boxes to grab the geode. "Stella, you may have done it." Grabbing a letter opener from the desktop, she attacked the rock.

"Careful," Ryan warned, "you don't want to damage the evidence."

Breathing deeply, she tried to get her emotions under control. The image of her sealing up the rocks and packing them came clearly to mind. Wedging the tip of the opener in an area that was a little loose, she twisted the metal opener prying open the rock to reveal a small blue pill. "Here it is." She held the tiny pill in her hand. The four of them peered at the pill. The sound of a twig snapping broke their silence.

Simpson made eye contact with each one of them. He motioned them closer. "It's time to go, sooner than I thought. They will be watching our cars. How did you get here, Korman?"

"Came through the woods," Ryan indicated by gesturing behind the house.

Simpson narrowed his eyes. "Listen well. Ryan will take the lead. No noise, we'll discuss more in the car. Amy, tune your radio to some talk radio. It might fool them into thinking we're still in here for a little bit, not long. Let's go."

Chapter Seventeen

Amy's hand rested lightly in Ryan's back as he guided them through the dark woods. The tree branches filtered out most of the meager light a crescent moon offered. Stella's fingertips held tightly onto her belt loop. Simpson brought up the back, walking sideways with his weapon at the ready. What if Simpson was the real threat, not all these unknown people, or even Theron? What if they weren't running from danger, but running into it?

Ready to call a halt to flight, she turned to look at her house. Shouts and a few flashes of lights came from the bedroom where she'd pulled the comforter up over the pillows making it look as if someone was in bed.

Simpson caught up to the stalled group. "Get moving. That slight whine was a silencer. We're dealing with pros. Wouldn't be surprised if they blow the house to cover their tracks."

As if on cue, a large boom erupted, sending a fireball upward. "My house!" she exclaimed, while Ryan sped up dragging them up the hill. Simpson was on their side. Stumbling after Ryan, she fought the urge to stare back at her house. All her dreams and hopes for the tiny cottage were gone.

The car gleamed in moonlight as if a beacon. Ryan ran toward it, towing the rest of them behind in a parody of a childhood game. He unlocked the doors to have Simpson grab the keys. "I'll drive. It will be easier than explaining where we are going. Women, get in the back and stay down. There may be shooting."

Stella's eyes widened as Amy pushed her in. The female was going to have to toughen up to survive in the world of investigative reporting. Crouching in the back of car, she struggled with the seatbelt. It would be a shame to die in a car accident going to this much work to live.

Ryan slammed the passenger door. "This is a stick. Can you drive a stick?"

Simpson shoved his phone at him. "Push three, and tell him we'll be there in twenty minutes." He shoved the car into gear and took off leaving a bit of rubber in the process.

Ryan remarked more to himself, than anyone else, "I guess you can drive a stick."

"Yeah, I can. I can drive a semi, a tank, a tugboat, a plane, even one of those jetpacks like in those spy movies. The ability to drive any type of vehicle has saved my life more than once."

The car weaved down the deserted road with lights off hitting almost every pothole. She could imagine Ryan wincing at the damage inflicted on his classic vehicle. Still, he hadn't lost his house. Wondering about it, she yelled her question over the car and road noise. "How hot will a fire from an explosion burn?"

Making rapid turns in succession, Simpson replied, while watching the rearview mirror. "Four thousand, especially if thermite was used. Probably was. It even burns when wet. Makes it hard to put it out. Normal fires burn around eleven hundred Fahrenheit. I imagine an arson investigator can determine it was a bomb. Our friends back there may have done us a favor."

Ryan looked behind them. "What are you looking for? Any particular vehicle?"

Making another left turn, then a right, Simpson replied, "No, not a clue what they might be driving. Look for anything that keeps following us is the tipoff. That is what the turning is about. Once we get to the highway, I'll put on the headlights and get lost in the traffic. Dallas is always good for endless streams of traffic."

They drove in silence for a few minutes while everyone kept checking for possible followers. One helpful citizen flicked his lights, letting them know they forgot to put theirs on. Simpson put their lights on, only to flick them off after the car passed. As if suddenly remembering Amy's question, he answered, "Because an explosion burns so hot, there would be no human remains. I thought having our cars nearby would verify we died in the explosion, but the cars could melt if close enough to the fire. The best that can happen is they'll assume we were caught in the explosion when we don't show up for work."

Stella looked up from her rapid texting. "I guess I don't have to worry about anyone taking care of my houseplants. You could just drop me off."

Amy looked at the text. "Following up on Amy Newkirk story, more dramatic developments." She grabbed the phone from the protesting woman. "You can't send this." Simpson half-turned, grabbed the cell phone and tossed it out the partially open window into the heavy traffic.

"What did you do?" Stella exclaimed, looking back at her phone only to watch a semi roll over it.

"Saved your life. Thank me later. Phones have GPS in them. Your text message would serve as enough of a beacon for them. Toss out your cell phones. Your life is worth more than a smart phone. Folks burned up in an explosion would not have been texting or moving. Capesch."

Ryan tossed out his phone while Amy pawed through her purse for her prepaid phone.

Simpson threw over his shoulder, "Don't worry about the prepaid. I doubt you registered it under your name. Did you give anyone the number?"

"No, I didn't. The service I used didn't require a great deal of information. I used the name Kitten Lefaye," Amy admitted.

Ryan leered at her. "Sounds like a stripper name."

Amy shoved him, causing Simpson to clear his throat. "There will be plenty of time to play after you make it out of this meltdown alive. Get out your phone. I am going to give you my number to put in it. Remember once you call, leave the area immediately. If someone, somehow, can trace the phone tower, you don't want to be nearby."

Amy carefully placed his number in and read it back, even went so far as to call to make sure it worked. "Once we get there, what will we do for money?"

Simpson tossed a wallet he pulled from his chest pocket at Ryan. "There's five hundred dollars of small bills, plus a couple of prepaid credit cards. Use the money first. People are sometimes funny about accepting the prepaid cards, often wanting some ID. Just in case, I included identity cards."

Ryan pulled out a driver's license. He read the name. "Brian Mathers. I live at 476 Novel Drive, in Astoria, OH."

The traffic thinned out, and they made a hard left, driving along high security fences. Simpson turned the lights on and glided to a stop by a hangar where a prop plane waited. "Here you are, you two, you know what to do. I'll handle it from here."

A man approached the open driver's window. "Got them here with two minutes to spare."

Simpson nodded at the man. "You knew I would. Same drill as usual. "

The man laughed. "You need to get in another business." He motioned to Ryan and Amy. "You can call me George. Not my real name, but it will serve."

They could hear Stella complaining. Ryan looked back at his car. "Do you think he'll take good care of her?"

George smiled ruefully in the dim light. "There's not a female he can't handle."

"He was talking about the car, not the woman," Amy explained.

"Oh." George opened the plane door, waving them in. "That's a different story. There's a decent chance it might survive."

Ryan moaned a little while settling in his seat. Amy felt bad for him. If he'd kept his distance, none of this would have happened. She patted his shoulder. "Burton is okay."

"You're right." Ryan looked at her with gratitude. "More importantly, we'll both live and look forward to a future together. "

"That's right," she agreed eagerly, hoping to hide her own doubts about survival. She settled the backpack full of geodes and evidence on her lap.

George started the engines and asked, "Where to?"

"Thelma, Wisconsin," Ryan offered.

"Is that the city or the county?" George asked as he typed information into his computer.

"Can't call it a city. It is more a wide place in the road. Why?" Ryan eased his seat back. Amy followed his actions.

"Need someplace to land. Any long straight expanses, abandoned roads, airstrips, even unused schools. While I can do a short runaway, I do need some space," George confided with a cocky grin.

"Why can't we fly into an airport?" Amy wondered aloud.

"Part of the reason is we aren't filing a flight plan. We are also literally flying under the radar. Some kid will look up tonight and see a plane so close he'll swear he could touch it, which won't be too far from the truth. I may take some out of the way routes to avoid detection. The government is not whom we're hiding from, but they have less than secure sites. So why give them the info?"

"Right," Amy agreed, wondering how she could be starring in her action adventure epic. Her house turning into a giant fireball would have been enough. Teamed with Simpson's cloak and dagger routine and Indiana Jones wanna be with his bomber jacket and fedora piloting the plane, it was too much. Maybe she'd close her eyes and realize it all was a bad, convoluted dream. Her eyes drifted to Ryan's weary, stubbled face. Well, he was the one good thing about the whole experience. Her eyes shut as the plane powered up. The movement of it taxiing into place for takeoff jostled her. The low timber of male voices drifted between the noise of the engine revolutions.

"There is some kind of funeral home near my parents' cabin. It went out of business being in the middle of nowhere. I do remember them having an extensive parking lot. They took over a failed grocery."

"Sounds like a classy place. People must just be dying to get in there." George laughed at his own pun.

Ryan answered in total seriousness. "Apparently not or they wouldn't have gone out of business."

His reply made her smile. God, she loved that man. What? She opened one eye staring at her newly realized love. Hell, she was afraid this might happen when she slept with him. Why did it have to happen now when she had too much to think of, such as staying alive and finding Mary Beth alive?

George said something about the capacity of his fuel tanks and having to land somewhere to fuel up. It was the last thing she remembered.

Morning light came through the windscreen waking her. Cramped from sleeping strapped into her seat, she stretched. Where was everyone? A peek out the small side window revealed the men walking across a parking lot riddled with cracks. In the distance, she saw a warehouse structure with gold letters, picking out the words Madeline's Mortuary, Home of the Tasteful Goodbye. Amy decided it was more than the location that did the business in. She climbed out of the plane to join the men.

Morgan K. Wyatt

Ryan turned at her approach and pulled her into a much-appreciated hug. "Sleeping beauty is awake. Well, it's time to grab breakfast and hit the road."

"Hit the road, how?" She smothered a yawn with one hand. George pointed behind her with a grin. Why a man in the cloak and dagger occupation could be endlessly amused puzzled her to no end. She turned in the direction, he indicated.

A battered motorcycle waited. "It's a motorcycle," she said, stating the obvious. "Can you drive a motorcycle?"

"You're in luck. Having a father who went through a mid-life crisis, I learned how to handle one."

The faded vinyl seat had a spider web of cracks while long scrapes decorated the dark blue body. "It's not in the best of shape."

Ryan caressed the handlebars with a grin. "She might not win any beauty contests, but her engine is sound and the tires are new. That's what counts."

The tires did look new and had a deeper tread for all terrain climbing as opposed to a smooth road.

Ryan slid a leg over the bike "Luckily, George had this on the plane. It wasn't easy to wrestle this bike out of the cargo hold. It weighs a ton."

George smirked at them. "Naw, maybe six, seven pounds at the most."

After a quick meal of granola bars and water, Ryan studied the map before strapping on his helmet and handing her the other one. The day was crisp, and the leaves were turning. It wasn't a bad day for a ride if it didn't end in trying to grab evidence before the strong hand of Theron smote them out of existence.

She padded out her rock-filled rucksack so it wouldn't hurt too much. "It's not that I don't trust you, George, but I have control issues that means the bag stays with me," she offered when she saw his eyes resting on the backpack. He laughed and waved them off.

Ryan drove through the winding roads as if sure of his destination. The motorcycle started to climb. The paved road gave away to gravel flinging stones until they finally reached the cabin. A beautiful lake shimmered in the distance. He stopped, letting the engine idle. "Not there yet. The bunker is higher up due to the water table."

Tightening her arms around his waist, she leaned into his back as he forced the bike over rough terrain. Reaching an area with a few large boulders and scruffy pines, he killed the motorcycle engine. Pointing to two cylinder rocks with a third flat stone on top, Ryan said, "I marked the bunker's location. Remind you of anything?"

Trying to see the rocks as a symbol as opposed to a bunch of rocks, she thought she got it. "Pi, right. I recognize it as the symbol for Pi."

"You got it. For your efforts, you get a kiss." He placed his lips on her hair.

"Really, you call that a kiss?' Amy grabbed the front of his jacket and pulled him in for a real one. Standing on her toes, she landed her lips on his, thinking for a brief second this was her first kiss when she knew for sure she was in love with Ryan. The kiss deepened on its own until they stumbled into the Pi formation.

Ryan's eyes twinkled. "That's what I call a kiss. What caused you to stop holding back?" He walked to an area between two pines and started kicking dirt away exposing a metal door.

With his back turned to her, she managed to say the words, "Looking death in the face made me realize how much I didn't want to die, that and loving you."

His head jerked up to stare at her. "Come closer. I want you to know the combination of the family bunker since you'll be an official partner."

Squatting on the ground next to him, she watched him punching in numbers. "Isn't that your birthday?"

"It is. Good of you to remember. Then it's my mom's birthday. My dad was big on obvious things. The door clicked. Pushing it open revealed a cavernous dark hole. Reaching inside, Ryan pushed a button that turned on some low lights. "I charged up the battery when I was here a couple of months ago. I knew then, something was up. On one hand, you made more time for me, you were more aware of your surroundings, but, on the other, you were frightened and refused to tell me why. I was more than happy to hide your package. Want to tell me what's in it?"

She followed him down the flimsy stairs to a small windowless room that was worthy of a vintage movie set. A folding table was piled high with board games and puzzles, and a tiny kitchenette had flats of bottled water and canned goods.

"Wow, your parents were really prepared. The box is the computer I had all the smuggled Morpheus files on. I gave Stella the USB without the chemical formula. I figure no one needs that. I thought of getting rid of my computer, but I lived in fear of someone finding it and the recipe."

Ryan walked to a large portrait of dogs playing poker. Placing it on the floor, he revealed a safe. "Want to guess the combination?"

She hazarded a guess, realizing if anyone with a touch of intelligence suspected Ryan, there would be no duct-taped box inside. "The same as the bunker door." Inhaling deeply, she held her breath until he reached inside and pulled it out. Letting her breath go in a gasp, she grabbed the box. It felt the same. "You never opened it?"

"You told me not to." He pulled a pocketknife from his pants.

Opening the knife, she attacked the box. "I had a whole plan. I made CDs with information, even flash drives. In all, I eliminated ingredients. I figured it wouldn't be too hard to find people as devious as Theron's higher-ups. I was going to release the information at some Internet café, something I saw on a movie once. I even had the envelopes inside to mail the data to major news organizations. I was so careful. Wore latex gloves, used preprinted labels, everything, before I forgot who I was. When you came back from hiding my package, I was clueless who you were."

Placing a hand on her forearm, he stopped her shredding the tape. She turned to meet his somber continence.

"I came back and heard about your runaway marriage. I could have kicked myself for not making my intentions clearer. Then, in the hospital, you kept calling me Dr. Korman, which almost broke my heart. Everything we shared from the hot air balloon ride to the turtle races disappeared. I was a stranger to you, not the man who loved you desperately and was trying to woo you in my own inept way. I knew then, they'd done something to you. I wasn't sure. Maybe if I had been faster with my own covert research, I could have prevented it."

Placing the knife on the package, she covered his hand with hers. Turning her head slightly to look up at him, she said, "I know you now. Together we can expose Theron's evil machinations. Know a coffee shop or library where we might download the files?"

Kissing her hair, he murmured into it, "One or two. More in the next town depending on how far we want to travel."

Exhaling, she allowed herself to lean back against him. Amy closed her eyes for a second, allowing Ryan to wrap his arms around her, which gave her the illusionary sense of security. Then again, how much safer could you be in a bomb shelter in the middle of nowhere? How long had she been little more than a zombie scientist? "Do you think we were always drugged?"

Ryan leaned his head against hers for a second. "No, I don't think we were, but I wonder if it was always in the works. Think about the people they employed. Brilliant minds, introverts, worker bees with no social network to comment on if things didn't seem right. They always offered free food and beverages. In the beginning, we did things together, even though it was forbidden, and you acted more like the woman I chose to mentor, but then you became driven, all work, all the time."

Just a second more of feeling secure and reasonably happy before she shifted back to the reality of running for her life. "I can remember dinner in a swanky restaurant and you discussing the newest pharmaceuticals." His laughter vibrated between their two bodies. It added more to the feeling of intimacy rather like some emotional super glue.

"Do you have to keep bringing that up? That's one memory I hoped you'd forget. I knew we couldn't fraternize, but I believed if I could convince you of how perfect we would be together that we could run off and marry. It would be a done deed. I also rationalized that we were both too important to Theron to fire. If they did, we would still have each other. I ruined it by talking drugs instead of telling you how I felt about you. Is it any wonder I'm alone?"

Their elegant dinner together made more sense. "Ryan, when you were opening the bunker and told me to watch the combination because I would need to know it since I would be part of the family, was that a proposal?" Surely not.

His laugh was a tad self-conscious. "Yeah, pretty lame, I know. On the flight here, I kept thinking what if this is the only time we have together? I want to make it count. If nothing else, I want you to know where you stand in my life. What's your answer?"

She drove her elbow backwards a little, earning an "*Umpf*" for her efforts. Straightening, she turned and looked Ryan in the eyes. "I'd say you need to work harder on your proposal. That's what cued me to my fake marriage. There was no great proposal scene. I plan to survive, as do you. With that in mind, I want a great proposal. You'll agree that I deserve it. Once we save the world, you can work on planning it."

Ryan grabbed her shoulders to pull her in for a fast, hard kiss.

Slightly dazed, Amy asked, "What was that for?"

Ryan grinned. "You just agreed to a pre-proposal, which takes some of the pressure off."

Rolling her eyes, she went back to ripping open the package. Opening it, she shook out the pre-stamped envelopes, latex gloves, a battered computer and power cord. Slipping on the gloves, she checked the envelopes, then, sealed them. "We can drop these off at the nearest mailbox. They are small enough that we don't have to enter the post office to mail them."

Ryan walked closer to stare at the array of evidence. Amy held up a pair of gloves to him. "No thanks, I'm off today. I'll just watch you. You thought of everything. I never want you working against me."

Opening her backpack, she pulled out the rocks and wedged the computer, power cord, and envelopes inside. "If we can pry open these rocks, I can remove the evidence, which will make it easier to carry."

Ryan began opening drawers in the tiny kitchen cabinets. "Here's a butter knife, which should work better." They both began forcing the thin blades through hairline cracks in the stones sometimes using the other rocks to hammer the knives in. Rocks popped open revealing a pill or two, and tiny vial. "You even got the liquid form. How did you manage that?"

Amy shook her head. "Do you really want to know?" At his avid look, she continued, "I took advantage of men's natural aversion to anything to do with menstruation."

"Ick, you got me there. What happened?" Ryan popped opened another rock revealing folded up paper. He began to unfold it.

"As you well know, we women don't carry purses because of the search, but I needed tampons for my period. Therefore, I started bringing this plastic case full of tampons at that time of month. The first couple of times they thoroughly examined the case, embarrassing both of us. Then they stopped. I figured they were well aware of my cycles, as they seem to be of my food preferences. I carried them in at my normal time, but one applicator had the vial shoved up the cylinder I'd carefully covered up with the plastic tampon sleeve." She smirked, thinking Ryan would find the story amusing, but his interest was on the paper in his hand.

"I see you found the recipe."

His only response was "Un-huh." Amy searched through the cabinets for something to store her evidence in. Carrying the small container over to the table, she asked, "Is it what you thought it would be."

Ryan looked up, his brow furrowed. "Some. I recognized Acetylcholine as a memory blocker. Sometimes it's in your OTC sleep aids. Then there's Chloral hydrate. It is a hypnotic sedative, although it has a limited time span. Some of these, I've never heard of, and I doubt you could find them in your local pharmacy. It is no wonder the employees enjoyed endless free food. Working the employees long hours while pumping them full of sedatives, it is no wonder they stumbled home and went to bed. Forget the contract. They had no energy left to do anything."

Amy plucked the list out of his hand and placed it in the container. "You seemed to have more energy than most. Why weren't they suspicious?"

Ryan closed the safe and replaced the picture while talking. "They were at about three or four years into the project. I kept getting questions about coffee or if I had lunch at the cafeteria. Clemmons personally passed on cases of vitamins I was supposed to take daily, which I assured him I did. I also imitated the slightly dazed appearance of the other workers. Most importantly, I never questioned anything."

Working her arms into the backpack straps, Amy admitted, "Questioning was my mistake. If you thought people might be drugged, why did you never say anything to me?" Ryan's bewildered expression answered her inquiry, more than words could. "Oh, you did say something to me. What was my response?"

Indicating the steps, Ryan waited until her head was clear of the opening before turning off the lights. Sliding the bunker door shut behind him, he reinitialized the lock. He stood, dusting off his hands. Motioning to the backpack, he said, "Let me carry it."

Handing it over, she said, "You never answered my question." Her head swiveled automatically, checking the surrounding area for people among the pines, the start of a hardwood forest, and a shimmering slice of lake. Sadly, every unknown face became a threat. Still, who would be out here in the middle of nowhere on private land?

Ryan mirrored her motions, peering into the distance. "I hinted around several times to see what you knew. Each time you never bit, never responded. It made me wonder if my suspicions were correct. I respect your mind more than my own. My chemist friend, at first, had personal issues that prevented him running the test in a timely fashion. Finally, I got back the list of ingredients from the blood samples I sent him. The issue with the blood was the individuals could be taking other pills. The problem with the vitamins is they might not have represented what folks inside the corporation had. Even though Theron employed me, I spent most of my time outside the confines, which meant my security clearance was lower. In retrospect, maybe I didn't need to be drugged as much."

Amy considered his words while he guided the motorcycle along the overgrown path, which led back to the family cabin. A rustle in the bushes startled her until a black squirrel darted out, giving her an indignant look before scampering across the path. It took them only a few minutes to reach the cabin.

Swinging her leg over the bike, she waited for Ryan to cut the engine before replying. "Makes sense. Why drug the people who aren't giving you any trouble. On the other hand, drug up the troublemakers. Guess that explains why I was drugged." Her half-hearted laugh emerged from her throat. People often mistook her for a rule follower, and she was, until she decided the rule needed to be broken.

Ryan bumped her shoulder as he walked beside her. "One of the reasons Theron offered such generous medical benefits was to have access to the employees' medical records. They needed to know the dosage they could use, the side effects of combining medication they already were on, even if they were pregnant."

"Pregnant?" Not that she was, but maybe she could be. The last time at the motel, they forgot to use a condom. "What's wrong with being pregnant? I can't remember anyone having a baby. Theron workers tended to be poster children for the Zero Population League."

The rustic cabin was visible through the spruce branches as they walked along the perimeter of the lake. Ryan's head swiveled side to side as they strolled. "It's a beautiful day for a hike," he announced out of the blue. Lowering his voice, he added, "If anyone was watching us, I didn't want to give them a clear trail to the bunker. It may end up being our safe hole."

The thought caused her to shudder. The fact she might need an underground sanctuary was bad enough. Better to have one than not to have one. She grunted her discontent, causing Ryan to smile. He pulled out a set of keys, located the right one, and put it in the heavy padlock. Setting the padlock aside, he undid two more locks and pushed the door open.

Amy started inside, but Ryan's outstretched arm stopped her. "Let me check everything out. The locks may not have stopped anyone who entered through the back window."

Great, she thought, watching Ryan and her backpack enter the cabin. Ryan disappeared from view, causing her heart to race and blood pressure to shoot up. His "All clear," shout allowed her to enter. Her eyes roamed over the contents of the small cabin. A plaid sofa and chair dominated the living room. Photos crowded the fireplace mantle. Amy drifted closer, picking up a snapshot of a younger man with Ryan's distinctive features proudly holding up a

Morgan K. Wyatt

fish. What a cutie, even then. Amazing, somehow she had missed the man's latent sex appeal.

Noticing the picture she held, Ryan said, "Thought I was ready to be a professional fisherman with that five pound largemouth bass."

"Notice you didn't go pro. The world of medicine would be a poorer place." She placed the picture on the mantle, hearing his soft swears. "What is it? I mean besides being chased by people who want to kill us."

Sticking his hands in his pockets, Ryan just shook his head. "It's me. I had such grandiose plans that I would doing something that matters. I started out well. Published much talked about papers, even served on a think tank for a few months, then I was enticed away by Theron, and in turn, I enticed you. Not exactly helping the world."

"Hey," she said, as she interlaced her fingers with his, "we are going to save the world from becoming mindless clones under the rule of some nefarious despot. That has to count."

Pulling their joined hands up to his lips, he landed a kiss on the back of Amy's. "I thought we could wash up some, eat something, change clothes, and head out to town to mail your packages."

"It sounds good, but eat what? Wear what?" she asked, still keeping her fingers interlaced with his.

Pulling her into the kitchen, he opened a cabinet full of canned goods. "Not the tastiest assortment, but it is food. My dad even got K-rations from a service friend. You can actually buy them. Most have a chemical pack that even heats them up. You have your choice."

Kneeling, she read the labels and withdrew one that promised to be beef stroganoff. "I'm betting this is not part of my farm to table diet."

Ryan selected chicken chow mein and demonstrated how to heat the meal. "Most of the mixtures aren't too bad. You just don't want plain meat because it is as tough as shoe leather. The water will be cold because the generator isn't going. I'm not sure if we want it or not because it is noisy and will only signal our presence."

Digging into a stroganoff, she bobbed her head. Holding up a laden fork, she said, "I thought this would be horrible, but it's not too bad. Even tastes like real food. Well sorta. So tell me about the clean clothes I am going to change into."

His eyes roamed over her body as if gauging it.

"Stop it. We don't have time for that. We have a world to free from possible domination."

Ryan chuckled as she hoped he would. "Truth is I was wondering if my mother's clothes would fit you. She carried a bit more weight than you carry but was always fond of the elastic waistband. I thought we could disguise ourselves as middle-aged lake people. We will have to be sure to wear fishing hats too." He chased the last bit of chow mein noodles around his tin as he spoke.

A few minutes later, a little chilly from a rain water wash-up, Amy emerged from the bathroom in purple stretch pants and a brightly flowered top. "New from Paris," she mocked and twirled in a circle.

"Great," Ryan remarked and handed her a fishing hat bedecked with an occasional silk flower. "Put this on."

Shoving the flower-decorated cap on her head, she noticed his frown. "What's wrong? How could I put a hat on wrong?"

"It's the hair. Pull the hat down more. Men will remember a good-looking blonde-haired woman with a great body. The clothes do a fair job hiding the great body, but once they see your hair, they will wonder about the body under all that fabric. Better if they don't wonder."

Amy wedged the hat down over her ears. "So do you think I am a good looking blonde with a great body?"

Ryan put on his fishing hat, completing his wardrobe change. "The fact you don't know that's what I think is more damning evidence against my courtship style." He took two steps and swept her into his arms. "Know this. I have loved you for as long as I've known you. I did pick you to mentor because of your brilliance and undergraduate distinction. Part of me picked you because I just wanted you around. Your keen intellect, your smart mouth, your snapping turtle tenacity all wrapped up in a killer package. I think the male residents I passed over had a clue."

Amy's eyes twinkled. "That would make you chauvinistic," she teased, dropping a quick kiss on his lips.

Ryan took the kiss as an invitation, deepening it, causing Amy to forget for a second the reason behind their impromptu trip, but it rushed back all too fast when the kiss stopped. "As for me picking you, if you mean to imply that I am an intelligent man, then you'd be right. Let's go save the world."

Amy donned the backpack since it would be easier to cling to Ryan's back without the pack between them. Inhaling deeply, she thought this is it. *My real intention before I forgot everything.* Slinging her leg over the bike, her mind catalogued everyone who was involved in the mission. Anyone could be the break in the chain that could get Ryan and her both killed.

Ryan expertly guided the bike through the winding roads allowing Amy time to analyze the facts. Stella and Simpson didn't know their final destination. Sure, George knew they were in Wisconsin. Even if the cheerful pilot took a bribe, there were miles and miles of hardwood forests to search.

Houses and buildings started to line the road the closer they came to an actual town. Guiding the bike to the side of the road, they slowed to a stop.

"Might want to don those gloves now. It would definitely look suspicious if you don them in front of a mailbox," Ryan added, pushing the bike kickstand down. Amy carefully slid off the back. Ryan dismounted and stood in front of her to shield her from curious eyes.

Ready. They both mounted the bike. They spotted their first mailbox in front of a convenience store. Amy dropped her first envelope addressed to CNN in Atlanta in that one. She decided to put them in different mailboxes. In the end, the same post office would process them, but she didn't want to take any chances.

They eventually stopped at a familiar looking fast food restaurant. "I heard they have Wi Fi here. Trying to attract the coffee house crowd, even have power bars for people to plug their computers into, which will work out well since your battery is most likely dead."

Amy headed for a table in the corner while Ryan went to the counter. At the closest table, two mothers gossiped while their young children flung French fries at the floor. An elderly man in overalls, nursing a coffee, smiled at her. She looked away not wanting to invite contact or remembrance.

Unzipping the bag, she removed her computer and power cord. Plugging in the cord, she mentally crossed her fingers and pushed the power button. What if it didn't work after being stored in the ground for a couple of months? She exhaled as the familiar Windows logo chimed. "Thank God."

Ryan approached her carrying a small plastic tray with two cups and something else on it. He slid in on her side, wedging her in, but giving her a feeling of security too. "My parents always sat on the same side of the booth. I used to think it was because they had me, but now I realize they just wanted to be next to one another. It was a tragedy they died before their time, but I guess it was good they went together."

He placed her tea in front of her, along with a fruit pie. "Thought we might want to celebrate."

Amy shook her head. "Not until I'm sure."

She had bookmarked all the news places she wanted to contact. Instead of using her own email, she used their contact pages. Who knew how long it would take them to get to them, but outside of emailing and snail mailing, she was unsure what else she could do. Couldn't exactly hold a news conference. She'd tried to get the information out through Stella whose contribution failed before it ever happened.

Attaching the appropriate file to the contact form, she clicked send. The missive went. The women next to her still gossiped. Their kids were out of fries, and one was reaching for the mother's oversized drink. No fanfare, no rain of bullets, nothing. She reached for her lukewarm tea.

Sipping her tea, she watched Ryan peck out a few words on the keyboard. "Hah, I thought as much." He turned the computer screen to Amy so she could see what he was reading. The bold headlines denoted that a major pharmaceutical company went up in flames last night. Several fire engines filled the picture frame, but she still recognized the parking lot where she parked the last several years. A few taps brought her to the article.

> *Late last night, nearby residents of the pharmaceutical giant heard a loud boom. The sound dismissed as coming from the nearby airport until flames shot into the sky. Night watchmen at the plant called in the fire. Seven stations responded to the large fire without much success putting it out. Water transported the fire to different areas of the complex. A HAZMAT unit assisted in dousing the flames. The flames burned extremely hot for hours, even destroying cars close to the building. The facility is a total loss. Theron's CEO has not responded to inquiries about the nature of what production was in process when the facility blew.*

She pushed the computer back to Ryan. "It makes me feel better, but I am still not a hundred percent convinced of my safety." The pie's aroma tempted her. Opening the packaging, she asked, "What do you think will happen to everyone?"

Using a bent knuckle, he rubbed his forehead. "I would think the supply of the drug, or at least the majority, was destroyed in the fire. Your fellow workers will come out of their chemically induced state and awake to the real world. Imagine Clemmons is on his way to his little love shack in Bali, with Belinda his secretary, or some place that doesn't have an extradition treaty."

The chunk of apple pie lodged in her throat. She had no doubt the man had the recipe. All he needed was willing workers, always easy enough to come by when you waved money, even easier when you drugged them. Grabbing the pack, she rifled through it finding her prepaid phone. Turning it on, she noticed it was almost out of power. A quick riffling of the bag didn't yield a charger. "Damn," she said, earning a glare from one of the gossipy mothers.

Oh great, their children trash the place, but she got the Medusa stare for one cuss word. "Let me out, I need to get outside and try to make a call." Ryan stood to allow her to exit. She slid out the side door, but stood in front of a window, only a few yards from Ryan and the food-flinging tots.

"God, let this work." She punched in Simpson's number. It rang a few times. She heard the phone pick up. "Clemmons is running, has a place in Bali." The phone chirped as it died. Great, she'd never know if he got the message or not. She needed a charger. Sometimes motels, even truck stops had some charger on steroids that would charge your phone in a minute. That's what she needed.

Before she could tell Ryan what they needed, he came out with the backpack and a serious expression. Grabbing her arm, he urged her in the direction of the bike. "No time to talk now," he said, as he started the machine.

Amy tightened her grasp, and he sped up as he left the town limits. She wanted to live, and it felt like Ryan was determined to get them killed. After several traumatic minutes, he switched off the cabin road, even turning into the underbrush at one point to come up behind the cabin. Stopping the bike, he said, "Let's get rid of that computer."

"What?" She swung the backpack in front of her and hugged it as if it were a child.

Urging her back into the underbrush, he made a zigzagging path to the bunker. "Back at the restaurant," he gasped the words as he ran toward the destination, pulling Amy behind him, "I saw two foreign-looking guys, the ones Simpson told us about."

Amy jogged after the man she formerly thought was one of the most brilliant minds she knew. "You never saw the men Simpson mentioned. How do you know these guys were it?" A stitch was working its way into her side when they stopped at the tumbled down PI marker. Thank goodness.

Squatting on the ground, Ryan pecked the code into the lock. "I don't know, but put it this way, why would two foreign men shown up in Bertha, a town so small it isn't even on a map? I am pretty damn sure one was asking for information, and I think he said Korman, hard to tell with the accent."

A sense of dread dropped over her like a blanket. "I thought this was all over."

Ryan took the bag from her and motioned her in. He slid the door closed, which made an ominous clicking sound. There was finality about it. If people ever did use it as a bomb shelter, they entered it expecting the world they knew to vanish. She could definitely relate. "What's your plan?"

The dog picture rested on the floor as Ryan manipulated the number pad on the wall safe. "For now, we are going to have to leave the computer in the bunker. I am the only living person besides you who knows the bunker exists. Then we will have to try to get to Madison and turn ourselves over to the authorities, who will put us in protective custody."

"You hope, "Amy added.

Ryan turned to stare at her. "What do you mean?"

Taking a deep breath, she held out both hands. "Why would they believe us? You have to admit it sounds far-fetched. Right up there with alien abduction."

Placing the picture on the wall, he fiddled with the keypad. Amy looked at her watch then back at him. "We need to get out of here. What are you doing?"

"Changing the combination. If we have operatives smart enough to track us to the cabin, then I am betting they know my family's birthdays. Most passwords are pet or children's names, while combinations are birthdays or anniversaries. I'll need to change the outside one too."

Amy's heart raced like a Greyhound. They needed to be gone, far away from the place. Her teeth worried her bottom lip until she tasted blood. Ryan ushered her up the steps, where he repeated the procedure. Her clenched fists left crescent-moons on her palms.

Ryan stood, staring at her lip. "What's wrong with your lip?"

"Let's just go." She tugged at his hand to get him moving. Together they picked through the underbrush trying to be as silent as possible. As a kid, she used to enjoy pretending to be a pirate or an Indian princess. Part of playing usually involved sneaking up on Remy. Who knew she'd ever make use of her pirate skills?

The coast was clear around the cabin. Rushing across the open ground, they reached the porch. Cowering behind a rustic rocking chair, she barely breathed, as the various locks were opened. "Inside," Ryan said, pulling at her jacket. Her noodle-like legs caused her to stumble. Ryan grabbed her shoulder before she kissed the floor. Ushering her to a chair, he helped her sit. "Stay there," he ordered. "I am going to see if there is anything in this cabin we can use."

Grabbing a flowered tote bag, he worked his way through the house. Throwing in bottled water, a few K-rations, then he headed to the bedroom. Amy wondered if she should help him, but why would she know where anything was stored? It sounded like he said something. She almost answered when she realized the voice didn't come from inside, but outside. Another male voice answered. Amy slid from the chair and crawled to the window. Peering out, she spotted the two men. If she had any doubt about their identities, the guns in their hands pretty much screamed that they were the enemy.

Lucky them. The friendly people in Bertha gave good directions. The image of Ryan practically dragging her into the living room drew her eyes to the door. It was unlocked. A two by six piece of wood stood beside the door ready to ram through supports on either side of the door. Two large steps got her to the door. The wooden bolt proved to be heavier than she expected, but she still managed to get it in place smashing three fingers on her right hand in the process.

"Hey, look at what I found," Ryan said, standing in clear view waving a pistol.

Amy turned ready to warn him about the intruders, but a bullet shattered the window glass doing the job for her. Ryan hit the floor. She stayed, splayed against the door, her eyes fixed on his body. Did the bullet hit him? Was he dead? Oh no, it was all her fault. Determined to make the bastards on the other side of the door pay, she crawled toward Ryan and the pistol he held. His head came up reassuring her he was still alive.

Her breath came out in a whoosh she didn't even realize she was holding. Their eyes met, an entire discussion about love, life, and the possibility of a future was in the brief look. Ryan crawled to the kitchen. She followed. Squatting by the sink he whispered, "They will get in eventually. Our best bet is to get on the motorcycle and leave before they find it. We need a distraction."

Opening the cabinet under the sink, a number of cleaning products crowded the space. "Bless your mother for not only being tidy but also environmentally incorrect. See if you have any foil. We are going to make some mini-bombs. I'll need empty water bottles too."

Ryan poured the water on the floor, not daring to stand up to empty it in the sink. He handed the bottles to Amy who carefully dispensed the cleaning product into the empty bottles. "Should I ask where you learned such a questionable skill?"

Handing him a piece of foil, she said, "Start making foil balls. Once I drop them in and seal the bottle, the chemical reaction starts. At best, it will make some noise and scare the men. It may do nothing, but holding onto an exploding bottle will blow your fingers off. Rough neighborhood, there was more than one kid missing fingers."

Laying the bullets in a line, he began to load the gun. "My dad obviously didn't expect he'd need much ammunition. I have five bullets, that's it. Let's hope the gun works. I have never seen my father fire it, but I did remember him buying it after a nearby robbery. We should go out the back bedroom window if possible."

Amy nodded her agreement stuffing the foil balls in her pockets and capping the bottle. They scuttled to the bedroom hearing the men trying to open the door. A heavily accented voice yelled, "Let us in. We can help you."

Spotting them, one of them took a shot at them that grazed Amy's cheek. "Help I can do without." Ryan's look veered between alarm and pure male aggression. "Keep going, escape is our only chance."

The wooden window fought being opened, forcing Ryan to knock out the window glass, alerting the men of their location. He stepped through the broken window and reached back for her hand. Instead, she handed him two bottles she just finished assembling. "Shake them up hard, it speeds up the reaction."

One of the intruders tore around the building, startling Ryan into throwing both bottles in his direction. They rolled intact to his feet. The man picked up the bottle, looked at it curiously. "Are you throwing the formula at us?"

Amy slid out of the window with four other bottles in hand. Damn it, it looked like the chemicals lost their potency. Then the bottle blew, surprising all of them. The partner who approached from the other side came to a stop when his partner started screaming but had the competency to hold onto his weapon. "Drop it," he ordered.

Amy took the opportunity to shake and lob a bottle at the gunman. Shaking another one, she aimed it at the second man. Unfortunately, the bottles seemed to be on a delayed signal. The gunman kept firing. One bullet went through the flowered hat, which thankfully had a little extra space in the crown.

With pistol in hand, Ryan fired in the direction of the approaching gunman. The gunman stumbled about the same time the two bottles blew. Grabbing her hand, Ryan tugged her into a run, heading toward the motorcycle. Aware she was jiggling her armed mini-bombs, she threw them behind her. The bullets pinged all around them. Ryan jerked but continued to pump the motorcycle starter, which refused to catch.

Amy asked, "Do you think they did something to it?" Not once did she think she would die in a gunfight.

Ryan passed the pistol back to her. "Four bullets left. Hold them off. I think I flooded it."

Okay, no two ways about it. It was time to call on some of those various deities Aunt Remy was so fond of asking to help her. "Spirits good and kind, god and goddesses divine, listen to my cry for assistance." She aimed the gun at the flash of color in the shrubbery. An angry spat of what she was sure was swear words confirmed she either hit her target or got mighty close.

The motorcycle's engine roared to life. "Hang on," Ryan warned as they took off through the brush. They bumped over the rough terrain avoiding the main road. Just as well, the main road seemed to be full of cars with flashing lights and dark SUVs and men in swat uniforms.

Her mouth near Ryan's ears, she yelled, "Police." He steered the bike toward the cars and the impromptu roadblock they'd set up. A group of armed men turned their way. For a moment, it looked like they'd escaped the bad guys only to end up shot by the authorities.

"Don't shoot them," George popped out of black SUV, surprising Amy. She'd have bet George did not exactly operate on the side of legality.

The armed men lowered their weapons. Simpson came around a van surprising her even more. "Where are they?"

Ryan pointed in the direction of the cabin. "Left them up by the lake. One might be missing some fingers."

A team leader gave the signal, various men slipped into the woods, and a few got in an unmarked car and drove. Beth hurried to her side to help her dismount from the motorcycle. "Beth?" Ryan opened his mouth to exclaim. "Is there anyone who isn't here?"

Simpson saluted the doctor. "Clemmons didn't make the closing act of his snake oil medicine show."

Ryan swore before saying, "Figures that villain would get off scot-free." Using his foot, he pushed the bike's kickstand in place.

"Dr. Korman," Simpson called out, "I said he didn't make it. Entirely different thing."

"Oh, I understand." Ryan nodded.

Amy understood too, just as she was willing to bet Simpson knew a great deal about the facility exploding.

Beth herded them toward the van. "We have a medic who can examine your gunshot wound."

Amy fingered the graze on her face. "It's nothing really. Clean it out and slap a bandage on it, and I'll be fine."

"Not you, Ryan," Beth answered, directing her attention to Ryan who was being helped by Simpson.

"Let me help," she wrapped one of Ryan's arms around her shoulders, staggered a little under his weight. No time to act like a girl, she admonished herself.

"I think I'm going into shock," Ryan said in breathy voice. "I know the signs," he added before collapsing.

"Do something!" Amy screamed as two men rushed forward to take Ryan from them.

Wait, I'm a doctor. She tried to push her way into the ambulance. Simpson held her back. "You're in no condition to help. Let Beth do her job."

Beth was a doctor. She always thought she was a scientist. Still, that didn't answer why she was here. "Have a seat." The weary man waved her to a canvas chair.

Someone handed her a bottle of water. Holding it up to the light, she checked the seal before twisting it open. Taking a swig of water, she relaxed in the chair. Maybe she could relax. "Tell me."

"Beth was hired to do research like you. After she started work at Theron, the FBI recruited her to be its eyes and ears. Beth never received the projects we wanted to study, not like you. It would have been better to try to recruit you, but she knew enough to recognize signs of people being drugged." He took a sip from the cup one of the people handed him.

Beth having medical knowledge made sense. In her less drugged moments, she remembered that Beth seemed a trifle more personable than the other employees did. "Why wasn't she drugged?"

"As far as I can tell, she was. Some of our doctors worked on a solution that would do a type of detox. She tried hard not to eat too much, making more a show of eating. Lost a few pounds on this assignment. Mary Beth was one of ours, too. I thought it was a mistake to have two women named Beth, but that's their real names." He finished his cup and placed it on the ground. He fished out a cigarette pack and shook out one.

A complaint about smoking welled up in her, but she checked it. He did save their lives. She should be able to put up with some smoke. "Is Mary Beth alive?"

Cupping his hand around the flame, he concentrated on lighting the cigarette. Once lit, he took a deep drag. "I know, nasty habit. I'll give it up once I take a less stressful job, which I am seriously considering. Mary Beth is fine. She knew something was up, so she chose to disappear on her own."

Beth popped out of the ambulance. "Ryan's stabilized. He's asking for you."

The words propelled her out of the chair. She covered the distance in a few lunging steps. Beth put her hand out. "Slow down before you have a heart attack. Bullet went clean through, didn't touch the bone, but he has lost a lot of blood. We are going to take him to the hospital and see if we can't fill him back up. I assume you want to ride in the ambulance."

Putting her chin up, she stared Beth down. "Try to stop me."

Beth put up both hands as if trying to ward her off. "Not me, I've seen what you can do. It's all over the Internet and in the papers too. No one claims responsibility for all those downloaded files, but I know it was you. Somehow, you managed to do what I couldn't in the two years I've been undercover."

Amy managed a tired smile as she hauled herself up into the ambulance. Ryan was strapped down to a gurney looking pale and worn. An IV dripped saline solution into his veins. At the sight of her, his face split into a goofy grin. "There's my fiancée," he cooed.

His slightly slurred voice indicated that more than saline dripped into his veins. Kneeling by the gurney, she took his hand. "I thought we talked about asking me properly. Just because you probably saved my life and got shot in the process doing it, doesn't—" She stopped, considered her words. Yep, risking his life repeatedly did qualify as a proposal of sorts.

Ryan grinned up at her. "How about a kiss, sweetie?" Without hesitation, she kissed him on the lips in front of the attendant. She expected some action on his part until she realized the man was unconscious.

* * * *

After spending a fitful night in a foldout chair in Ryan's room, Amy woke when Simpson walked into the room. He nodded at Ryan. "Still under, I see. I came to say goodbye and clear up a few things."

Yawning, she blinked, then, stretched and stood. "Okay. What do you want to know?"

"The recipe. Does it still exist?"

"It does," Amy pointed to her head, "but I still have memory issues. Have a nice life, I guess. I can't thank you enough for deciding to be on our side." She held out her arms for a hug. The man blushed, and then awkwardly walked into her embrace. Amy squeezed him as hard as she could, then let go.

The door closed softly behind him, and Amy stood staring at it, puzzled by the man. Ryan's voice startled her.

"Why didn't you tell him about the computer?" He carefully pushed himself up in bed, trying to keep his IV hand free of the entangling cords.

Padding over to his bedside, she half-perched on the bed. "Truthfully, I was never totally sure he was one of the good guys. He was this time, but why put the temptation out there?"

Ryan reached for her hand and grasped it. "Did I mention how much I love you?"

Amy shot him a coy look. "Maybe, but I never tire of hearing it. Tell me again."

Scooting to one side of the bed, Ryan invited, "C'mon up here, so I can show you properly." Amy scrambled up beside him, tucking her body under his shoulder and laying her head on his chest.

His stubble caught on her hair as he dropped kisses on her hair.

A throat clearing caught both their attention. A trio of lab-coated doctors stood just inside the room. One of them was Beth. She smiled at the two. "Looks to me as if someone is ready to go home."

One of the male doctors added, "Looks like he's UP to going home." He chuckled at his intended pun.

Beth rolled her eyes. "Don't worry. I'll get Ryan out of here in time for you both to get breakfast."

"Thanks," Amy offered, but realized she had a host of other issues, such as finding a place to live. Good chance the explosion destroyed her car, too. "I am not sure how we will get home."

Ryan sat a little straighter and moaned. "My car." He cut his eyes to Amy and added, "That's not important as long as I have you."

Amy snorted her disbelief. Maybe he could fool himself that the loss of the classic car didn't devastate him, but she knew better. Stella entered the room, swinging a familiar set of keys. "I'm here to drive you home."

Ryan's eyes lit up. "In a certain gold Mustang convertible?"

"Of course," Stella said. "I never drove a stick, but your security buddy said it wasn't that hard."

Amy and Ryan said together, "I'll drive."

Stella grinned. "Beau said you might say that."

"Beau." Amy rolled the name around on her tongue. "Is this Beau the same gentleman who drove us to the plane?"

"Yes, he's not too bad once I figured out he wasn't going to kill me. We got on much better after that. In fact, I kinda found him attractive in a sorta understated way. Did he say where he was heading?"

"No, he didn't." She shook her head at the wistful look on the woman's face, wishing she had different information. "Rest assured, if he wants you to find him, you will." Well, at least Stella didn't wait years to make the move on her object of affection.

Ryan made a shooing motion with his hand. "Leave the keys." Both Stella and Amy laughed as they left to stand in the hall.

"Thanks for the scoop. I'd like to follow it up with an interview. How about it?" Stella probed with a hopeful smile. Hospital staff passed by, pausing to cast an interested look in their direction. Gesturing to the gawkers, Stella announced, "See that, you're famous."

Amy could hear Ryan moving around in the room. She wanted to help him, but she realized a man had to do some things himself, which included putting on his pants. She'd work on taking them off. Remembering Stella, she turned away from her vigil on the closed door.

Pulling Stella into a hug, she surprised a nervous giggle out of the woman. "Of course, I'll do the interview. It is the least I can do. First, Ryan and I are going to take a well-deserved vacation."

Ryan opened the door. "Vacation sounds good to me. We'll have to make it pet friendly or see if our pet sitter might extend her time."

Amy hooked her arm with Ryan's. "Pets are staying home since we'll be on our honeymoon."

Ryan patted her hand as they walked toward the elevator. "Are you proposing to me, darling?"

Amy grinned. "I believe I am."

Furrowing his brow, his countenance turned troubled. "Oh dear, I was hoping to be proposed to on a moonlit carriage ride."

She swatted him. "Stop it and just say yes."

Ryan stopped and planted a kiss on her lips. Staring into her eyes, he said softly, "I've been saying yes for years. Unfortunately, it took almost dying for you to finally ask me, properly that is."

"Ah, yes that. I guess it took losing everything, including my memory to realize what really mattered." She returned his kiss.

Stella mouthed 'meet you downstairs' before she walked away. Ryan returned his attention to Amy. "What matters?" he whispered the words into her hair.

She moved her hand up to his cheek, rubbing the back of her hand against his three-day beard. "You, loving you, you loving me, us."

"Is that all?" He turned his head to kiss her hand.

Amy thought she'd summed everything up. Everything she previously considered important was gone. Wait, she knew what she forgot. "The children, Samson and Burton."

Ryan laughed, shook his head, and hit the down button. "Tell you what. You drive us to my house, while I conserve my strength. Once we get there, we can work on creating some less hairy offspring. How does that sound?"

The elevator doors dinged open to allow a pair of elderly women to exit. Amy dropped her hand to lace her fingers with his. "That sounds like a project that will need our combined skills for a successful outcome."

They stepped into the elevator. An intern who was hurrying to catch the elevator got sight of the two and slowed his pace enough to miss the elevator. Ryan nodded at the intern who came to a brief halt in front of the elevator door.

Ryan called out to the man, "Thanks. Dr. Newkirk and I need to do some private consultation about an upcoming procedure."

Amy smirked up at him. "Aren't you ashamed of yourself?" She snuggled into his arms.

"Nope, not at all. The way I see it I waited most of my life to have you in my embrace. I am taking advantage of every opportunity to have you in my arms." He rested his chin on her hair.

The hospital smell of disinfectant and alcohol wipes lingered on Ryan's skin, but enough essential male smell reached her nostrils. Aunt Remy complained they couldn't see what was right under their noses. Maybe she should have said they couldn't smell what was under their noses. Thank goodness, they finally did.

The End

About the Author

Morgan K Wyatt, raised on a steady diet of superheroes, believed she could fly at a very young age. After using trees, barn lofts, sliding boards, and even a second story window as launch pads, she found her flying skills were limited to fast and downward. By the age of nine, her dreams to be a superhero needed some modifications, which caused her to turn to writing and horseback riding as alternatives to flying.

At the age of twenty, she had another chance at superhero greatness as being one of the few female soldiers trained for combat. The fact that women will be able to serve in combat soon indicates that all the witnesses to the grenade incident have retired. The grenade incident didn't prevent her two sons or daughter-in-law from enlisting in the service. Having different last names probably helped.

Morgan recently retired from teaching special needs students to write fulltime, instead of in the wee hours of the night. With the help of her helpful husband and loyal hound, she creates characters who often grab plot lines and run with them. As for flying, she prefers the airlines now.

www.morgankwyatt.com
Other books by Morgan
The Reluctant Cougar
Cub in Blue
Puppy Love
Unexpected Cougar
Incognito
Dangerous Curves
Perfect Stranger
Blind Date

Escaping West
Undercover Rebel
Rebel Bride
Rebel Heartsong
Seeking Shelter
The Soul Mate Search

Secret Cravings Publishing
www.secretcravingspublishing.com

Made in the USA
Lexington, KY
12 January 2015